KILLING CRITICS

CAROL O'CONNELL

BERKLEY BOOKS, NEW YORK

THE BERKLEY PUBLISHING GROUP
Published by the Penguin Group
Penguin Group (USA) Inc.
375 Hudson Street, New York, New York 10014, USA
Penguin Group (Canada), 90 Eglinton Avenue East, Suite 700, Toronto, Ontario M4P 2Y3, Canada
(a division of Pearson Penguin Canada Inc.)
Penguin Books Ltd., 80 Strand, London WC2R 0RL, England
Penguin Group Ireland, 25 St. Stephen's Green, Dublin 2, Ireland (a division of Penguin Books Ltd.)
Penguin Group (Australia), 250 Camberwell Road, Camberwell, Victoria 3124, Australia
(a division of Pearson Australia Group Pty. Ltd.)
Penguin Books India Pvt. Ltd., 11 Community Centre, Panchsheel Park, New Delhi—110 017, India
Penguin Group (NZ), 67 Apollo Drive, Rosedale, North Shore 0632, New Zealand
(a division of Pearson New Zealand Ltd.)
Penguin Books (South Africa) (Pty.) Ltd., 24 Sturdee Avenue, Rosebank, Johannesburg 2196,
South Africa

Penguin Books Ltd., Registered Offices: 80 Strand, London WC2R 0RL, England

This is a work of fiction. Names, characters, places, and incidents either are the product of the author's imagination or are used fictitiously, and any resemblance to actual persons, living or dead, business establishments, events, or locales is entirely coincidental. The publisher does not have any control over and does not assume any responsibility for author or third-party websites or their content.

KILLIING CRITICS

A Berkley Book / published by arrangement with Hutchinson, a division of Random House U.S. Ltd.

PRINTING HISTORY
G. P. Putnam's Sons hardcover edition / June 1996
Jove mass-market edition / July 1997
Berkley mass-market edition / May 2010

Copyright © 1996 by Carol O'Connell.
Excerpt from *Shell Game* by Carol O'Connell copyright © by Carol O'Connell.
Cover images: "Frame" copyright © Olinchuk, "man outline" copyright © by Nix, "splatter" copyright
© by Sergieiev/Shutterstock.

ISBN: 978-0-425-23806-6

BERKLEY®
Berkley Books are published by The Berkley Publishing Group,
a division of Penguin Group (USA) Inc.,
375 Hudson Street, New York, New York 10014.
BERKLEY® is a registered trademark of Penguin Group (USA) Inc.
The "B" design is a trademark of Penguin Group (USA) Inc.

PRINTED IN THE UNITED STATES OF AMERICA

10 9 8 7 6 5 4 3 2 1

Many thanks to the people who answered my questions and extended their courtesy.

Dianne Burke, Search & Rescue Research Associates, Tempe, Arizona, for her patience and diligence. (LFQY01A@prodigy.com)

Robbin Murphy, Creative Director of artnetweb, for a tour of the system. (http://artnetweb.com/artnetweb)

YTNOP Music, for the use of an atmospheric Jean-Luc Ponty instrumental.

FOR MY FATHER

He was one of those quiet heroes who worked until the day he died. He was also a man who could do a financial transaction on a handshake; he bought our first house that way. And people who've known him since he was a child will tell you he never told a lie in his entire life. What spare time he had was spent in public service; what spare cash he had was given away. This remarkable man filled a church when he died, and the planet was diminished.

PROLOGUE

SPEAKERS WERE HIDDEN IN EVERY WALL, THEIR CLOTH covers painted over many times to render them invisible and to baffle the sound of Jean-Luc Ponty's *Civilized Evil*. Throughout the evening, the dark sweet music of the jazz violin had been muted—strings and drums subdued to the level of a backdrop for a hundred inane conversations. A ripple of notes chaining into chords wove around the art gallery patrons as a subliminal entity. The crowd inhaled the music with every breath, and it hovered over their food and wine.

Dean Starr's head nodded, almost imperceptibly, to the beat of a drum just beyond the reach of his awareness. Much was beyond him this evening. In fact, he had just been stabbed and hadn't the wit to realize it.

Drugs and wine had sabotaged the switchboard operator of his brain. All internal lines of communication were botched, and trauma was never connected to pain. He had felt the contact, but knew not what it was, for he could not see inside himself, could not grasp the damage from the steel needle of the ice pick. And now the blood was leaking from the chambers of his heart. Weakening without understanding, Dean Starr slipped to the floor, his head gently settling to the hard wood as though to a pillow.

A card wafted down to his chest. His eyes rolled toward the small white rectangle, but he was unable to read it, and felt no inclination to lift his head. Liquid warmth was spreading outward from the center of his back where the tiny hole was—the small back door to his damaged heart.

Lizard skin shoes approached his prone body in the company of patent-leather pumps. Now, other shoe styles which he approved of joined this pair. His slow eyes roved from sequined bows to golden buckles. And there was the sound of shoes behind his head, a light dancing-shoe scuffle mingling with the tap-tap of stiletto heels, the tinkle of champagne glasses, and the chatter of mouths opening and closing to say nothing that was any longer intelligible to him—if ever it had been.

A woman's gloved hand reached down for the white card and picked it up, the better to read it. The owner of the glove tilted the card as she was putting it back where she had found it—on his chest. Now he was able to read the single word *DEAD*.

And then he was.

Long after all the pretty shoes had departed for the evening, a pair of black shoes approached the body. These shoes extended out from the blue cuffs of the gallery rent-a-cop's uniform.

"Christ," said the owner of the black shoes.

In this one word, he gave away his lack of sophistication and education, his utter ignorance of the fine arts, for he had instantly realized that this was a dead body lying in a red spread fan of blood—and not a piece of performance art.

CHAPTER
1

ALL AROUND THE FRENETIC CIRCUS OF TIMES SQUARE, car lights blinked and traffic lights glared. Above the din of horns and shouted obscenities, neon signs flashed and clashed with messages on every surface that was for sale. The wraparound sign on the old Times Building sent headlines in a band of bright letters running around the facade. Mounted over the running words was a giant motion picture screen with an ever changing array of full-color commercials.

At street level, less electrifying messages rode the backs of men with sandwich board signs. Pedestrians moved in quick streams of intricate traffic patterns, flying through the rush hour, dodging those who moved into their path to hand them bright-colored ads for local stores. The beggars also worked this fast-paced stream, moving along with their marks to flash broad smiles and holler pitches for spare coins. And on every corner, there was a great war of odors from the street vendors' carts, as pretzels battled with roasted animal parts.

Only two people, a man and a woman, were not in motion, and the whole world moved around them.

The woman stood near the curb, flashing white teeth and large breasts. Both her profession and her unnatural shade of red hair fit well with the advertising atmosphere. "Care to dance?" she called to every passing stranger. And then her eye fell on the elegant lone figure in the expensive suit.

With a predatory stare, she watched this man from the distance of a few squares of the sidewalk. He didn't belong here. She checked the length of the curb for the limousine that should accompany such a man, but there was none in sight.

He was staring up at the roof of the building across the street. Only this afternoon, a derelict had hovered at the edge of that roof. And then, the ragbag had spread her skinny arms on the wind and sailed off the high brick wall. So like a bird she was, even as she fell, and caused no more than a brief interruption in the flow of the square, only the time it had taken to improvise the foot traffic around the body and over it, and some had trodden on it. But to compensate for that indignity, the dead woman had received two minutes of fame on the evening news.

Now the man in the expensive suit seemed fixated on that same ledge. The woman strolled over to him and lightly touched his sleeve to call his attention back to the earth, to her.

"Sugar, if you're waitin' on another jumper, I'd say you've got some time to kill." She rolled her shoulders back and thrust her breasts out in a none too subtle offering.

"Thank you." He inclined his head, and she knew if he'd had a hat he would have tipped it. "But I'm afraid I have an appointment," he said, addressing her as a lady and not a whore.

His dark hair was threaded with silver, and his moustache did not quite conceal the line of a faded scar. The scar made him look a little dangerous, and she liked that. And there was something about his mouth that would make any woman wonder what it might be like to sleep with him. She was wasting her time here, and she knew it. Yet she lingered awhile. Perhaps it was the challenge of those eyes hooded in shadow.

She came closer.

The beams of a turning car flashed on his face, flushing out the shadows with brilliant light. And now, though it was spring and the evening was mild, she wrapped herself in her own arms. Her sudden shiver was not caused by any expression of his intentions, for surely he had been born with those eyes.

Imagine a baby with eyes like that.

Obediently, her imagination conjured up the face of an infant with alien irises the color of blue frozen water, and with black pupils like onrushing missiles.

Well, ain't that cold?

She looked up to the man with another question in her thoughts. *Did your mama shiver when she suckled you?*

In a burst of intuition, the woman, who truly understood men, realized that this man's entire life had been shaped by his eyes, which could not convey any semblance of humanity—only bullets and ice.

She forgot the pitch to sell her body. In silence, she stepped back and watched as he turned away from her and entered the Gulag. The restaurant's glass door swung shut behind him.

The Gulag was brightly lit to obliterate any trace of ambiance which might induce the patrons to linger over their food. *Eat and get out!* said the overhead fluorescent lights. The strong aroma of coffee dominated the single room, riding over the stale odors of bygone meals.

J. L. Quinn threaded his way through tables of tired conversations and the quiet islands of solitary book readers. A cockroach ran for its life across the cracked linoleum in advance of the man's handmade shoes. Quinn sat down at his regular table, a small square of Formica in company with two plastic chairs.

Few people knew that he frequented this place. Those few had often pressed him with variations of "Why in God's name would you eat in a hole like that?" The famed art critic always responded with high praise for the cheeseburgers. *This* from a man who had authored four books on fine art, whose suits were tailored by maestros, and whose moustache never trapped crumbs.

He glanced at his watch. Detective Sergeant Riker would be arriving soon. Riker's urgent business could only be the recent murder of that hack artist—and this made him smile. The police department was so right to suspect an art critic. In his youth, Quinn had taken a postulant's vow to kill off bad art before it could spread.

Near his table at the back of the room, a long countertop bore the ravages of the last shift of rush hour in the deserted dishes and crumpled napkins. The two men seated on counter stools were not regulars, and unlike the other patrons, they eyed him with grave suspicion. In unison, they bulked up their shoulders to make themselves larger than they were. By the warehouse logos on their T-shirts, Quinn guessed their vocations as manual labor, and in their expressions, he intuited avocations of mindless violence.

Out of habit, the art critic touched one finger to the scar above his moustache. The two customers abruptly ceased to ogle the man who smelled of money. They swiveled on the counter stools to turn their backs on him. Quinn flirted with the idea that his scar had the power of a talisman. This was the single fanciful thought in his otherwise pragmatic mind.

His regular waitress was standing at the next table, piling dirty dishes on a tray. She saw him now and walked to his table to take his order. He noted all the signs of the long day's warfare in the food stains on her clothes. The blue-jean legs below the hem of her apron were stained with an artist's rainbow of oil paints.

"I'm waiting for someone, Sandy. Will you give me a few minutes?"

"Whenever, Mr. Quinn."

She was his type, attractive and intelligent, but she was a painter. He had never bedded an artist, though not for the lack of offers. A sense of ethics had always prevailed and prevented any forays into the art community. There were women enough elsewhere when he wanted one.

Sandy deposited a second menu on his table as she passed by with her tray artfully balanced on one arm. "For your friend," she called back over her shoulder.

He glanced at the door. Detective Sergeant Riker had arrived.

Though more than a decade had passed since they last met, Quinn recognized the man's slouching silhouette on the other side of the glass, which was too fogged with grime and scratches to allow for much more detail.

Sandy was already appraising Riker as he pushed through the door, and by the dip of her mouth on one side, the waitress judged him to be a bad tipper. Her eyes opened a little wider as the man with two days' growth of beard walked to Quinn's table and the art critic stood up to greet his guest.

At fifty-five, Riker was not much older than himself, but Quinn thought the detective wore his years less well, and certainly with less style. He would not have been surprised to learn that Riker was dressed in the same suit he had on twelve years ago when they had sat down to this same table to discuss a more personal murder.

As Riker shook hands with Quinn, there was a tone of apology in the rituals of "Hello" and "Good to see you again." There was great regret in the detective's brown eyes as he took his seat opposite the art critic.

One might believe Sergeant Riker's suit had been slept in. Not true. The wrinkles were determined by the way the garments landed when tossed onto some piece of furniture or, missing that mark, the floor. And the network of red veins might mislead anyone who didn't know how red his eyes could be when he was living in the bottle. This evening he was only showing the wear of a night without sleep, and the heavy reading of old case files.

"Thanks for seeing me on short notice, Mr. Quinn." He noted the art critic's tan, a side effect of having a summer home in the Hamptons. Quinn's glowing good health and trim figure fit well with Riker's idea that money could buy absolutely everything. Now he caught his own pasty, dregs-of-the-booze reflection in the mirror behind the counter, and he turned away.

"I assume your visit concerns the death of Dean Starr," said Quinn in his cultured voice, which exuded breeding and a privileged education at the finest private schools on the eastern seaboard.

"Yes, sir, it does," Riker said, with a rough New York accent that spoke of a night school education, paid for by blue-collar jobs. The policeman looked down at his hands. The left was scarred with a bullet wound, and the right still bore the marks of a felon's teeth. He knew these hands could never, in one million years, touch the cool fair skin of the women Quinn was accustomed to.

Riker had always understood the art critic's attraction to the Gulag. This place was Quinn's source of women, the rare animals with beauty and talent. He had to trap them in their natural habitat of poverty, and the restaurant was a low-budget haven for actresses and writers.

"Mr. Quinn, did you read Andrew Bliss's column yesterday?"

"No, I'm afraid not."

Riker pulled a folded newspaper clipping from his inside pocket. "I'll cut to the best part." He held it at arm's length and read with the squint of a man who would not wear reading glasses. " 'The new art wave was first heralded by the graffiti artist who defiled the city walls—artist attacks architecture. Then it progressed to the vandal artist who scarred the work of others—artist attacks art. And now we see a further escalation in the performance-art murder of Dean Starr—artist attacks artist. This is the new wave—full-blown now—Art Terrorism.'" Riker spread the clipping out on the table and looked up at Quinn.

"It's absurd, of course," said Quinn, "but quite interesting if you know Andrew. Have you met him?"

"No, I left messages for him, but he never called back. I'm gonna try to catch up with him at Starr's wake."

The art critic's handsome face had hardly aged since their last meeting. There were no deep lines about the eyes to say the man had ever laughed out loud. Quinn had a limited range of expression, devoid of emotion even when he smiled, only communicating cool indifference and élan. Riker might be the only man alive who had ever seen him cry. And that had been an eerie sight—tears falling from dispassionate, ice-blue eyes.

"Mr. Quinn, do you see a direct connection between Dean Starr's death and an artist?"

And maybe another connection, an old connection?

"Not really," said Quinn. "I suppose you could call the murder performance art, but it wasn't very sophisticated—labeling the body that way. You wouldn't actually have to go to school to do a thing like that."

"You said if I knew Andrew—"

"Well, it's interesting that Andrew Bliss would do anything this progressive on his own. He usually follows some other critic's lead. Naming a new wave in art—that's pretty daring. It might be the most courageous thing he's ever done, however misguided and ridiculous." Quinn pointed to the clipping. "May I?"

Riker turned the paper around and pushed it to the other side of the table. Quinn ran one finger down the lines of type, reading rapidly. Riker wondered if he did not detect relief in Quinn for what he had *not* found in Bliss's column.

"It's a bit of a stretch," said Quinn, "from vandalism to murder."

Riker leaned back in his chair. He could not shake the old memory of the night J. L. Quinn had cried. Riker had given the art critic shelter in the back of a squad car and kept guard over the crying man until Quinn was in control of himself again. Tonight, Riker was debating whether or not to prepare him for what was coming. Could he afford that?

No, he could not.

Inspector Louis Markowitz could have kept pace with Quinn, but the old man was dead, and Riker had drunk away too much of his own store of brain cells. He needed an edge in dealing with this man. He put his compassion away and proceeded like the good cop that he was.

"Would you take a look at this?" Riker pulled a plastic bag from his pocket and slid it across the table. Inside was a letter, neatly typed and unsigned. "Don't take it out of the bag—it's evidence."

Quinn silently read the text which Riker knew by heart: 'There is a direct link between Dean Starr and the old murders of the artist and the dancer. Twelve years ago, you knew that Oren Watt's confession was a fraud.'

Riker reached across the table to tap the plastic bag with one finger. "Someone sent a clipping of Bliss's column to Special Crimes Section, along with this letter."

If Quinn was jarred by this reminder of his young niece's murder, he gave away nothing, not even by the lift of an eyebrow. "I would have thought Koozeman was the obvious connection, since all three murders were done in his gallery. Are you really taking this letter seriously?"

Riker nodded. "The envelope was addressed to me. Not too many people would remember the name of a case detective on a twelve-year-old homicide. And the writer thinks Oren Watt's confession was a fake. Would you say that indicates an inside view?"

The art critic lit a cigarette with steady hands, and no waver in the flame. "You're reopening the old case?"

"It was never officially closed." Riker fumbled in his pockets for a pack of cigarettes, and then a second thought stopped him. His own hands were not so steady before that first drink of an evening. He had missed his breakfast beer and worked straight through his lunch beer. "Markowitz never believed Oren Watt was the killer. And as I recall, sir, neither did you."

Still no response from Quinn. The man seemed bored by it all. What the hell was going on behind that mask?

"Both killings had the same method," said Riker, "if you consider the old double homicide as performance art. Do you? The body parts in the first—"

"The bodies were arranged as artwork," said Quinn behind a haze of curling blue smoke. "I see the association, but I don't know that it's a strong one."

"Well, a killer has his own style. It's what we call his MO—*modus operandi*. Now Andrew Bliss is saying an artist killed Dean Starr. Could he be right? Could you call this an artist's style, the way the murder was done?"

Quinn's eyes followed the twisting plume of smoke. "The majority of artists in this town are mediocre hacks. Most of them have no style at all."

"Did you send that letter, Mr. Quinn? You see, twelve years ago, everyone was so sure we had the right man. It was such an ugly murder—everyone in this town wanted to believe Oren Watt did it—except Markowitz and you."

"Sorry, Sergeant. I didn't write that letter."

"Do you know anyone else who thought Watt's confession was a fake?"

"Aubry's father, for instance? No. My brother-in-law believed Oren Watt was the killer. He was rather unhappy when Watt's psychiatrist started hawking drawings of his child's body parts. But he's gotten on with his life.

When Watt was released last year, Gregor never even commented on it.''

"Mr. Quinn, I need to identify the new player, the one who wrote this letter. What about Aubry's mother, Sabra? Do you know where we can find her?''

"No idea. I haven't seen my sister in years." His eyes ceased to follow the smoke and suddenly locked onto Riker's. He leaned forward. "*You* always believed Oren Watt killed my niece. Have you questioned him about Dean Starr's murder?''

"No.''

"Interesting. And what about Koozeman?''

"I haven't even talked to him. I have a direct order to stay away from the principals in the old case. And I'd appreciate it if you'd keep this conversation to yourself.''

"Understood, Sergeant." As Quinn sat back in his chair, his eyes never leaving Riker's face, it was clear that he understood on many levels. If the wrong man had been sent to the asylum, if the butcher had been at large all this time . . .

Riker lowered his eyes to keep Quinn from dicking around in his mind. "I just follow orders, sir. I'm only a working stiff.''

"I suspect you're much more than that. Markowitz thought very highly of you.''

Riker studied his hands. If Markowitz had such a high opinion, why hadn't the old bastard shared more of the case? *Ah, Markowitz, always holding something back, even holding out on his own men.*

Riker retrieved the plastic evidence bag and held it up to Quinn. "This letter says there's a link between Starr and the old murders. I need that link.''

Quinn was silent, eyes drifting to that place beyond focus where the thinking is done. Then he waved one hand to show that he had come up empty of possibilities.

Riker looked at his wristwatch, and reset it to the time of the wall clock. He pulled a small notebook and a pen

from his shirt pocket. "Just for the record, sir . . ." Every
move, every word conveyed the tired resignation of end-
game. Riker's eyes were cast down as his pen hovered
over the open notebook. Then he looked up at Quinn,
with the pretense of an afterthought. "What if Oren Watt
was the wrong man? Suppose Dean Starr was the one
who slaughtered your niece? Oh, Christ, the things he
did to her. 'Slaughter' is the only right word for it, isn't
it, sir? Who could blame you if you stabbed the sick
bastard with an ice pick?"

Riker waited on a sign of damage from his salvo, some
emotional disturbance in Quinn. Had he been hoping for
fresh tears? No, he never wanted to see a sight like that
one again. But there should be something—jangled
nerves, if not tears—and there was not. He had just
bludgeoned this man with the worst memory of his life,
and all for nothing.

The art critic wore the trace of a smile, as if to say he
understood and there were no hard feelings. Then he ab-
sently touched one finger to the scar above his moustache.

The Koozeman Gallery had the proportions of a modest
gymnasium. High bare walls glistened with the sheen of
a recent whitewash. The floors had been waxed and now
were beaded with the spilled wine of reporters.

The press corps was feeding by the back wall on the
far side of Dean Starr's coffin. Mountains of food were
laid out at long tables and lit by ceiling track lights, as
though the Fourth Estate might ever have trouble locating
the staples of caviar, smoked salmon, and a spectacular
array of strange but edible objects skewered on tooth-
picks. Glasses were filled by gallery boys in bow ties,
black pants and starched white shirts. They passed among
the throng of reporters, carrying magical, inexhaustible
wine bottles. The tone of the babble was jovial, all li-
quored up for the show.

The night's main attraction sat on a long pedestal at the center of the large room. The white coffin wood was covered with four-letter words and bad drawings of obscene gestures. One small and gangly man stood behind a lectern near the casket. He seemed too young for vestment and a clerical collar. Horn-rimmed glasses greatly magnified his eyes. His gaze was fixed on the bare surface of the lectern as he tried to pretend this funeral service was not odd and unseemly, even by New York standards.

Rows of empty benches were lined up in the staggered height of bleachers at a sporting event, and this, J. L. Quinn pointed out to Sergeant Riker, was not far from reality. The art critic and the detective nodded to the little minister as they approached the coffin together.

"Oh, sweet Jesus," said Riker, as he looked over the scrawled writing on the white wood, and then walked around it to read all the obscene words on the other side. "Damn kids."

"Oh, no," said the critic. "You don't understand. This is art. See?" He pointed to the lower right-hand corner of the coffin. "That's the vandal artist's signature. You might recall the name from Andrew Bliss's column. Later on, they'll dump Starr's body into a pine box and auction off this one."

"You're kidding me, right?"

"No, I can't do that. I have no sense of humor."

Riker looked down on the remains of Dean Starr. "Pretty messy corpse."

Quinn leaned over the edge of the casket to study the face of moles and pockmarks, the thickened body straining at the buttons of a purple leather jacket, thighs threatening to split the green leather pants, creating the illusion of life in the stress of dead cow's hide.

"Actually Starr looked about the same when he was alive," said Quinn. "I would've expected an autopsy to do more damage."

"Well, the chief medical examiner was out of town, so we got the discount version. That's why my partner's picking up the paperwork to have the autopsy done over. So the guy was always that ugly? Is his hair supposed to look like that?"

"Yes. It's a neo-Mohawk. They had to trim the spikes to fit the coffin. You're not really getting the full effect."

"But this is no punk kid. This guy's gotta be what?"

"Fifty-two years old."

They took their seats in the bleachers, sitting front row center and facing the remains of Dean Starr. Beyond the coffin were twenty feet of empty space and a pure white wall. A few people, clutching black-bordered invitations, filed past the deceased. Their heads turned briefly to look at the carnage of the food tables by the back wall. Perhaps deciding the refreshments were not worth the battle, they chose seats in the middle rows.

Riker's head swiveled slightly to admire a passing wine bottle in the hand of a gallery boy. He turned back to the white wall and sucked in his breath as he recognized Avril Koozeman, the gallery owner, a bald, heavy-set man in a dark suit.

What the hell?

Koozeman had suddenly appeared at the center of the blank wall beyond the coffin.

Where did he come from?

Koozeman was walking toward the coffin with enough momentum to suggest to Riker's cracking brain that the man had just walked through that solid wall. Now the detective was torn between giving up drink and the longing for a triple shot of whiskey to make this idea go away.

As the gallery owner came closer, Riker focussed on Avril Koozeman's small, regular features, an ordinary face but for the black, unruly eyebrows tangling above his small gray eyes. The man carried his bulk in a way that alluded more to prosperity than to overeating. Koozeman leaned over the coffin and stared at the corpse for a moment. His expression was inappropriately cheerful.

Riker took out his notebook and leafed through it, as he leaned closer to Quinn. "He owned a piece of the dead artist, right?"

"Yes, fifty percent of all sales."

Koozeman walked to the bleachers and smiled benignly on Quinn, who nodded in reply. The large man snapped his fingers and two gallery boys ran up to him with trays of wineglasses in three of Riker's favorite colors: red, pink and white. Riker accepted a glass, following Quinn's lead and choosing the red. Koozeman was still smiling as he turned and walked over to the feeding frenzy on the far side of the room.

Riker shook his head. "I don't get it. Starr was a real moneymaker for Koozeman, wasn't he? What you call a hot property?"

"The hottest," said Quinn, tasting the wine and approving it.

"So why is he smiling?"

"Well, he has an inventory of work. After Starr died, Koozeman raised the price two hundred percent. Of course he's smiling."

And now, another man, slender and slow-footed, made a more ordinary entrance, not emerging from a wall, but by the more conventional front door. An escaped shock of light brown hair hung over one eye, and his tie had gone awry, but otherwise, his well-styled clothes put him in the same species as J. L. Quinn. He seemed to drift toward the coffin by accident. In a confusion of manners, he sighed at the little minister and waved to the corpse.

Riker was watching the man and flipping through his notebook. "Should I know that guy?"

"That's Andrew Bliss," said Quinn. "The art critic who wrote the review on Starr's death."

"Not one of your favorite critics?" Riker made a note.

"Actually, he writes very well, but he always waits

until the other reviews are in, and then he goes whichever way the wind blows. That's why his last column was so unusual.''

Riker found the background sketch in his notebook. According to the bio, Andrew Bliss was forty-eight years old, but the detective was looking at the face of a boy. This illusion was helped by Bliss's large blue eyes and full lips. Riker felt suddenly uncomfortable. Old children were wrong in the world.

"And how did Mr. Bliss feel about the dead artist? Was he—''

Conversation broke off as a gallery boy replenished Riker's wine. He looked down at his glass, and Quinn graced him with a smile.

"It's because you're with a critic. The boy won't allow your glass to go even half-empty. He could be fired for that.''

Riker stared into his wine and wondered how his own religion would square with the gallery philosophy, for he believed it was a sin to allow a glass to remain half-full.

He looked back to the second row where Andrew Bliss was seated. And now Riker noticed that Bliss's gray hairs were fast overtaking the light brown. As he stared at the man with the young face and the old hair, Riker noticed the reddened nose. Broken veins? The slackness of the jaw, the slow-moving eye which was not obscured by strands of hair, all were familiar signs he remembered from his own shaving mirror.

So Andrew Bliss was a drunk.

"How did Bliss and Starr get along?'' He chugged back his wine, and in sidelong vision, he saw a gallery boy snap to attention.

"Hard to say,'' said Quinn. "I only saw them together one time. Andrew seemed a bit tense at the gallery opening.''

"You didn't tell me you were at the gallery that night.''

"Ah, but you knew, didn't you, Riker? I'm not exactly a low-profile guest at a function like that. And now you want to know if I was there when he died. Do you know the exact time of death?''

"The jerk who screwed up the autopsy didn't get the stomach contents. We know he was alive at seven-thirty, and the security guard found the body at ten-fifteen.''

The gallery boy was back and weighting down Riker's glass again.

"I was there until eight o'clock,'' said Quinn. "I never saw anything suspicious, unless you count the artwork.''

Riker tipped back his glass, the sooner to forget Koozeman's walk through the solid wall. He might need reading glasses, he would cop to that, but there was nothing wrong with his long-distance vision. And what about the myopic hundred guests at the Dean Starr show? "I still can't believe Starr got stabbed in a room full of people and nobody saw it.''

"Well, Koozeman's patrons are a rather self-absorbed group,'' said Quinn.

The reporters were being led away from the feeding tables by Avril Koozeman. He was flanked by gallery boys holding wine bottles as lures. Bearing full glasses and paper plates filled to overflowing, the ladies and gentlemen of the news media settled into the remaining seats.

One rowdy press photographer in the back row yelled, "Bring on the noise!''

The minister cleared his throat, and tapped the microphone on the lectern.

Riker was feeling the ten cups of coffee drunk before all the wine was slugged back. Seeing no signs with familiar men's room symbols, he pressed his legs together as he leaned close to Quinn and whispered, "So where is the can?''

The minister's voice was amplified in volume, but carried little weight with the crowd as he began to speak over the babble of conversation. "I'm afraid I know very little about Mr. Starr. I'm told he's only been an artist for a short time. I know nothing about his life before that. Perhaps I may call on others to help fill in the gap.''

Riker's I-got-to-pee-or-die body language was escalating with the crossing and recrossing of his legs.

Quinn inclined his head toward Riker. "Sorry?"

"Where is the toilet?" Riker spoke with the slow careful enunciation of foreigners and drunks, and in a volume to be heard above the minister, who was making his second appeal.

Quinn pointed to a hallway off the main room. "It's that way, first door to your right."

Quinn turned back to the second row and nodded a greeting to Andrew Bliss. It was a courtesy of long acquaintance, but not friendship. He noticed that Bliss was not his usual twitchy self today. In fact, the man was so inebriated, it could only be inbred good manners that kept him from sliding to the floor.

"Hey, Bliss," called one of the reporters from the back row. "Loved the art terrorist column. How come you didn't throw in the old Oren Watt murders?"

Ever the chameleon, Bliss's complexion changed from a rosy, sotted flush to a pale cast of clammy skin, perhaps the better to blend in with the dead man. Summoning a burst of energy, Bliss gathered up his raincoat and fled the gallery with unnatural speed.

Now Quinn displayed that flicker of emotion that Riker had been hoping for in the restaurant.

He resumed his mask and willed his mind to other things—the increasingly rowdy guests and the little minister, who solemnly shook his head, taking this afternoon's entertainment far too seriously from Quinn's point of view.

A young woman entered the gallery and set off a flashbulb in the camera of a drunken, yet discriminating photographer in the bleachers. The light show spread across the rows in a chain of pops and blinding lights, accompanied by the music of low whistles.

She was tall, and it took Quinn's eyes a while to travel over all of her. The black leather running shoes were top-of-the-line. Though he could not see the back pocket of her jeans, he knew it would bear a designer's name. A long black trench coat was draped over the shoulders of her blazer, which was cashmere, and her T-shirt was silk. He would bet his stock portfolio that her curls were styled in a Fifty-seventh Street salon, but not dyed there, for this was that most unusual creature, a natural blonde in the spectrum of burnished gold.

In every other aspect of her, a lifetime's experience in stereotyping humans had failed him. He could not hazard her occupation or her exact status in the world. All he knew for certain was that her eyes were green, and if it was true that one could read another's soul by the eyes, this young woman didn't have one.

She sat down next to him. Her perfume was expensive and discreet.

He knew they had never met; one did not forget such a face. Yet she was familiar.

Riker was back from the men's room and tugging on his sleeve. "Be careful of that one. She carries a big gun."

Quinn smiled indulgently.

"Okay, watch this." Riker leaned across his person to say, "Hey, Mallory. You got the paperwork on the stiff?"

She reached into her blazer, which had an inside pocket. The garment was obviously tailor-made. Women who bought their clothes off the rack were denied such pockets. And now her upper body was turning toward him, her hand pulling out folded sheets of paper, and he could see the large gun in her shoulder holster. She ignored him, passing the fold of papers across his body as though he were merely an inconveniently situated object.

And now he placed her, but he had to travel back many years to do it. She was the child of Special Crimes Section.

He had only seen her on a few occasions in Inspector Markowitz's office. All those years ago, he had found it amazing to see a little girl moving in and out of discussions of murder. She had been stealthy, appearing suddenly, lighting by the desk to hand Inspector Markowitz a stack of printouts, and then off again, later returning to Markowitz to wheedle money for the candy machine. In passing, the child had glanced at the art critic, found him uninteresting, and passed on.

"That's my kid," the inspector had told him then, behind the child's back and with obvious pride. Though Quinn later realized that pride was not in the child's beauty but in the quick intelligence behind her glittering eyes. He then learned that the girl frequently came in after school to jump-start the glitch-ridden computer system for her foster father. Markowitz had not resisted the urge to brag.

"Kathy can do anything with a computer," Markowitz had said. *"This afternoon, she taught it to fetch the newspaper."*

The proof of this was in the copy of a crime reporter's column, a fresh spate of information leaked from NYPD. It contained a plethora of typos and misspellings and could only have come from the city editor's personal computer. This had been part of Markowitz's plea for special cooperation, for concealment and covert assistance. And so Quinn's conspiracy with this policeman had begun over an illegal computer theft by the baby hacker, Kathy Mallory. The other documents she produced had led them down dark streets of utter madness and up steep inclines of theory. The child had been a prolific thief.

"I was sorry to hear of Inspector Markowitz's death,"

he said to the young woman beside him. "I liked your father very much."

And this was true. Markowitz had been a man of deep grace and charm, undisguised by his excess poundage and a bad suit. When Quinn had read of the man's death in the papers, he felt the planet diminish beneath his feet because this policeman was no longer among them. He could count on three fingers the people who had so affected him.

"I believe I was of some assistance to your father. If I can help you, of course I will." He handed her his card, and with it the unlisted number which was given out to few people in this world.

"I'll need to talk with Gregor Gilette," she said. "You might be able to help with that. We can't work the old case in the open, so you could prepare him for the interview, ask him to keep it quiet."

"That would be difficult. He spent so many years getting over his daughter's death. He won't want to deal with this again."

"Well, that's too bad, because it's going to happen. It's all new again. I'm starting over."

Her speech patterns spoke of good schools beyond the salaries of most city employees. Whatever the cost and sacrifice, Markowitz had invested wisely in his foster child.

Her tone of voice strictly defined who was in charge here. And when Quinn ventured the proper form of address, he learned that he was to call her, not *Miss*, not *Ms.*, nor by her given name, but only *Mallory*, and he was not likely to forget that—ever.

"It's impossible to get an appointment with Gilette," said Quinn. "He's in the middle of preparations to unveil his new building. I might be able to manage a brief social meeting. He'll be at a charity ball at the Plaza. My mother hosts that ball every year."

Even before she spoke, he realized he had been telling her what she already knew.

"I've seen the guest list," she said.

"I could arrange an invitation."

"It's been arranged."

Apparently, she didn't really need him at all; that was made very clear as she turned her face away from his.

"Mallory," said Riker, "is the meat wagon out front?"

She nodded. Riker walked across the room and placed the papers in Koozeman's hand. When Quinn looked her way again, Mallory was staring at him. The long, slanted eyes were beautiful and unsettling. Her expression was inscrutable, though he did detect a kindred coldness there.

"Riker tells me you're hoping to tie Dean Starr to the old murder case."

"I won't discuss that here." She turned toward the coffin, dismissing him again.

Neither of them noticed the reporter taking a seat behind them at that moment. A pen scribbled furiously behind their backs.

Riker was back again, checking all the rows and asking, "Where did Andrew Bliss go?"

"He left right after you went to the men's room," said Quinn. "The other children were teasing him about his column."

Suddenly he found himself sitting alone, watching Riker and Mallory moving across the wide floor toward the door. A reporter fell over his own feet to leave the bleachers and catch up to Mallory. He stepped into her path, and a second later, stumbled backward, though Quinn could swear she never touched the man.

The place Mallory had occupied was now filled by the less attractive person of a reporter, a man with sparse hair, a wide girth and grinning nicotine-yellow teeth.

"Mr. Quinn, would you say this death is a great loss to the art community?"

"Oh, I don't think so. There are perhaps ninety thousand other hack artists in New York to fill the void."

"What's your personal response to the death of Mr. Starr?"

"One down and eighty-nine thousand, nine hundred and ninety-nine to go. Is there anything else?"

"Yeah. Don't you think it's a little odd they didn't arrest Oren Watt?"

Quinn's posture was aloof, his expression slightly bored, but beneath the skin, where everyone's innards were equally inelegant, was the sickening confusion of emotions tied to his niece and all her butchered body parts.

Emma Sue Hollaran, head of the Public Works Committee, had pinned him to this appointment. Thus pinned like a butterfly, Andrew Bliss had been drinking steadily, wings astiffening throughout the day. Emma Sue, root of every bender, probably had no idea that he was drunk each time they met, for she never saw him in any better condition. She must believe he lay over every armchair as a second skin to the brocade, and that his eyes were always languid.

Among the evolved humans, Andrew was too quick to be kept track of. His normal everyday eyes were rocketing pinballs, powered by manic energy. And when he was in the depressive stage, his eyes were dark crawling slugs. But tonight, he was merely in the bag and unfocussed.

He stood up on wobbly legs and walked to the French windows, which opened onto the terrace. He inhaled the fresh air and eyed the near ledge.

If she doesn't shut up, I'll jump.

Ah, but they were only five flights up, and the fall might not kill him immediately. He abhorred messy scenes. He was trapped then, escape cut off—so scowling Emma Sue might have the pleasure of doing the same to his soft parts.

She droned on in a testy nasal twang. Few of her words penetrated his skull. Only the tone was clear. She was pissed off.

What is it this time?

Did she hate his review of her pet artist of the month? And however did she get those boys into her bed? Who had so much ambition and such control of the flesh as to keep it from crawling off the bones when she touched him?

There was one ugly drawback to being mercifully swacked out of his mind: his reaction time was poor. He was not quick enough to dodge the flying spittle as she stomped toward him.

At some point in her fifty-one years, Emma Sue must have noticed that people would not come close to her, not within spitting range. He credited her alienation from all things human and good to this one tragic flaw. Even with her gift for self-delusion, how could she be unaware of it?

The darker possibility was that she was aware of it.

As a personal quirk, spit did have its fascination. This woman was not a hairy biker, but a power broker in the art community, directing the funds of every architect's budget to include the mandatory bit of sculpture which graced, or more frequently wrecked, each public plaza.

Her most glaring visible flaws began with the ankles of a plow horse. From there up, she bore a family resemblance to a succession of other animals, despite years of cosmetic surgery. No reputable doctor would touch her, for the best of surgeons could not make a muzzle into a human-scale nose, nor could they enlarge upon the piglet eyes. And so she had been relegated to the hacks of Fifth Avenue, putting all her faith in a good address.

She had the look of a jury-rigged job in the misalign-

ment of her features. Deep chemical peels had tightened
the skin of her face to expose the contours of fat deposits
and bulging veins. The flesh was scarred and discolored
beneath many coats of concealing makeup. And yet, with
each new procedure, the magic mirror of her mind was
telling her that she was becoming more beautiful.

On the upside, her wardrobe was flawless—and here
he complimented himself. It was his chore, as her personal advisor, to dress her properly, though not literally.
Saliva was their only intimacy.

Though her face was still puffy from her last surgery,
her makeup was perfect, and kept perfect throughout the
day, thanks to his scheduling of pit stops at the makeup
counters of Bloomingdale's. Now, out of habit, he
checked her fingernails. Perhaps he should send her back
to the shop for a nail wrap. It was always something,
wasn't it?

What is she going on about now?

Ah, the new artwork for the Gilette Plaza. So old Gregor hadn't left her any room to sufficiently vandalize the
plaza of his new building? Really? Brilliant man—the
only architect in New York who'd found a way to foil
her.

All her verbal defecation was being sifted and sanitized
through a gauze of alcohol. His thick wine stupor prevented her from knotting his insides while she damped
his skin.

What now?

Oh, that. Of course he had attended the funeral. He
was an art critic, wasn't he? Her feud with Koozeman
shouldn't be allowed to interfere with his own job. That
was asking too much. He had half a mind to leave, and
perhaps never to return. She'd be ruined then, wouldn't
she? Who but himself would tell the ignorant bitch when
she had lipstick on her teeth? This heinous symbiotic
relationship worked more in her favor than his.

What? Oh, right.

He bade farewell to the wine as he felt its effects abandoning his brain cells, being displaced by chilling sobriety.

The upper half of the office wall was solid glass, a wide window on the larger area of Special Crimes Section, where uniformed officers and civilian clerks moved in crisscrossing patterns through the labyrinth of file cabinets, desks and chairs. A score of taxpayers and suspects sat with detectives under the bright lights of the second shift. Across the room at the far desk, one of the taxpayers was crying. Her face contorted with pain; her mouth opened wide.

The woman's scream never penetrated Lieutenant Coffey's office. On his own side of the thick glass, it was a drawn-out silence that disturbed Jack Coffey. The muscles of his neck tightened as every quiet second was adding to the tension of the room.

Detective Sergeant Mallory had turned her back on him and faced the wall of glass. Her blond hair hung in curls over the collar of a long, black coat. Only a few inches of her blue jeans were visible below the hem. And now Coffey noticed Mallory was wearing her formal black running shoes tonight—all dressed up for the funeral service.

Sergeant Riker had made no such effort for the murdered artist. He was slumped in a chair by the desk, staring at his scuffed shoes. Coffey's first indication of trouble was the absence of Riker's cigarette smoke and sarcasm. This evening, the man was actually deferring to his younger superior officer, and this worried Coffey. How much damage could they have done tonight?

"The focus is on the murder of Dean Starr," said Coffey. "We are not resurrecting the old Ariel-Gilette case. Is that real clear, Mallory?"

Was she even listening to him? Jack Coffey thought not. His own ghostly reflection wafted in the glass behind

Mallory's, the image of a man thirty-six years old, not tall or short, hair and eyes neither dark nor light—best described as average in every aspect but his rank. In a bygone era, Coffey would have spent five more years in the slow mentoring process before he got his own detective's shield. Now, the younger investigators dominated every squad room. But at twenty-five, Mallory was the real standout. And in this young woman, Coffey could see all the flaws and virtues of the new NYPD cult of youth.

Lieutenant Coffey looked from one detective to the other. Riker was too easy a target. There were entirely too many things he could threaten this sergeant with; first among them was the aroma of wine imbibed on overtime. Jack Coffey was not one to press unfair advantage on a man.

So he turned on Mallory.

"Sit your ass down, Mallory! I want to see your damn face when I'm talking to you. I don't want to hear any crap later on about how you didn't quite hear a direct order."

She turned to glare at him. Well, that was something. Even Riker was impressed enough to lift his sorry head.

"I want to know where these orders are coming from." Her tone of voice put her on the borderline of insubordination. She had been straddling that line from the moment she walked in the door with Riker. Coffey had to admire her tactics. Whenever she was in deep trouble, she always went on the offensive.

She continued, not waiting for his reply, not wanting to lose momentum. "Oren Watt is out of the asylum less than a year, and we've got another body fixed up to look like a work of art. That bastard should be sitting in an interview room right now. Don't you think it's just a little strange that we can't touch him?"

Her sarcasm stayed within the gray zone, where Coffey could not challenge her without playing the fool.

"You know she's right," said Riker. "This is trouble. The press is already carping about it. Everybody's gonna think it's odd if Watt doesn't make the short list."

"Oren Watt has been vouched for," said Coffey. "He was never in the gallery the night Dean Starr went down."

"Who vouched for him? His quack psychiatrist?" Mallory faced the window, stepping on his authority by the simple act of turning her back on him again.

"Senator Berman vouched for Watt," said Coffey. "You might remember Berman. He was the police commissioner when you were just a little girl."

Riker was trying not to smile, and Coffey knew he had scored a game point by knocking Mallory down in size. He walked over to the window, tapped her on the shoulder and said, "Sit *down*, Sergeant."

She shrugged off the trench coat and folded it neatly over one arm. And now, as though it were her own idea, Mallory pulled up a chair and settled into it. She stretched out her long legs, and avoided looking at him—yet another sign of trouble.

He addressed both of his detectives. "Senator Berman says Oren Watt wasn't there, and none of the other guests saw him either. When Berman was the commissioner, Oren Watt's art show was the biggest, bloodiest case of his career. Watt's face was all over the papers for months, so it's not likely the senator would forget what the bastard looked like. None of us will. If Berman says the man wasn't there, we take his word for it."

"*You* talked to Senator Berman?" There was a light incredulity in her question. It was a well-placed shot, for he had not been allowed near the senator.

Good guess, Mallory. "Blakely interviewed him."

"That figures," said Mallory. "The chief's one hell of a political animal, isn't he? So this is all coming down from Blakely's office, right? Twelve years ago, it was

Blakely who tried to force Markowitz to close out the double homicide.''

"That's bullshit, Mallory! It made sense to close out the case. Watt was insane—he couldn't stand trial, and you *know*—''

"And what about the gallery owner?'' Riker's voice carried a suspicious amount of respect this evening. "Do we ever get to talk to Koozeman?''

"No,'' said Coffey. "We already have his statement from the first officer on the scene.''

"He should be at the top of the suspect list.'' Mallory turned to Riker. "Can't you just smell the money? I want to go over Koozeman's books.''

"You don't go near him!'' Coffey's gut sent him a sharp message of pain, and then he realized that she was only torturing him for fun. *Well, shot for shot, Mallory.* "If you can't follow orders, I'll bury you in the computer room, and you'll never get out on the street again. Is that understood?''

Oh, she didn't like that one bit.

He could see her return volley coming, the predictable threat to quit the force. The slight lift of her chin was all but telegraphing a reminder that she could make twice the money in the private sector. Maybe she would escalate her illegal, unauthorized fiddle and become less than a silent partner in Charles Butler's consulting firm. Coffey stood a little straighter, squaring off his body, gearing up his mind for the inevitable fight. Just let her try to jerk his—

"You're right,'' she said softly. "It was a bad idea to go after Watt. And the less the gallery owner knows, the better.''

What did she expect him to do with all this excess adrenaline? Maybe she was hoping it would burn a hole in his veins.

She crossed the room to settle on the corner of his desk. One long blue-jeaned leg draped over the edge of it. One black running shoe dangled as she smiled. He had to wonder what she was planning to do to him. Boxing with Mallory so fascinated him, he was ruined for every other form of blood sport.

"You think I don't understand your position," said Mallory. "But I do. If Blakely found out you disobeyed an order, he'd go after you, wouldn't he? It makes a lot of sense to keep a low profile."

He was digesting her if-you-only-had-a-spine implication when she reached down to the canvas tote bag on the floor and pulled out a set of photographs.

"These are the old shots of the dancer's funeral." She held out one panoramic view of a large group of people. "The Gilettes hired security to keep the circus out. Only friends, relatives and police. Look at this figure two heads away from Markowitz." Mallory was pointing at the one outstanding mourner, remarkable for his height of six four, and his large nose. "Look at that. It's Charles."

Charles Butler had been one of her foster father's closest friends. Though Louis Markowitz came from humble environs and Charles was descended from Park Avenue stock, commonalities had outweighed their differences—Charles was also a charming man with a giant brain. But years before Charles and Markowitz ever met, they had attended a funeral together.

"This is gold," said Mallory. "I've got my own connection to the Gilette family, and I can work it quietly. Charles has Social Register connections and art connections. He spends a fortune at the galleries. You want to keep it quiet, right? Do you know anyone more discreet than Charles Butler?"

Coffey knew he was about to be sucker-punched, but not quite how she was going to do it to him.

"Riker and I can work the case out of the office in Charles's building," she said. "It's perfect. Nothing in print lying around for a clerk to sell to a tabloid. And if

Blakely asks you what's going on, you won't know, will you?''

Did she really think he was that stupid?

"Oh, but I like to know what's going on with you, Mallory. Just every damn minute of the day."

"Markowitz never did."

True. When Markowitz had command of Special Crimes, things had been quite different. Every time she had illegally raided a computer to pull information, Markowitz knew he could claim the ignorance of a computer illiterate. Well, he had inherited Markowitz's job, but thanks, Mallory, he would rather run the place his own way.

He pulled his sportscoat from the hanger on the back of the door. "We're going to run a clean investigation." He put one shirtsleeve into the coat to signal to his detectives that this meeting, in fact, this *day* was at an end. "I give the orders, Mallory, and you follow them. It's a novel idea, but you'll get used to it."

"I have to work the old case to—"

Well, that tears it.

"The old case is off-limits." His coat was off again and roughly slung over one arm as he turned on her. "Off-limits! That's the last time I'm going to tell you, Mallory."

Her body was stiffening. Her leg ceased to dangle over the edge of his desk. The running shoe was frozen at an angle of tension. He never moved, but in his mind, he was putting up his own fists as they squared off from opposite sides of the room.

Well, good. Let's get this out on the table. And right now!

"Twelve years ago," she said, voice on the rise, "Markowitz didn't just *think* Watt's confession was a fake," louder now, "he *knew* it!"

"Markowitz doesn't work here anymore! That case is closed!"

"Not officially! Markowitz never closed it!"

"Well, *I'm* closing it! Don't you remember? Watt confessed!" he outshouted her.

"Markowitz didn't—"

"The hell with Markowitz! That wasn't the only time your old man screwed up!"

Riker shot him a warning glance. *You've gone too far*, said the slow shake of the sergeant's head. The last time her father made a bad mistake, the only bad one in living memory, it had gotten him killed in the line of duty.

Coffey felt the heat rising in his face. Why had he said it? Markowitz had been his mentor, quietly cleaning up the debris each time the rookie had made a mess of something. The old man had given out more second chances than Coffey deserved. And now he had just thanked him.

Forgive me.

Too late—Mallory was staring at him with solid hatred.

She eased off the desk and came toward him. Coffey recognized the gait of the pugilist. Her hands were curling into fists, and there was a physical menace in the movement of her body. In peripheral vision, he could see Riker rising from his chair with the same idea and perhaps a plan to slow her down before the damage was done. But Mallory stopped dead, her face a bare three inches from Coffey's.

"All right," she said, "forget Markowitz."

As if he could.

"Blakely's interference is as dirty as it gets," she said. Actually, she spat the words out. "I can link the old double homicide to Dean Starr—a fresh murder, and suddenly the chief's hot to bury it." Her voice was on the rise again. "And all you can say is the case is *off-limits?* Don't try to snow me, Coffey. I'm not a kid anymore."

And she couldn't be snowed when she *was* a kid. She was not much changed over the years he had known her. The anger had always been there, beneath the tightly controlled veneer of manners. Her foster mother, Helen Markowitz, had installed that rough coat of etiquette on Mallory's psyche when she was ten. When that good woman died four years ago, her handiwork had not faltered. When Louis Markowitz died, it had developed cracks to drive a truck through, yet somehow it held.

Mallory's voice was lower now. "You want me to work around department politics? Okay, I will. Let me run this case my way, and I promise nothing will come back on you."

The orphan standing in front of him now was hardly helpless or pitiable, was she? But a ten-year-old street kid was always lurking under the skin of her, peeking out to remind him of her baby days on the road, stealing every necessity, biting every hand that tried to reach her.

Until Markowitz.

As much as he had loved Louis Markowitz, sometimes he cursed the man for dying and leaving her so alone.

Mallory walked over to the desk and pulled another photograph from her tote bag. She came back to him and placed it in his hands—a present.

It was one of the old crime-scene photos of the artist and the dancer. He had never wanted to see this piece of cruelty again, and now he could not look away. It was truly stunning, the effect of these two young corpses, eyes wide for the camera. He was staring into the heart of Special Crimes Section, the core purpose of its inception—the abyss—and it was looking back at him.

Suppose Markowitz had been right? What if the butcher was still out there?

He met her eyes as she took the photograph from his hands. Seconds dragged by as Coffey and Markowitz's daughter played the staring game which would determine where the power lay. And now, she confounded him by dropping her eyes and giving him the scoring point of the match, in full view of Riker, and thus saving his face.

"Okay, Mallory. You and Riker work it your way."

• • •

Andrew Bliss had no memory of crawling out of Emma Sue Hollaran's apartment. When vision and mind achieved parity of clarity, he was standing on the first floor of Bloomingdale's.

Of all the department stores in all the world, only Bloomingdale's had parishioners, and Andrew was one of the faithful. His greatest fear was not death, but being locked away from his store of choice. It was a psychedelic womb. His *raison d'être* was here in the mazes of color and light, a vast array of goods on floor after floor, enough to shut down the neural synapses of the novice shopper. There were no less than five restaurants in Bloomingdale's, if one counted the espresso bar, but his favorite was Le Train Bleu, and he was on his way to it.

On the first floor, the salesclerks held fragrance bottles in a vaguely threatening manner, fully prepared to recondition any offensive odors which might enter the store on two legs. Other women with perfect makeup and clipboards were suggesting to shoppers that their faces would not do, in fact needed to be completely made over.

Nearing the escalators, he observed the confusion of an amateur shopper, and he knew the woman was searching for a way to get to the cleverly hidden second floor. Sometimes even hard-core veterans couldn't immediately find their way to the escalators. Andrew could do it blind drunk, and he did.

One hard-boiled shopper found the escalator too slow. She ran up the moving staircase, leading a charge of tourists who chatted only in Japanese. "Trust me," the woman said to the confused faces of a party of obviously non–English-speaking people. "I know where to find it. I know their stock better than they do." Her foot soldiers smiled and nodded. Somehow she had communicated product without foreign-language skills. Well, product was everything, wasn't it? Truly transcendent.

He changed escalators on the second floor and rode

upward and onward, heading slowly toward last call for wine at Le Train Bleu. Rising to the third floor, he rode into the spectacle of a raven-haired mannequin in a silver gown, all dressed up to go dancing. The mannequin reminded him of Aubry Gilette, the young dancer who had died with artist Peter Ariel. On the fourth floor, two workers passed the escalator with a headless, handless mannequin, and this was Aubry too.

On the fifth floor, as he stepped off the escalator and walked to the next moving staircase, he looked down at the carpet, which had always brought to mind the color of red wine. Now it was more the color of blood, blood all over the floor, every bit of it. He nearly slipped in it, so complete was the illusion of the guilty eye.

Finally, he stepped off the mechanical stairs on the sixth floor and headed for Le Train Bleu. The restaurant was open late this evening to cater a party of fashion designers. He approached the maitre d' and extended his invitation. The man smiled at his most loyal patron and escorted Andrew through the space arranged in Orient Express ambience. The dimensions of the pale green room, the banks of square windows, and every appointment of brass, wood and crystal kept to the design of a train. Crisp white napkins graced linen tablecloths, and plush green chairs completed the atmosphere of fine railway dining from an era gone by.

His personal shopper, Annie, was seated at his usual table. He was oblivious to the crowd as he sat down. He beamed his widest smile on Annie, for she was his treasure. She made his lunch and dinner reservations, called for his cabs, did his shopping, and rearranged his business appointments when they interfered with special shipments and sales.

"Annie."

"Yes, dear?"

"I'm going to change my life."

"Yes, dear."

Annie had her own style—minimalism. Each day, she wore the same dress, a classic black shift which never showed stains. He often wondered if she washed it out each night, or might she have a closetful. In the time he had known her, she had gone from salt and pepper to solid white hair. Her fingernails went everywhere naked, and she wore slippers around the department store. He tolerated the slippers and the lack of polish because he loved her best.

"You know, Annie, I worry about this place when the lights go out. But I imagine the security is rather good. I suppose they just let a pack of dogs roam at will— something like that?"

"No, the dogs go around with a guard. Employees have been here pretty late some nights."

"So they give the employees lots of overtime, do they?"

"No, dear. That was in the holiday season. No one does overtime this time of year."

"Annie, tell me more about the store security. I find this fascinating."

"Yes, dear."

Riker turned on the wall switch and an overhead light bounced off the rows of metal filing cabinets. There was no one on duty in the records room this time of night, no one to remind him that the law forbade smoking in public buildings. The antismoking activists closed in on him tighter and tighter every day—for his own good, they said. But though he coughed himself to sleep every night, and the stale smell of smoke clung to all his clothes, this dirty and unhealthy habit had become more and more attractive. Now it was a bona fide sport, a real challenge to find the odd room where he would not be caught. He reached in his pocket for the outlaw cigarettes.

He heard the door open behind him, but had no time

to turn around before a hand grasped his shoulder. It was not a warm and friendly grasp. Riker turned to face a young man with unruly blond hair and the much put-out pout of a giant five-year-old with a goatee. Dr. Daily was the newest staffer of the Medical Examiner's Office, and the younger man was wearing a very unfriendly expression. Riker looked down at the hand riding the material of his suit. Riker's expression said, *Back off*.

Daily's hand dropped to his side.

Prick.

"Well, Daily, you're working late tonight."

"All right, Detective, what's the deal? Why does NYPD want Slope to redo my autopsy?"

"Nothing personal, Doc. We were just wondering how that ice pick could've ruptured the heart from the back. We only want a second opinion is all."

"It was an ice pick. For Christ's sake, you found it next to the damn body."

"It probably was a pick. But it couldn't have been the one we found by the body. That was the bartender's. No blood traces."

"So the blood was wiped off. So what?"

"Naw, Heller would've found something with his little bag of chemicals and magic dust. He's the best forensic man in the country. The FBI's been trying to seduce him away from the force for years. Oh, and the bartender's pick was too short."

"What the hell does it matter if it was one ice pick or another one?"

"Well, Daily, it's always a good idea to know what the weapon looks like, just in case you trip over it while you're making an arrest."

"Okay, so you know it's a long ice pick. What does that—"

"And it makes the case a little more interesting if the weapon was brought to the gallery. That makes it premeditation. We gotta nail these things down in case the perp tries to claim temporary insanity, crime of passion. We also thought it might be nice to have a few blood samples, stomach contents, stuff like that.''

''I should think it would be obvious he wasn't poisoned. So I'm being criticized for trying to save the taxpayers a little money? Is that what you're telling me? Do you know how much it costs to run those tests?''

''Well, my partner likes these little details.''

Riker smiled. He had made book that Slope would fire this kid long before the probationary period was up. He had picked the early date in the office betting pool, and he was hoping this would be the autopsy that won him the big bucks.

Mallory walked through the swinging door, followed by Dr. Edward Slope, the chief medical examiner. They walked to the far side of the records room, where Slope busied himself at a filing cabinet and spoke to Mallory in a low voice. He handed her a manila folder and disappeared down an aisle of cabinets. Riker heard the angry slam of a metal drawer from a distance of two rows of tall steel files. He wondered what Mallory had done to brighten Slope's evening.

Dr. Daily was staring at her now. All animosity forgotten, he punched Riker lightly on the arm in the spirit of just-us-boys.

''Nice piece of ass,'' said Daily, with a wide grin. As the young doctor swaggered off in Mallory's direction, Riker only regretted that he had no time to place a side bet on Daily's life expectancy.

Riker watched the young man begin the courtship dance, strutting up and down in front of her, picking up a chart, pulling out a drawer and checking a file. When at last he came to rest beside Mallory, his height was even with hers at five feet ten, and Riker could swear the man was stretching his neck to be taller.

Mallory continued to look at the photos. She put all but one of them into her tote and glanced at her watch.

The doctor must be feeling the pressure of impending loss of opportunity. Now he was puffing out his chest and his young ego.

Riker winced because he knew what was coming next.

"I'm off duty now. I thought we might go out for a drink," said Daily, as though he were offering to do her a favor.

"Why would I want to do that?" Mallory's face was incredulous.

"Excuse me?"

The words *Fuck yourself* were in her eyes, but she would not say them. Her foster mother had not liked such words, and Mallory continued to defer to Helen Marko-witz long after the woman had died. So now she only stared at Daily for one chill moment, just long enough to shrivel his testicles with frost and drive his penis back up into his body cavity in a mad quest for warmth and survival. Satisfied that Daily was indeed self-fucked, she resumed her study of a dead body, apparently finding it a thousand times more appealing.

The young doctor looked quickly to Riker, who refrained from laughing aloud. Daily turned back to her. "I just thought—"

He was talking to the air. The door was swinging in her wake.

He walked back to Riker, pointing one thumb toward the door. "Frigid little bitch, isn't she?"

"Naw," said Riker. "That ain't it."

"So just what is that cunt's problem?"

"You don't know about Mallory? Nobody told you?"

"Told me what?"

"She's an escaped nun," said Riker.

Chief Medical Examiner Edward Slope rounded a wall of filing cabinets to stand just behind Dr. Daily, the most junior member of his staff. The overhead light gave the elder doctor's gray hair the shine of silver. Slope was a tall man, and his stony face was better suited to a general than a physician. When he cleared his throat, it had the effect of a gunshot.

The young doctor spun around to face his superior. Daily was all startled like a bird, and less the man now.

"She can't have a drink with you," said Dr. Slope, in tones of reined-in anger, "because I don't think her mother would've approved of your language." Slope bent down to bring his face level with Daily's and to destroy all sense of personal territory. "Her parents were my oldest and dearest friends."

After the younger doctor had fled the room with as much decorum as fear for his job would allow, Slope turned on Riker.

"Now what was all that crap about an escaped nun? Satan has no *nuns*."

A long string of psychiatrists had told him that depression crept up on one so slowly and with such stealth, no victim could point to the hour of its arrival or even the day. But this was not true. Andrew Bliss could point out the very moment in the first whispers from the back of his own mind, which said to him, *You are human garbage.*

He had thought of visiting his current psychiatrist, but they would only have gone round and round again over the lithium. The lithium made him into a contented cow with slurred speech and hand tremors for all his waking hours, and he had long ago decided he would not forgo the epiphany of his euphoric highs in order to escape the black holes of depression. He preferred to self-medicate with alcohol, but the glow of it was wearing thin, and the calming effects were dissipating now.

The roller coaster was revving up its engine once more. The conductor of his moods was crying, *All aboard, Andrew, and away we go!* And he was climbing, soaring in his mind, looking toward the radiant lights of Bloomingdale's ceiling. *Gathering speed, Andrew. Never mind that safety belt, boy.*

He raced up the mechanical stairs, and two blue-haired dowagers bounced off the rail at his passing. He roughly shouldered a tall brunette who was young and a true child of New York City. But Andrew was one second gone before she thought to put her knee into his groin; he was moving that fast in the body, and his brain was fairly electrified as it sped along its single rail.

In the late hours of the night, when the store had been swept free of consumers and staff, Andrew emerged from the shadows of Bloomingdale's with a shopping list. He consulted his watch and then his notebook. The watchman and his dogs should be patrolling the second floor.

He stepped lightly on the frozen mechanical staircase, heading toward the rug department. Oh, but on his way he must rip off a dozen raincoats. He would need at least a dozen to make a canopy. A small refrigerator was copped from the employee lounge. Housewares provided the electric espresso maker. He ticked off other items on his list: satin sheets, ten down quilts for his mattress, tulip glasses, a reclining chair and a reading lamp. An hour later, he leaned against the furniture dolly which he had boosted from the stockroom. Leverage was everything. He wasn't even sweating.

Andrew saw motion among the clothing racks, the shadow of a lithe and graceful dancer, sleek and young. *No, wait.* It was not a woman, but a large security dog. He had mistimed the watchman's rounds. He quickly sprayed his entire person with perfume, the better to smell like Bloomingdale's.

CHAPTER
2

THE BASEMENT WINDOW GAVE HER A GROUND-LEVEL
view of the suburban backyard, with its green lawn and
shade trees. This had been Louis Markowitz's piece of
the American dream.

The glass pane was streaked with water from the lawn
sprinkler, and the grass was neatly trimmed. Mallory
knew this was Robin Duffy's work. Markowitz's old
friend and neighbor did what he could to create the illusion that people still lived there. The old lawyer had
raked the leaves in the fall, shoveled the walks in the
winter, and brought her offers from young families who
wished to buy the place and bring it to life once more.
But to Robin Duffy's consternation, Mallory always refused to sell, and she never explained her reasons for
wanting to keep a house she would never live in again.

When was she here last?

She could not remember if it had been weeks ago or
a month. She reached up and opened the window. A fresh
breeze cut through the basement to kill off the musty
smell of abandonment.

Helen had been the first to abandon the house when
she died under a surgeon's knife. Then Mallory had
moved out of Brooklyn and into a Manhattan condo with

no reminders of home and grief. Markowitz had spent his last years working late hours to avoid coming home to empty rooms, unoccupied furniture and all the memories of Helen ganging up on him in the dark. After Mallory had put her father in the ground and finished his last case, she rarely visited the old place, though this was home and always would be.

No, she would never sell the house, never evict the Markowitzes, or what survived of them in closets, boxes and drawers, from the attic to the basement. She could not imagine an afterlife for them—so where were they, if not here?

Today she had one more piece of her father's unfinished business, and she had come home again to look for answers among his personal notes in the boxes and files of his disorganized, unfinished life.

She ran her fingers across the dust which had accumulated on the record albums of the swing bands and the cassettes of the Rolling Stones. There were also ancient reel-to-reel recordings, Markowitz's prized collection of vintage radio programs from the late thirties and forties. She blew more dust from the elaborate recording equipment she had brought to the house a year before his death. She had used it to preserve his most precious recordings on CDs before the old-fashioned tapes could rot on their spools.

Markowitz had been unreasonably happy when she told him he could play the CDs over and over, and never wear them out. She opened the plastic boxes now, all of them, and then she smiled. Though she had a mania for order and neatness, she was pleased to see the CD covers and discs completely mismatched to tell her he had made good use of her gift in the time that was left to him.

Now Riker sat in Markowitz's favorite chair. Helen had wanted to throw it out. To save it, the old man had dragged it down here to his basement sanctuary. He had never been able to throw anything away. Once she had chided him about that, but today she was counting on it.

Riker was bent over an open cardboard carton. "Your old man's filing system really sucks." He reached into the box, his fingers raking through the mess of matchbook covers, notepaper, one cocktail napkin, three dinner napkins, and all the assorted materials that would take the scratch of a pen or pencil. He read some of the notes and shook his head. "I've known Markowitz forever, but his shorthand still throws me. It could take a year to wade through this, and another year to make sense out of it."

"We'll just separate the critical notes by the dates. He dated everything." Mallory pulled up a small wooden chair which had been her own when she and Markowitz spent the rainy Saturday afternoons of her childhood in the golden age of radio, sipping cocoa and listening to the opening lines of The Shadow—*Who knows what evil lurks in the hearts of men?*

Riker held up one paper napkin, yellowed with age. "This might be worth something. The date is right. Listen to this. 'Weight twelve pounds, four ounces with bone. Started twelve-oh-five a.m. Finished twelve forty-five a.m. Time out to rest, five minutes. Time out to send the kid back to bed, fifteen minutes. Dull now. The next one would take longer.' Now what's that about?"

She took the napkin from his hand. The date was four days following the murder of the artist and the dancer. How old had she been then? Twelve? She looked at the time and the reference to the kid. Herself? It couldn't be. She had never been allowed to stay up that late.

Suddenly she remembered exactly when Markowitz had written that note. She looked up to the basement ceiling, as though she could see into the kitchen on the floor above them.

All those years ago, she had left her bed and gone down the stairs, minding the steps that made the most noise. She went stealing through the rooms of the dark house, hours beyond a child's bedtime. Young Kathy had been heading for the kitchen, tantalized by the knowledge of half a pie at the back of the refrigerator. Food was never begrudged in this house. Food was love. But being caught out of bed so late on a school night, that was another matter.

She had come upon Markowitz standing at Helen's chopping block and working over a leg of beef with a meat cleaver. So intent was he on his hacking, he never heard the small bare feet on the tiles as the child slipped into the kitchen behind his back. She retrieved the cordless electric meat carver from a drawer, making no sound until she switched it on and the metal came to life in her hand, motor buzzing, the serrated blade working back and forth.

Markowitz had whirled around in a near pirouette, so graceful for a man his size, excess weight hanging around his belt as a tribute to Helen's cooking. He had been shocked to see the child standing there in her pajamas. There were sweat stains under his arms, and his face was flushed with unaccustomed exertion.

"Kathy, I swear I'm gonna hang a bell on you."

And then he had thought to look at the kitchen clock, wiped his hands with a dish towel and scribbled a note on a white paper napkin. He smiled down at her and ruffled her hair. When he smiled, she smiled. It was an uncontrollable reflex, even when she was angry with him, and sometimes it drove her nuts that he could make her do that against her will. She recovered her solemnity quickly and held out the meat carver.

He had thanked her for it, and agreed that yes, the electric knife would be a lot faster than the cleaver. Then he read her mind and pulled the pie from the refrigerator and set it on the kitchen table. He poured them each a glass of milk, and they sat down together in companionable silence for a few bites.

"So, what's the deal with the meat?" the child had asked, nodding toward the chopping block with some

suspicion. Not counting this slice of pie, she knew all food came from Helen's hand, not his.

"Don't talk with your mouth full," he said.

When she had demolished her pie to the last crumb, Markowitz motioned her to stand, turned her around and gave her a very gentle push in the direction of bed and sleep.

Now Detective Sergeant Mallory sat under a bare lightbulb in the basement, staring at the notes on the age-yellowed napkin. She handed it back to Riker.

"These are the old man's stats for the time it took to cut through the meat and bones of Peter Ariel and Aubry Gilette."

Morning came with rude bright light, which penetrated the tender, pink membranes of his eyelids. When Andrew Bliss opened his eyes, he wondered if the bedroom ceiling didn't look rather like the blue sky, replete with fleecy clouds. He rejected this as impossible and closed his eyes again. But now there were car horns in his bedroom as well, and they played havoc with the fragile nerve endings behind his eyeballs, where his brain was fermenting in yesterday's wine. Unaccountably, his hair hurt, but he would think about that later.

He pushed aside a layer of down quilts, which he instantly recognized from Bloomingdale's Domestics display. Memory was stealing up on him. He looked around at the cables and the tall pipes, the black ductwork and vents, the surrounding buildings, and the mountains of stolen goods.

Of course.

In a salute to recovering memory, he slapped his forehead. He instantly regretted that. Holding his poor, freshly injured head, Andrew murmured an apology to it as he began to rise.

On your feet now, one leg next to the other. Good boy, you remembered.

He was attired in striped silk pajamas. A matching robe was laid out on an armchair. How had he gotten that heavy chair up to the roof? Ah, well, in the manic phase nothing was impossible. The door of Bloomingdale's roof was set high in a narrow shaft of brick standing twenty feet above the rooftop. The exit was sealed with industrial tape and bound by a heavy chain. The metal stairs leading from the door and down to the roof had been ripped away and twisted outward to hang in the sky as a staircase to nowhere. A second roof exit, resembling a storm cellar, was set into the ground. Half of this door had been barricaded with two steel beams and six large wooden cases topped by a pile of designer raincoats. The door handle was clear of debris, but useless.

Well, haven't I been thorough. But why?

It was a mercy the espresso maker from Housewares was already plugged into the roof cable. He could never have found the electrical outlet this morning, certainly not before a cup of coffee. He switched it on and smiled feebly when the red light glowed.

While the espresso machine was busy, he surveyed his new domain. Bloomingdale's roof was an island, one city block square and bounded by heavily trafficked streets on all sides. Ah, paradise. The potted palm tree in the corner might have been some idea of homage to other island exiles with a preference for sweaty tropics.

The espresso machine ceased its gurgling. When he looked down, he noticed the bullhorn plugged into the same outlet. What had he planned to do with that? And the binoculars? Or might this be something he had already done? He picked up the binoculars and adjusted the lenses in time to see a pigeon magnified to the proportions of Godzilla. Startled, he nearly dropped the glasses. He was unaccustomed to nature in the raw. He refocussed the lenses on the street below, and the next sighting was no less shocking.

Oh, the clothes, the clothes these people wore. How

did these idiots manage to commit so many really criminal offenses in a single outfit? Had they not eyes to see?

It was coming back to him now.

Right.

He picked up the bullhorn in his free hand and cleared his throat, amplifying his phlegm a hundredfold. It worked.

But where . . . Oh, right.

He had broken into the security office last night. This was one of the bullhorns they used for fire drills.

Through the telescoping lenses, he scanned the sidewalk again. A heavyset woman was strolling past the store—*his* store. Oh, this was really too much. He raised the bullhorn and inhaled deeply. "No you don't!" he blared in a voice so powerful it caught his hangover off guard, and the reaction time for pain to set in had a long lag. "You there! You in the black and white dress. Madam, you know damn well you're too heavy to wear horizontal stripes. Your friends have all told you that. Might I suggest a dark rose ensemble to go with that Mediterranean coloring?"

The woman, trapped in the twin lenses, moved her head quickly from side to side. Her mouth fell open, and her head slowly bowed. As she turned away from the store, a newspaper fell from her hand and marked the spot where Andrew had scored his first direct hit. The young woman settled into the gait of an old woman, meandering down another street which was not Andrew's street and of no concern to him. He had already moved on to the crime in progress at the bus stop.

"Oh, you can't be serious!" he screamed. And now delayed reaction set in. His brain was throbbing and thrashing against the sides of his skull in a mad attempt to get free of it. In a lower pitch, and with the pathos of genuine agony, he said, "You can't possibly take that gorgeous Armani creation on the bus."

The perpetrator in the Armani suit was all eyes, and his eyes went everywhere.

"That's right, you know what you've done wrong. Now go and flag down a cab. Show some dignity, for Christ's sake. Let's try and live up to the clothes, shall we?"

And the man did indeed put out his hand and flagged down a cab to carry him away as quickly as possible.

Andrew went back to his bed of ten down quilts and rested his damaged head on a pile of silk pillows. His head lolled from side to side as he took stock of his campsite. Fortuitously, he had remembered the larder of Le Train Bleu, and apparently he had removed their entire stock of premium wines. The cases were stacked in a solid wall of champagne and red wine. Cartons of imported cigarettes were strewn everywhere.

Did Bloomingdale's sell . . . ? Oh, right.

He had raided the locker of an executive.

Well, here was a snag. He had not had the foresight to steal a portable toilet before sealing the exits from the roof.

What about the fire escape?

No escape. The emergency exits were all interior. He looked up at the metal staircase which no longer led to the roof door. Distressed and mangled steel angled oddly away from the brick structure. Had he really done that? But how? Drunks could be so ingenious. He might have to get drunk again to figure out how he had managed it.

What else? Was that a year's supply of espresso beans from the gourmet selection on six? It was.

Oh, joy.

He opened the half-size refrigerator. No cream. He was inconsolable. Ah, but two magnums of wine were cooling with companion tulip glasses. Light flooded his soul again.

And food?

None. Not any in the refrigerator, nor among the boxes

and cartons. He counted fourteen smoking jackets, eight Dresden teacups, nine pairs of silk pajamas, two potted palm trees and no food.

During the bender, while he was in the genius mode, he must have resolved the problem of solid-waste disposal by eliminating the solids. Quite sensible. He could piss his liquid wastes over the side of the wall.

He returned to his post at the edge of the roof and slung the strap of the field glasses around his neck. He took up his horn just in time. There was another blight on the street. "You . . . in the too-mauve-for-words pantsuit."

The mauve woman stopped and looked everywhere but in the right direction.

"Up here," he guided her. "I'm up here with the pigeons and God. Look up! Good. What are you trying to do to me? Do you want me to hurl myself into the street? You can't get away with that pantsuit, and you know it. Give yourself up on the second floor. Surrender to Alice. She'll know how to deal with you."

The woman was entering the store. So far, the pedestrian masses were rather good about taking creative direction. So he had finally found his true vocation—fashion terrorist.

Now if only he had his personal shopper, his life would be complete. He leaned over the roof once more and screamed into the bullhorn, "Annie! Annie, where are you?"

Charles Butler unsheathed his blade and slashed open an envelope. He was arrested for a moment by the shining surface of his antique dagger.

Mrs. Ortega had been polishing things again.

He would rather have the ancient piece of silver clouded with tarnish. He never cared to come upon his own reflection, or even the knife blade's width of it, by surprise. But every now and again, he must endure a time when his housekeeper would go mad with metal cleaners, of which there were as many varieties as there were metals. And for a time, he could go nowhere in his own home without some bright piece of Mrs. Ortega's handiwork throwing back the image of a man whose nose was too long, and whose eyes resembled heavy-lidded hen's eggs with small blue irises.

Now he sat quietly awaiting his visitors' knock on the door. No doubt the people advancing down the hallway were known to him. He hadn't buzzed anyone into the building, so one of them must have a key. That narrowed the field to his tenants, his cleaning woman or his business partner. And of course the visitors were on their way to his own door, for this suite of offices and his apartment across the hall occupied the entire second floor of the SoHo building.

This particular room was the reception area of Mallory and Butler, Ltd. Queen Anne reigned with Louis XV in period furniture with graceful curving legs, which seemed always on the verge of dancing. Each morning, Charles sat down to this antique desk, opened his mail by the light of a tall triptych of arched windows—and wondered what his partner might be up to.

She so seldom stopped by anymore. He understood.

A consulting firm could not hold much allure for Mallory. The rather academic problems of quantifying, qualifying, and finding homes for the oddly gifted could hardly compare to the problems of Special Crimes Section. These days, she only stopped by to play with the computer toys she stored in her private office.

The footsteps in the hallway stopped. Now the door was opening without the customary knock. Only two people ever did that, Mrs. Ortega and Mallory. But his cleaning woman never traveled with an entourage.

Mallory was first into the room, carrying a large and dusty cardboard carton. She was in a black mood by her tone as she said to Riker, "I want to find that little twit, Andrew Bliss, and right now."

Behind the safe cover of his own carton, Riker was making facial expressions to indicate that she was a brat. He in turn was followed by a young uniformed officer with his own load of boxes, and these bore the stamp of NYPD. The parade trooped past his desk with two "Hi Charles"'s from Mallory and Riker. And then the door to Mallory's private office closed behind them.

Minutes later, the uniformed officer emerged, nodded to Charles in passing, and left him to wonder what was going on. Of course he could guess. He had read the morning paper. But most of the cartons had borne stamps from the NYPD evidence room. Now that was a problem, because they couldn't possibly have four cartons of evidence in a brand-new case which, according to the newspaper, involved a single ice pick, no suspects and no leads.

Riker emerged from Mallory's office, leaving the door ajar. "Charles, I'm gonna make coffee. You want some?"

"Oh, yes. Thank you." He would have asked after Riker's health, but the man was already ambling down the short hall leading to the office kitchen.

Charles leaned far over the desk to see through the open door. Mallory's office might as well have been in another building in an entirely different solar system, where extreme order and high technology prevailed over charm and antiquity.

Mallory was sitting cross-legged on the floor, her back turned to him as she lifted something heavy out of a carton. It was an axe wrapped in clear plastic. The axe handle was short, and the blade was no wider than the meat cleaver in his kitchen. He didn't care to hazard a guess at the stains visible through the clear cover.

What does an axe have to do with an ice pick murder?

Mallory's head turned quickly to catch him in the act of watching her.

Of all the bizarre talents he had ever been asked to study, Mallory's were the most convoluted. In addition to her gifts in the computer mode, she had a hyperawareness of her surroundings which he found inexplicable.

She smiled unlike any other woman. Her expression now said, *I caught you.* But her smiles had a wider spectrum of meanings, which included, *I'm going to get you for that,* and he never wanted to be the recipient of that one. It was so seldom that she smiled for happiness. He suspected there was not much of that in her life. He had known her for years, and yet she was still a great mystery to him. He had once asked Riker what Mallory did with her off-duty hours. Riker had advanced the theory that she went into a closet at night and hung from the rod by her heels like a vampire bat.

Now she beckoned to him. He left the room of beloved antiques and crossed over the threshold of her office and into the world of high technology. Three computers dominated the room, metallic cyclopes, each with a large gray terminal eye. Other machines kept them company in links of cables and wires. The office furnishings were metal with cruel sharp corners. Technical manuals sat in perfect order on the purely functional shelving.

And then there was the incongruity of a bloody axe.

Mallory pulled open the flaps of another carton. Inside was a jumble of papers in all shapes and sizes. Charles recognized the scrawled lines of Markowitz's handwriting on napkins, matchbook covers and envelopes. Mallory brushed these papers aside to reveal an old photograph. Wordlessly, she handed it to him. He recognized his own likeness first, all six feet, four inches of himself towering above the surrounding crowd of people. And then his eyes settled on the image of a dear friend, the late Louis Markowitz. It was a younger version of the man, perhaps by ten or twelve years. Louis's hair was only beginning to gray in this photograph. The excess of forty pounds was there, and carried with the same élan, but the lines of his face were not yet so deep.

"That was taken at Aubry Gilette's funeral," said Mallory.

Charles looked down at the photograph with wonder. If he had only been standing one place to the right, he might have had the pleasure of Louis Markowitz's company years earlier, and his own life might have been that much richer for it. He missed Louis sorely; he missed him every day.

And what effect had Louis's death had on his only child? Well, no outward effect at all. He often wondered if, in the secret life of Kathleen Mallory, she didn't spend part of her time in grief. He would never know. She was an intensely private person. There were questions one could never ask her, such as, *Does it hurt you still?*

Riker entered the room, juggling three coffee cups and the morning paper. He placed one cup in Charles's free hand, and leaning down, he gave one to Mallory. Riker drank deeply, rushing caffeine into his veins until his eyes were all the way open.

"I don't think you're gonna find a money motive in this one, kid." Riker hunkered down beside her. "That must put a real crimp in your day."

"It could be revenge," said Mallory. "I like that one, too."

Riker held up the newspaper, folded back to the page Charles had been reading. "You wanna see your reviews?"

The headline at the top of the column read: NYPD HUNTS ART TERRORIST. In the subheading it said: Connection to Oren Watt?

Riker was grinning. "I think they've really captured your style, kid. Listen to this. 'Detective Sergeant Kathleen Mallory would have walked over the body of the

Times reporter had he not scrambled to get out of her way.' "

"And it's a good picture, too," said Charles, bending down to admire her portrait over Riker's shoulder. "It's worthy of a frame. But what did you do to the reporter?"

"I never touched that bastard."

"She told him to get the hell out of her way or she'd shoot him." Riker handed the paper to Mallory. "You're damn lucky he had a sense of humor. We don't want any more bad press on this case." As Mallory held the paper, Riker tapped the caption under her photograph. " 'The photogenic green-eyed blond detective.' I like that line."

"On the next page," said Charles, "there's an interview with the FBI spokesman. The reporter was questioning him on the terrorist aspect of the murder— something to do with a critic's column on art terrorism. The FBI man says they're looking into it."

"Oh, terrific." Riker slugged back the last of his coffee. "Damn that jerk Andrew Bliss. Now we got feds in the house. Commissioner Beale's gonna have an aneurysm. A damn swarm of feds with psychiatric Ouija boards."

Mallory said nothing. In her own critique, she dumped the newspaper into a wastebasket. She pulled four plastic bags from the carton and read the labels. "What about all this hair and fiber evidence? Was all of this accounted for? I can't find the forensic reports."

"Never developed it," said Riker. "The gallery was a public space with heavy traffic. All of it was collected and tagged, but most of it wasn't worth the tests."

"That doesn't sound like Markowitz. He was a detail freak."

"After Oren Watt confessed to the murder, we couldn't justify the budget for any more lab work. Blakely did everything but handcuff Markowitz. The chief just wanted the case wrapped and forgotten."

Oren Watt? Charles stood over Mallory's desk and

looked down at the labels of other evidence bags. Each one bore Oren Watt's name. "Why are you going back into this old murder? They have the man who did it. They caught him twelve years ago."

"No they didn't." Mallory turned back to the carton and pulled out a paper bag. It came apart as she handled it, and a shred of stained clothing fell to the floor. "They caught a man to do the time for the murders. That's not quite the same thing. Watt didn't do it."

Riker lowered his head only a little and turned his face toward the window. Charles recognized the subtle meaning of this simple gesture. Apparently, Riker did not share her theory.

"What about these tracks?" She held up a bundle of photographs. The first image was a pattern of red footprints on a hardwood floor. "Men's shoes, women's shoes." She shuffled the photographs like a deck of cards. "There aren't any notes on half of these prints." By her tone of voice, she seemed to hold Riker responsible for this oversight.

"Damn waste of time," said Riker. "Someone called an anonymous tip to the press that night. The news crews beat a patrol car to the scene by five minutes. They contaminated the evidence before the uniforms showed up. We corralled some of the reporters to print their shoes for elimination, but we didn't get all of them."

He took the photographs from her hand, riffled through them, pulled one out and turned it over to display a label. "This one has notes. It's tagged for Oren Watt. That's one set of footprints we had an easy match for. And his shoes were still bloody when his psychiatrist surrendered him to the police."

Charles had the sense that Riker was playing a game of push and shove with Mallory. She chose to let him play alone. Her voice was casual, and her face turned down to the contents of the carton. "Any idea who tipped off the newspapers?"

.

"Probably Oren Watt," said Riker, draining his coffee cup. "Watt wouldn't be the first psychopath with a craving for publicity."

"Oren Watt didn't do it." There was a definite edge to her voice this time.

"Both things could be true," Charles suggested in the gentle manner of a peacemaker. "Watt could have made that call whether he did the murders or not."

Mallory nodded, seeming to like that idea. Riker would not look at her. He moved away to stand by the door and stare into his empty cup.

Charles stepped between them. "What can I do to help?"

"You're taking me to the ball tomorrow night," said Mallory.

"You can't mean the Manhattan Charities Ball. Is that tomorrow?"

"Yes, Charles." She stood up and walked to her desk.

"But no one actually *goes* to the ball."

"You buy the tickets every year." She opened the desk's center drawer and pulled out the printed invitations and receipts. Mallory held them up to him, as though she had just caught him in a lie.

She must have retrieved the invitations from the wastebasket in the reception room where he filed them every year. She could only have found the receipts in his private files. One day they really must sit down and discuss what his privacy meant to him, as opposed to what little it meant to her.

For the moment, he only shrugged. "Well, of course I buy the tickets. It's a charity event. My mother was a friend of Mrs. Quinn's. We've always bought the tickets, but no one actually *goes* to the ball."

"The mayor goes," said Riker.

"Well, yes, but he's not—" Here Charles stopped himself from saying that the mayor did not come from a Social Register family, that he was merely the leader of the largest city on earth. "Yes, I suppose the city's power structure will be there. You're quite right. But *I* don't know anyone who goes."

"J. L. Quinn will be there, and you know him." Mallory turned to face the rear wall. It was covered with cork and functioned as a giant bulletin board. "You were at Harvard the same time Quinn was."

Charles wasn't about to ask her how she knew that. He was staring at her computers, which sometimes did double duty as cyberspace burglary tools.

"Well, Quinn *has* to go," he said somewhat defensively. "His mother hosts the ball."

"And Aubry's father—the architect, Gregor Gilette?" She pinned the old photograph of Aubry's funeral to the wall. "He'll be at the ball. You know him, too, don't you?"

As if there was any doubt in her mind about any sector of his formerly private life. "Gregor also has to go. He was married to Mrs. Quinn's daughter."

"Sabra?" Mallory walked back to the carton and sifted through the paperwork bundles, scanning a page in each one. She turned to Riker. "Just the one name everywhere Aubry's mother is listed. Why isn't it Sabra *Gilette*?"

Riker shrugged. "Sabra was her full legal name, just the one name."

Mallory looked to Charles for enlightenment.

"Sabra renounced the family name and walked away from the money. Then she became wildly successful on her own. She was an enormously talented painter. Later, she set a legal precedent when she married Gregor Gilette and refused to take his name. She—"

"Do you remember seeing Sabra at Aubry's funeral?"

"Yes, it was the last time I ever saw her."

Mallory was deep in the interrogation mode now. She had reached her limit for six minutes of semicivil conversation. "Did you like Sabra?"

"Yes, very much. I also liked her work. I have one of her early paintings." Suddenly he wished he had not told her that. And now she would want to know—

"Where is it?"

Charles and Mallory walked across the hall to the apartment which was his residence. Beyond the foyer, a bank of tall windows made the front room light and airy, despite the heavy furnishings in dark woods spanning four centuries of craftsmen. All that belonged to his own era were the contemporary works of art. They should not have worked well with the older pieces, and yet they did. The colors of a splatter painting agreed with the bright details of the Persian rug and the upholstery of a George III side chair. Another abstract repeated the rococo lines of a Belter sofa.

They walked down the wide hallway, where late twentieth-century drawings were on close hanging acquaintance with framed pages of illuminated manuscripts. At the end of the hall, he opened a linen closet and pointed to a framed canvas sitting on the floor, face to the wall. He lifted it carefully and handed it to her. The painting had a lonely, sad feel to it. One small pale worm of an element writhed in a maelstrom of powerful bold color.

"Don't you like it, Charles?"

"I like it very much. It's one of her most accessible works. I bought it at a Christie's auction a few years ago."

"Why do you keep it on the floor of a closet?"

He shifted uncomfortably, not wanting to answer her. He kept it in the closet because what it communicated was so obvious, so blatant that his cleaning woman, Mrs. Ortega, had readily understood it. That high school dropout who loved baseball and hated art, Mrs. Ortega, had understood the painting so clearly that Charles had been embarrassed when the normally hostile cleaning woman had gone out of her way to be nice to him for several weeks after she had seen the painting on the wall of his front room. *So this is what your guts look like,* Mrs. Ortega's uncharacteristic kindness had said to him, *you poor jerk.*

Now he wondered if Mallory was drawing the same inference.

"Charles, can we hang this in my office for a while? Just till I wrap the case? Oh, and your collection of art catalogs? Do you have one of Sabra's museum retrospective?"

They returned to the office with the painting and the catalog. Mallory set the canvas against the cork wall, which Riker was littering with clippings, photographs and reports. Mallory followed behind him, straightening every sheet with machinelike precision. Finally, she slapped Riker's hand away and forbade him to touch the board at all.

Charles sat at Mallory's desk. Riker looked over his shoulder as he turned the pages of the museum catalog, hunting for photographs of the elusive Sabra. Here and there, Charles would point out a turned face, the line of a cheek. A hand raised to blind the camera's eye.

"What's with this broad?" said Riker. "There's not one clear photograph of her."

"She hated the sight of a camera," said Charles. "Sabra was always reclusive. She very rarely appeared in public. An agent submitted her work through one gallery, and I'm not sure she ever met with the gallery director."

Mallory turned away from her work on the cork wall. "Was it Koozeman's gallery?"

"Oh, no," said Charles. "Sabra was a major talent. She showed in the most prominent gallery on Fifty-seventh Street. In those days, Koozeman only had a small storefront gallery in the East Village—the one where Sabra's daughter was murdered."

"Here's one of Sabra's kid." Riker pointed to the photograph of a young woman standing by a painting. "Pretty girl. Did you know Aubry very well?"

"No, not really," said Charles. "Just a nodding acquaintance. These were people I ran into at weddings and
funerals. I'm usually excused from christenings and grad-
uations. I did see Aubry at the gallery shows. Sabra rarely
attended her own openings, but Aubry and her father
never missed one."

Mallory was flipping through a notebook, checking off
items. Now she hovered over Charles and dropped a card
on the desk in front of him. "I made a hair appointment
for you."

"Pardon?"

"You need a haircut. My stylist will take you this afternoon. That's your appointment card."

"But this salon—"

"I know. They only do women. But I leave large tips.
They'll do you. So we have a date, Charles?"

"For the ball? Oh, yes."

Oh, God, yes and absolutely.

Since his teenage years, it had been his fantasy to walk
into a grand ballroom with a beautiful woman on his arm.
In earlier fantasies of childhood, he had seen himself in
the bedtime story of Pinocchio, the long-nosed puppet
who ached to become a real boy. Now, in his fortieth
year, as he looked across the room at young Mallory, he
realized he had grown up into Cyrano, another poor hapless longnose who fell in love and found it to be a bleak
place where he lived by himself.

And what of Mallory's perceptions of this strange one-
sided romance? He wondered if she didn't see him as a
large and friendly, slightly shaggy dog in a three-piece
suit.

As if in answer to his innermost thoughts and fears,
she patted him on the head and told him to get out of
her chair.

He had only closed his eyes for a moment, and then he
had fallen into a deep sleep. In the next moment, his head
exploded.

"ANDREW!" screamed the voice from hell.

Emma Sue?

Oh, no. She had her own bullhorn. If there really was a God in New York City, how did He coexist with Emma Sue Hollaran? The woman's normal speaking voice had the unholy pitch of a cat set on fire. Now she was electrified, insanely amplified. And for the first time in years, he was not fortified to withstand it. This time, he was sober and all soft underbelly.

Brain asloshing, moving slowly, minding the pain, he crept to the short wall at the edge of the roof.

"GOOD MORNING, ANDREW!"

His body jerked back, the involuntary motion of a man whose head has been struck by a grenade. He ventured a second glance over the side. Another woman was taking the bullhorn away from Emma Sue.

Oh, thank you, thank you, whoever you are.

She must be from the haute couture police, for Emma Sue was dressed in the most awful rag. It had to be some wardrobe relic from the days when she was allowed to dress herself without his advice. Well, if this alone did not demonstrate his indispensability. The dress was a bright pink billboard plastered on her meaty frame, advertising choice cuts of bovine flesh, thick flanks and overhanging rump. And what was she doing here? He had only wanted her to handle a simple press release.

He picked up his bullhorn and aimed at her like a gun. Oh, would that it were a gun. "Emma Sue, go inside and have someone dress you. Now, before someone sees you."

She was going inside. And he knew it would be a while before she dared come back. Wasn't he brilliant? Oh, she must be seething. How secure was the roof door?

"Mr. Bliss," said the more civil woman now in possession of the bullhorn. "I'm Harriet Marcan. *Women's Wear?*"

"Call me Andrew. What may I do for you?"

"I'd like to interview you, Andrew. May I come up?"

"Not possible, I'm afraid. The stairs are torn away from one door and the other is barricaded. You simply can't get here from there." Annie had joined the reporter on the sidewalk. "But of course," he continued, "I have no objection to the interview."

"It's a bit awkward, isn't it?" With one hand, Ms. Marcan tossed off the flyaway gesture of *You're kidding, right?*

"I can fix that," said Andrew. "Annie, have an armchair and a table brought down from Furniture on the fifth floor. And arrange a champagne brunch for our Ms. Marcan."

Across champagne glasses and through dueling bullhorns, Andrew explained his *modus operandi* to the reporter from *Women's Wear*. Fashion terrorism was the only way. She could see that, couldn't she? For terrorism was horribly effective, wasn't it? And who could fail to notice, in a daily perusal of the *Times*, that it worked best when there was a base of genuine and justifiable outrage. The world might not approve the methodology, but they did sit up and pay attention. And they became, against their collective will, aware of wrongs done.

So now there was a homeland for the beautiful people. Nothing fancy, just the one square block of Bloomingdale's. And tomorrow? The entire island of Manhattan.

"Sorry, I'm digressing. Terrorism will out. You'll see."

J. L. Quinn followed her through the door with a few minutes' distance between them. When he entered the Koozeman Gallery, it took him another minute to locate Detective Mallory among the bustle of art handlers, a tour group and the television crew.

Mallory stood by the entrance of the main gallery, removing the yellow strips of tape which had marked the crime scene. The television crew poured into this room as the last tape was stripped away, and she stood aside.

Oren Watt, confessed murderer in a dark suit, was leading the parade of cameras, women with clipboards and men with sound equipment and lights. The flesh of Watt's head shone through the stubble of close-cropped brown hair. His dark glasses only concealed small, ordinary eyes, and could not begin to disguise him. His most prominent feature was an overlarge mouth, which made a long, thin-lipped line across the lower face, as if someone had drawn it there, and drawn it badly. The small ears were another odd feature, only half finished in their details. Perhaps his mother had pushed him out of the womb before her work was quite done. Watt's child-size pug nose fit well with this theory.

When the trample of feet had come to rest in this room, Oren Watt was approving the placement of his artwork. The rather bad drawing of a dismembered foot was held to the wall at different levels and locations by a young woman in the art handler's uniform of black jersey and jeans. The confessed murderer shook his head and waved the drawing farther along the wall and higher. The art handler was quick to follow his instructions, for this was the Monster of Manhattan, wasn't it? The gallery worker was so young—Oren Watt had probably been the bog-eyman of her childhood nightmares.

Mallory was the only one in the room who seemed bored by Watt. Quinn watched her as she turned her back on the Monster of Manhattan, and walked along the opposite wall, where the drawings were lined up awaiting the hanging process. Her face gave Quinn no clue to her thoughts as she scanned the artwork. Perhaps she was wondering which of the body parts belonged to his niece, the dancer, and which to Peter Ariel, the young artist who had died with Aubry. The sketches were all so badly drawn, there was no gender differentiation.

The sidewalk tour gathered at the entrance to the room. Two of the party snapped photographs. None of them needed their tour guide to tell them this was Oren Watt. One man nudged another to whisper that Watt was even uglier than his television image. The entire tour group stared at the strange-looking man as though he were a zoo specimen, and by Quinn's lights, this was close to the truth.

Quinn kept track of Mallory as she wandered out of the main gallery and into a smaller room where the real art was hung. He followed her, wondering what he might say to make this meeting seem accidental.

The tour group was pulled away from the spectacle of the monster and led into the smaller room by the guide-cum-art-maven, who was babbling banalities. Twelve pairs of feet trooped up to the drawing Mallory was admiring. Conversation stopped as the group's leader rambled on about the lines of the work, the texture of the paper and the artist's intention—as if he had a clue.

Quinn appeared on the far side of the group. Respecting the etiquette of the docent's lecture, he kept his distance and his silence, and never looked at Mallory directly or acknowledged that he was aware of her. The tension between them was strung across the baffle of words and a score of tourists.

He studied her now, as she studied the minimalist piece on the gallery wall. What held her attention was a soft embossing of three delicate lines of paper. The strokes were exquisitely feminine, as were the lines of a dreaming nude. There was no frame. It was fixed to the wall with four pins. The stock was pristine ivory and the embossing was visible only in reflective light, so faintly were the lines raised. He would later return to the gallery and buy it. Later still, he would put it away in a dark portfolio because it reminded him too much of Mallory.

Her head turned slightly, and for a few minutes they did the children's dance of the eyes, each stealing glances at the other. And so their conversation began before they ever said hello.

• • •

Emma Sue Hollaran pulled the ball gown out of her closet. She held the hanger at arm's length and studied the formfitting sheath, which was not intended for dancing beyond the confines of the box step. Before she even tried on the gown, she knew the long zipper would be a problem over the thighs and buttocks.

And she was right.

A full-length mirror of three panels afforded a global view of her body. The zipper held, but oh, what it held. The fabric was straining over large bumps and accentuating lumps.

She reached out to the telephone and tapped out the clinic's telephone number, a number she knew by heart. After the frustration of dealing with the receptionist, who had no time slots left to give her, she screamed, "He'll see me, or I'll turn him in! I'll burn his ass!"

And indeed she could send the plastic surgeon to jail if she chose to. He'd done procedures on her after four other surgeons had turned her down. Once he put her near death—never mind that it was at her own insistence. He had taken out more fat than her buttocks, stomach, arms and double chin could safely part with at one session with the high-tech vacuum cleaner.

The thighs had been left undone in the doctor's haste to change her skin color from blue to something more like live flesh. After that near-death experience, she had been wary of having her thighs done, but now she had no choice, did she? And the buttocks had grown back to their former substantial proportions. Now that was definitely a breach of contract. Liposuction promised svelte forever, and lied.

When the receptionist returned to the phone, an opening had magically appeared in the doctor's schedule.

"Where is Mallory?" asked Charles, freshly barbered—styled, actually—and smiling.

Riker was seated at the desk in Mallory's office. "She's out." Now he looked up and whistled. "That's a great haircut, Charles."

Charles agreed. He was very pleased with himself today. Mallory's hairstylist had convinced him that giving more volume to his hair would call attention away from his large nose. The man had cut his locks with the skill of a sculptor, and the effect was striking. Charles thought it highly unlikely that his nose could be minimized by a blow dryer, but he had managed to sustain this fairy tale all the way from Fifty-seventh Street to SoHo. And he had yet another reason for good spirits. He had something to contribute to the case.

"But where did Mallory go? I have good news."

"She's at the Koozeman Gallery." Riker removed a carton from the desk and settled it to the floor. "The mayor ordered us to take down the crime-scene tapes. Seems they were getting in the way of the television crews. God forbid a homicide investigation should hold up a television shooting schedule. Get this, they're doing a documentary of the old murders, and Oren Watt is the technical advisor. They want to reenact it in the Koozeman Gallery."

"What uncanny timing." Charles was staring at the cork wall. It was a bizarre combination of Mallory's ultraneat positioning and Markowitz's sloppy handwriting, interspersed with bloody photographs of footprints and articles of clothing. It was almost a chessboard.

"Yeah, those television jackals move fast," said Riker.

"But it's the wrong gallery. The murders were in the East Village location."

"Charles, it's only television. No one expects *real*. So what's the good news?"

"I found Andrew Bliss."

"Nice going. Where is he?"

"At Bloomingdale's."

"You think he might be there for a while?"

"I know he will."

Riker was rising from his chair when Charles waved him to sit down again. "No, there's no hurry. He's there for the long haul. You see, my hairdresser—*Mallory's* hairdresser—is having an affair with an off-Broadway set designer whose brother is one of Bloomingdale's executives. They were talking on the speakerphone while I was having my hair cut. According to the brother of the Bloomingdale's man, Andrew Bliss outfitted the roof as a luxury campsite. Then the chairwoman of the Public Works Committee sent out a press release declaring Andrew Bliss an artwork in progress. And an ACLU attorney is meeting with the store's law firm to discuss freedom of speech versus liability. Bliss has already done his first press interview. Now he's an official performance artist."

"Oh, great. Another performance artist." Riker began to push the telephone buttons. "Let's see what we've got on the little bastard."

While Riker was talking to the desk sergeant in the East Side precinct, Charles turned his attention back to the cork wall. All but a few of the pictures and reports belonged to the old murders of the artist and the dancer. As he walked the length of the wall, he was aware of the father's brain merging with the daughter's. Here was Louis Markowitz's mania for detail matching Mallory's obsession with neatness. Every bit of paper was equidistant from each other, but the significance of some items should be beneath Mallory's contempt for the small details. And she usually tossed out whatever did not agree with her.

Riker held the telephone receiver in the crook of his neck as he tapped his foot and played with his pencil, all the signs that his call had been placed on hold.

Charles continued down the length of the wall. The fine detail work was already falling away. Louis Markowitz's influence was passing off. Most of Louis's paperwork had related to Aubry Gilette. Now Charles encountered a smiling publicity photo of Peter Ariel, the artist who had died with the young dancer. All that accompanied this photo was a medical examiner's report.

After a few minutes' conversation, Riker put down the phone, and none too gently. "We can't touch Andrew Bliss. No interviews, nothing. Bliss's personal shopper signed a charge for the merchandise. Then his lawyer showed up with a check to cover damages to a roof staircase."

"But surely this is criminal trespass."

"The store isn't filing a complaint. They like the little guy. He's their most loyal shopper. And he's good for a five-minute spot on the evening news." Riker put his feet up on the desk and slumped low in his chair. "I don't understand this, Charles. I thought the guy was a professional art critic, and now he's a damn performance artist."

"Well, there's quite a bit of crossover in art. Artists sometimes write art criticism the way authors review books by other people. No reason why a critic shouldn't make art."

"But isn't that a conflict of interest?"

"Perhaps, but crossover is common practice. Take your most recent dead artist, Dean Starr. As you know, that wasn't the name he was born with. His—"

"Starr is an alias?" Riker pulled out his pen and notebook and scanned the first page. "All the identification on his body was in that name."

"Sorry, I assumed you knew." Charles retrieved his discarded newspaper from the wastebasket and opened it to the obituary columns. He tapped the boxed mention of former art critic, current murder victim, Dean Strvnytchlk. "That's it. Under his original name, he used to publish a rather bad magazine of local art coverage. He was the chief art critic. He also contributed reviews to local tabloids."

Riker stared at the obituary. "How do you pronounce that?"

"Too many consonants. You're on your own." Charles opened a desk drawer and pulled out a pair of scissors. "If you followed the art news, you would have seen a review of his own show written under his real name."

"The bastard reviewed himself? You're kidding me."

"Not at all. There's historical precedent—Walt Whitman once reviewed his own work anonymously." Charles carefully cut the obituary from the paper, trying to make straight edges so as not to annoy Mallory with an imperfection. "Starr's gallery dealer, Koozeman, is also a critic. He writes a regular column for an international art magazine. Oh yes, it goes on all the time."

Charles tacked the obituary on the cork wall below the medical examiner's preliminary report on the death of Dean Starr. And now he noticed the next item on the cork wall was a blank sheet of paper. On closer inspection, this paper covered a photograph. He turned to Riker. "What's this about?"

"Mallory did that for you. It's the crime-scene photo of the old double homicide. She covered it over because you knew Aubry."

Charles and Riker exchanged a look which acknowledged that neither of them had believed she was capable of this delicate courtesy.

Mallory paused near a pile of the television crew's paraphernalia. Quinn watched as she neatly snatched up a clipboard. Anyone might have believed it belonged to her as she studied the pages on her way out the door.

He caught up with her on the street outside the Koozeman Gallery. "Hello again."

She nodded, acknowledging that she recognized him, but not that she was particularly pleased to see him. She turned away and walked down the street.

"I wonder if you could explain something to me." He walked beside her, matching his steps to hers. "The drawings of the bodies? Oren Watt has been selling them for years, and I still can't believe he's being allowed to profit on murder."

"He gets around the profit-on-crime laws because he was never brought to trial." One hand shaded her eyes from the light of the noonday sun as she looked up at him. "But your family lawyer would have told you that."

It was impossible to miss her suggestion that he was making up useless small talk. And of course, he was.

A warm breeze ruffled a bright silk banner overhead, and he could follow the wind down the SoHo street with the lift and swirl of similar banners which hung out over the sidewalk to advertise galleries and trendy boutiques.

He was walking faster now, to keep pace with her, and casting around for some bit of unfoolish conversation that might hold her attention for a while.

Mallory broke the silence. "Did you know Koozeman scheduled another show of Dean Starr's work?"

"Yes. I thought it might be going up today. I was surprised by the Oren Watt drawings."

Her face was telling him she didn't think he was all that surprised, and he wasn't. She quickened her steps, putting some distance between them. He walked faster.

"Koozeman never handled Oren Watt before," he said, in self-defense. "So, it *is* odd."

"Koozeman says he's not handling Watt." She consulted the stolen clipboard as she walked. At the top of the first sheet was a network logo followed by a schedule of places and dates. "He says it's a temporary installation. The television crew rented the space for the day." She made a check mark by the Koozeman Gallery and this day's date. "The Dean Starr show goes up in three days. Do you know why Koozeman's so hot to have another showing of Starr's work?"

"He'll want to take advantage of the publicity on the murder. Also, he has to unload the work as fast as he can. It's such a crock, it even strains the credulity of the amateur collector."

"What about the artist who died with Aubry? Was he any good?"

"Peter Ariel? Well, for a dead junkie and a third-rate hack, he had one hell of a run on the secondary market. But what a critic thinks of his work doesn't matter."

"Explain." It was an order.

He obliged her. "Collectors don't listen to art critics anymore. They listen to their accountants, who tell them how the artist is doing in the primary market. Then, they can make projections on the staying power in the secondary market."

"What is this, Quinn? Are we talking art, or stocks and bonds?"

"Same thing. The actual art means very little in the greater schematic of finance. The initial buyers paid a low price for Peter Ariel's sculptures. After his death, the work was worth a small fortune on the resale market. The early resale buyers were ghouls who collect souvenirs of messy homicides. The amateur collectors misunderstood, bought the work at the inflated price, and held on to it too long. Once the ghoul market was saturated, the price declined to the cost of the artist's materials."

She stopped walking, and he stopped. By only standing there, she was tethering him to the same square of the sidewalk. "You never mentioned any of this to Markowitz, did you?"

Now how did she manage to frame a question as an accusation? "No, I didn't. The focus was always on Aubry, not Peter Ariel."

She resumed her purposeful walking, and he kept pace with her, still tethered. "There was another artist mentioned in Bliss's review—Gillian, the vandal artist. What do you know about him?"

"He has an exhibition of photographs in a gallery at the end of this block. You might find it diverting."

"Photography? I thought vandalism was his style."

"Wait till you see the photographs, Mallory."

They entered the Greene Street gallery by way of a narrow stairway to the second floor. The rough steel door opened onto a large white space filled with light from loft windows lining the street front. People were milling around, some looking at the photographs on the wall. A man stood by a desk, holding sheets of slides to the light. Done with one sheet, he tossed it onto a pile at his feet and went on to the next.

Quinn pointed to this man. "Some artists spend a hundred hours on a single painting, and the gallery director spends a minute looking at twenty slides of their work. Occasionally, I time them. Call it a hobby. This man's about average, a minute an artist."

They drifted to the collection of photographs on the near wall. The work was an amateur's effort in bad lighting, with no eye for composition. The first photograph was of a crack in an old statue. Gillian's signature was printed in the fresh wound. All the rest were much the same, differing only in the statuary. Each work of art was harmed by a chip or a crack and signed by the assailant.

Mallory looked bewildered for a moment, but made a quick recovery. "Is this what I think it is?"

"Vandalism of priceless art? Yes. There's a more interesting show in the next room." He took her arm and guided her into the adjoining gallery space.

"At least it doesn't smell," said Mallory, counting the spilled garbage cans. There were twelve in all, contents strewn about the floor. He led her down a clear passage, sans garbage, saying, "I want you to know that the garbage was authentically spilled, and not purposefully arranged this way. The artist is a purist. He has integrity."

"You're kidding."

"Yes, but it's also true."

Other people stood in ones and pairs, inspecting garbage spills. One young man, wearing the art student's slashed-at-the-knee-for-no-good-reason blue jeans, was standing in the corner making notes on the half-eaten guacamole which he had found in the garbage spill that he was fondest of.

"So why doesn't it smell?" she asked.

"The gallery owner thought it might put off the paying customers. It's coated with resin. The artist didn't like that. He wanted it to rot naturally."

"Naturally—he's a purist."

"Now you've got it, Mallory."

"And that show in the front room, the vandalism?"

"All the statues are from the Greek collection of a major museum, and they don't want to encourage any more of this. The museum director gave me a 'No comment,' but I noted all the statues had been removed. When they go on display again, there won't be any trace of the damage."

"I bet they bought out the show."

He nodded. "You're right, they did. This show will close as soon as their check clears the bank. They were very good-natured mugging victims. Rumor has it they ransomed the negatives, too."

"I just can't believe this," she said.

"New York City. What's not to believe?"

Twenty minutes later, Quinn was sipping espresso under the green awning of a sidewalk cafe on Bleecker Street and ferreting out Mallory's tastes in art. It seemed she only liked minimalism, and only because it was neat and clean, not cluttered with tony metaphors and messy paints. She had no use for any extraneous line or shape.

When she was done, he said, "Well then, why not take a blue pencil to James Joyce, edit out all the extraneous stuff that doesn't really further the plot? Most people don't understand the metaphors anyway. So we could probably whittle *Ulysses* down to a manageable short story."

He was smiling now, because *she* was smiling, and he was helpless to do otherwise. He wondered where she had learned that beguiling trick. An old memory brought him up short, as he realized she was perfectly mimicking the smile of the late Louis Markowitz. He was startled, but also confident that it did not show.

He continued as though nothing had happened, as though he had not just seen a ghost. "And then we'll have literature that's more accessible to a thirteen-year-old subnormal. Why make people reach for art, when they can pick it up off the floor?"

Her hand went up to say, *Enough, I get the point*. He went on anyway. And so began Mallory's first lecture on the other language, the metaphor of subject, the symbolism of object, the poetry evoked by color and shape, by texture and line, what was said by the immediacy of a single violent stroke of a brush or the subtle shading of a pencil.

And then she asked, "So where's my metaphor in the garbage and the vandalism?"

"All right, you win." He sensed that winning was the main thing with her, the very key to her. "You're still planning on attending the ball tomorrow night?"

"Yes, and I still need an interview with Gregor Gilette. You've got that covered, right? He'll keep it quiet?"

He smiled and let her take that for a positive response. "But you must let me help you with something else. The opening for the next Dean Starr show is by invitation only. I could have Koozeman invite you."

"I don't need an invitation—I'm the police. Riker says you weren't planning to review the first Dean Starr show. So I have to wonder why you were there that night."

Like Riker, she had saved her best cut for last. Her style, however, was a departure from her partner's—not a blunt and clumsy accusation, but a trap. She only stared

at him now, defying him to lie to her and try to get away
with it.

"Riker was right, I never review hacks. A bad review
is counterproductive. Repetition of the name is fame in
New York City. I only went to the opening for the food
and wine. It's so rare to find hors d'oeuvres served in
galleries anymore."

"Seriously."

"Seriously, Mallory, you can hardly believe I went
there to appreciate art."

The woman ceased to drag her rolling wire cart, which
was partially covered by a tarp. Tired, she leaned on the
cart handle as she watched the art critic leaving the
Bleecker Street cafe with the young blond woman. Quinn
held open the door of a small tan car. The young woman
disappeared into it and drove off. Now he crossed
Bleecker Street and approached the woman with the wire
cart. He looked into her eyes, where it was winter of
weak iris skies and clouding cataracts. He nodded to her,
and a bit of paper passed from his hand to hers as he
passed her by.

Her palsied hand jolted the cart. Trembling fingers
pulled back the tarp as the woman peered inside it, eyes
fixing on a tea tin, believing she had heard a thought.
Snow drifted through her mind and she lost the threads
to where she was and why she was. The dead child's
brains gently remembered for her. "Move on," urged the
voice from the tin. The woman nodded and moved on
down Bleecker Street.

She seemed a collection of things found and put together. Her four skirts were a concert, whispers of dead
leaves shushing along toward Lafayette and turning south
on that street. Her head of iron-gray hair wobbled on a
slender bird's neck. She crossed wide Houston with her
free hand tucked in, giving one arm the appearance of a
useless wing, atrophied or broken.

She tripped on the curb and lurched suddenly, upsetting the cart. The tea tin went tumbling as the cart settled in a gutter. The tin was rearranged among the other contents layered over and around it. A crusted knapsack spilled a shiny stream of bottle caps, broken pins, tin silverware and other small found things—pretty only, good for nothing.

The woman righted her cart and veered east on Houston. Forgetting, minutes later, that the dead child's brains had ever spoken, she turned a corner onto Essex Street. Trash cans seemed to grow there in abundance. She looked over her newfound wealth with the eye of a connoisseur. A flash of metal caught her eye with a ricochet of sunlight. There, on one trash can, was a knife. It was crack-toothed and broken-handled, but still good for cutting meat. She stared at it until the voice from the tea tin cautioned, "Forget."

But the mad persistence of memory won out. She began to shake. A cold miasma of fear settled about her shoulders and forced her to her knees and to ground. She clawed at her hair, eyes bulging at what memory was showing her, sobbing, shuddering, screaming, screams quieting now to moans as the dead child's brains called up the blessed snow of forgetfulness.

Emma Sue Hollaran was sedated when her body was being transferred to the operating table. The nurse partially draped her in a green sheet. Her exposed legs were marked in sections with black crayon lines like the diagram of a cow in a butcher shop.

Her eyes slowly roved the small operating theater and the familiar gowned figures of the surgeon and the nurse. Another familiar person was the anesthesiologist. Since this man spoke not one word of English, she was certain that he was not certified to practice medicine in this country. So she could assume he worked cheap, and she never complained.

The plastic surgeon's face hovered over her for a moment before her eyes closed, and her mind was swept away in the anesthetic whirlpool. She was well beyond feeling the first stroke of the scalpel as it cut into her body.

A long hose was inserted into a bloody hole in her left thigh. The music of youth and beauty began with squishy suction noises, the siphoning of fat sucking to the steady beat of the motor which powered the wildly upscale vacuum cleaner. What came out of her was the color and texture of yellow chicken fat, grease and blood. Another hole was made on the inside thigh, and the ugly bits of her body collected in a glass jar at the end of the hose. Another hole was cut in her skin, and another for the next leg—more globules slopped into the jar.

In a dream state she heard a voice say, "Time to roll the meat."

More holes were made in the back of her knees. The long rod was moving under her skin, minding the black marks of the butcher shop diagram. The vacuum cleaner was slurping up fat, ripping away pieces of her body with its greedy incessant sucking.

Two hours later, her eyes were open again. The surgeon was standing over her, saying a polite variation of *You're nuts—totally insane!* His exact words were, "At your insistence, I removed more fat than I should have. You're going to need rest for at least three days, if not longer. No lifting, no bending, no stairs. Going to a dress ball is absolutely out of the question."

"Bullshit."

The Manhattan Charities Ball was a networker's dream. Every power figure in the city would be there. But best of all, Gregor Gilette would be there. She was nearly ready for him. Her triple chin had been suctioned away to a mere double roll of flesh. And her legs would be svelte beneath the tight wrap of a ball gown that was not designed for dancing, and most certainly not designed to be worn by the likes of Emma Sue Hollaran.

"So how's Doris?"

Dr. Edward Slope pushed back the Plexiglas face guard and looked up at her with a quizzical eye.

Kathy Mallory was one of few cops who could make idle conversation over the open chest of a dead man. The only thing that bothered him was that she *never* made small talk.

Now he left his assistant the chore of bagging the body parts and replacing them in the open cavity. He removed his gloves and gown as he walked Mallory to the door of the autopsy room. "Doris is just fine." He tossed the bloody garments into a disposal bin. "She wonders why you never come by for dinner."

"And Fay?"

"Oh, you know kids. Last week she wanted to be a veterinarian, and now she's decided to be a musician. I can see the tuition bills rolling in from Juilliard now."

"Is she giving you any problems?"

"We're working it out."

"So you're going to keep her?"

"She's a little girl. It's not quite the same as returning an unsatisfactory pet to the Puppyland Kennels. And Doris is already planning on grandchildren. You could say it's a done deal. So now you're doing civilized small talk. Helen would be proud of you, Kathy."

"Mallory," she corrected him. "So, can we talk body parts now?"

"Sure." He plucked a file from the rack and held the door for her. The air in the hall was warmer, and the odor of death was exchanged for the strong disinfectant smell of chlorine.

His office farther down the hall had the smell of stale cigar smoke, and a hint of the aftershave he slathered on for his wife's sake. "You're lucky Starr's gallery dealer didn't want to waste money on embalming.'' As he sat down to his cluttered desk, he waved her to a leather armchair. "So tell me what you want first. Markowitz would've wanted to know what he had for breakfast.''

"Did he die instantly?''

"No, by the blood flow, I'd give him a full minute to live.''

"I want to know why he didn't scream. He'd just been stabbed. That must have hurt like hell.''

"Not necessarily. He had enough drugs and wine in his system to dull the pain of major surgery. And the back isn't the most sensitive area of the body. You'd be surprised how many people have reported not realizing they'd been stabbed in the back. They know something's happened. There's a localized pain, but they're not aware of the penetration. I can tell you there's evidence of long-term drug habituation.''

"Same as Peter Ariel, the artist who died twelve years ago.''

She handed him a copy of his own autopsy report on Ariel. He scanned the lines, and finding the entry he wanted, he nodded his head. "Both artists used the same combination of drugs. It's a heroin cocktail with some interesting additives. Why in God's name are you digging around in that old case? It was over and done with twelve years ago.''

"It's being reopened . . . quietly. We never had this little chat, okay? So, the heroin cocktail gives me a link to Peter Ariel.''

"Well, no it doesn't. You won't find the exact same combination. They have brand names now. Even if the combo is close, a lawyer could argue that link is no stronger than two people sharing the same blend of tobacco or coffee beans.''

"What about the weapon?''

"I agree with the first postmortem. Ice pick probably. But you were right, it couldn't be the one they found by the body. It had to be at least six to seven inches in length. I'm guessing the point of the weapon was filed down. The rod was thin for an ice pick, and razor sharp. No tearing on entry. Very smooth, very neat. There wouldn't be any blood splatters on the clothing of the killer. It's the perfect weapon for a public killing.''

"I need another link to the old murder.''

"Frankly, outside of the drugs, I can't see the similarity at all. The first crime was brutal, insane. Kathy, I don't—''

"Mallory," she corrected him as she always did. They had played this game for all of the five years since she had joined the police force and forbidden him to use her given name.

"Well, you're still Kathy to me. I've known you since you were ten.''

"Eleven,'' she corrected him again.

"Ten. You lied that extra year onto your age. You put it past Helen Markowitz, but you never fooled me. So don't expect me to treat you like a cop, when every time I look at you I see a ten-year-old brat. You haven't changed all that much, *Kathy.*''

"Mallory.''

"All right, what else do you want from me?''

"I want to know about the detail that Markowitz held back.''

"I have no idea what you mean. We never discussed the case after the autopsy. I know Markowitz didn't believe it was Oren Watt, but I did.''

"I know the old man was holding out—that was his trademark. There was something he didn't want anyone else to know, not even his own men. It was a real bad year for department leaks. It seemed like every damn detail of a case wound up in the tabloids. He knew Oren Watt was lying when he confessed. I know the old man had something, and he used it to trip up Watt. It was something about one of the bodies, wasn't it?''

"That was twelve years ago. I've worked on a great many bodies since then."

"This was the most brutal homicide you ever worked on. Don't tell me the details just slipped your mind. You know what I remember about that year?"

"You were only a little kid, and you lived inside a computer. Don't go telling me that Markowitz discussed this case with you. He wouldn't—he didn't."

Slope was right about that. The old man had only given her shopping lists of things he needed from other people's computers. And Mallory had never cared to ask what the information was for. She had been perfectly focussed on the wonderful novelty of sitting at a computer terminal in a police station and raiding cyberspace for all the data she could steal, stealing until she was sated with theft. And getting away with it—that was the best—licensed to steal. It had been one great year.

"I'll tell you what I remember best," she said. "It was the weekly poker games. You missed three games in a row that year. Everybody knew you'd had a falling out with Markowitz. But I'm the only one who knows why. You were a long time forgiving him for asking you to bend the law and hide the facts."

"You're blowing smoke, young lady."

Slope had been the best poker player among Markowitz's old cronies. His face was always a model of composure, defying even God to guess what cards he held.

She reached into the pocket of her blazer and pulled out a sheaf of yellowed pages bearing the seal and signature of Chief Medical Examiner Edward Slope. She set the papers down on the desk in front of him and tapped them with one long red fingernail. "This is the *first* autopsy report on Aubry Gilette. It's dated two days earlier than the report on file."

"Where did you get that?"

Slope reached out for the papers. Mallory was faster,

picking up the report and casually turning it over in her hands.

"I found it in the basement of the old house in Brooklyn. That's where Markowitz kept his personal case notes."

She leafed through the pages. "It's much more interesting than your *amended* report. I think Aubry Gilette's brain weight is a bit light. I have a weight of three pounds, one ounce for Peter Ariel's brain—that's standard, right? But there's barely six ounces left of Aubry Gilette's brain. I didn't see any mention of missing organ parts in your *second* report, the official report." As though she were merely confirming the time of day, she asked, "Now falsifying an autopsy on a homicide—that's a felony, isn't it?"

Edward Slope stared at the pages in her hand, his head shaking slowly from side to side. "Why on earth would Louis have kept it?"

"He probably wanted to protect you. If anything had gone wrong, he could have substituted this original for the one on file. The signature copy is the only one that could come back on you. None of the duplicate copies would be admissible in court."

She understood the shock in Slope's eyes. In her hand was damning proof of the worst crime in his profession—the collusion of police and ME to falsify and suppress evidence. "If you remember any other *irregularities* in the old case, call me."

She slipped the papers back into her pocket.

"I think you can trust me with this," she said softly, with only a suggestion of sarcasm, "because you know how well I can keep a dirty secret. You can trust me because you know I wouldn't rat on you if you broke a hundred laws." Her eyebrows lifted with the afterthought of a third reason for his trust. "Oh, and I'm a cop."

•   •   •

Night and dark came on. Andrew Bliss settled down with a new bottle and looked up at the stars. There were hardly any. He had to hunt them down with his binoculars. They were faint, pathetic things, washed out by the glittering cityscape, only pinholes in the ceiling. He believed the poetry of stars would be more deservedly dedicated to the dazzle of city lights. The traffic of headlights and turn signals kept to the rhythm of classical symphonies. Great buildings loomed as shimmering behemoths footed in concrete. Poetry was here in every physical metaphor. An aureole of light crowned the city.

God lived here. Screw the cowboy lore of the western Big Sky Country. Mere stars could not compete with this.

CHAPTER
3

EMMA SUE HOLLARAN HAD AWAKENED ON A BED OF pain. Now she lay nude under the four-poster's canopy of red velvet, which matched the flocked red-on-gold wallpaper. The carpets and curtains were deep purple, the sheets were shocking-pink satin, and every red lampshade was rimmed with black tassels. A player piano was all that was needed to complete the cliché of an antebellum brothel.

As the plastic surgeon examined Emma Sue's swollen thighs, her maid of the week paced the length of the bedroom, eyes cast up to heaven and muttering prayers or curses in a language her employer had not yet been able to identify. The succession of maids had all been illegal aliens, the cheapest labor to be found. Some had done only a single day in hell, and others, like this one, had lasted an entire fortnight in Emma Sue's employ. She could not remember the maids' names from day to day, week to week, and so had taken to calling all of them Alien.

"Alien, stop that damn pacing!" she screamed.

This week's Alien stepped quickly to the bed, having recognized only her own new name in the spate of words. She looked down at Emma Sue's bare body and turned away in disgust to resume her pacing and muttering.

Emma Sue was a mass of red splotches from hips to knees. The swelling made her legs twice as big as they had been before the fat was suctioned out. She stared down at the offensive limbs.

"Drain that crap out!" she screamed, more outraged than pained.

"I warned you," said the surgeon. "This was entirely too much to—"

"Make it go away!"

"Don't you remember when we did your abs and buttocks? You were swollen then, too."

"Don't you remember? My stomach and butt were swollen because you nearly killed me, you idiot! You drained me then. Do it now."

"I drained an infection. This is just the normal post-op swelling." He was writing on his prescription pad. "I want you to take these pills. The swelling will go down in two to three weeks. Try to—"

"Weeks? You moron, I haven't got two to three *days*. The ball is tonight!"

"You can't possibly go anywhere."

"Watch me."

Within the hour she was attached to the medical apparatus. She did not seem to mind the sight of fluid draining into her veins from a plastic bag attached to a long pole, nor the other fluid coming out through the series of drains plugged into her legs. The maid fled the room, as the doctor monitored the cortisone IV. The air was foul. The doctor's face was going to that pale vomit shade of green, and then he too left the room in search of a toilet.

The bad drawings of body parts had been taken down, and gone was the babble and the crush of television people and tourists who had wandered in off the street. The last cable for the camera equipment was pulled out of the wall and rolled up by a crew grip.

His back turned on the door, Sergeant Riker stood alone in the quiet emptiness of the high white walls. The room was all too familiar, a long rectangle, coffinlike in the convergence of parallels toward the end of the room. Though this space was vast, there was the feeling of walls closing in, the coffin lid coming down on him. Koozeman's new location was upscale, high-rent SoHo, but it was only a larger version of the old gallery in the East Village, the site of a crime so brutal, the photographs had never been published.

Twelve years ago, in the blood and butchery of a double homicide, Riker had come close to understanding art. Never had he seen anything so compelling. The image of the bodies would never leave him.

On that long-ago night, he had reported to the crime scene, pressed through the crowd and past the guards at the door. Two rookie officers had been standing in the room with the bodies. The young cops were statues, struck silent and still by shock. Flashbulbs had gone off from every angle, and everyone was blinded by the light. The dark shadowy bodies were the stuff of bad dreams, but they took on a terrible clarity with each blast of light, intermittently real and illusory.

The forensic technicians had gone about the night's work with only the exchange of necessary words. Orders were issued in the low tones of talking in church. There had been no black humor that night. The youngest officer had looked on the bloody face of the dancer and cried. Riker had gently wiped the boy's face and sent him away.

Now his reverie was broken. He was aware of Mallory standing beside him, waiting.

"The room in Koozeman's old East Village gallery was smaller," said Riker. "But it's the same layout. The killer didn't do them at the same time. Peter Ariel died first. Markowitz figured the perp laid in wait for Aubry."

Mallory moved to the center of the room. She was

reading from a yellowed sheet of paper. "Quinn had blood on his shoes."

"Yeah, we all did," said Riker, pulling out a cigarette to kill the phantom smell of blood and spoiled meat, urine and feces. "You had to be there. You can't tell what that scene was like from the paperwork and the shots. Then Aubry's father shows up. He'd been waiting for her in a coffeehouse three blocks west of here. Aubry was hours late. Her father called everyone she knew to track her down. She was supposed to meet Quinn at the gallery earlier that night."

The sudden appearance of Gregor Gilette had been the last heartbreak of the night. The artist, Peter Ariel, had been bagged and placed in the meatwagon. They had put the parts of the dancer into another bag and were loading her onto the gurney. Turning away from the ambulance, Riker had seen the damndest thing, a man running toward him, stumble-running, strewing red roses everywhere. They were lifting the gurney into the ambulance. The doors were closing as Gregor Gilette reached the vehicle, and he was pounding on the doors even as they closed, pounding to be let in, yelling, *"Aubry, Aubry!"* Markowitz had pulled the man away from the ambulance doors, pinning his arms and holding him close. And then Edward Slope had tried his hand on a living patient with a merciful hypodermic to kill the father's pain.

Mallory was only a little older than the rookie officer who had cried for Aubry Gilette. What would Markowitz think if he knew his kid was going into this black hole to finish what he had begun?

"I still want to talk to Andrew Bliss," said Mallory. "What about fire code violations? He botched the roof staircase—that's a legal fire exit."

"I already thought of that. Somebody with influence got the commissioner of the fire department to look the other way. A lawyer from the Public Works Committee has a restraining order to prevent any interference with his free speech, so we can't bring him down. And we can't go up to the roof with a copter either. Blakely would find out you're working the old case."

"Well, there's ways and ways." She looked at her watch. "I've got that damn press conference in an hour. Did you make any progress on Sabra? Any idea where she might be?"

The woman was lying under a blanket of newspapers in an abandoned building on Essex Street. She had crawled through a basement window the night before and now lay dreaming late into the morning. It might as well have been night, for no daylight penetrated the window after she had replaced the boards, fitting nails to holes. A candle sat dark in a dish, burned to the end of its wick.

In dreams, her child stood on point in satin toe shoes, reaching up to a soft golden glow just above her straining fingertips. Suddenly, her soft red mouth formed the oval of a scream as the ghouls came dancing by her. Greedy mouths with yellow teeth sucked the wind from her throat. Clutching at the poisoned air, hand to her mouth, the child went reeling and running. And as she ran, she heard the sounds behind her of feet slapping floor, and sickly mucus noises. Phlegmy voices sang to her in a hellish choir. To her side the ghouls came dancing, eyes sewn shut, hands locked in prayer and grown together, skin merging into skin. Their mouths moved as one, making foul wind and words, weaving chains of obscenities. Then the child had lost her shoes, and through her tears, she could see her legs were gone.

The child's mother opened her eyes in that dark and airless place, believing she was blind. Her hands were clenched together on her breast and she screamed out curses, damning God and all His minions, until the dead child's brains said, "Hush, now. It's only a dream is all."

She slowly made out the dim contours of the tea tin

on the top of the cart. The dead child's brains crooned on, "It isn't real, only dreaming."

Sabra rose to a weary stand in sleep smells of used linen and dried urine.

Chief of Detectives Harry Blakely lit up a cigar in the close space of the hallway. His pasty white jowls jiggled as he rolled the cigar from one side of his mouth to the other. Draping flesh closed his eyes to gun slits, and the rolls of his chin obscured the knot of his tie. "The commissioner's in a really pissy mood today, Jack."

Lieutenant Jack Coffey could well understand that. He was looking through the glass window of the pressroom door. "I still can't believe that FBI agent is here. Beale hates those bastards."

"You know the routine, Jack," said Blakely. "They need a little good press after that last hostage situation blew up in their faces. So we're gonna let them put on a little dog-and-pony show for the reporters. The press just loves all that psychiatric bullshit on the killer profile."

"The profile of a psycho, right? Christ, I can see the headlines now. 'Crazed killer loose in Manhattan.' They're gonna blow the case all out of proportion, and you know it. I thought you wanted a quiet investigation."

"Doesn't matter now."

Blakely exhaled a cloud of smoke, and Coffey stepped back to the wall, his usual position in all his dealings with this man. He could feel Blakely's smoke all around him, stealing into his hair, his clothes, his skin. He knew the smell of Blakely would hang on him for the rest of the day.

"I think we might give this case to the feds," said Blakely. "They really want it, and we have enough bodies to go around. They're so pumped up on this profile, they tell me they can wrap the case in two weeks."

"Why not give your own people two weeks? The Bureau has no jurisdiction."

"Oh, officially the case will stay with NYPD. I thought I'd assign it to Harriman and let him work with the feds."

"Harriman's a worthless idiot. He's just treading water waiting for his pension to kick in." It was a fight for Coffey to keep the frustration out of his voice.

"Who cares?" Blakely's smile was unsettling. "He only needs to show up for the collar and the closing press conference. The feds promised to kill the Oren Watt connection. So I did a little deal with 'em. I'm gonna put Mallory on something else."

"I'll bet this isn't Beale's idea," said Jack Coffey. "He hates feds with a passion."

"Commissioner Beale has all the political savvy of a twelve-year-old girl. I hope you're not suggesting that we actually let him run the police department."

"He specifically asked for Mallory at this press conference. He wants her on this case. What's he gonna say when he finds out you climbed into bed with the FBI?"

"How would he find out, Jack? All he knows about his own police department is what he reads in the papers and what I tell him. Beale promised to play nice with the feds today 'cause I told him it might save the city a few million in lawsuits if they took the heat off Oren Watt."

"How are you gonna tell Beale we're giving the whole case to the feds?"

"I know how to handle him I'm not worried about it. Now we've got another case we need Mallory on—computer fraud. We're sending her out to Boston to follow up on a similar case. Boston's cooperating. So tell her to pack her bags and drop off her case notes on my desk tomorrow morning."

"I want Mallory to stay on this case."

"That's tough, Jack. I don't think I owe you any favors this week. Here she comes now. Don't tell her she's being reassigned until after the press conference.''

Mallory walked up to Coffey as Blakely turned and headed down the hall at a faster pace than his usual rolling mosey. She stared after his retreating dark bulk. ''I guess he's pissed off about the article in yesterday's paper.''

''No, Mallory, that's been smoothed over. Blakely understands how it happened. He's been misquoted often enough.'' He motioned her to look through the glass of the pressroom door. ''You see that guy at the end of the platform? He's FBI. It's going to be a joint press conference.''

''Why would the feds want in?''

''The art world makes sexy press. Blakely only wants them to support the idea that Oren Watt is not a suspect. The feds agreed, so Blakely did a deal.''

She turned away from the window. ''I don't like the sound of that.''

''Commissioner Beale wouldn't like it either if he had any idea what was going on.'' He stared through the window, eyes on the far door beyond the dais. ''If the feds get a piece of this case, they'll go for a quick and dirty wrap. They'll pick up all the neighborhood freaks, and nail the one with no alibi.'' The back door of the pressroom was opening to admit Commissioner Beale and his entourage. ''It's time, Mallory.''

They pushed through the door and into a loud room, filled to capacity with television crews, photographers and reporters. Bright, white-hot camera lights were trained on the long table which spanned the dais. Clusters of microphones in nests of wires were set before each of the three chairs. The short gray police commissioner was climbing the two steps of the platform. As he moved toward the center chair, flashbulbs went off, and thirty mouths closed simultaneously.

Coffey took her arm and pulled her back into the reach of intimate conversation. ''Mallory, I don't care how you do it. Just go up there and dazzle the shit out of them. Do whatever it takes to make Beale and the department shine. NYPD is in control of this case. You got that?''

"Right."

"You smoke over the old case and concentrate on the new one. The feds' interference is driving Beale nuts. He's the one you need on your side, so do all the damage you can."

She was smiling, and that worried him. But Commissioner Beale's little washed-out gray eyes actually sparkled when Mallory walked up the stairs of the dais and took her seat beside him. She looked out over a sea of faces and bright flashes from every quarter of the room.

When Beale introduced her, he mentioned that, in the area of computers, Detective Sergeant Kathleen Mallory had no peer. There were other words to the effect that she could turn water into wine. And now the old man gave a terse introduction to the special agent from the FBI, who apparently was not so talented in Beale's estimation.

Special Agent Cartland shuffled his papers and looked up, smiling for the cameras with the practiced ease of a fashion model. He was the perfect specimen, a walking argument for eugenics, with youthful good looks, light brown hair and strong white teeth.

Coffey stood at the back of the room and watched Mallory seated at the left hand of the commissioner. Coffey suddenly understood why Beale had asked for her. Harry Blakely had underestimated the little man in the gray suit. Commissioner Beale understood image and press and public relations. Mallory, tall and wonderfully made, was more than a match for the FBI agent. If she only sat there and said nothing, Beale would have won the argument that God was on the side of the cops and not the feds.

A reporter was rising, hand in the air. "Agent Cartland, what's the FBI interest in this case? The terrorist line in Bliss's column?''

The FBI agent leaned into his collection of microphones, each bearing a network logo. "If the case did develop along the lines of terrorism, we would certainly take a very active interest. Terrorism is an area best left to experts.''

Well, this was not part of the deal.

Coffey could see that Beale was not at all happy with that remark. The commissioner's little head swiveled right, in the manner of a schoolteacher about to pounce on a student who has gotten out of line.

Beale spoke into his own group of microphones. "There is no planned FBI participation in this case. The press is making an unfounded and highly sensational connection to the old murders of Peter Ariel and Aubry Gilette. Special Agent Cartland tells me the FBI has a profile on the perpetrator that puts that speculation to rest. You may proceed, young man.'' And the implication was that the young man should proceed with extreme caution.

"The FBI is always willing to help local law enforcement in the art of profiling a suspect," said the smiling, unflappable Agent Cartland. "Based on the evidence of the crime scene, we can give you a rather detailed portrait of the man.''

"Why do you think it's a man?'' called out a feminine voice in a sniper shot from the back of the room.

"The overwhelming majority of psychopaths are male.''

A reporter stood up in the front row. By the back of his dark-skinned, bullet-shaped head, Coffey knew the man. It was McGrath, a seasoned journalist who had swapped lies with Markowitz for several decades. McGrath was recognized with a nod from Beale.

"So we're looking for an insane killer?'' McGrath addressed his remark to the FBI agent. "Say—oh, shot in the dark—someone like *Oren Watt*?''

Beale's right hand wormed around the microphone at the center of his cluster, and his knuckles went white, as though he were choking it. He managed to lock eyes with the agent before the younger man responded to McGrath.

"Well, there are similarities," said the FBI agent, and Beale covered his face with one hand. The agent continued. "In the old case of the artist and the dancer, the perpetrator used a fire axe he found at the crime scene. The killer of Dean Starr used an ice pick, also a weapon he found at the scene. And the word 'dead' was written on the back of one of the gallery's business cards. Both the old killing and the recent one showed lack of premeditation. Both crimes were the spontaneous acts of disorganized personalities."

McGrath remained standing, holding the floor. "Oren Watt arranged the body parts as artwork. The killer of Dean Starr arranged the body as performance art. You don't think that calls for a little planning?"

The agent's smile was benign. *Let me lead you out of ignorance*, said his tone of voice. "These things were done after the fact. The act itself was not planned in advance. Neither perpetrator brought weapons or materials to their respective crime scenes. As to the arrangement of the bodies, a psychopath will often indulge himself with ritual mutilation of the victims, or some personal theme in writing or acts performed on the corpse. But the killer in this instance is not Oren Watt. The murder was cleaner, quicker, less violent. The brutality always escalates in the second kill. It never lessens."

"So you think our guy is a young Oren Watt in training."

"He fits the same profile as Watt. He acted spontaneously, with no fear of discovery. The trigger for the act was probably a recent traumatic event in his life. For example, he may have recently lost his job. We're looking for a white male between twenty-five and thirty-five, no close friends, no stable relationships with women, no social graces. His father died or left the home when he was very young. He lives alone, or with his mother. He doesn't take proper care of himself, he's badly dressed. Now, about the shabby clothing—in SoHo that would not be a standout feature. It would even have helped him to blend in with the crowd at the opening.''

"Hey, Mallory," sang out a veteran cophouse reporter in the back. "You goin' along with this line?"

Commissioner Beale was staring at Mallory, hope in his eyes as she spoke into her own cluster of microphones. "No, but all the FBI errors are understandable."

The FBI agent was frozen in his best public-relations smile, and Commissioner Beale was grinning with joy and real malice.

"The FBI only asked for the crime-scene photographs and the preliminary ME report," said Mallory. "They specifically asked us not to send our own conclusions. They said it would *taint* their profile." Now she picked up a document and scanned it, as though she did not know it by heart. "According to this preliminary report, the wound was consistent with the ice pick found at the scene. Apparently, the FBI was satisfied with this."

She crumpled this document into a ball and tossed it back over her shoulder. Then she leaned back in her chair to look at the FBI agent behind Beale's back, and she gave him that special smile which women reserve for addled children. She was all business again when she turned back to the reporter.

"But NYPD had a major problem with a four-inch pick penetrating six and a half inches of fat and muscle to rupture the heart from the back. So we asked for a more extensive autopsy. Now we know that the weapon is much longer. No such weapon was found at the scene, so we assume the killer brought it to the gallery and took it away when he left."

In his rush to contradict her, Agent Cartland leaned too far into his microphones, brushing his teeth against the soft cover of one. "It might be a mistake—" The microphone squealed with feedback as it was dislodged from the cluster.

Mallory rose gracefully to pass behind Commissioner Beale's chair. She adjusted the FBI agent's microphones. And now a crowd of reporters grinned as Mallory gave Agent Cartland lessons in the proper distance from the mike.

When she was seated again, the agent, dignity shot to hell, continued. "It would be a mistake to *assume* that because the weapon wasn't found at—"

"Oh, it's no mistake." Mallory smiled at him to say, *You lose, sucker.* "Further evidence of premeditation is the card found on the body. True, it doesn't take long to write the word 'dead,' but the letters were printed with a straight edge—like a ruler—to avoid handwriting analysis. And there were no fingerprints on the card. The perp either wore gloves or handled the card by the edges. So we *assume* he brought it to the gallery. The card was used to disguise the act and allow the murderer time to escape unmolested. The killer chose a perfect weapon for a crowded room—no blood splatters. A lot of thought and planning went into this crime."

"You think it was a man?" asked McGrath.

"A woman could have done it," said Mallory.

"It does take some force—" the agent began.

"*I* could have done it," said Mallory. "The weapon only had to penetrate one layer of light material, and more fat than muscle. It was a clean thrust between the ribs, and it cleared the vertebrae. The weapon was much thinner than the average pick, and probably needle sharp at the point." She nodded to a reporter in the back row.

"Mallory, are you going to ask the FBI for a revised profile?"

"What for? When we know why it was done, we'll know who did it."

"So you don't like the crazed-killer line, Mallory?"

"I suppose it could have been a more organized psychopath, or it could be a money motive. Revenge is good—I've always liked that one. We found evidence of habitual drug use in the second autopsy, so it could also be drug-related."

If Beale smiled any wider, he would hurt himself.

"What about Oren Watt?" yelled another reporter.

"He didn't do it."

"You sure about that, Mallory?" asked McGrath.

"Dead sure."

"Because the murder was *neater* and *cleaner*?"

"No, nothing that cute, McGrath. You and I both know it would be impossible for Oren Watt to go anywhere unnoticed. He's more famous than a rock star. The room was crowded that night. Not one of those people could place him at the scene of Dean Starr's murder."

"Can you tell us anything about the killer?"

"The killer was reasonably well dressed. This wasn't the typical art show. The opening was black tie, invitation only, and it was a money crowd. Mr. Koozeman tells us that at least ten percent of the gathering crashed the party, but a shabby dresser would've been stopped at the door. So we have very little interest in the unemployed, badly dressed psycho in the FBI profile."

"You think the killer was an artist?"

"Well the idea was just creative as hell, wasn't it? It's someone with a background in art, but it could just as easily be a collector."

Another hand went up, and Coffey noted that all requests for time were going through Mallory now. With a curt nod, she recognized a woman in the front row.

"What about this art terrorist angle, Mallory?"

"That's a joke. Only the lunatic on the roof of Bloomingdale's has made that connection so far. Oh, and I believe Agent Cartland mentioned it."

"So the FBI is dead wrong on almost all counts, is that what you're saying?"

"But we certainly appreciate all their help," said Mallory.

The reporters politely restricted themselves to sniggers and other sounds muffled by tight lips. When the FBI agent had lost his ramrod posture to sink down in his chair, and Beale's eyes were glistening with emotion, a small sprinkling of applause followed Mallory as she left her chair on the dais and walked toward Coffey at the back of the room.

Coffey put one hand on her shoulder and walked beside her through the wide door and down the quiet hallway. "I've never seen Beale look so happy. After that performance, you could commit murder and not wind up on Beale's shit list."

"Really?"

Coffey only had one bad moment, when it crossed his mind that she might translate that into a free kill. The moment passed in confidence that Markowitz had raised her to repress any grossly antisocial acts. But he wondered what the FBI profilers might have done with Mallory's psych evaluation. He made a mental note to hunt down all her records, and to destroy the most damning lines. He was a good political animal, and if this case should go wrong, he would not like to find himself in front of the Civilian Review Board explaining why NYPD had a sociopath on the payroll.

A tall man was blocking the hallway. As they drew nearer, he recognized him, though he had only seen J. L. Quinn on two or three occasions. The man's remarkable blue eyes drew Coffey in with fascination and then repelled him with their coldness. The art critic was a handsome man, and ageless. His ice-blue eyes were fixed on Mallory now, and Coffey felt suddenly protective. He wondered if Mallory understood how politically well connected Quinn's family was. Would she even care?

Quinn dismissed Coffey from the immediate universe with a nod of recognition. He focussed all his attention on Mallory, as though they were alone. "I stopped by Special Crimes Section. They told me I could find you here. I thought we might have lunch. Perhaps we could discuss what else I might do to help you with your investigation."

"I think we've covered that, Quinn." She started to walk past him.

He put his hand on her arm to detain her. She looked down at his hand, and he drew it back as though she had burned him.

Coffey willed her to be careful. This man was money, influence and power.

"There must be some other way I could help," said Quinn with insistence and the confidence that came from background, wealth and the sure knowledge that he could crush her if he wanted to. He would not be put off by her, yet she seemed determined to do just that.

Jack Coffey was suddenly very alert. There was something not right about this man. All his instincts told him a likely suspect was the one who tried to insinuate himself into the investigation. Well, maybe the attraction to the case was something as simple as Mallory's pretty face.

She was staring at the man as though he had just crawled out of a sewer. "Quinn, I'm sure you told me everything you knew."

The implication was *What use are you to me?*

"Well, I expect you'll be taking the case in new directions. You may have new questions," said Quinn. "I'm at your disposal. Ask whatever you want of me."

"All right," said Mallory. "I want to know who your sister's friends are. I want to know all the places where Sabra hung out before she disappeared."

Now Coffey saw regret in Quinn's eyes. The man had not foreseen this. Twelve years ago, he had gone to a great deal of trouble to keep the police away from his family. And now that he had given Mallory carte blanche, how would he get out of this?

He wouldn't.

Suddenly, Coffey understood that Mallory had spent the last few minutes digging a deep hole for Quinn and covering it over with twigs and branches. And now she had him. It was the old man's style. Markowitz would have been proud.

And what's this? Plaid trousers? *Flared?* Andrew Bliss leaned over the wall, bullhorn at the ready, target in his sights.

"You down there, the man with the plaid clown suit!"

The man stopped.

"Yes, *you!* The sixties are done. Get yourself a life. Men's—on the first floor—and hurry, for God's sake."

It was afternoon when he saw Annie on the sidewalk. She was smiling up at him and making the round "okay" with thumb and forefinger. Bless Annie, she had worn black pumps for the occasion. Now she gestured to the mobile news unit pulling up to the curb. More publicity, and hallelujah. Annie was motioning with a sweeping gesture which encompassed the small crowd massing at the foot of the building, and then she blew him a kiss.

Throughout the day, crowds gathered and dispersed, as he periodically retired into a bottle to rest his voice and kill the pain of the previous night's bottles.

There was one small horror, realized on his second day out: he had no shampoo, deodorant, soap, none of the little niceties. And today, he was down to his last bottle of designer water for his morning espresso. He had thought to cart up two potted trees, but no toothbrush or paste. Though he had many changes of clothing, his body had begun to stink. His hair had become greasy and matted. Experimental bathing in champagne had only brought down a plague of flies. And then there was nothing for it but to get drunk and drunker, until he could no longer feel the flies running barefoot through his hair.

A fat dollop of water splashed the bridge of his nose, calling his attention to the sky and the coming rain. He began picking through the mounds of material, sheets, towels and silk pajamas, searching for the rope with which to make his canopy of raincoats. Now he uncovered a woman's hand, and he drew back too quickly, losing his footing and landing on his rear end with a look of dumb surprise. On all fours, he crept close to the hand protruding from the pile of cloth. It was a mannequin, of course, but why had he brought it up to the roof?

He uncovered the mannequin woman with raven hair, a silver dress and dancing shoes. He dragged it off to a far corner of the roof and put a sheet over it. He retreated and sat down with his back against the opposite retaining wall, arms hugging his knees. He began to rock from side to side. Now that the mannequin was laid out and draped like the dead, it frightened him even more.

A small bell tinkled over the door as Mallory and Quinn passed under the amber light of the old Tiffany lamp. "That lamp was purchased in the early fifties," said Quinn. "Every stick of furniture can be dated to that era. This place was Sabra's favorite hangout."

They settled at one end of the bar. There were patrons up and down the length of mahogany. Mallory picked up a cocktail napkin and stared at the logo for the Hilda-Godd Bar. "I thought it was called Godd's Bar?"

"Well, Mike Godd died twenty years ago. Hilda Winkler is still alive, but she might as well be a ghost. Her name just dropped out of use. See that old woman over there? Even the bartender doesn't know this, but that's Hilda, the owner."

An old woman sat in the far corner of the room, and tipped back a sherry glass. In the way of a specter, she kept to the darkest shadows of the place.

"Regulars of ten years' standing have no idea who she

is. The bartender only knows that the old lady drinks
sherry and never pays a tab. She's there when he comes
to work in the afternoon, and still there when he leaves
at closing time.''

The phone was ringing, and the bartender moved up
the length of the bar to answer it.

"Watch the old woman now," said Quinn.

The bartender picked up the phone and said, "This is
Godd, whaddaya want?" and the old woman shuddered
when he did this, as though she might be wondering if
she was the ghost, and not her long-dead partner, whose
name lived on.

Quinn looked toward the lineup of drinkers at the bar
and then over his shoulder to the scattering of patrons
among the polished tables. "Almost all of these people
are painters or photographers."

A young man dropped a coin into the jukebox, an elaborate art deco piece of ornate zigzag lines and curls of
bright, colored lights. The music pouring out of the box
was the big-band sound from a time when the old woman
had been younger, prettier, more alive than the other permanent fixtures of Godd's Bar. Mallory recognized the
music from Markowitz's record collection in the basement of the old house in Brooklyn.

When she was a child, Markowitz had played the old
records for her and taught her how to swing to the big-
band music which had filled the basement with a fifty-
piece orchestra. The dancing lessons had begun with the
waltz, leading into bebop and then on to rock'n'roll—
the old man's real passion. But she suspected Markowitz
had harbored a special feeling for the early fifties. He
would have loved this place.

She was intent on the bartender's back, waiting for him
to turn around. When he did turn, he read her lips as she
ordered a scotch and soda. He smiled and nodded at her,
added a word each to two different conversations, mixed
a tray of drinks for the cocktail waitress and splashed her

scotch into a glass without a spill or a wasted motion. It was a magic act. He moved up the length of the bar, dancing to the music from the jukebox. One hand ringed a twist of lemon around the rim of the glass as he set the napkin in place on the bar. The glass appeared to settle there of its own accord, so sly was the hand. Long dark hair grazed his shoulders and he seemed to have no bones. Now he produced a bottle of sipping whiskey from the backbar and poured a neat shot without Quinn having to ask for it. The bartender was introduced as Kerry.

"Thanks again for the gig at Koozeman's," Kerry said to Quinn. "The opening is gonna be a big night. He packs a lot of money into those crowds. It's a networker's dream."

"Don't mention it," said Quinn. "I did it for selfish reasons." Turning to Mallory, he said, "Kerry is one of my best sources for news in the art community."

Now Kerry was pointing to a patron sitting alone at the other end of the bar. "He just got the commission to shoot the plaza of Gilette's new building. Gilette's bringing down the wooden construction-site walls so they can photograph the place before the sculpture is installed."

Quinn turned to Mallory. "Every time a building goes up, the architect is obliged to let the city put its own sculpture in the plaza. It's usually something pretty awful. The architect always likes to get the *before* shot so he can remember it the way it was meant to be."

Style, thy name is Kerry. She watched the bartender dance away to pour another round for a patron. Without facing Quinn, she asked, "Why were you at the old East Village gallery on the night of that double murder?"

"Don't you ever shift out of the interrogation mode? I told Markowitz. I'm sure he left—"

"I don't care what you told him. I can place you in each of Koozeman's galleries at the time of two different homicides. That's bound to make me curious, isn't it? Now talk to me.''

"I was told to meet Aubry there. A message was left at the newspaper in her name. Later, I figured that I'd been set up. The killer wanted to be critiqued, or that was your father's thought.''

"Was it? I don't think you cared what Markowitz thought.''

"Pardon?''

''I think you spent all your time steering the old man in the direction you wanted him to take. I think you were obsessed with your own theories.''

"You're interrogating me, aren't you?''

"Cops do that.''

"Are you considering me as a suspect? You think I murdered Starr? That's ridiculous. The only kind of artist a critic can kill is a good one. Mediocrity is indestructible. You can step on it and flush it down the toilet, if you like. Not only will it survive, it actually flourishes in the crap.''

While she quietly ruminated over his toilet metaphor, he signaled Kerry for another round of drinks.

The jukebox was playing a tune from the late forties. All the records were perishable vinyl, played with needles to grooves. Mallory understood to the penny at what great cost these collectible recordings were rounded up, played until worn and replaced with others.

She listened to the clear, sweet notes of the girl singer and wondered who she might have been. It was a distinctive voice, but she didn't recognize it from Markowitz's collection. She left the bar and walked to the jukebox. The song was ended, the record slowed and stopped. The singer's name was on the record label below the name of the band, and in very small type—Hildy Winkler, the owner of the bar. So Quinn had missed that, or else he would have thrown it into the tour ramble. What else might he have missed?

Hilda Winkler was shaking her head slowly as she waved one hand at the wide plate-glass window. Mallory caught the motion out of the corner of her eye. The old woman's face swiveled quickly back toward the bar, and she was surprised to see Mallory staring at her. It was guilty surprise, a look Mallory knew well. She smiled at the elderly bar owner, just the line of a smile to ask, *What are you up to, old woman?*

Mallory turned to the window in time to see the back of an old hag dragging a wire cart down the sidewalk.

So that was it. Just waving off the riffraff. *Move along*, was all the old woman on the inside meant to say to the crone on the outside, *No loitering, no rest for you—not at my door.*

Charles rang the bell again. Punctuality was her religion. He was genuinely stunned that Mallory was not at home. They had agreed to meet at eight o'clock, and it was ten of the hour now.

He stood outside Mallory's door as people passed by him on the way to a party in the apartment at the end of the hall. And every passerby looked at the man with the flowers, the tuxedo and the foolish smile. He was so transparently in love, they could read the plaque bearing Mallory's apartment number through his soul.

The elevator announced itself with a metallic ping. The doors opened and Mallory appeared, striding down the hall, a canvas tote bag slung over one shoulder. "Hi, Charles."

"You're not dressed."

"You said eight o'clock." She looked at her watch. "It's only ten of eight now."

He followed behind her as she pressed through the door, dropped her tote bag on the rug and disappeared into her bedroom. "Clock me," she called back to him as the door was closing.

He sat down in a massive armchair. He wished everyone's furniture was so accommodating to his large frame. Every object in this room had been selected for simplicity of form and function. If he didn't know this was her apartment, there would be nothing to give him a clue to the inhabitant's character. This was a non-atmosphere, impersonal, with no imprint of background. All the furnishings were expensive, but nothing was sought for show. There was a Spartan quality to the bare walls where the giveaway photographs and paintings should be. There was not a single bookcase to tell anyone that Mallory had a life of the mind. Her reading matter was squirreled away in her office at Mallory and Butler, Ltd.—all manuals for machines, and no literature to show even a passing interest in human beings. He looked around him again. Yes, he could believe that a machine lived here.

The tote bag toppled over on its side and a slew of photographs spilled out onto the rug. He was staring down at the image of a man's severed head. He looked away. He knew this must be the head of the artist who had been murdered twelve years ago. Though the photographs had never been published, no adult living in New York City had been spared one gruesome detail of the deaths in the old Koozeman Gallery. He did not want to look at the photograph, but could not help himself.

When his gaze was drawn back to the picture on the floor, the bloody head was partially obscured by one green satin dancing shoe.

Beauty triumphed over bloody violence. His eyes lifted to the stunning sight of Mallory, green eyes and flowing green satin, waves of golden hair curling just above her bare white shoulders. He would have wagered anything that no other woman in Manhattan could have managed this in less than an hour. She had done it in less than five minutes. But then she was beautiful in blue jeans. She needed little else but the red lipstick to go with her flawless red nails. More would have been less.

• • •

In years past, the ball had been the social event of the season and quite successful on this account. However, as a charity function, it never failed to lose money. The most lavish gala of New York society drew funds from the families of the Social Register Four Hundred and many power moguls of *Fortune*'s Five Hundred, but it rarely turned much profit to the coffers of any worthy cause. Most years it ran to red ink, and this year the ball had barely broken even.

The elderly chairwoman, Ellen Quinn, was photographed in the act of handing an envelope to the administrator of the Crippled Children's Fund. There was, of course, very little in the envelope, the chairwoman hastily explained in a whisper, and alas, no more was forthcoming. And so the administrator of the fund was photographed with an authentic expression of shock and slack-jawed surprise.

Charles made an entrance with Mallory. They passed through the great doors and into the spectacle of cathedral-high ceilings and a chandelier of a thousand lights, a room of silks, sequins and brilliant color interspersed with black tuxedos. A full orchestra was on the bandstand in black tie. The acoustics were marvelous. Music swelled to all points of the room, and perfumes swirled past them on the dance floor. Mallory walked close beside him, her hand on his arm to complete the overload of all his senses.

As Charles and Mallory moved through the crowd, heads throughout the room began to turn, each head alerting the one behind. The ball photographer abandoned his model of the moment to flash picture after picture of Mallory, exploding the flashes only a few feet before her eyes. The photographer's former model, the director of New York's largest bank, was left to smile foolishly at nothing at all in a pose with his wife, who also continued to smile.

Other women in the room were carefully coiffed and

lacquered. Eighty-mile-an-hour winds could not have dislodged a single hair. Mallory's hair waved in natural-looking rivers and curls of blond silk slipping over silk, moving as she moved. Her eyes had a charming, startled look which was largely attributable to flashbulb blindness. People continued to stare, some boldly, some covertly, at the young woman in the sea-green satin ball gown.

Charles danced one dance with her and then lost her to another partner and another. The dancing men came in legion. The ball gown lived its own life, capturing the lights and threading them into the fabric. Twirling amid the green satin fireworks, Mallory seemed not to touch the ground at all.

J. L. Quinn captured her for a waltz. They made a striking partnership, opposites of dark hair and light, turning, twirling. The other dancers slowed to watch the pair, and some of them altogether stopped. The fascination for beauty overcame envy in the pinch-faced women with too little flesh, and the men with red-veined noses and too much flesh, socialites who had no breasts, and the gangly boys who had no beards.

Charles stood alone, not dancing and not wanting to watch anymore.

Quinn held her out to admire her, and then pulled her close again, dancing her toward the center of the room. "My God, it must have been sheer hell growing up with a face like yours."

"I'll tell you just one more time," said Mallory. "Dance me over to Gregor Gilette and change partners with him. Do it now."

"And give you up? I'd rather be killed outright."

"I'm a cop, I can arrange that."

Contrary to a direct order, Quinn was not leading her in the direction of Gregor Gilette, but quite deliberately leading her away. She regretted leaving her gun at home.

"There's really no need to disturb Gregor. I can tell you anything you need to know," said Quinn.

He probably could, but *would* he? She didn't think so, not without a weapon to his head, and perhaps not even then. "Did your brother-in-law have any enemies twelve years ago?"

"Of course he did. He's a profoundly talented architect. You can find a list of his enemies in any copy of *Architectural Digest*."

"What about the art community?"

"He and Sabra had a few common enemies. I suppose Emma Sue Hollaran would be at the top of that list. The woman scorned—you know that song."

"She was involved with Gregor Gilette?"

"Only in her dreams."

"So she was jealous of Sabra."

"Yes. The animosity was rather overt. Hollaran used to be an art critic for an upscale newspaper that's since gone under. The editor thought her barnyard critiques would make a nice contrast to the good writing in the other columns. She tried to destroy Sabra in the column. But Sabra's work was critic-proof. Now Hollaran is on the Public Works Committee and perfectly positioned to go after Gregor in a more direct fashion."

Mallory caught sight of Gregor Gilette dancing closer. "Did you ever talk to Gilette about my interview? Did you even ask him if he'd cooperate off the record?"

"He can't go into that horror again. I want you to stay away from him."

"Is that his decision, or yours?"

"It doesn't matter."

"You didn't talk to him, did you? I thought you wanted to help me."

"I do, Mallory. But there's nothing Gregor can tell you."

"You stopped the police from interviewing the family twelve years ago. You're not going to do it again."

"Oh, but I will. He's been through quite enough. Now that's the end of it."

Quinn's elderly mother waltzed by in the arms of a young man. The old woman was a graceful dancer, but Mallory noticed the wince when the young man pressed her hand for the turn. Mrs. Quinn was probably arthritic, though she hid the pain well.

So, the old lady was fragile. Good.

"You know, Quinn, I don't think anyone ever got around to interviewing your mother, either. She looks like she's pushing eighty."

Quinn held her away at arm's length as though she had just bitten him, and rather viciously. "There was never any reason for the police to talk to my mother. No one even suggested it."

"I can question Gregor Gilette. Or I can go after your dear old mother. *Choose one*."

And now they had come to a standstill in the center of the room, as all the dancers swirled around them.

"You know I could—"

"Have me fired? And I suppose you thought Marko-witz was afraid of losing *his* job? He wasn't! Markowitz let you get away with a lot because he figured he could use you. You were his tour guide through the art com-munity. But I don't think you were as useful as you could've been. I think you held out on my father, and I think you're holding out on me."

"You can't possibly believe—"

"It's a given. Everybody does it. Who wants to strip naked for a homicide investigation? If you want to go after my badge, go for it. But if you get it, I'll have to get even with you, won't I? I'm good at revenge. I'll turn your life inside out, and I know how to do that. I'll see you in tabloid hell. You only think you know what naked is. And you don't want to think about what I could do to an old woman like your mother. I could do her with my eyes shut. Now change partners with Gilette."

• • •

Emma Sue Hollaran began the tortuous journey across the ballroom floor. She was moving slowly, smiling despite the pain and nausea. Her swollen, bruised legs were encased in the tightest long-line girdle made. Every step was agony in this grotesque parody of the little mermaid of fairy tale, whose every step on human feet was the thrust of knives through her soles. Emma Sue was in constant pain now, but she had become accustomed to it over the years of surgeries.

Resplendent in her designer gown of iridescent colors, she was closing the distance on Gregor Gilette. He was stirring every part of her mind and the nether regions of her body where pain could not obliterate simple longing, ungodly desire that never ended. Once she had sent him love letters every day. He had never answered one of them. It was Sabra who eventually responded, if one could call it that.

Ah, but Sabra was gone, and Gregor was back from his long exile in Europe.

Emma Sue Hollaran banished Sabra from her thoughts and all the way to hell where she belonged, for Gregor Gilette was turning around now. Any moment he would see her in her finest hour, her new-formed body, her much worked-over face.

She was closer to him, nearly there, almost within touching distance. And now she was staring into his remarkable eyes, which penetrated her facades and knew her secrets; they probed the places of heat and sex, all the soft places. She felt herself being drawn into him as if she had no more substance than light. For this one stunning moment, she was young again, with all her possibilities intact.

Her hand fluttered up to her chest to quell the havoc there of blood rushing unchecked through her veins, heart pumping faster, chasing blood with blood, filling her with warmth and flooding her face with a vivid redness. Every step toward him was a knife wound, but she would have endured much more for this moment of triumph. She had waited so long.

And now.

His eyebrows shot up with recognition—followed closely by the revulsion in his eyes.

He turned away from her as introductions were being made to a young woman in a green satin gown. And now, Gregor and this woman were revolving, spinning away from her, locked in one another's arms, moving across the floor with grace and speed.

He was out of her reach.

She turned away from the dancing pair and, trembling, she walked aimlessly through that room, awash in physical pain and the worse agony of humiliation. Finally, she summoned a cab to take her home to a bed that was too wide.

At fifty-eight, Gregor Gilette was far from old. His white hair was incongruous with the bull's chest and the limber, supple motions of the body. His golden-brown eyes were remarkably young, and the craggy contours of his face also insisted on youth and strength. It was a face where paradox lived, beautiful and yet strikingly grotesque, animal sensuality and keen intelligence.

"I like your work," Mallory said. "I was wondering what kind of sculpture was planned for the plaza. I understand the chairwoman of the Public Works Committee is an old enemy of yours. Does that worry you?"

Gilette laughed. "Emma Sue Hollaran? She's not big enough to be an enemy. She's a barnyard animal. A small one."

She could hear the trace of a foreign accent, not the French of his father's people, but a lingering influence of his Hungarian mother. According to Mallory's background check, he had immigrated with his mother at the age of seventeen. In his spectacular rise from poverty and obscurity, he was the American dream machine at its best. And his daughter had been the American nightmare. Aubry had won the national lottery of the victim with the most extensive media fame.

"This new building is your first American commission in years, isn't it?"

"So you do know my work. Yes, this building is my swan song. It's the last commission I will ever take. I want to end my career at the height of my powers."

"I suppose you spent all this time in Europe because New York had too many reminders of your daughter."

"No, that's not it. I carry reminders of Aubry everywhere I go. I must have a hundred portraits of her. No, my problem was just the opposite. Here in New York, no one ever spoke of her anymore. Friends and relatives were all afraid to mention her name, afraid to cause me fresh pain. In every day which excluded any mention of my child, I felt she was being erased."

Charles was surprised to see Mallory leaving with Gregor Gilette. As she was passing through the doors, he saw her turn to search the sea of faces, and finding his, she waved. There was the lift of one white shoulder to say, *It can't be helped.*

The tilt of his head to one side asked, *Why not?* But the doors were already closing behind her. The tight line of his mouth wobbled in a foolish, self-conscious smile.

The music began again and the dancers whirled around the floor, making a circle of hushing fabrics, a rushing blend of perfumes, a mosaic of brilliant color and motion all around the solitary man with the sad face, who was staring down at his shoes.

Just as Andrew Bliss had assembled his canopy of raincoats on a loose net of ropes, the rain had stopped. Well, that was life. Now a wet breeze licked the edges of his designer raincover. Traffic noises were sporadic. The night was cool and ten-thirty dark. A heavy truck was making wet static in the street below, and now a car. A siren, far off, was fading down some other street. And on the street below, two boom box radios dueled rap music to heavy metal.

Exhausted, Andrew fell on his bed of quilts and relapsed into fitful sleep, mangling satin sheets into a damp and winding rope. His dream blew apart in pyrotechnics of brilliant red flashes. His hands clutched the air, reaching for the blasted color fragments.

He mimed a scream as his body jerked with spasms and slowly folded in on itself to resemble a twitching fetus with hands pressed to its gut. The dream slid away from him, the pain subsided and his body unfolded in a free fall, floating down into deepest sleep.

"No, I never dream," he would say, when conversations turned to that subject. And he believed that this was so. He never did remember his dreams, though this one had been much the same every night.

His face was composed now, the flesh smoothed back. He was forty-eight years old, and there should have been at least a character line, a laugh line about the eyes or mouth, but there was nothing there. No ancient scar to prove any rite of passage. But for the size of his body, he might have been a child.

He was child-size in his dream, and the world inside his head was bright as day and hot, a touch of hell in the afternoon. He rode silently, covertly inside a bag lady's trolling cart, resting on a buttonless blue coat, the find of two trash cans past. A salty drop sweated down his shaded face. He made no sound, lest she find him there and drive him out. No free rides in New York City. In the rolling wire nest of junk, he found a Chinese fan, cracked lacquer and one hole, but useful still and soothing. Now his hand found the axe, wet and red. He screamed, but only the smallest squeak could be heard, no louder than the creaking cart wheels.

The old woman stopped the cart. "Get out! Get out!" the woman screamed, baring toothless red gums. "No free rides in New York City."

He stepped out onto the sidewalk, watching her move on, laboriously rolling down the steamy street with her wire cart.

A group of adults loomed over him, angry and pointing to the body of a young woman lying at his feet. Her face was a mask of blood, and yet she would not die. He turned his back on her, and listened to the sounds of her struggles. What kept her alive? He turned back to look. A blade was cutting into her neck, aborting the scream in her throat. Next, it cut through her outstretched hand, shredding it. He covered his face and turned away. By the sounds, he understood what was happening behind his back. He could hear the sounds of gurgling blood in her throat and the soft suction noises of the blade working in and out of the flesh. The blood ran over his shoes in a trickle, and the trickle widened to a steady stream of rich red, and her banging heart beat out more blood to feed the river.

He woke up screaming. The rain had begun again.

The plaza was covered by scaffolding and wooden boards. He handed her the umbrella and gestured for her to step back as he pried open one of the boards and removed it. Mallory and Gilette stepped through the wooden fencing and entered the dark plaza. He led her across the paving stones, explaining the placement of each object and what he had done to foil Emma Sue Hollaran's plans for this space.

"She really hated your wife, didn't she?"

"Yes. But someone had to stop Emma Sue. Sabra thought the woman was crazy, and she didn't want her near Aubry."

"Dangerously crazy?"

"Perhaps. Emma Sue was stalking me. She telephoned

and sent me letters every day. We were constantly changing the phone number, she was always getting the new one. She could simply not believe that I wanted nothing to do with her. Sabra took her letters and gave them to a tabloid reporter. Instead of printing them, the reporter sold them back to Emma Sue. The harassment stopped, but then she went after Sabra in her column. When that didn't do any damage, she finally just ceased to be a problem.''

''Until now.''

''Yes, but I think I've minimized the damage she can do.''

Mallory approved the layout of the plaza. The fountain was the centerpiece, a work of art in itself, and there were generous paths between it and the groupings of benches, but her eye for perfect symmetry could find no place to put another object.

''You haven't left her any room for a large sculpture.''

''Exactly. Whatever they put here, it will have to be something rather small.''

The plaza itself was a perfect work of art, and nowhere in the scheme would it accommodate another structure. A strand of young trees lined the space and would not permit anything but birds among them. Benches had been built up from the plaza floor and could not be moved aside. Anything placed near the fountain would block the carefully planned walkways.

She entwined her arm with Gilette's and led him to a bench by the fountain. Water music and sporadic sounds of traffic mingled with the rustle of the trees in a warm wind.

''I want to talk about the night Aubry died.''

''You're wondering if I can do that? I prefer to talk about the time when she was alive—but yes, I can manage it.''

''Let me give you a scenario for Aubry's death. You tell me if this works for you. Suppose she wasn't the

target that night. She might have come on the murderer
in the act.''

He nodded. ''That would make sense. If she heard
someone calling for help, she would have gone running.
She was at her physical peak, and she was fearless. You
don't know the chances she took as a dancer. Every leap
might have been the injury to end a career. Yes, it could
have happened that way.''

''She was in good shape. If she came on a murder in
progress and she wasn't taken by surprise, the bastard
who killed her would have had to catch her first—if it
happened that way. You'd have to figure it was someone
large or in very good shape.''

''Yes, I never understood how Oren Watt could have
done it, unless he came on her from behind. He was a
junkie, wasn't he? Maybe he had help.''

''So you had reservations about Watt? I had the idea
that you were always convinced that he did it.''

''Oh, I'm sure he was there. He did confess. Jamie
took the blame, you know. My poor brother-in-law
thought someone had set him up and used Aubry for bait.
Oren Watt was an artist. He would have fit with that
idea.''

''Oren Watt didn't become an artist until he made his
confession. Before that, he was a junkie who delivered
pizza and did occasional drug deals with the deliveries.
I wonder if he even knew your brother-in-law was related
to Aubry, or if he even knew Quinn was an art critic.''

It was dark, but she could follow the changes in his
face as he digested this. This was news to him. Had he
been lied to or sheltered? ''How well did you know the
gallery owner, Avril Koozeman?''

''We crossed paths at a few art functions. And once
or twice we've bid against one another at auctions, usually charity affairs.''

''How well did Sabra know him?''

''They knew each other quite well in their younger

days. They exhibited in the same gallery.''

"Koozeman was an artist?''

"Oh, yes, and a good one.''

"So he's been a gallery owner, a critic *and* an artist?''

"It's not so strange. People often float among related fields. A police officer might become a security expert or a criminal, or both, yes?''

"It's been done,'' said Mallory. "So you thought Koozeman was a good artist. And what did Sabra think of him?''

"She had a very high opinion of his work. She said there was a dark genius to it. But Koozeman wasn't willing to pay the dues, so he applied his genius to promoting others. He tried to lure Sabra into his stable of artists, but by then she was established, a rising star. She was quite beyond him.''

"Did he hold a grudge?''

"No. I wouldn't think so. He was always a driven man, too fixated on his own life. He's made quite a success of his gallery over the past ten years or so.''

Mallory looked around the plaza. "It's too bad your wife can't be here to see this. You haven't seen her in a long time, have you?''

"No. Sabra disappeared soon after Aubry died. I blame myself. I was so deep in grief, I didn't see the changes in her, until she cut off her beautiful hair. She left me. She didn't stop to pack a bag. I found all the cut strands of her hair lying on the floor of our bedroom. She didn't even take that.''

"Did you try to find her?''

"Of course.''

"But you never saw her again?''

"No.''

She wondered if she believed everything this man told her. And what of Quinn? He behaved like a man with a reason to lie, to cover, but for what reason? Who was Quinn shielding? Not Gilette.

"You really have no idea where she is?"

"None. If I knew, I would be with her now. I'm still very much in love with my wife."

And there was truth in this. His eyes were looking at a memory, and it was beloved. He turned to face her now, back in the present and curious. "Why are you so interested in Sabra? Do you think she might be able to tell you something about that night?"

"Maybe. I'll never know. The police weren't allowed to question her after Aubry died."

"She could not have stood up to any stress."

"Maybe she could stand it now. I'd like to talk to Sabra, but she's sunk below my radar. She's living under an alias, or she's—"

"Dead? Yes, I've thought of that possibility, but she would never commit suicide. It's against her religion. Would it help you to know that she was in an institution for a few years? It was a voluntary commitment."

"What institution?"

"If I had known the name, I would have settled the bill. She never used our insurance policy. She had to be there under an assumed name. My detectives couldn't find her."

"So how did you find out she was hospitalized?"

"Word got back to me. I won't say from whom. It was a private affair, and I am a great respecter of privacy." He looked away, and then his face came back to her, smiling with a change of subject.

"The man you came with, Charles Butler? I can't say I know him well. I only saw him at family gatherings, but I did watch him grow up from wedding to wedding, funeral to funeral. I'm sure I remember him far better than he remembers me. He was so remarkable in any company—and I'm not referring to that magnificent nose. I gather he's not a close friend of yours?"

"He's a very close friend." He was her only friend. "Why did you say that?"

"Well, he must be devastated now. I don't imagine he enjoyed losing you that way."

"Charles? He understood why I had to leave."

"You think he understood why he was left to look like a fool in front of all those people?" He put up one hand to silence her, to stop her from denying she had done that. "When Charles was a little boy, his freak intellect made him a thing apart from other children, a different species. The things the *normal* children did to him—just following their nature, never missing an opportunity to be cruel. But you're not a child, and you say you're his friend."

"I *am* his friend."

"I wonder, Mallory. Would he have left *you* behind?"

"It wasn't like that."

"Oh, but it was. I've seen it before, at every wedding and funeral. His mother would shoo him into a crowd of children. The little monsters would torture him for a while, and then they'd run off. He would just stand there, very quiet, with this stunned look in his eyes. I think the cruelty always baffled him. That's what I saw in his face tonight as we were leaving the ball—he really didn't understand."

Gregor Gilette was searching her face, probing her with his eyes. He seemed surprised by what he had just found. "Mallory, you don't comprehend any of this, do you?" He brought his face closer to hers. "No, I can see that you don't."

Mallory looked down at her watch. "I have to leave now—I've got work to do. I'd like to talk to you again. Can I call you?"

"Yes, of course." He pulled a pen and a card from his pocket and scribbled a telephone number on the back. "I'll look forward to it."

Charles stirred in the night, rising to half-consciousness with the light pepper of pebbles on glass. With mild annoyance, he rolled over and pressed his face into the pillow. He came rudely awake to the sound of a breaking windowpane, and his eyes snapped open in time to see a dark object fly into the room and land on the carpet amid a sparkling shower of glass.

Well, now he was wide awake. He rushed to the window and threw up the sash, ready with a small store of words Riker had taught him to relieve the angst of just such a moment. He leaned out the window, prepared with an opening gambit to cast aspersions on the parenthood of the rock thrower.

In the street below was a beautiful woman in a shimmering green ball gown. She was standing in the soft rain and staring up at him. The drops pocked her gown with dots of a darker green. Her face was misted and shining, her white skin luminous. Her hair glistened with rain and lamplight. She blew him a kiss, and in the next moment, she was gone, hurrying up the narrow street toward the wide busy lanes and bright lights of Houston. He leaned far out the window and watched until the last bit of her gown had disappeared into a yellow taxi.

When he finally stood back from the window, he wore the most foolish grin a human could wear outside of captivity. His hair was soaked through, and now he realized he was standing on broken glass. It had just dawned on him that his soles were bleeding, when he noticed the object at his feet—masonry which he hoped was a chunk off someone else's building. A bit of paper was bound to it by string. He knelt down and untied the wet knot, carefully unfolding the limp paper as though it were a precious relic. He lifted his message to the window. By this poor light, he read the words, "I'm sorry."

When he considered the source, this was nearly poetic. And to think, he had once criticized her for not having a jot of romance in her soul, or for that matter, a soul. And who but Mallory would have come up with the original idea of tendering an apology by rock?

• • •

In its original form, the newspaper clipping had been Sabra and Gregor Gilette's wedding portrait from the society pages. It had shown only a small part of the bride's face, only one eye unobscured by her flowers. Half that photograph stared back at Emma Sue each night from the ornate picture frame on the bedside table. She had cut off Sabra's side of it in the way of a jealous lover. How she had hated Gregor's wife. And yet, perversely, her most prized possession was one of Sabra's paintings.

In her young years, before she had become a mover and shaker in the New York art world, Emma Sue Hollaran's taste in art had always run contentedly with reproductions of Americana by the painter from Maine. His work was as quiet and unchallenging as wallpaper in the portraiture of neighbor folk and peaceful landscapes of an America that she never lived in, a made-up place that she might visit for a moment before turning out the lights.

All those years ago when she had seen the first of Sabra's paintings, she had physically recoiled. It was the shock of cold water and the disorientation of a sleepwalker called rudely awake. It thrilled her. Sabra had painted a place that Emma Sue had known in her fantasies. The work was done in vibrant reds. The upper portion was a jagged raging violence and the lower part, a rolling, bleeding passivity. She stared into the painting, believing for one full second that she might actually enter it.

Untutored in abstract art, she had forced representation onto the canvas, and reorganized the atmosphere of raw sex, until the violence became a tumultuous fiery sky, roaring over the gently sloping earth below. Rushing across the red plain in the distance, coming ever close, was a churning blood storm. This, too, was another country. It was young, and it was passionate. She remembered it well from dark rooms where she had sat alone with imaginary men who really loved her.

The painting had been hung on her bedroom wall all those years ago. Even when she had come to hate Sabra, Emma Sue could never bring herself to destroy the painting. All these years later, she still found herself staring at it for hours, her head pressed into the pillows, hand hesitating on the lamp switch, watching, waiting for the passionate blood storm to come, in the delusion that, for her, it had not already passed her by.

She turned off the lamp and plotted in the dark.

Gregor would be sorry, very sorry.

Mallory had doffed her ball gown and her yellow taxi cab. Long after midnight, she had returned to what she was, a cop in blue jeans, carrying a large gun in a shoulder holster and striding across a rooftop on the east side of town, ten flights in the air.

Riker waved one arm to say hello. He had his binoculars trained down on the roof of Bloomingdale's across the street. He was focussed on the thing beneath the makeshift canopy of raincoats. The wind whipped at the canopy, and a coat flapped up to expose the mannequin in the silver ball gown. Andrew Bliss was tenderly draping the plastic figure with a raincoat, as though he thought she might be cold.

"Strange little guy," said Riker.

"What's he doing?"

"I think he's starting a new religion. Right now he's lighting a candle in front of a giant Barbie doll."

Mallory took the binoculars, and watched Andrew light the tall formal candles of a silver candelabra set on a table before the mannequin. "It does look like an altar, doesn't it?"

She had been schooled in two religions, Jewish and Catholic. Both lit candles, but this little rite of Andrew's was closer to the church than the temple. Now Andrew was making the sign of the cross. It was this very act, performed unconsciously as a child, which had tipped

Helen Markowitz off to her real mother's religion, and the foster mother had felt an obligation to condemn Kathy Mallory to four years of parochial school.

"Riker, how much food do you think he has in that little fridge?"

"No food. I saw him open it an hour ago. It's packed with wine and one bottle of water. There's no sign of food anywhere."

"Take off, Riker. Get some sleep."

"G'night, Mallory."

After the rooftop door had closed on Riker, Mallory plugged in her directional microphone and scanned the roof, counting up wine bottles. When she focussed on Andrew again, he was stumbling to his bedding of quilts. He must be tired and weak from the dearth of food and the glut of wine. Yet he did not sleep except in starting fits. He was having nightmares, if Mallory understood those screams. She could remember a childhood of screaming herself awake in the night as Andrew did all the night long, until the candles failed, burning to the nubs and going out.

When he woke again, an hour shy of daylight, he discovered his melted candles, and he went ballistic. She watched him tearing through his entire stock of goods until he found another candle. He lit it and went back to sleep.

Curious.

It wasn't fear of the dark. Electric light bloomed everywhere on the roof. She counted ten lamps tied by a network of extension cords. The candles must mean something more to him.

Just before daybreak, he fell into an exhausted sleep with no more screams, and he did not wake again before Mallory left him.

Gregor Gilette remained in Godd's Bar until closing time. Then he sat in an after-hours bar until near sunup, pondering the possibilities of dark genius.

When he did go home to his Fifth Avenue residence, he was weary in so many ways. He went to the large kitchen at the back of the apartment. He selected a bottle of red from the wine rack and carried it through the rooms, slowly working the screw into the cork.

Gregor unlocked the door of the only room in the apartment which his housekeeper was not obliged to clean. He entered his den and sat down in a chair opposite the enlarged image of a bloody severed head. He casually fumbled in a drawer for his cigar cutter. Behind his chair, Aubry's murdered face, in full color with open, staring dead eyes, seemed to watch as he struck a match to a Cuban cigar, and then poured his wine into a goblet.

He turned to his left, seeking an ashtray. He was so accustomed to the wall covering on that side of the room, he never even glanced at it. From the baseboard to the ceiling molding, the wall was splashed with a collage of photographs and yellowed newspaper clippings, held in place by nails driven into plaster. Four of the photographs were large and glossy, in full color, and the predominant color was the blood of wounds.

The young woman in the photographs was more recognizably human in the newspaper clippings below. Each clipping told much the same story. Each said, in much the same wording, that here was a wildly talented young dancer who was going somewhere in this world.

There were retractions printed in articles at the base of the wall, which said in varied garish tabloid headlines that they had lied; she had died; she would never go anywhere now.

CHAPTER
4

THE KITCHEN WAS RIKER'S FAVORITE ROOM AT MAL-
lory and Butler, Ltd. It was a bright and airy space, a
proper sit-down kitchen, where the best of conversations
took place in the company of people he cared for, and
the coffee was always first-rate.

Riker slumped low in his chair and came to grips with
the early morning. His daily routine had been so completely upset that he did not even have the continuity of
his customary hangover. Mallory had taken the late shift
on the roof, and yet she looked fresh and new. When did
she ever sleep?

She set a platter of croissants and cheeses on the table.
There was also a side dish of jelly doughnuts as a special
concession to himself.

Charles stood at the counter, bending down to read a
light display on the coffee machine. In the kitchen of
Charles's apartment across the hall, he still used a manual
bean grinder, and brewed the coffee, drop by drop, into
a carafe. Here he dealt with a computer which organized
the grinding and brewing, set the richness of the flavor,
and all but fetched the mugs from the cupboard after
announcing that the coffee was ready. This room was the
middle ground between Charles the lover of all things

antique, and Mallory the machine. Now Riker noticed the recent addition of a microwave oven sitting on the counter in company with a small television set and a radio with a CD player.

So Mallory was dragging Charles, appliance by appliance, into the twentieth century.

"I would think Oren Watt was still the most likely suspect," Charles was saying.

"No one saw him there." Mallory laid the silverware on the table.

Sunlight slanted through the squares of the kitchen curtain and made a bright chessboard on the gleaming hardwood floor. The cleaning woman, Mrs. Ortega, owned the credit for the polished woodwork and all the odors of cleaning solvents that lingered for a day after her visits. Riker envied Charles the services of Mrs. Ortega. His own place had not had much of the dust disturbed in all the time he had lived there.

Charles turned to Mallory as he was pouring coffee into generous mugs. "If you took more of an interest in the fine arts and attended a few gallery openings, you would know that no one has any idea what's going on in the room. They stand in front of the artwork in little clusters and gossip. It's not like anyone is watching the room or even looking at the art. Actually, Oren Watt could've done it."

"No, Charles, he couldn't."

Riker noticed that her attitude in dealing with Charles was the same one she might use to housebreak a pet. Of course, she had no pet but Charles. Her voice was softer as she went on. "I watched him at the gallery installation for the television film. People stared at him everywhere he went. His face is a standout, and they all knew who he was, even though he'd cut off his hair and wore dark glasses. It was creepy. I don't care how crowded the room was, or how preoccupied the guests were. Whoever was there and not dead would've noticed him."

"I'll make a bet with you." Charles carried the mugs to the table. "If I can prove that Oren Watt could've done it, you pay for lunch. Deal?"

Riker grinned. "I didn't think you were much of a betting man, Charles."

"It's a science experiment with him." Mallory sat down at the table and selected a golden croissant. "He can never win at poker, and he doesn't know why. So he'll keep doing experiments until he figures it out."

"What's to figure out?" Riker reached for a doughnut and studied it with grave suspicion, wondering if he could eat it without a beer to wash it down. "You play poker with sharks, Charles. Doc Slope was born with a poker face. Rabbi Kaplan is a walking book of knowledge on human nature, and Duffy's a goddamn lawyer. A genius IQ won't save you in a game with that crew."

"Riker's right," said Mallory. "The game is tonight?"

"Yes, in my apartment." Charles sat down to breakfast with a bright smile. "Incidentally, I *have* figured out how to win at poker, and tonight I'm going to win big. And this morning I'm going to beat you, Mallory. Do we have a bet on Oren Watt?"

"You're on."

"Oh, I have your research." Charles placed a bundle of Xeroxes by Mallory's coffee cup. "These are samples of Dean Starr's reviews under his real name. He was not a brain trust. Just barely literate." He set another bundle on top of this one. "And these are all the articles that appeared following Watt's confession. The first fifteen stories are descriptions of an affair between Peter Ariel and Aubry Gilette."

Mallory scanned the first two sheets. She turned to Riker. "According to Markowitz's notes, Quinn said there was no personal relationship between the artist and the dancer. That's it? There was no follow-up on these articles?"

"I did the follow-up," said Riker. "Quinn was the spokesperson for the family. According to him, the parents had no idea she was having an affair until they read about it in the newspaper. I talked to all the people quoted by the reporters. I had the feeling they didn't really know Aubry at all. That happens sometimes. Everybody wants to get their name in the papers."

"So all we've got on her relationship to the painter is what we read in the papers? Is that what you're telling me?"

"Quinn told us no one who really knew her could corroborate it."

She handed him one of the sheets. "It seems Andrew Bliss knew her, and *he* corroborated it. He had his own newspaper column, so it's not like he needed to break into print."

Riker read the short interview where Bliss was quoted, and he knew he was reading it for the first time. "Damn." He looked at the date of the article. It was a full month after the case had officially shut down, but Markowitz had still been working it. So this had gotten by them.

She plucked the sheet from his hand. "Didn't Aubry have any friends who could help you sort this out?"

"Naw. She was a lonely kid. She didn't have any friends at all."

Mallory pulled an old battered notebook from her pocket and opened it. Across the table, Riker recognized the scrawl that had been Markowitz's handwriting. She flipped back the first three pages and put her finger to one note. "Aubry was twenty years old. She attended the same ballet school for six years."

"A couple of girls who took classes with her were interviewed. None of them ever saw her outside of class."

Mallory scanned two more pages. "What about this

Madame Burnstien? It says Aubry took classes with her for the entire six years.''

"We couldn't get a statement from Burnstien. She's old but she's fast. The first time, she gave Markowitz three minutes. The second time he tried to talk to her, she gave him the slip. I think Quinn had something to do with that. All the family information came through him, and he was really tight with the personal stuff. Maybe the old lady was close to the family."

"I want to see this woman."

"Lots of luck, kid. Markowitz could charm snakes, and he couldn't get anything out of her. So I figure *you* haven't got a prayer. I got five bucks says you can't get near her."

"Deal."

Jack Coffey stood before the desk for a full minute before he was invited to sit down in the leather wing chair. Coffey stared at the window beyond Blakely's head while waiting out the ritual of being ignored. This set his status in the world far below the level of the chief of detectives, a man with more important things to do, or such was the chief's own personal mythology of himself. On his rare visits to the Special Crimes Section, Blakely carried his bulk like he owned all the real estate he walked upon.

Coffey studied the man behind the desk, who filled a chair to overflowing, his body gone to soft flab, and skin the sallow color of sickness. The office had the smell of opulence, an odor that always made Coffey suspicious. The rugs were not the standard city expenditures on civil servants. The desk was miles too broad to have any efficient use. All over the walls were souvenirs and proofs of power. Blakely appeared in photographs with famous and important people. Every portrait represented the currency of a favor owed or a favor paid.

Two years ago, Coffey had been invited to sit down in Markowitz's office for a chat with an FBI agent. The agent had asked him if he thought the mob owed Blakely any favors. Coffey had said no to the agent, never mentioning the rumors that said otherwise. He remembered Markowitz nodding his approval behind the agent's back. It was best to keep the dirty stories in the family, and stories were all they ever were. But now Coffey looked at the photographs again, almost expecting to see Blakely frozen in a warm handshake with a Mafia don.

He continued to wait while Blakely read his newspaper. From the opposite side of the desk, Coffey stared at the upside-down photograph of Mallory in a ball gown, dancing with a white-haired man. A cup of coffee sat at Blakely's left hand and the aroma blended with a hint of rot. The patches of bad wood in the exposed floor near the baseboards might account for that, but he could not lose the idea that the decay originated with Blakely.

The chief folded back the paper to frame the photograph. He held it up to Coffey. "You've seen it? This shot of Mallory and Gregor Gilette?"

"Yes, sir. She went to the ball with Charles Butler, an old friend of Markowitz's. Butler has some social connection to the Gilette family. It's only natural that she should dance with the man. She probably danced with a lot of men."

"I thought I told you to pack her off to Boston."

"That was before the press conference."

"Nothing has changed, Jack. She goes."

"This can't be the commissioner's idea. He loved every minute of Mallory torching that fed in public."

"She's going today. She can embarrass the feds in Boston, too. I know what you did at that press conference, Jack. You sicked her on that poor bastard, Cartland. And I know why you did it. And it worked for a while. Beale thinks she walks on water. But now it's time for her to move on to another case. We'll leave it to the feds to clean up the Starr murder."

"They'll screw it up."

"And they'll take the heat. This time you will do what I tell you to do."

"What's the real reason for losing Mallory?"

"I don't need one, Jack. Insubordination is a bad mark on the record of a man who's bucking for a captain's rank."

"Who suggested it? The city attorney? Is he that worried about a lawsuit from the crazy artist? Heat from the Quinn family? Or maybe it's Senator Berman. It wouldn't look too good for the ex-commissioner if it turned out Markowitz could have proved Watt didn't do it—if his hands hadn't been tied."

"Jack, think about your pension, your job. Oh, and your promotion, which is all but in the bag as we speak. Then shut your mouth and get out of my office while you still have all of that in your future."

Andrew Bliss understood what it was to suffer for one's art. As he leaned over the retaining wall, he felt dizzy. He pulled back and pondered the vitamin content of wine. He was weakening more each hour now, and his stomach was a churning knot of cramps.

Lately, the avenue had been dominated by Kmart escapees. That tyranny must end, and he didn't care how he brought it about. He had no time to ruminate on the morality of terrorism. He was on a mission. Ruthlessly, he would strike out at every passing offender.

And he had been true to his cause, jump-starting his heart each morning with espresso and Russian cigarettes which were actually manufactured in New Jersey. The traffic-watch helicopter flew by. Andrew returned the cheery wave with a harsh critique of the traffic reporter's tasteless, low-rent, polyester jumpsuit. The copter veered off sharply.

And to every ragged panhandler, he screamed, "GET A JOB AND A CHARGE CARD!"

After a time, Andrew's bullhorn fell silent. Green-haired children from SoHo and tourists from Iowa were allowed to stroll the avenue unmolested.

No sign of life could be detected around the canopy of raincoats, nor through the leaves of the browning potted foliage which Andrew had thoughtfully watered with wine.

The Koozeman Gallery was quiet today. And the walls were bare. The gallery boy left them alone in the main room, where Starr had died. Charles scrutinized the floor, disappointed that there was not at least the drama of a chalk outline to mark the place where the dead man had fallen. "Where was Dean Starr standing when he was stabbed?"

Mallory walked to the center of the right-hand wall and paced four feet straight out. "Here. Slope said he lived for at least a full minute. So he might have been able to walk a few feet in any direction, but this is where he fell."

"So he might have been standing closer to the wall." Charles ran one finger along the painted surface behind her and smiled broadly. "I bet I can sneak up behind you and stab you."

"Yeah, right."

The sarcasm was well placed. Sneaking up behind people had always been her own special talent. How many times had she frightened him out of his skin, coming up behind him when he was convinced she was rooms away or even miles. Well, this would be fun. "Lunch, right? That's the bet."

"It's a bet, Charles. Go for it."

Charles left by a side door leading to a back room, saying, "I'll be right back. Don't move from that spot."

Three minutes later he opened a section of the wall behind her and said, "Mallory, you're dead. Oh, and you owe me one lunch."

Mallory turned slowly, and he was somewhat disappointed that she hadn't jumped. Had anyone ever taken her by surprise?

She examined the section of wall. There was a beveled overlap at the edge of the wall, and a similar overlap lined the edges of the door. "It's a perfect job. Nearly seamless."

When she opened the door wider, she saw the white curtain hanging over the opening. She looked up to the overhead track lights which illuminated the curtain, killing the dark hole of the small hallway beyond and maintaining the illusion of an unbroken wall, even when the door was slightly ajar. "Perfect." Now she closed the door, and the wall became a single plane. She pushed lightly on the wall. The door opened. "Pressure lock. Just perfect."

"Like his shows. You never see anything but the art. Let's say you had an interest in a particular artist, but his work wasn't on display. Koozeman would position you with your back to this wall. A gallery boy would open the door, hand him a painting, and you'd think it had just materialized behind your back. He's always been quite a showman. It's the main reason I attend his openings— for the magic act."

Three gallery boys entered the room with buckets of whitewash, a ladder and brushes. One boy stood off to the side, unraveling the cord on a large industrial waxing machine.

"Koozeman had the place freshly painted and waxed for the funeral," said Mallory. "Why is he doing it again?"

"Well, that's pretty standard. You said there was artwork on the wall during the filming of the television movie. Now they'll fill in the holes in the wall with plaster and paint again. Then the floors will be waxed."

"He always does that?"

"Yes, always."

"Did you ever go to one of his shows at the old East Village location?"

"Yes, a few times. Where shall we have lunch?"

"Did he do this in the old days, too?"

"The painting and waxing? Yes. Everyone does it. It's standard."

"Thanks, Charles. Now I'll tell you why Oren Watt couldn't have used this door to kill Dean Starr. When Koozeman did his little trick on the patrons, he was the one who positioned them. No one behind the door would know who was on the other side unless Koozeman was doing a planned setup. So an accomplice would have to position the victim, and then signal Watt to come through the door and stab the man. According to Watt's confession, he works alone and never plans that far ahead."

"All right. I'll pay for lunch. Where shall we go?"

She was distracted. He followed her gaze to the entrance of the gallery, where J. L. Quinn was standing. How long had he been there?

"Mallory, isn't this the second time he's found you at Koozeman's? It can't be coincidence. He's stalking you, isn't he?"

"Or maybe he has some connection to Koozeman. We'll do lunch tomorrow, Charles."

"I was expecting the Gulag," said Mallory, looking around at the appointments of the Tavern on the Green. She approved the cleaning job on the clear panes of glass looking out on Central Park, and she ignored the gang of tulips just beyond the window in a riot of color, each bloom openmouthed and screaming at the sun.

Quinn was reading the wine list. "Unless you have a preference, I'll—"

"Frog's Leap Cabernet Sauvignon, 1990," said Mallory. "That year isn't on the wine list. They only have a few bottles left. You may have to pay more to get the waiter to look for it."

Quinn set down the menu. He seemed only vaguely disquieted by the fact that she might be accustomed to this place where one did not escape the table without a substantial outlay of cash. She sat back and watched him through half-closed eyes, wondering what other small cracks she might make in his composure.

When he had ordered the wine and the lunch, he folded his arms and leaned toward her. "Well, what shall we discuss? Art?"

"Marketing."

"Same thing."

"A lot of money flowed through Koozeman's hands after Peter Ariel was killed. But most of it didn't stay in his bank account or his investment portfolio." And it never appeared on Koozeman's tax returns, but Quinn didn't need to know she'd found a back door to the IRS computers.

"Part of the money would have gone to investors. Koozeman was small-time in those days, so we can assume there was substantial backing to promote Peter Ariel. I imagine you've seen Koozeman's old gallery in the East Village."

She nodded, though she had never seen it except in cyberspace visions of paperwork, rent estimates, map locations and a floor plan. Now she thought she might make the trip to the East Village to check it out in the dimensions of real time and space.

A plate of appetizers appeared on the table with the unobtrusive flash of a waiter's sleeve.

"There were no profits on Peter Ariel's show," she said. "Not on paper. But Ariel was dead less than three months, and suddenly Koozeman was paying ten times the rent for his new SoHo location. His investors paid for that, even when he had no buyers for the art?"

"The investors *were* the buyers." The wine arrived and he paused for the rituals of reading the label and testing the contents. "It's difficult to launch an artist in

the primary market, particularly a sculptor like Ariel—
no talent. Sometimes a dealer creates an artificial market
to get the ball rolling.''

"The primary market—you mentioned that before."

"That's the initial sale. The secondary market is the
resale of work. If you can generate a lot of hype, the
demand for the art will exceed the supply. Then you go
back to the buyers of the early work, and you broker
resales for a share of the profit.''

Salad plates appeared with the finesse of fine service,
and disappeared to be replaced with main courses. Between the leafy vegetables and the red meat, she learned
the fine points of faking success in the art world—the
kickbacks to grant committees for impressive lines on a
résumé, the trade of advertising money for guaranteed
reviews, and even the publicist's fees.

"I can't question Koozeman on the old case," she
said. "How do I find out who participated in the sales
of Ariel's work?''

"You don't." Quinn caught the waiter's attention and
mimed the word "coffee." "Even if you could approach
Koozeman, he wouldn't give you any names. That list
would be the most closely guarded thing he possessed.''

"Because he doesn't want the police to bother his cli-
entele?''

"Because some of the people on that list are probably
not paying any capital gains taxes or sales tax.''

"He ran a tax scam?''

Conversation stopped as coffee cups were filled.

"I don't know that he did anything illegal—I'm only
speculating. You said there were no profits on paper from
the last Ariel show. Let's say most of Peter Ariel's work
was reported damaged on the night of the murder. In a
tax audit, Koozeman would only have to produce the
police report and letters from the initial buyers saying
their money was returned to them because the work was
damaged prior to delivery. But they might hold on to the

work, and Koozeman might not actually return the money.''

''So he voids the check transactions by claiming refunds in cash. Then the cash goes into a safety deposit box?''

''*If* it happened that way, the initial buyers would make a substantial tax-free profit on a cash resale. No capital gains tax for the initial buyer, no sales tax for the resale buyer, no income tax for Koozeman.''

''Could he use the same racket to sell what's left of Dean Starr's work?''

''I hardly think so. He actually did make a few sales the night Dean Starr was murdered. But the art is such a crock, the A list people wouldn't touch it. The work was bought by ignorant gate crashers. For the second showing, he'll probably sell directly to the amateurs.''

''So the primary market is the A list.''

''Right. That would be the money people. They're not art lovers—only looking for investment ventures. Now if an artist dies with a lot of notoriety, that's a windfall profit. The art is knowing when to unload the work before its value falls off.''

''So the A list unloads on the suckers from the B list.''

''And they may in turn sell to a C list, the ultimate morons who get stuck with worthless art. C list buyers are corporate collections and banks. They rarely notice they've been duped because the cost of the work is added to the asset value of the company. It's a hidden loss, a worthless holding that won't show up in an audit. And now you know all about art.''

''But I don't know anything about Aubry's mother. Why aren't there any photographs of Sabra?'' She had expected some reaction to that, but his composure never faltered.

''You can blame my father for that.'' He leaned toward her. ''My mother was every bit as beautiful as you are, Mallory. That's why my father married her.''

Over another cup of coffee and dessert, she learned
that Quinn's father had not been married long before he
discovered what hell it was to live with a woman obsessed by mirrors. One night, when Sabra was only
twelve, her father said to her, "It's a pity about your
beauty. If only you had been born ugly or even ordinary,
you might have developed an intellect." He was drunk
when he said that, but he meant it. He was afraid for his
daughter.

Sabra had marched up the stairs and destroyed all the
mirrors in her bedroom. Later, the Quinns began to notice
the sabotage of family photographs all over the house.
Eventually, she had destroyed every likeness of herself.
She never wanted to see her own face again.

"It may seem mad to you, but I thought it was rather
brilliant. It gave Sabra great focus, and she did develop
that intellect and more. She was a creative genius. So
perhaps you can also blame my father for her talent."

"But eventually she did go insane."

"She went through a bad time of it when her child
died."

"Her husband says she was crazy, certifiable. And she
spent some time in an institution."

"Gregor said that? Well, perhaps by New York standards she was always mad. She never took money from
the family. That was insane, wasn't it? With no help at
all she made a startling career. Her museum retrospec-
tives traveled the world. But she probably did need professional help getting through the aftermath of the
murder."

"Sabra was a strong woman. I have to wonder what
pushed her over the top."

"Sabra adored Aubry."

"That's not enough. We all lose people. And how is
she living now? She doesn't paint anymore. Hospitals are
expensive. Gregor says she never used their health insurance plan, so her money had to dry up eventually.

Wouldn't she go to her husband or her family if she needed money to live on?''

"I only wish she had.''

Mallory knew he was lying, but she didn't call him on it. *"Let them lie,"* Markowitz had told her. *"They always tell you more with the lies than you will ever get from the truth.''*

She sipped her coffee, and stared out the window. "You know, when you ask a civilian the names of the artist and the dancer, they only remember Peter Ariel.''

"Of course. The cliché romance of the starving artist who's only discovered after his death.''

"But if you ask a cop, they only remember Aubry's name. That was your work, Quinn. You led the investigation back to Aubry every time, even though Peter Ariel was the most likely target.''

"Oh, *was* he? Then why did the chief medical examiner back up my point of view? Twelve years ago, he supported Aubry as the primary target.''

She watched Quinn and the young woman from the vantage point of a pile of garbage fresh from the restaurant's kitchen, the spill of an overturned can. She didn't notice the odor of fish heads mingling with the warm aroma of dog turds and the smell of fruit. Nor did she feel any curiosity about the young woman. This was simply all the spectacle offered to her at the moment, watching them together as they left the Central Park restaurant.

The woman with the wire cart was not so old as she appeared. Just as money could keep age at bay for a while, the dearth of money could and did accelerate aging. The lack of a roof to keep off the elements could ravage the skin and prematurely wrinkle the spirit. There were gaps between the teeth she had left to her. Her hair was iron gray and unwashed since that time, months ago, when she had been herded into the women's shelter, stripped and deloused as the matrons watched from the door of the gang shower.

Now she spoke to the tea tin on the top of her cart, and nodding to it, she moved away with the cart in tow. Cart wheels squeaked, and aching feet with swollen ankles dragged across the gravel path. Her breathing was the wheeze of bad lungs as she strained to pull the cart which had grown heavier with each passing year on the streets of New York.

Coffey sat back in his chair, holding the telephone receiver a short distance from his ear. Commissioner Beale had a high irritating phone voice, and he tended to yell like a boy in the days when telephones were tin cans and wires.

"Yes, sir," said Coffey. "I'll pass your compliments along to Mallory before she leaves for Boston. . . . Yes, sir, Boston. Chief Blakely's pulling her off the case and sending her to . . ."

Coffey held the phone farther from his ear. "Well, Blakely felt the case might go high-profile if Mallory . . . Yes, sir, the photograph of the ball. . . . Oh, you're putting me in a hard place, sir. Blakely gave me a direct order to send her to Boston, and I would never . . . Yes, sir. I'm glad you understand. . . . Well, no, sir, I wouldn't mind if you had a word with him, but I'd appreciate it if you'd leave my name out of it. He might get the idea I was going behind his back to keep Mallory on the case. . . . Thank you, sir."

Coffey set down the phone. When he turned to his reflection in the glass wall of his office, he thought he recognized a Mallory smile on his face.

The rabbi's desk and chair were the heart of this sun-bright room filled with books and papers, warm wood, and white curtains that lifted with every breeze from the open window.

Rabbi David Kaplan was a long, elegant figure in a dark suit. His graying beard was close-trimmed and did not conceal the leanness of his face. His eyes conveyed the tranquillity of a drowsing cat, and this *was* deception. In every meeting with Kathy Mallory, all his senses were in play, and speed of mind was paramount in all his dealings with her. His old friend Father Brenner had learned this lesson the hard way and too late.

Helen Markowitz had sent her foster child out among the Catholics to honor a covenant with Kathy's birth mother, a woman Helen had never met. Kathy had never spoken about her first mother, and so Helen had to intuit the wishes of this woman who had taught her child to make the sign of the cross. It was the only stitch of evidence to link Kathy with a past. Protestants did not make such signs, so it was determined that Kathy must have begun life as a Catholic. Helen had honored that original intention—up to a point. The experiment had ended badly.

The child was sent back to frustrate Rabbi Kaplan until her religious education was deemed complete. His greatest frustration had been the fact that she was his brightest student, and he could not separate the makings of a scholar from the greater talents of a thief and a gifted liar.

When she was well into her teens, he had offered her a choice of which faith she would continue in. She had chosen Judaism on the grounds that Jews had no place called hell.

If he had been marginally successful in keeping her from the flames of the Catholic hell, he had not brought her any nearer to God. She had been insulted by his efforts, believing that deities of every faith were no more than fairy tales for slow learners. But for some strange reason, the Christian devil was very real to her. She had met him somewhere out on the road in those first ten years of life, the years she shared with no one.

Despite all the traps he set for her, all the lost leaders he had put out upon the air between them, he had learned very little of her origins. Through the years, he had continued with his gentle probes into her past, and she had fended them off with agility. And so their relationship had always been a bit like a badminton game.

The rabbi set the black telephone receiver down in its cradle and looked across the desk to the child he loved as much as his own. "All right, Kathy. You have an appointment. Madame Burnstien will look at you."

"*Look* at me?"

"She must have assumed I was sending her a dancer. She hung up on me before I could correct that assumption. It's just as well. My wife tells me Madame's whole life is the ballet. If you're not connected to that life, you don't exist. The woman only accepted my call because Anna's charity group donates scholarship money for the ballet school."

"Markowitz couldn't get anywhere with her. What do you suppose he did wrong?"

"Well, your father's best weapon was charm. As I recall, the scum of the earth could be quite taken with him."

"So we know that doesn't work on the old lady."

The rabbi only smiled at the idea that charm might be an option for Kathy Mallory. "Now, you will mind your manners with this woman. You *will* address her as *Madame* Burnstien. Helen raised you to show respect for the elderly. Of course, Madame Burnstien is a lot tougher than you are."

"Yeah, right." She was not at all impressed. "I have a photo of her at Aubry's funeral. She must be pushing ninety by now, and she walks with a cane."

"My wife tells me Madame eats dancers for breakfast."

"I still think I can take her two falls out of three."

"And I understand she's very good with her cane. I

only saw it once—it's formidable.'' He stopped smiling and leaned toward her, all serious now. ''When I say Madame Burnstien is tough, I'm not being facetious. She survived two years in a Nazi concentration camp. I don't know what you could have in your own history that even comes close to that horror.''

''*Four* years with the nuns at the academy.''

''You're so competitive.''

''So what's the best approach?''

''The key to Madame Burnstien is respect. Try to earn it without bloodshed.''

Mallory stood on the sidewalk staring up at the old brown building reported to be the finest ballet school in the country. It had been a factory once, and now eight stories of lofts had been converted into rehearsal halls and classrooms. Girls and young women hung off the fire escape, dangling limbs sheathed in bright-colored leg warmers. Some smoked forbidden cigarettes, others lifted their faces to the weak light of the sun, leaching what warmth there was so early in the spring.

The rabbi's wife, Anna Kaplan, had warned her that today there would be at least a hundred children underfoot. When Mallory passed through the front doors, she entered a wide room with high ceilings, where pandemonium ruled. Small breastless girls and a sprinkling of boys bore numbered cards hung around their necks with strings. Mothers hovered over them, clutching the leg warmers and costumes, harried and frazzled women consumed by the tensions of audition day.

The front desk was besieged by shouters and elbowers. A man with a phone attached to one ear was holding four separate conversations. And above all of this, a loudspeaker called out numbers, and children were separated from their mothers, taking positions on one side of the room.

Beyond this crush of tiny dancers stood a young

woman close to Mallory's age. They exchanged a look across the room. At first the other woman's expression recognized Mallory as neither mother nor novice, but a fellow creature of the ballet. She smiled and shrugged to say, *Awful, isn't it?* But now her head tilted to one side with the realization that Mallory was an altogether different animal, and interest intensified as Mallory moved toward her, advancing on the mob of children. They parted for her in a wave, the act of one mind in many small bodies.

"Where can I find Madame Burnstien?"

"Third floor. The stairs are quicker. The elevator takes forever." The young woman pointed to a narrow staircase several feet away. She called a loud warning after Mallory. "If she's not expecting you, she'll nail your hide to the wall."

A hundred small faces turned in unison, eyes rounding.

"I can handle it," said Mallory. "I went to Catholic school."

Fat chance old Madame Burnstien could outdo an insane nun.

Mallory took great pride in her enemies, and she was particularly proud of Sister Ursula.

She climbed to the third floor and stopped at the wide-open door to a rehearsal hall. There were other students in the room, leaning against the walls and seated tailor-fashion on the floor, but all Mallory could see was the single dancer hurtling through space in a powerful swirl of music, her body arching in the leap—call it flight— and at last touching to ground in tattered red satin shoes.

She wore bright purple tights and leotard, and brilliant orange wool covered her legs from ankle to knee. A long braid of lustrous black hair floated on the air behind her as she stepped and turned before the mirrored wall. And now she began to twirl like a dervish, sweat glistening on her young body, spinning madly, wonderfully, and finally coming to rest before a white-haired woman with a wine-dark dress and a cane.

This old woman only frowned, declining any comment with the slow shake of her head, and disappeared through a red door, slamming it behind her.

The young dancer's head bowed. Her body seemed to be losing strength, all confidence and power gone now.

Mallory watched her for a moment, trying to understand her and failing. The ballerina should have known how wonderful she was, but apparently she did not.

Markowitz would have understood. It had been his gift to sit across a desk from strangers, and then to steal inside of them, peek out through their eyes, walk in their flesh, go where they go, and then to know what their soft spots were. He had called it *empathy*.

Mallory had none, and she knew it. She might be adept at crawling into the living skin of a killer, but never would she be able to go where the ballerina goes.

Now she crossed the wide room, passing by the defeated dancer, to knock at the red door. After a full minute the door opened, but only a crack.

"Yes?" said the old woman facing her. Madame Burnstien was small and slight, hardly threatening. Her white hair was captured in a bun, and every bit of skin was a crisscross of lines. The only hand visible through the crack of the door was a cluster of arthritic knots wrapped round the cane.

"I'm Mallory. I have an appointment with you?"

"You are Rabbi Kaplan's young friend?"

Mallory couldn't immediately place the woman's accent, but then Anna Kaplan had said that Madame Burnstien hailed from too many countries to call one of them home. In youth, she had danced for the whole earth. Mallory could not believe this crone had ever been young.

"Rabbi Kaplan said you would see me."

"I said I would *look* at you, and I have. You're a beautiful child, but you are too tall. Go away now."

The door began to close. Mallory shot one running shoe into the space between the door and its frame. The old woman smiled wickedly and showed Mallory her cane, lifting it in the crack-width of the door to display the carved wolf's head and its fangs.

"Move your foot, my dear, or you'll never dance again."

The cane was rising for a strike.

"Madame Burnstien, you only *think* I won't deck you."

The old eyes widened and gleamed. The smile disappeared and her brows rushed together in an angry scowl as the cane lowered slowly. There was exaggerated petulance in her cracking voice. "I like determination, child, but you waste my time. You are still too tall."

"Everybody's a critic." Mallory showed her the gold shield and ID. "I want to talk to you about Aubry Gilette."

"I have had many students. Aubry was a thousand dancers ago. What do you expect me to remember of one girl?"

"Oh, I think you remember her better than most. Don't make me show you the autopsy photo. You're old. It'd probably kill you."

"Dream on, child." The wicked smile was back, and the door was opening.

Madame's office was generous in size, and showed Charles Butler's penchant for antiques. The light of the corner window washed over an ancient ornate desk piled high with large paperbound books, sheets of archaic penmanship and notes of music. All but one brocade chair was filled with costumes. Every bit of the far wall bore an autographed photo, or a drawing of a dancer in motion. The only respite from the dance was a small painting behind the desk, a still life of flowers. Mallory had attended Barnard College long enough to recognize a Monet. She knew this must be the real article, for she had already learned that the old woman was death on second-best. Her eye moved on to a larger canvas hanging on the next wall, and this she recognized as Sabra's, even though there was no signature.

"So Madame Burnstien, you knew Aubry's mother well?"

"Very good, my dear. That's a portrait of Aubry."

There was someone dancing in the painting. Although the subject was abstracted, there was a figure there, ephemeral, shimmering, flying over a wide space. Action strokes gave it life, and the space surrounding it pulsed with color. Fuchsia juxtaposed with brilliant greens and vied for the foreground to create a depth of field that confounded all laws defining the flat planes of canvases. Flourishes and dabs of paint had the rhythm and the punctuation of music. Mallory turned away with the afterimage of a full ballet and even its score.

"Do you know what happened to Sabra?"

The old woman sat down and averted her eyes. "Has there been an accident?" One gnarled hand went to her breast.

"Not that I know of. She disappeared years ago. Do you know where she went after she left the asylum?"

"No."

This was the simple truth. There was no pause, no telling sign of a new furrow in the old woman's face, or a nervous shift in her body. And there was no hint of a question or a surprise in her eyes. So she was close enough to the family to have known about Sabra's asylum years.

"You were at the funeral. I saw you in the old photographs. What was Sabra like that day? Was she already crazy?"

The old woman shook her head. Frowning, she waved her hand as if to chase away the words. Mallory came closer and leaned down to meet Madame's eyes. "Maybe I should have asked if you'd seen Sabra recently."

Madame Burnstien said nothing. But that was something. There was no convenient, polite lie to fill the gap. This woman might be capable of deception, but the outright lie was not Madame's style. So Sabra was alive. She backed off now, to give the woman space.

"All right, then tell me about Aubry and the artist she died with. Was Peter Ariel really her boyfriend? Or was there someone else?"

"She had no lovers."

"She was a very attractive woman, and these days, twenty is old for a virgin."

"The world changed, the ballet did not. It's a grueling, demanding profession. Aubry had great ambition. She had no time for friends or lovers. This is what she loved." Madame Burnstien pointed to a large photograph of a dancer's ruined feet, half-healed sores and open wounds, all the punishment of the cruel shoes. "When Aubry was not performing in her ballet company, she was here, taking classes. The classes never end, you know, not for your entire life span as a ballerina."

"She had some connection to that gallery she died in. There was something going on in her life. She could have been meeting her boyfriend in the hours after the lessons and performances."

"No, she couldn't!" The cane beat the floor with a thud and left a round impression in the rug. There were many such impressions about the room.

"You can't know that, not for sure." Mallory leaned back against the red door. "You weren't with her every minute." Her words were taunting, to lead the old woman into the fray. She had learned a great deal from the rabbi. "You were only her teacher. She could have had a hundred boyfriends."

And now the old woman sat up a little straighter, head lifting, rising to the bait. "Aubry could not have been carrying on an affair, not without my knowing. Dancing takes tremendous strength, great care with one's health.

I myself was overtrained. My arthritis began when I was only a little older than Aubry. A dancer needs rest above all things. Aubry retired as early as her evening performances would permit, and she was here *every* morning taking class. There were no late-hour bruises to her eyes. Aubry only danced!'' Lower and less emphatic now, ''She never had a life.''

Mallory folded her arms in the skeptic's pose which the rabbi used when he thought she might be lying.

Madame Burnstien rose from her chair. The pain of movement was concealed well, but not completely. There was evidence enough for Mallory to know the arthritis had taken over the entire body of this former prima ballerina.

The old woman stood by the window, her back turned to Mallory when she spoke. ''You saw all the children downstairs? Out of the hundred, perhaps one will make it, perhaps not. And all the children who are *not* chosen— I like to think they have escaped.''

Mallory moved behind her, coming upon her so quietly that the old woman started at her first words. ''According to the newspapers, Aubry and the artist had an affair. An art critic named Andrew Bliss said—''

''A pack of lies.''

''People who knew them both were quoted—''

''All lies!''

''Or maybe you're lying to me now.'' But she knew that Madame Burnstien was not. When the old woman spoke next there was no confrontation, no defense, only the simple facts of Aubry's time on earth.

''She only danced. She never really lived. And then she died.''

''More blackmail, Mallory?'' Edward Slope made two notations on a chart and set it down on the table by the gutted male cadaver and former taxpayer. ''What do you want now, the pink slip on my car?''

He pulled off his gloves and slapped them down on the body which had done nothing to offend him. She held her ground. No emotion whatsoever, and that never failed to disturb him. He suspected this was her method of getting a rise out of him, forcing him to fill the emotional void from his own store of frustration.

"Just a few questions," she said. "Did Markowitz ever ask you how much time it would take to cut up the two bodies?"

How in hell did she know that? He turned away from her as he pulled off the bloody surgical gown. "Yes, he did ask. But I was angry with him. I told him to buy a leg of beef and figure it out for himself."

"That's just what he did." She pulled a yellow napkin out of her pocket. "It took him a long time to cut through that leg. That gave him a lot of trouble with the time frame of the murder. It looks like there had to be more than one person working on the bodies. I think that was another reason he wouldn't close out the case, another thing that wouldn't fit."

He took the napkin from her hand and read the log of cutting meat and bone. "Poor bastard. I could have helped him with that. But you were right, we weren't speaking then." He handed the napkin back to her. "The killer worked the limbs at the joint. Easier that way, though I couldn't tell you how much time was saved."

"Can you think of anything else that might help?"

"I suppose you could say the joint cuts were an oddity, and I should have told him that, too. In most dismemberment cases, the fool takes the leg off at the bottom of the torso, not the hip joint—cuts through the bone when he doesn't have to. The bones at the joints weren't cut, but I did report the damage from the axe. He might have misread that. And I suppose I misled him with that leg of beef."

"So would the joint cuts indicate some knowledge of anatomy? Like art school anatomy?"

"It might."

"Oren Watt never went to art school."

Slope thought she delivered that line with entirely too much smugness. He could fix that. "It might also indicate that the killer had simply carved his share of Thanksgiving turkeys. Nobody cuts the bone of the drumstick. But Helen always served a roast for Thanksgiving, didn't she? So I can understand how that one got by you. But you're so stubborn. I have to worry about what else you might be missing. You just can't admit that Oren Watt could've—"

"One more question," she said. "Why did you back up Quinn? You told him Aubry was the most likely target."

"Yes, I did. I also told him I thought Oren Watt was the most likely suspect. I still believe that little bastard did it. Why must you go back into that case again?"

"Why did you support the idea that the girl was the real target?"

"Because she was the only one to suffer. The other one was hacked up postmortem. I know you read the report. You could probably recite it by heart. But it's only a collection of data to you, isn't it? Try to imagine it. She was crawling when the attacker followed her along the length of the floor, inflicting blow after blow. That was something that bothered Markowitz a lot. The girl was the victim of unmistakable savage rage."

"It's a pity you and Markowitz weren't on speaking terms after the autopsy. Markowitz questioned Watt on Aubry. Watt didn't know her at all, not the first thing about her."

"So he didn't know her. So? Perhaps he hated *all* women. It was a lunatic act and a crime of rage. You have the evidence of madness in my original report. He took a damn souvenir, her brain, for Christ's sake!"

"You still don't get it, do you? It was the brain that Markowitz used to rule out Watt's confession."

"You don't know that." He knew she was running a bluff. Sometimes she forgot he had been playing poker for decades before she was ever born. "You're only guessing."

"Yeah, but I'm real good at that. Call it a gift. And I know my old man's style. You weren't talking to Markowitz. You were angry with him. You never talked about the case again. It would have been a bad subject after what he asked you to do. Now suppose Peter Ariel was the primary target. What then? If Markowitz was alive, standing here right now, would you have anything else to tell him? Would you change anything?"

In a way, Slope felt that Markowitz *was* alive. He sensed the man's presence every time she was near. She was a living reminder of a lifelong friendship. Even in death, Markowitz stubbornly refused to abandon her, forcing everyone who had loved him, to love his daughter too.

"No, Kathy, I wouldn't change a thing."

"Mallory," she said with insistence.

"Kathy," he said with great deliberation. "One day your father's friends will all be dead, and there'll be no one to call you Kathy. That's my biggest fear for you. Terrible thing being loved, isn't it? It's like a debt hanging over your head, and it pisses you off, doesn't it? Well, good."

She was angry now, and that was good too. Her anger was his only method of ferreting out her humanity in what limited range of emotion she possessed. She returned his broad smile with an icy glare. She advanced on him, gathering size as she closed in on his person, one hand rising to within striking distance of his face.

After she had gone, and the door was closing behind her on its slow hydraulic, he muttered, "Perverse little monster." For she had touched his face so gently and kissed his cheek. She had left him disoriented, flailing for understanding in her disturbing wake, and she had done that to a purpose. He knew it—for he truly believed it was her mission in life to confuse him.

The photographer set up the tripod on the sidewalk, facing the plaza of Gregor Gilette's new building. Workmen were pulling down the last section of the wooden wall to reveal the graceful stone arch. This gateway to the plaza mimicked the shape of the building's lower windows.

When the photographer was done, the workmen would replace the wooden panels, and they would remain in place until the plaza sculpture was installed for the dedication ceremony.

Emma Sue Hollaran stood by the pile of wood sections, her face red and pinched, railing at the workmen, who only shrugged their shoulders and said they had their orders. Emma Sue, mover and shaker of the Public Works Committee, turned ungainly and charged on the young photographer, who took her for an infuriated bull, cleverly disguised as a smaller, dumber animal.

"I never authorized any of this!" she yelled.

The photographer screwed a filter onto a lens and bent over the camera, making adjustments that didn't need to be made, hoping that she would simply go away. Stupid idea. Looking down at the camera, he could also see her legs, sturdy little fireplugs rooted firmly to the pavement.

"Young man, I'm talking to you."

Gilette waved the photographer back, and now the architect stepped forward to loom over her. Gilette smiled as he looked into the angry slits of her eyes, with an intensity that forced her to step back a pace. "The photographer takes his orders from me."

She had been planning to say something to him. What was it? She could only stare. He was so close. She couldn't think.

Emma Sue had always been protected from her own mirror by a doting father who had insisted that she was truly beautiful. She was protected also by her father's land and money, never suffering the plight of the homely girl at the school dance. Considered by every farmer in the county to be a good catch, landwise and moneywise, she was sought after by every landowner who had a son of marriageable age. She had always danced every dance and happily trod on the feet of the handsome, wild boys who feared their matchmaking fathers.

And money had protected her from her own dull-wittedness, with a generous endowment to an Ivy League college. Money could do anything. With money enough, black could become white and a bleating barnyard animal could become a peer of the art community in the art center of the world.

And yet, with all her protective armor, she was pinned like an insect and hadn't a grasshopper's wit to get loose. She could only stare at Gilette. He was so much more than just a man. There was something else in play here. He knocked the wind out of her by merely looking into her eyes and showing her something she couldn't buy.

There was sex going on here, on the sidewalk in the daylight, in public view, and it was indecent and raw and—she could only stare. *Would you care to dance, Gregor?*

No, his eyes said, *not with you.*

Ugly and lonely and witless, she turned and walked away with slow agonizing steps, size nine shoes clattering on the sidewalk, lost now in the sounds of Manhattan traffic.

People had begun to drift through the arch and into the plaza. A policeman asked Gilette if he wanted them cleared out. Some of them sat on the benches in the open light, some took the shade under the ash trees that formed the plaza walls, and two children dipped their hands in the water of the fountain. Gilette shook his head.

"No. Let them be."

He looked into the photographer's lens to see the fountain through the camera's eyes, bringing it into sharp focus. A young Spanish sculptor had won an international competition with this design to match Gilette's own skill for making marble flow like water. The lines of the fountain carried the eye along with a fluid grace that defeated its own hard substance, echoing the lines of the building's facade, and stone called out to stone across the plaza.

Reflections of the water played over the faces of two boys, and the camera's shutter clicked.

An old man flung one brittle arm across the back of a bench, which curved to fit the contour of his body. He lifted his face to the light and smiled peacefully, and a shutter clicked.

A young woman in a yellow dress stood in the lush green shadows of the young stand of trees, starting as a flock of birds settled in the branches overhead.

A derelict hesitated at the arch and turned to the place where Gilette stood. The man's face, with five days' dust and beard, was washed new with dazzling light, and a shutter clicked.

The television crew was unloading equipment from the large trucks. All about him was the hustle of people passing to and fro, laying cables and checking sound equipment and cameras, a babble of orders and questions.

Oren Watt stood at the outer edge of the fray, with the sun on his face. Perhaps that was why she just seemed to appear there. One moment the sidewalk across the street had been empty, and now she stood there, smiling at him. He remembered her from the Koozeman shoot. She was the one who had removed the tapes on the gallery where Dean Starr had died. The young woman had smiled at him then, too, though not exactly a smile, more like bared teeth.

Now she pulled a black wallet out of her blazer and opened it to display a badge. The sun hit the metal and shot his eyes with gold. A truck lumbered between them, and when it had passed by, she was gone.

"I thought you were the technical advisor, Oren."

He spun around to see her standing behind him. She was looking down at a clipboard.

"Did you tell them they were shooting in the wrong place?"

"What do you want from me?"

"I once asked a nun that same question, same words. You know what she said? 'I want your soul.' " And now she was walking away from him, making a check mark on her clipboard as she left him.

"Well this is wonderful," said Charles, as he stood at the desk in Mallory's office and pored through the contents of the brown bag. He held up a brand of mustard he had never seen before. And a full complement of foreign beers filled out the bottom of the sack.

"Sorry about lunch," said Mallory. She was sitting at one of the three computer terminals which dominated the room.

"Have you given any thought to how Quinn knew you'd be at the gallery today? Perhaps you don't know much about his habits. New York is overcrowded with galleries. What are the odds he was just passing by? He's stalking you. He's not dangerous of course, but still."

"He's tied to my money motive for the old murders. Maybe he's worried that I'm making connections he wouldn't like."

"You're wrong, Mallory. Quinn's presence kills your money motive."

"Like hell it does. Having Quinn view the bodies fits very nicely with money. He's an important critic. It all fits."

"No, Mallory, the fact that Quinn was called in is an oddity. It doesn't fit at all. He couldn't have been called there for publicity value. The murderer would have called in a hack critic for that.''

''A review from Quinn is gold.''

''Well, no it isn't, not for a bad artist. There was a time when a critic could launch a career. But not anymore. Today, the artist is promoted with media hype and a gimmick, not a critique. To have Quinn see the murder as artwork, well, that would only be important to a really talented artist. That description doesn't fit Peter Ariel, Dean Starr or Oren Watt. It only makes sense as revenge against Quinn. You may have to accept his idea that Aubry was the primary target. The only other reasonable theory is a random act of insane violence.''

''I'm swimming in people who made money on those deaths. I'm right about this.''

''Why are you so stubborn about the money motive?''

''I need it for the Dean Starr murder. Without it I've got nothing. If it's a random act of violence, then the killer disappears into the crowd, and there's no trail.''

She wasn't with him anymore, she was so intent on her computer screen.

''What are you doing?''

''I'm breaking into an artist's network through an internet server.''

She looked up at him and smiled. He must have found her smile disquieting, because now he was leaving her, softly closing the door behind him, not wanting to witness any breaking and entry.

She had taken quite an interest in the artnets over the past few days. Once into the system, she proceeded immediately to the forum under the heading of Bliss's Last Column. She passed over the familiar two-day-old comments of artists and interested parties, and happened on a conversation taking place in real time. Two of the players were opting out to a private room. She went into the data base and plucked the passwords to diddle the cyberspace lock so she could follow after them. Invisible to the screens of the others, she stole up on the more intimate conversation printing out before her eyes and learned that Andrew Bliss had spent two years in a seminary, studying for the priesthood.

Robin Duffy sat at the card table in the den of Charles's apartment. His beer rested on a coaster, and his pile of change lay in the center of the green gaming surface. An overhead light exaggerated Duffy's jowls and gave him the look of a bulldog. He was pouring out his troubles to Rabbi David Kaplan. Though Duffy was a devout Catholic, this man would always be his rabbi.

"I got another offer on Markowitz's house today, Rabbi. Why won't the brat sell it? I hate to see it empty every day. It doesn't make any sense."

"It's Kathy's home." The rabbi's face was composed in a serene smile. His elbows were propped on the table as he scrutinized his cards. "That old house is all she has left of her days with Helen and Louis."

"Naw, I don't think that's it. She hardly ever goes there, and she never stays the night. It should have a nice family in it, some kids—life."

"My parents died before I turned twenty," said Charles, looking down at his own cards. "It took me almost another twenty years to sell their apartment."

"Well, I know seventeen-room condos don't move all that fast," said Edward Slope, "but twenty years?"

"It was home. I didn't always live there, even when my parents were alive. I spent most of my life at schools. But it was home."

"Kathy should have a real home," said Duffy. "Gimme two cards. She should have a husband and kids, lots of kids."

Edward Slope put down his cards and looked to some distant point in the room. "I'm trying to picture a world with a lot of little baby felons who look like Kathy."

The largest pile of change was in front of Edward

Slope. The rabbi's pile and Robin Duffy's were smaller but respectable. As always, the obvious loser in this first hour of the game was Charles Butler, who had gambled wildly at the start, and now nursed a rather small pile of quarters and dimes. For the next round, the rabbi held the deck, and five cards were dealt to each player, four cards facedown and the last card showing. The high card, an ace, fell to Charles Butler.

"Don't pick up your cards," said a voice behind his chair, Mallory's voice. The other players looked up in unison.

"Trust me, Charles," said Mallory. "Just let the cards lie there facedown. Now ante up."

He put his quarter alongside the other three quarters in the pile at the center of the table, not knowing what his hand held, only trusting Mallory. As he looked around at his friends, he saw three suspicious faces focussed on her. All of these people had known her since she was a child. And now his trust in her increased.

"If you want to play, pull up a chair and do it properly," said Edward Slope.

"I don't need a chair in the game to beat lightweights like you."

There were raises of quarters around the table, and she nodded to Charles when it was his turn. "See that raise and raise him another quarter."

They went through this ritual until the pot at the center of the table had grown considerably. Charles had only three quarters and a small assortment of dimes and nickels left to bet with. According to the rules of long standing, when he lost his change, he was out of the game. His faith in Mallory was flagging. Logic dictated that he could be cleaned out by the player with the largest store of change, and that was Edward.

"Too rich," said the rabbi, as he folded his cards. "I'm out."

It was Robin Duffy's play. "Give me a minute," he

said, rearranging his cards to make it seem like he had at least two pair. Now he looked to Charles's hand with only the single ace showing. The graduate of Harvard Law School continued his deliberations over the twenty-five-cent bet.

"I've got a question for you, Doctor," said Mallory, with such exaggerated formality, Charles had to wonder what they were feuding about now. It was always something. "How long can a person live on liquids but no solid food?"

"Depends on the liquids," said Edward. "Not long if all you've got is water, maybe ten, twelve days. Some people have fasted for months on fruit juices, and vitamin supplements."

"Suppose the liquid is wine?"

"You can kiss that idiot goodbye. He'll be severely weakened after a few days with no food, and probably hallucinating. He might last a few days more before dehydration kills him. Alcohol is a diuretic."

Robin Duffy put in his quarter and met the last raise. Edward Slope pitched his coins to the center of the table, and raised the bet with a dime.

"Ante up, Charles, and raise him a quarter."

"But shouldn't I at least have a look at my cards? I *am* getting rather low on change."

"Bad idea, Charles, just let them lie there."

He did as she told him. Then Robin Duffy folded his cards, eyes fixed on Charles's ace.

Mallory stood by Edward Slope's chair now. "Let's say the fast has been going on for three days, and he has a bottle of water. What would you add to the diet if you only wanted to keep him conscious and functioning?"

"Oh, crackers or bread would be the simplest things for the body to break down and utilize quickly." Edward pitched his quarter into the pile, and raised by only a nickel this time.

"Meet that and raise him a quarter, Charles."

"If I raise him another twenty-five cents, I'll be down to fifteen cents."

"Do it."

Charles laid his last quarter down in a raise. And Edward Slope folded his hand. The doctor looked up at Mallory, and something passed between them, part anger, part admiration. Charles looked from Edward to Mallory.

"You knew he was going to fold."

"Yes, Charles."

"But how could you possibly know?"

"Dr. Slope is a gentleman of the old school." Mallory spoke to Charles, but fixed her eyes on the doctor. "That's what Markowitz called him. The old man always did this to him early in the game, but only when the game was at our house. Markowitz would bet his whole stash and win the pot every damn time."

Charles knew something was going by him but not what. "Mallory, I don't see the—"

"Charles, you're his host, and the night is young. He wouldn't let you lose everything and then just sit out the rest of the game. Of course, when Markowitz did this to him, the old man always looked at his cards. But you can't do that. You couldn't run a bluff if I put a gun to your head—not with that face."

And now Charles's face was a signboard advertising all his frustration and incredulity. "But you've put me in the position of taking unfair advantage of Edward."

Three men looked to the ceiling, but held the line at not laughing out loud.

"That's right," said Mallory. "Now you've got it. Try not to lose that pile, okay?"

Edward Slope pointed to Charles's cards. "Okay, let's see 'em. What were you holding?"

Mallory quickly reached across the table and grabbed the deck of cards. She swept up Charles's five cards and mingled them into the deck with the waterfall shuffle of a seasoned gambler.

Edward Slope looked down at the hand which held his beer bottle in a death grip. "I know you only did that to drive us nuts."

Robin Duffy leaned toward the doctor. "And you always said the kid had no sense of humor."

Mallory settled behind the rabbi's chair. "I've got a religious question."

Edward dealt the next hand. "Rabbi, if you want to keep my friendship and esteem, you'll tell her to get lost."

The rabbi was staring sadly at the deck of cards in the doctor's tight fist, the deck which contained the insoluble mystery of Charles's winning hand. "Edward's right. You do a thing like that, and then you ask for my help?"

"You're my rabbi, you have to help."

"All right, you got me twice in one night. What is your question?"

"I need to know what you have to do to get kicked out of a Catholic seminary."

"Kathy, as I recall, Helen gave you four years of a very expensive Catholic school education. Go and ask Father Brenner. He's semiretired now, but I believe he's filling in the vacation schedule at St. Jude's this week."

"Father Brenner and I aren't exactly on friendly terms. Maybe *you* could ask him."

"It's been what, maybe ten years now? He's not one to hold a grudge. It's not as if you broke that nun's leg."

After Mallory left the room, the other players fixed on the face of the rabbi in dead silence. He cast his sweet smile on each player in turn, which was easy because he was holding the best cards of the evening. But he never said another word about Kathy Mallory and the nun, not even when they withheld his sandwiches and beer for a time. He would not talk.

Gregor Gilette stood in front of the church, hatless in the drizzle.

He began as a pilgrim, climbing the steps vast and gray, leading up to the church doors. He had come here to find his wife. This was Sabra's church, not his.

As a small boy he had once wandered into a Catholic church, where he was dazzled by the spectacle of flaming candles and stained-glass windows lit with images of heaven and hell. He had stared at the tortured figure on the cross beyond the altar and then looked up and up to the high ceiling with its carved, curving beams. Sky high it was. As a child, he'd had the sense of a magical place. It had frightened him, and filled him with awe.

Gregor had come at the right time in his life. He was only twelve then. The following year he would not believe in anything magical, under pain of ridicule by peers. Then, the boy had put this feeling away with the comic books and the toys, and had forgotten where he left it.

Now the man remembered. He had come back for it.

Unshaven, unbeliever in this holiest of places, he was looking here for Sabra, though she was probably miles away and worlds, sitting somewhere cradling her own mind like a child upon her lap.

It was magic, it seemed, that sent her over, so he lit a candle now to bring her back. But how far and from exactly where? She had begun to leave him on the day Aubry died, growing farther and farther away, killing him as she left him, going away from him, bit by bit of her mind, and then altogether gone and taking her body with her.

Once, Sabra's life had been filled with glorious color. Color had throbbed about her in an electricity of bright scarves, textured stockings and summer dresses of impossible combinations of purples and greens. When she lived alone, her apartment had been alive with color. The rugs and drapes held vibrant, clashing conversations. Each careless thing that lay strewn about the rooms would contradict the thing it lay upon.

This had been a part of the excitement of her, the wild

charm of Sabra. After they were married, he began to work his changes on her, maintaining all the while that he loved her as she was. First he changed the shape of her body with their only child. Then he refurnished her environs, save for the rocking chair that had been her mother's, all that he approved of, good solid wooden thing. But glaring prints of rugs and drapes were cast out with the trash and the multicolored coat.

Standing in the perfect quiet of the church and gazing up at the stained-glass windows, he saw again the wild colors in a jam of rolling rainbows, escaping down Bleecker Street in the junkman's cart. And he watched Sabra running after the cart, shaking her fists at the junkman, and returning triumphant with her coat of many colors.

Oddly, it was never Sabra the mother he saw whenever she walked into a room in middle age with thickened waist, but wild Sabra, her bright colors flashing and waves of jet-black hair.

And then insanity had come to their house with the death of Aubry.

It seemed as though it happened in one night when Sabra came downstairs, very late, to sit in her mother's chair. At first he thought she'd come to keep him company as he grieved for Aubry in the dark. Then as he stared at his wife and she took form in the poor light from the street, he realized that her lustrous black hair was gone. Her crown was a cap of stick-out hair, and in some places she was shorn to the gleam of white scalp. Then Sabra had begun to rock, slowly at the beginning and then faster and faster, rocking furiously. Laughing like a mad child, she spilled out onto the floor, and crawled like a baby to the stair.

Twelve years later, Gregory Gilette lit a candle for his wife, and then another candle, and another. He went on to the next statue and the next, lighting all the candles. One by one, he begged the saints who stood above the flames, did they know where his Sabra was? Did they know the way she had gone and, most important, the way back?

The poor Protestant atheist, rational man of show-me country, broke down like a child when stones would not consult with him.

And that cat-size creature at the far side of the roof, twitching and compulsively rubbing its hands. Was that a mouse? Surely not. Mice were cartoons, and rather cute. This was something loathsome.

Tonight, the creature had come close enough to be splashed with champagne. Not to waste the wine, Andrew made a cross in the air above the scurvy animal, and he christened it Emma Sue. Then he tried to smash it out of existence with the bottle. But he was too slow— the empty bottle too heavy.

His head lolled back and he was staring up at an empty sky. Empty? He was too tired to crawl to the edge of the roof where he had left the binoculars. He shivered and hugged his knees to his body. His naked eyes drifted slowly from side to side, scanning heaven, searching for the stars.

But they were gone.

He fell into a light sleep, awakening at the thud behind him. He turned around slowly to see the brown paper bag, torn open to reveal a small loaf of bread.

A miracle.

He fell on the loaf, ripping the cellophane wrapping away from the bread. He broke the loaf open and smelled it, and then he wolfed down the sweet, white, fibrous, glorious bread, his gift from the sky.

So, there was a God.

Riker had a few bad moments watching her make the drop from the edge of Bloomingdale's roof to the narrow ledge beneath the top-floor window. When she was safely inside the building, he breathed again. He trained the binoculars on Andrew Bliss and watched him feeding on the loaf.

Riker's binoculars strayed to the surrounding buildings and then down below to the stream of late traffic. Ah, New York, all decked out in city lights like sequins on her best dress—all dazzle and smart moves. He had seen the city in harsher light, and he knew she was really a whore, but that could be fun, too.

He had underestimated Mallory's time in crossing the street and climbing to this tenth-floor roof. He turned to the right, and she was standing beside him, looking down on Andrew Bliss.

"Mallory, there's gotta be a better way to feed him. That ledge is dangerous."

"Yeah, right. A little old lady wouldn't have a problem with that ledge. The roof would be crawling with reporters right now if the bastards weren't afraid it would kill their story. Whoever Andrew's hiding from will get to him eventually."

"Didn't Markowitz ever tell you it wasn't nice to hang a taxpayer out as bait?"

"I think he did run that by me once." She checked the bolt action on the assault rifle, and aimed the sight on the roof of Bloomingdale's to test the night scope. "Charles thinks Quinn is stalking me."

"Quinn has good taste. He only goes after the brightest and the best. You're his type, kid."

"So was Aubry."

"What are you saying, Mallory? She was his own niece."

"Oh, right, and murderers are such stand-up moral people. What was I thinking of?" She walked off to the other side of the roof and stood there staring down at Andrew, her pet mouse, as he was nibbling at his bread.

"It doesn't work for me, kid." And he suspected it didn't work for her either, but this was her idea of sport.

He turned the binoculars to all the dark corners of the roof below, and lost track of Mallory by sight and sound.

"But the killing of Dean Starr suits him," said Mallory, close to his ear now, spooky kid, back for another shot at him. "According to Quinn's bio, he's a fencer, a former Olympic champion," she said. "He'd know where to put the steel to do the most damage. And it was such a neat crime, wasn't it? No mess. And that suits him too."

"So now you're thinking revenge?" Riker shook his head and lowered the binoculars to face her. "Quinn's not the type to go on a vigilante solo."

"Quinn held out on the old man, and he held out on us. He knows what the connection is. Dean Starr was tied to the old murder case, but I'm betting he wasn't the only one."

"Well, you're not thinking that poor little bastard down there could have done murder with an axe?"

"Andrew? He knows something, and so does Quinn. I'm sure there's more than one killer."

"Why?"

"I don't think Starr could have taken the artist and the dancer down by himself."

"Peter Ariel was stoned on dope that night. A twelve-year-old could have done him in."

"But Starr was a junkie too. So what about the dancer? Physical peak, good reflexes and some muscle."

Well, the killer couldn't have taken Mallory down, but Aubry was not the same species. She had been young and protected. Mallory could only see the muscle of the dancer, the reflexes. That was as close as she would come to Aubry.

She paced behind him. "I think Quinn could tell us who wrote that letter to Special Crimes, but he won't. He wanted Starr dead. If he didn't do the killing, he's still part of it somehow."

"Truth, Mallory? I think Oren Watt killed the artist

and the dancer. But let's say he had some help, maybe Starr's help. If Starr's death was revenge, I'm on the perp's side of this one. You can't know what that crime scene was like. All the pictures and all the reports won't tell you. If Starr was part of that, I'm glad the freak is dead. If Quinn had any part of the killing, I'd rather give him a medal than arrest him.''

''When I catch the perp, I'm gonna bust him. I don't care who he is or why he did it. Those are the rules.''

He was startled for a moment. For she had been the child voted most likely to send the crayons outside the lines of her coloring books. Sometimes he forgot that she did have rules. Markowitz had given them to her, but they were the rules of sport. Markowitz had been ingenious at fashioning games for her, games to keep her alive, to help her pass for normal. She was a born competitor, and this had been the only way to reach her.

Now Riker almost felt sorry for the nameless, faceless perp who got between Mallory and what she wanted most—to win.

He watched Andrew gathering up the last crumbs of his loaf, then handed the binoculars to Mallory as he pulled back from the edge of the roof. ''You know the little guy is totally nuts.''

''No he's not. That's just the booze working on him,'' she said to the alcoholic standing beside her, ''and the guilt. I see he found another candle. What's the deal with the candles? Any ideas?''

''It's gotta be religion,'' said Riker. ''That altar with the mannequin is giving me the creeps. I say he's nuts, but I can't see him hacking up those bodies or slipping a pick into Starr's back.''

''He did *something*.''

CHAPTER
5

GREGOR GILETTE CARRIED A STEAMING CUP OF COFFEE to the kitchen table and set it down beside the morning newspaper. By lowering the window shade only a little, he demolished every tall building above the tree line of Central Park. Five flights above Fifth Avenue traffic, it was almost possible to believe that he was no longer in Manhattan.

He glanced across the table at an empty chair and an empty space where Sabra might have been, if their only child had not been slaughtered. At some point in the past decade, acknowledging Sabra's absence had become a part of his daily routine, and once more, he sat down to breakfast without her.

As he unfolded his newspaper, the jewel of his ring flashed a dazzle of blue light, calling for his attention as it often did. The stone was cheap. He wore it because it was the very color of Sabra's eyes.

The doorbell rang precisely on the appointed hour, and that would be Detective Mallory.

Gregor ushered his young guest into the kitchen and poured her a generous portion of coffee. Visually, she had lost nothing in the transition from ball gown to blue jeans. But her manner had altered. He thought she seemed somewhat mechanical in the small civilized comments of "How are you, sir?" and "Sorry to bother you so early." Of course, he realized she was not at all sorry to bother him, and now, done with courtesy, she launched into the business of her visit.

She settled a laptop computer on the kitchen table by her cup. "I need more information on the night your daughter died." She opened the computer, and then reached into her blazer pocket to draw out a plastic device with a ball at its center, which she plugged into her machine. "You were planning to have dinner with Aubry that night?"

"Yes. I was to meet her at a cafe in the West Village." He felt a vague disquiet. The night of the ball there had been conversation. This was interrogation, cold and impersonal.

"You brought her roses." She began to tap on the keyboard, not meeting his eyes, almost disconnected from him.

"Yes, the roses were red."

"Was it a special occasion?" Now she did look at him, and he wished she had not, for she might as well have been regarding his chair and not the man who sat close to her, sharing coffee.

"No. The flowers were to brighten Aubry's apartment—a gift from her mother. Sabra was a woman of extreme color, and Aubry was very austere. So, every time we saw our daughter, Sabra would give her a gift of color—a scarf, a bright ceramic bowl. Sabra believed one could die for lack of color, so she continued to feed color to her child."

"Where was your wife the night of the murders?"

"Sabra was visiting her mother, Ellen Quinn."

For a moment, he thought Mallory was going to challenge that statement, but her voice was casual as she said, "I had the idea Sabra and her family didn't get along very well."

"They didn't. But my mother-in-law was getting on in years, and Sabra was too big a person to hold a grudge against a lonely old woman."

"Do you know why Aubry wanted to meet Quinn at the gallery that night?"

"No, Detective, you have it wrong. It was Jamie who chose the meeting place. Aubry called me to say she would be late for dinner, because her Uncle Jamie wanted to see her."

And now he saw suspicion in her face, as though she had caught him in a lie, and he was puzzled over this. But as quickly as he put this together, the trouble in her eyes had resolved itself.

"You're sure *she* didn't ask to meet *him*?"

"Quite sure. She said Jamie wanted her to meet him at the gallery."

"She spoke to him?"

"No. He left her a message at the ballet school. When I couldn't reach Jamie by phone, I called the school's director. Aubry had used Madame Burnstien's phone to call her uncle at the newspaper. Her message had been garbled—too many instructions for the school receptionist to write down in a hurry. It was a clerk at the newspaper who told Aubry to meet her uncle at the gallery. When I spoke to that clerk, she looked up the name of the gallery on the message carbon."

"Did you and Quinn ever speak about this?"

"I honestly don't remember. There were so many things to distract me from the small details. My only child was dead, my wife was falling apart . . . there was the funeral to deal with."

"Who broke the news to Sabra?"

"Jamie did. He took care of everything. He made the funeral arrangements and hired security men to keep people away from us. Sabra was going to pieces. Then, as I told you, she left me and checked herself into an institution."

"You left for Europe after that?"

"Perhaps nine months later—only after it was made very clear to me that Sabra wouldn't see me. The breakup of a marriage is a common piece of damage when two people lose a child. I had been in Paris for only a year when I heard she left the institution and disappeared. I did what I could to find her, but I failed."

"Would you like me to find Sabra for you?" She looked up from her computer.

"The best private investigators in New York are still looking for her. I never stopped trying to find my wife. So, I thank you for—"

"The best PIs are ex-cops. They get most of their information from old buddies on the force. Now I'm a cop, and I'm better than the best you've got. And the service is free."

He liked arrogance, but he mistrusted youth. "My people have been working the case for years. They're familiar with every—"

"I'll bet you didn't have one decent photograph to give them."

"No, I didn't." He smiled at this reminder of Sabra's eccentric camera hatred. "I gave the investigators a photograph of my daughter. Aubry bore a strong resemblance to her mother."

"Sabra was in her forties when she disappeared. Now she's twelve years older. Your detectives are looking for a family resemblance to a twenty-year-old girl." She tapped the laptop computer with one long red fingernail, and then turned it so he could see the full screen. "This is an identity kit."

He leaned closer to examine a photograph of Aubry. "It is a strong resemblance to Sabra."

"But the daughter wasn't an exact copy of the mother, was she?"

"No. Aubry was very pretty, but Sabra was striking, dramatic. My wife was a great presence in every room she entered. . . . But the day of the funeral she seemed small and tired. The ordeal added years to her face. Grief is an exhausting thing.''

Mallory revolved the ball device wired into her computer. ''I'm aging the photo of Aubry.'' A moment later she said, ''Here, take a look at this.''

He left his seat at the table to stand behind her chair. And now he was looking at the woman his daughter might have become. Mallory was adding wrinkles to the brow. It was cruel, this aging process, but fascinating. She had taken away the softness of Aubry's face and created lines around the mouth. The delicate nose was slightly enlarged, and the eyes were given their own lines. The black hair had been lightened with strokes of gray.

''That's very good,'' said Gilette. ''Sabra's eyes were a bit larger and more expressive.''

Mallory enlarged the eyes.

''Sadder,'' said Gilette.

She dragged down the corners of the eyes.

''And the mouth was wider, the chin a little stronger.''

When she was done, he said, ''That's what Sabra looked like on the day of the funeral.''

Mallory folded down the top of her computer and picked up her car keys, preparing to leave him. Now she put the keys down again. ''One more thing—how well did Andrew Bliss know your daughter? I have an old newspaper article that quotes him as a personal friend.''

''Andrew? Well, he saw Aubry at her mother's art shows. He always made a fuss over her when she was a child. He even went to her recitals when she was a student at Madame Burnstien's school. I like him for that. My daughter was a lonely little girl. There was a quality in Andrew that could speak to her, child to child.''

''You were there every time they met?''

''No. They sometimes saw one another when he visited the ballet school—Andrew was a generous patron.

Sometimes he met with Aubry after her dancing class. When she was a little girl, Andrew would insist that she call home to tell us she'd be late.''

Mallory's eyes narrowed. "He was seeing her *alone* when she was still a child?''

On one level, he liked this young woman tremendously, but just now he wanted to smack her. "He and Aubry would have tea in Madame Burnstien's office after class. Does this sound like a sexual tryst with a pedophile?''

Apparently, it did. Her expression was cynical. She sat back in her chair, unconvinced that opportunity was not synonymous with the act. He thought her too young to be so hard on the world.

"Andrew was very kind to my daughter, nothing more. He might have been her only real friend. Their relationship was totally innocent, almost spiritual. My wife believed that Aubry and Andrew were like two lonely monks with different callings.''

"Andrew Bliss is a materialistic little bastard," she said, calmly, evenly. "All the papers are touting him as the fashion terrorist of New York. What do you think Sabra would say now? You think she might buy the pedophile angle?''

"No!'' The palm of his hand slapped the table hard. "And neither do I.''

Had she been baiting him? Yes, it was in her face. She had what she wanted from him, and damn the cost. Now he understood why Jamie Quinn had gone to such pains to keep the police from his door all those years ago. The questions, the insinuations—this was a rape of memory.

"Andrew's friendship with Aubry was innocent kindness. Nothing can dissuade me from that.'' He rose from the table, making it clear that it was time for her to go. "The suggestion of something sexual in her childhood is maddening. You have no sense of my emotions concerning my child, do you?''

"I think you'd like to kill the man who murdered her."

A cockroach floated dead among the slags of cream on the surface of his coffee. Riker shook his head and set the cup down on the bedside table. The roach must have been in the pan he used to heat the water. Morning light was diffusing through the dust-gray lace of a curtain. Layers of cigarette smoke had dimmed and yellowed the windowpane to make the daylight kinder to his emaciated features.

Now he parted the curtain and caught sight of Mary Margaret rounding the corner with her arms full of groceries and leading a parade of four children. Her body had thickened some, but her hair was the same carrot red she was born to. The children, redheads all, were laughing, and she laughed with them.

If only they had had children together, Mary Margaret might have stuck it out with him.

Naw, that's not right.

It was the drinking that drove her away, and not the dearth of babies. She was always meant for better than him, and the year after she left, she had found that better man.

She had lived three doors away for all these years, and they never spoke. He saw her most every day of his life, passing sometimes within touching distance, never daring to touch her once in all that time. He wished she had moved away from the old neighborhood when she left him. It would have been easier for her to leave instead of him. He had stayed here on this same street because she had stayed.

Every time he had seen her passing by his window with her brood of kids and her second husband, it had been a personal assault. In the march of children's feet, all ducks in a row behind Mary Margaret, Riker could see generations of the life he might have had. No problem with her second husband. No sir. Not a sterile drunk like the first one.

Perhaps he should have crawled off to die with his drunk's liver, years ago. What kept him alive he didn't know. He sat down on the side of the bed and opened the drawer of the nightstand. He reached to the back, hand combing through the debris until he touched the small paper envelope. Inside it was his wedding ring and a bullet with his name engraved upon it, his rainy day bullet.

He seldom opened the envelope. It had more magic for him when he didn't look inside. It was only important to him to heft the weight of the ring and the bullet in his hand, to know that there was one last place to go when he couldn't live in this one anymore.

He kicked a pizza carton out of his way as he walked to the bathroom. A nest of roaches fled the cardboard box and took refuge in another take-out container with remnants of rice and noodles. Now he stood before the mirror over the small sink where he shaved, when he shaved. He checked his eyes in the mirror. He saw dense red road maps with patches of brown where his eyes leaked through.

By nine o'clock, bits of tissue paper with bright red centers marked all the places where he had cut himself shaving.

Drunks should only be allowed to use electric razors.

When he was bereft of tissue, bleeding stopped, he dressed in his best bad suit.

"I have been given a sign that God is on my side in this," Andrew announced to the world, via his bullhorn. And now he cast a benevolent eye on the small crowd of ant-size, badly dressed people who gathered on the sidewalk below. He had come to think of them as his parishioners, his personal flock of insects.

"He would want you all to make the most of His gifts

to the world. Why do you think He created Blooming-dale's and Bergdorf's? Sinners, can't you see His grand design in Tiffany's?''

The crowd was growing larger.

Oh, thank you, Lord, fresh victims.

He sized them up in the binoculars, and couldn't get horn to mouth fast enough.

''You! Wearing that yellow, shapeless thing that makes your skin look sallow! Most of us have to hang out at laundromats to see that peculiar shade of polyester. Sinner, you'll find the Suit Collection on the second floor.''

And now another. ''Woman with the hideous purple tights. Don't you realize what a steady diet of champagne and cigarettes can do to the human body? I'm dying for your sins. Get thee to Women's Sportswear, third floor.''

He addressed the larger gathering. ''Remember, we are all God's creations, and we must dedicate our lives to the greater glory of His works. Charge card applications are available on the first floor. You may cosign a card for the less fortunate.''

He lowered the binoculars and bullhorn to uncork a new bottle and sip his lunch, forgoing the amenity of a glass. There were no glasses left. One blanked-out night he must have taken up the custom of smashing them against the wall each time he emptied one. Now he surveyed his plush aerie, ignoring the shards of broken glass and the growing litter of empty bottles. Even blind drunk, his taste in goods had been unerring.

And now he flopped down on his bed of quilts and stared at the mannequin behind her altar. He wondered why God had created Aubry if He was just going to kill her that way. It was all God's work and God's will, wasn't it? All of it?

Aubry the Virginal, the perfect sacrifice. How holy.

Oh, beautiful Aubry. God can be such a bastard, can't He?

• • •

Coffey stood in front of Blakely's desk until the chief of detectives made a guttural noise and pointed to the chair.

Now the great man deigned to lift his head and squint his small eyes at Coffey, as though trying to remember what the head of Special Crimes Section was doing here in his office.

"Well, Jack, Commissioner Beale wanted me to pass on his compliments. He's Mallory's number-one fan this week. Course that makes it more difficult to take Mallory off the Dean Starr murder."

"I was hoping you'd reconsider that."

"No, Jack, I don't think so. I want you to call Beale. Tell him it's your idea to pull Mallory and Riker off the case. As long as the FBI is out of the picture, he probably won't care if you have the janitor run the investigation."

"Mallory and Riker make a good team. I don't want to change the assignments."

"This is not a good time for you to be making waves, Jack. The paperwork on your promotion is sitting on my desk. You don't want it to park here for another year, do you?"

Coffey sat in silence. He had learned this from Markowitz. *"Let the bastard flap his mouth,"* the old man had said. *"Let him knock himself out, and then you're still fresh when you move in to shut his mouth."*

"You'd be the youngest captain on the force, Jack. Of course, Riker was the youngest captain we ever had. You didn't know? Well, that's not too surprising—he wasn't a captain for very long. This was on someone else's watch, before my time—remember that. He was just doing his job, and a good job, too. One night, he interviewed a twelve-year-old boy who gave him the license number of a limousine and a very detailed description of a man. So Riker ran the plates, and matched up the description of the perp with the owner of the car. Then he wrote up his report like the good cop he was. The kid was raped by a prince of the church.''

"So that was Riker's case? I heard the story about the arrest, but I always figured it was like one of those legends about giant alligators in the sewers. There's no trace of the arrest report ever—''

"You looked for it, didn't you? All the rookies look for it. Well, Riker's report disappeared, and as far as Riker knew, the prince went on doing little boys in the park. Riker objected to that. He received a warning from the guy who had my job—a threat's more like it—and then he got a promotion to captain. They were hoping he would get the drift. Well, that stupid bastard didn't have a captain's rank for five days before he goes out and busts a prince of the church with a kid in his car. Riker brought the cardinal in handcuffed. You can guess what happened next.''

"He was busted all the way down to sergeant.''

"No. He went back to the rank of lieutenant. And he still wouldn't stop. *Then* he was busted down to sergeant. By then his wife had left him, he was deep in the bottle and next to useless. The department would've eased him out, but Markowitz grabbed him off for Special Crimes Section and sent him to a clinic to dry out. Markowitz had more power around here than God Almighty. Nobody else could have saved Riker's ass. By the time Riker dried out, the prince was gone, and a new prince was in power.''

"Did Riker ever try to go outside the system?''

"No, he wouldn't do anything to hurt the department. He's a third-generation cop, just like Markowitz was. And who was he going to go to—the cops? Maybe the newspapers? The church is a major political power in this town. He had no evidence and the kid was gone.''

"What happened to the kid?''

"Who knows? Who cares? You've got a great future, Jack. You could learn from Riker's mistakes.''

"This case is small-time, compared to Riker's."

"Some very high-profile people could be embarrassed, Jack."

"A senator, for instance? And what's the old mayor doing now, running for governor, isn't he?"

"If Riker couldn't buck the system, what chance have you got? Call Mallory off."

"You'd never touch Mallory, would you?"

"Of course not. Her old man and me, we had a lot of history together. I think of her as my own—"

"You can't touch her, can you? She's got everything the old man had. She must know where every single body is buried. Markowitz wouldn't have left her defenseless in the shark pool."

"Careful, Lieutenant. I think you're bordering on insubordination here."

"Maybe there was more to it than leaving the homicide books tidy when the mayor and the old commissioner left office." Coffey was rising out of his chair. "Maybe they were afraid the real killer was somebody in a power position." He turned his back on Blakely.

"That's enough!" Blakely pounded his desk. "Come back here and sit down, Lieutenant!"

"Just call me *Sergeant*," said Coffey, closing the door behind him.

Orwelhouse Sanitarium had been home to Oren Watt for eleven years.

Mallory looked around at the trappings of the trendy New York asylum for the artistic and crazy. The reception-area walls were lined with cheap art in expensive frames. The furniture was chic and ugly, blending well with the loud geometric pattern of the carpet.

Perhaps the world *did* need a fashion terrorist.

In her pocket was Charles's daunting list of all the mental institutions in the tristate area. Charles had put Orwelhouse dead last. He had reasoned that because Oren

Watt was the star patient, this asylum would have been the last place Sabra would go.

Thank you, Charles.

Mallory had moved Orwelhouse to the top of her list. She was thinking along the lines she knew best—rage, obsession and revenge—which she believed were closer to Sabra's mind-set in the aftermath of Aubry's murder.

The receptionist was quickly exiting the internet server, blanking the screen of her desktop computer. There was time enough for Mallory to note the personal code and the erotic service the receptionist subscribed to, undoubtedly without her employer's knowledge.

Now the pinch-faced brunette studied Mallory, eyes traveling from the expensive running shoes to the designer sunglasses. Mallory flashed a platinum credit card as identification, and now the brunette's sudden toothy smile acknowledged her as a member of that exclusive sphere, the master class of money.

"I need a tour," said Mallory. "I have all the paperwork for admissions, but I want to see the place first. My mother is a wealthy woman, so I'm concerned about your security."

She was then introduced to a man with a used-car dealer's smile and a Savile Row tailor. During her guided tour of the facility, Mallory checked the electronic locks on the doors, asked about the front-end system of the computers, and noted the security cameras mounted on the walls. She was not impressed. This was going to be entirely too easy. Before her guide turned her over to the director's secretary, he had all but given her the keys to the door and the passwords for all the patient files. Best of all was the tour of the basement and access to the trunk line for the telephones.

Now she stood in the director's anteroom and put one hand in her pocket to depress the switch on her scrambler. The secretary's computer screen went berserk, changing all the text to math symbols.

"Oh, shit," said the secretary.

Mallory watched as the woman powered down to lose the glitch. When the screen came to light again, the scramble was still there, and there were many more "Oh, shit"'s before the defeated woman beat her hand on the desk.

"My computer does that once in a while," said Mallory. "Do you want me to fix it for you?"

"I'll give you my firstborn child," said the woman with the frazzled eyes. She stood up and pulled out her chair for Mallory. "Can I get you some coffee, hon?"

"Thanks. Black, no sugar." Mallory sat down at the computer station. When the woman was out of sight, she turned off her scrambler and restored the screen. Now she went into the main directory and created a back door in the system to bypass every security code. The coffee appeared beside the keyboard as she was calling up the secretary's word-processing program.

At the end of the afternoon, she was back in her office at Mallory and Butler, Ltd., sitting at her own computer. She waited for the trip lights to tell her she had access. The amber light glowed. The asylum's closed system was operating on the modem now, accessing the internet, which made it an open system with a back door.

As she tapped into the phone line for the Orwelhouse lobby, she found herself intruding on a sexual liaison. The receptionist was hooked into an internet service which catered to the erotically deprived. Mallory checked the user's personnel file with a purloined password. The receptionist was high school graduate Sylvia Ulner, who was passing for a psychiatrist on the anonymous internet connection. At the moment, Sylvia was typing out a pornographic analysis of her body for an amorous correspondent in a private cyberspace room.

Of course, there were no private rooms in cyberspace. Any cut-rate burglar knew there was no such thing as an inviolate system. But Sylvia and her keyboard stud were oblivious to Mallory's intrusion as they were busy violating one another.

Welcome to the goldfish bowl.

Mallory stepped lightly on the information superhighway, tiptoed past the lovers in the circuit boards, and entered the hospital system to roam the patient entries of twelve years ago.

There was no medication on the charts for Oren Watt or any of the other Outsider Artists, and no one was paying the bills. The accountant was reporting this group as a loss, though each had a growing trust fund for sales of insane artwork. The insurance companies of the non-artistic patients were paying the moon for drugs and counseling. She found only one female patient in Sabra's age bracket with no insurance and no scholarship. Well, that fit. Gilette had mentioned that Sabra never used their medical policy.

The computer called the woman Sarah, and itemized the counseling sessions and rounds of medication for depression. When Mallory called up the complete file, she was looking at the patient's photograph, a blurred face twisting away from the lens, unrecognizable but for Sabra's hallmark camera avoidance. The bills for her care had been paid directly by a blind account in a foreign bank until the account ran dry two years later. Her entire fortune was gone, and coincidentally, she was discharged that same month. No forwarding address.

Did the bastards give you bus fare, Sabra?

While the receptionist and her lover were trysting in cyberspace, taking off a hundred bytes of panties, Mallory was downloading all the patient files. The lovers were in printed throes of ecstasy as Mallory left the hospital records, closing the back door softly behind her.

MORE, MORE, MORE, wailed Sylvia at her keyboard.

Now Mallory scanned Sabra's file on her own system and at a more leisurely pace. There were reams of charts which only told her Sabra's deep sadness had never re-sponded to drugs or counseling. The personal notes of a psychiatric nurse mentioned Sabra's only close friendship with another inmate: Sabra and Oren Watt had been in-separable.

Riker walked into Coffey's office unannounced. He looked from the man to the bottle, which Coffey made no effort to conceal. That was a very bad sign. Riker pulled a chair closer to the desk and settled into it. Coffey wouldn't meet his face. A worse sign.

"I got ten bucks says I can guess what's goin' down." Riker put his money on the desktop next to the lieuten-ant's empty glass.

Coffey gave him a grudging smile and fished a back pocket for his wallet. He laid a ten-dollar bill beside Riker's, saying, "Go for it."

"You've been in here for less than ten minutes, and the glass is drained. Now that's criminal, 'cause it's a real good grade of sipping whiskey. Your knuckles are white, and you look like a man who shouldn't be allowed near a loaded gun. It's Blakely, right? He's messing with your command."

Coffey pushed both tens to Riker's side of the desk. "Yeah, he wants Mallory off this case. He wants that really bad."

"And he threatened you, right?"

Coffey nodded, as he reached into the drawer of his desk and produced another glass, holding it up to Riker as though he actually believed his sergeant might say no to a shot of whiskey.

"Well, I think he's overreacting," said Riker, accept-ing his glass and emptying it before he spoke again. "There's worse department cover-ups to worry about. This one is really small potatoes."

"Blakely's taking it pretty seriously."

"And I'm sure he's taking it personally, too. He's the

one who ordered Markowitz to close out the case."

"But the case stayed open. Blakely never screwed around much with Markowitz, did he?"

"Well, you have to figure Markowitz had something on Blakely—the things the old man got away with? Lieutenant, you know what your real problem is? You got your promotions on merit. You didn't come up through the patronage system. If you had, you'd have enough dirt to fend for yourself. You remind me of my old man. That's high praise, 'cause the old bastard was as straight-arrow as they come."

"Riker, why did you stay on the force after they busted you to sergeant?"

"Well, my old dad was a cop. My grandfather, too. There was nothing else I ever wanted to be. So I quit the force and do what? You think I'm gonna go be a hairball private dick? Gimme a break."

"You're fifty-five. You could retire with a nice pension and a few—"

"And put a gun muzzle in my mouth after the novelty wears off? Naw. I still got Markowitz's kid to raise. She thinks she knows it all. You can't tell her nothin'. She's gotta learn everything the hard way. Somebody's gotta be there with the bandages when she falls down and skins her little knees, or gets kicked in the head."

Rather normal people, suited and gowned, filled the gallery and mingled with the freaks of SoHo antifashion. Among the better dressed, there were many obvious cases of plastic excess and cut-rate work. With an unerring eye for aesthetics, it was not difficult for Charles Butler to guess which of the noses and chins had come from the store.

Charles took Mallory's arm to escort her around a leering little man in a long fur coat which probably concealed something lewd. Among the lunatics, his instincts were seldom wrong. Whenever he smiled in public, they gravitated to him, taking him for one of their own. He held his loony smile accountable for every mad confrontation on the streets of New York.

"Mallory, it's not the same crowd that would have been at the last Dean Starr show. If that group was the A list, this is definitely the C list, the incompetents of art collecting."

"How can you tell?"

"Koozeman brought out the circus freaks to entertain them. They'll want to tell their friends back home in the suburbs that they spent the evening with famous artists. Any freak will qualify in that role. In my experience, the real artists are fairly normal in most respects."

A young woman with a half-shaven head walked by in earnest conversation with a pin-striped suit.

"So Koozeman is trying to unload the unsold work in a hurry," said Mallory. "That fits. He put both galleries on the—"

"Check out the metal jacket on my tooth, here," said the small man in the fur coat, who had followed along behind them. Now the little man put himself in Mallory's path, and she was suddenly confronted with a wide, grinning mouth. A grimy finger pointed to the shiny metal crown reflecting a small silver cameo of her face between his lips. The tiny mirror was set slightly off center in a crooked line of yellow teeth. She backed up and stared at his sweating face above the collar of the fur, taking in the spiked hair, and the gold rings which pierced both his nostrils.

He grinned at her, all but salivating as he looked her up and down. "Would you like to see the jeweled safety pin in my dick?"

Charles pulled her away while she was still in the fascination mode and had not yet thought to bloody the little man.

Koozeman was advancing on them, smiling and openly appraising Mallory's black silk dress as he extended his hand to Charles. "Mr. Butler, how good to see you again."

"Hello, Koozeman. I believe you've met Mallory."

"Who could forget such a face? If I had known you were coming, my dear, I would have made up a guest list with a better class of collector."

Charles nodded to the near corner. "I see J. L. Quinn is here."

"Yes, he is," said Koozeman, as though he could not figure out why Quinn had come.

Mallory looked around at the walls, stark and bare but for the small red bits of paper held in place with pins. "So where is the artwork?"

"The artwork?" For a moment, Koozeman seemed baffled by the idea of art in his gallery. "Oh, the tickets. See the tickets on the walls? They all have numbers. Dean Starr did it with numbers."

"Pardon?" Charles knew he would regret asking for clarification.

"Numbers. See?" Koozeman waved a small red velvet bag in front of them, grinning like a master sorcerer. He opened the bag with a small flourish and offered Mallory a peek inside, wherein lay a pile of tickets like those on the walls.

"Every one of them matches up with an idea, just like the tickets on the walls. They all have numbers on them. Please pick one."

She dropped a white hand into the bag and pulled out a red ticket. It was number twenty-two.

"All right, Dean's idea for number twenty-two. Let's see." He pulled a folded sheet of paper from his jacket pocket. "Oh, yes. His idea for number twenty-two is a broad steel beam that goes half a mile straight up in the air."

Mallory seemed skeptical. "What for?"

"To make you uncomfortable. You can't see the base support, it just stands there while you wait for it to fall down. It's meant to be threatening. Not his most original theme, though. He's building on the work of a sculptor who once wrecked the side of a government building when the plaza sculpture fell down.''

''A half-mile beam. That's a rather ambitious project,'' said Charles, playing the good sport. ''How are you planning to fund it? With drawings—like Christo?''

''Oh, no. Dean never intended to create the pieces. He just thought of them.''

Mallory tilted her head to one side, and Charles wondered if she was listening for the audible snap of her mind, which could only be moments away.

''Well, of course. He just thought of them.''

Koozeman missed her sarcasm, as he took her hand and kissed it. ''You do understand. I sell the artist's thoughts, his intentions. Very pure, isn't it?'' He handed a price list to Charles.

Charles scanned the list of numbers accompanied by prices in four and five figures. ''And how are the sales going?''

''I've sold four of them in the past half hour.''

''You sell the artist's thoughts.'' Mallory gave equal weight to each word.

''Yes. I sit over there.'' Koozeman pointed to the side wall where an armchair sat on a platform. ''When you see a number you like, you come and tell me the number on the ticket, and I tell you the idea Dean Starr had for that number. Simple?''

Charles watched J. L. Quinn's approach. ''Charisma'' was a word he called up easily enough, but he was also searching for something to describe an animal so much at home in its body, too graceful to be human. Now this was art, he thought, as he soon fell victim to Quinn's talent for putting people at ease when he felt so inclined.

And then suddenly, Charles realized he had been robbed. Mallory was walking away with the art critic.

• • •

A matron, wearing a pearl choker, gasped audibly at the specter standing by the gallery window.

On the sidewalk outside the gallery, face pressed up against the window, a ragged derelict was holding a tea tin to her head and staring after the retreating figures of Quinn and Mallory. The woman's mouth was working in a furious agitation of red gums as she slowly withdrew into the darkness beyond the light of the window.

The matron with the pearl choker made a mental note to send a nice check to the Coalition for the Homeless and drained her full wineglass in one swig. What dark thing had lived and brooded on the wrong side of the glass, she did not want to know, but thought it might have come from hell and felt rather at home there.

Mallory stood very close to the wall, eyes level with ticket number thirty-four. "Tell me again about the metaphor, the poetry of shape and color—"

"That pertains to fine art," said Quinn.

"What's this?"

"The demystification of art."

"Well, thanks for clearing that up for me."

"It's not a technical term. It's a eulogy." Quinn only glanced in the general direction of a passing gallery boy, and two glasses of wine appeared in the next instant. He handed one to Mallory. "Actually, if Dean Starr hadn't been such a fool, I might have given him credit for ingenious parody. Go to any Whitney Biennial and you'll see scores of three-minute ideas executed by the untalented and curated by the blind. Starr just carried the premise a little further by not bothering to construct the idea. In fact, the more I think of it, the more I'm convinced that the idea for the tickets wasn't even his."

"Gregor Gilette said Koozeman used to be an artist."

"Yes, he was. You know, the tickets could be Koozeman's concept."

"What are you doing here, Quinn? You said you

didn't review hack artists. And I had the feeling Koozeman didn't expect you to show up tonight.''

"I've been planning a lengthy piece on Koozeman, not
Starr. He really is quite the magician. I could hardly ignore a thing like this.''

"How will you write it up?''

"I intend to promote Koozeman as a genius of the new
order. A genius of hype, and hype, don't you know, is
the art form of the era. He's truly a man of his times.
But it hardly merits writing. I can phone this one in.''

"Will anyone know you're kidding?''

"No.''

"What did you think of Koozeman when he was a
working artist?''

"I thought he was very good.''

"According to your brother-in-law, Sabra thought he
was a genius.''

"She was probably right. Some of his work was brilliant, and now he promotes hacks. Every third person you
meet in this town is a creative artist. If you have an old
can of spray paint knocking around in the garage, Koozeman can make you a star.''

"Must be tough for the people with the real talent.''

"New York City,'' said Quinn, as though the complete
explanation could be offered in those three words. New
York, he explained, was tough on every artist. In the
beginning, New York doesn't seem to notice them at all,
or so they think. They believe the city doesn't even know
they're alive. Then, one day an artist trips on the sidewalk and his hand hits the pavement and New York steps
on it and breaks all his fingers. New York has noticed
him. Then New York steps on his face and breaks that,
too, and that's just to say hello. ''So, who could really
blame Koozeman for opting to roll in cash instead of
always chasing after the rent money.''

Now Koozeman joined them with fresh wine and a
gallery boy at his side to take away their empty glasses.

"Quinn, you mustn't monopolize my prize celebrity this way." He made a small courtly bow to Mallory. "It was lovely the way you demolished the FBI. So these killer profiles of theirs are worthless?"

"No, not if they're done right. My own profile tells me the killer is successful. He's rich and getting richer. I smell money every time I think about the case. So I'm looking for someone with a soul that's interchangeable with a cockroach or an advertising executive."

Koozeman stared into his wineglass as he spoke to her. "And you think the killer of Dean Starr—"

"Oh sorry," she said. "I was thinking of the wrong murder. Sometimes I get confused. I understand you were once an artist. Is that true?"

"It was a long time ago." His words were halting.

"What kind of work did you do?"

"Nothing of any consequence." Koozeman sipped his wine, eyes reevaluating her over the rim of his glass.

"But I heard different," said Mallory. " 'Genius' is the word I keep hearing. Now let me guess. You were a sculptor, right?"

A few drops of wine spilled from Koozeman's glass.

Mallory didn't wait for her answer. She abruptly dismissed him with the turn of her back and drifted off toward the wine table, leaving Quinn to wonder. He turned to Koozeman.

If a face could fall, Koozeman's truly did. His mouth opened slightly as the jaw fell first, followed by the excess flesh of cheeks and jowls. And at last, his eyes dropped, staring at the floor now, as though it might be coming up to meet him at any moment.

Mallory was standing at the long table, looking from bottle to bottle.

"Can't make up your mind?"

She looked up to see the smiling face of Kerry, the bartender from Godd's.

"You know, what you drink at an art function is very important." Kerry said this as much to the small crowd gathered at the table as to Mallory. "It shows your true political orientation."

Heads turned. Kerry flourished a crisp white bar rag and continued. "A major gallery opening serves wine, champagne and sparkling water. Now, champagne," he said, holding up a bottle as a visual aid, "given the state of the world, is in the worst possible taste. It says, 'I realize that people in third-world nations are starving and politically oppressed, and I don't care.' "

Emma Sue Hollaran, wearing a knockoff silk blouse made by third-world child labor, sipped champagne and nodded reflexively before she could call the gesture back.

"White wine is middle of the road. It says, 'I have no political convictions of my own, but I would be happy to embrace yours if you would only explain them to me.' It's the wine of wimps."

The reporter from *StreetLevel Weekly* had been reaching for the white wine. He withdrew his hand as though it had been slapped.

"How about a nice glass of water?" another man suggested.

"Oh, worst possible choice," said Kerry. "Water says, 'I'm in complete sympathy with the plight of the homeless, and now I'm going to grind my heel into your face, you fascist pig.' Water is much too politically volatile. They really shouldn't serve water here."

"What's left?"

"My personal favorite." He held up a dark bottle. "Red wine only says, 'I don't care if I do spill this on my suit.' "

The sour-looking young man from *StreetLevel* set his glass of sparkling water down on the bar and edged toward the red wine. Then, perhaps thinking of the cleaning bill for his only good suit, he retrieved his glass of water and went off in search of some rich and pretty socialite whom he might kill with words.

As Emma Sue Hollaran walked away from the table with her champagne, Kerry formed his hand into a gun and shot her with his middle finger, thus combining an obscene gesture with an imaginary kill.

Mallory took a glass of red. "You have a problem with her?"

"I have a problem with art critics in general. I make exceptions for the good ones, but there aren't many like Quinn."

"I thought Emma Sue Hollaran was on the Public Works Committee now."

"She still turns in columns in the art magazines," said Kerry. "She likes to keep her hand in with the thumb-screws. But she'll get hers. I know where New York art critics go when they die, and it's not pretty."

"You mean fire and brimstone?"

"No, more like self-cannibalism. Critic's Hell looks just like New York—but without any artists. The critics have to make their own art and criticize themselves. So they start chewing on their own tails, and being what they are, they can't stop until they reach their necks, and . . ."

Everybody wants revenge.

While Kerry went on with the bitter details of the critic's afterlife, Mallory was watching J. L. Quinn in conversation with Emma Sue Hollaran. Quinn's polite mask was fracturing. He wore a nearly human expression of dismay. As Hollaran walked away, he emptied his glass in one swill—not his style. What had Hollaran said?

He turned to see Mallory watching him. He came toward her now, and set his empty glass on the table with a nod to Kerry.

"Take this." Mallory handed him her own glass. "You look like your stock portfolio just died."

"I've just been told the name of the artist who's doing the work for Gregor's plaza."

"How bad can it be?"

"It couldn't be any worse."

Kerry appeared with another glass of red wine and held it out to Mallory. She nodded her thanks, and turned back to Quinn. "Did she give you any idea what the plaza art will be like?"

"No, she didn't. Hollaran's forte is covert attack. It won't be anything small, I can guarantee that. I only hope its removal won't be too much of a problem."

"You can have it removed? I thought the law protected—"

"The law? Oh, yes, I bought off the law. I have the paperwork on my desk to remove whatever travesty she decides to install."

"You bought the *law*?"

"Mallory, you can buy anything in New York City."

"*I'm* the law."

"As if I needed reminding. Oh, please. We're both grown-ups. This town has not had six continuous uncorrupted moments since its inception. What can't you buy here? You can buy men, women, and children. You can have sex with them, or just remove the organs you need for spare parts. And it's not getting more corrupt, only more imaginative. Before we developed the technology, they only used the spare body parts for trophies and souvenirs."

"And artwork." She was staring at his face. "Where did you get that scar? Did a woman give it to you?"

"Charles Butler gave it to me."

Was he being sarcastic? No, he was serious. "Why?"

"You'll have to ask Charles."

The curator for a New Jersey bank's art collection looked down at his red ticket and asked the computer software king, "Would you be interested in trading my football arena filled with marmalade and great white sharks for your mile-long line of bustless but sexy blondes?''

Quinn watched her walk away from him. It seemed she was always doing that. She walked past a neighborhood junkie, apparently uninterested in his unlawful act of demonstrating a drug fix for a small group of well-dressed out-of-towners.

One of the nicely dressed people obligingly held a lighter under the junkie's spoon as the man filled his needle with a liquefied dope. The junkie expertly tied the elastic cord around his upper arm to make a vein bulge out. And now he inserted the needle, and the spectators watched him fly away to the land of Wynken, Blynken and Slow Death.

This was not the first junkie Quinn had seen up close.

He had seen Oren Watt outside the gallery on the night Aubry died. He had only taken note of the dark glasses and the bizarre mouth. All the other features had been wiped out by the headlights of three police cars, all trained on Oren Watt. His limbs had been jerking to a music of the mind with only half its notes intact. Between his lips, his tongue had darted in and out like a small pink mouse, keeping the rhythm of his spasms, as Watt's feet tap-danced in codes of pain. He had fallen to the ground, and then scrambled back to his feet.

''What a trouper,'' one cop had called out.

''Encore,'' yelled another.

And Oren Watt had done his junkie's song and dance one more time.

Quinn, Markowitz and Riker had been passing by the drug addict and his art critics in blue uniforms when Quinn brought the parade to a halt. He had pointed to the junkie, and Markowitz shook his head, saying, ''Not enough blood on him.''

Quinn remembered looking down at his own clothes that night, the blood on his shoes and pantlegs. And the policemen and technicians filing past them, going to and from the gallery, all had blood on them.

Koozeman jerked his head to the sound of her voice. She smiled. It had taken less than twenty minutes to instill this lab-rat reflex in the man.

"Miss Mallory." His smile was forced this time.

"Just Mallory is fine. I suppose your next opening will be an Oren Watt show?"

"No. I told you I don't handle him, and I never will. The television people only rented the gallery for the shooting. Just business. Nothing to do with art, really." He was perspiring, and his hand went to the knot of his tie, unconsciously working it loose.

Feeling the heat, Koozeman?

"Don't you think Oren Watt is a genius?"

"Of course not," said Koozeman. "He knows nothing about art, and it shows. He could never work outside that narrow market of ghoulish souvenirs. The drawings are poor by any standard. If you're thinking of investing—"

"No, but I am interested in art—more and more every day," said Mallory. "The most fascinating piece of art I ever saw came out of your old gallery in the East Village."

"But you would have been a child when I was in that location."

"I was. All I have now are the photographs of the artist and the dancer when the butcher was done with them. I study them every day, every damn day. I can't stop looking at them. I'd say there was a dark genius to the arrangement of the bodies. Wouldn't you?"

"In the context of the crime, perhaps—"

"But Oren Watt is no genius, is he?"

Koozeman's forehead was filmed with sweat. And now, not wanting to lose the momentum of a hit-and-run, she went off in search of Charles Butler. She had a few questions for him, too.

"The scar? Quinn told you about that?"

"He says you did it."

Charles took Mallory by the arm and led her to the only corner of the room unpopulated by tickets or patrons.

"I'll tell you some other time, all right? Here," he said, presenting her with a red ticket. "A souvenir."

Mallory looked down at her ticket. "I can't believe you paid good money for this."

"I didn't. Koozeman would never insult me that way. He gave me an obscene discount. I think he wants to cultivate me for the A list. I hope you like it. Dean Starr's idea for this one was an elephant museum. His plan was to reenact all the elephant jokes with stuffed elephants. The real thing. Only dead."

"Charles."

"Oh, lighten up. It's only a joke."

"So, that wasn't really one of his numbers."

"Oh, yes it was—one of his best."

She smiled at him. It was one of those rare smiles, not meant to convey anything threatening or sinister, but only the pleasure of the moment. And to think he had bought that pleasure with an elephant joke.

Then the moment was over, the smile was gone. "Quinn thinks these tickets were Koozeman's idea."

"Well, that would only fit if it was a joke. He's always been a man of extremes. But he—"

"Maybe it was a joke. I'll bet you even money that Koozeman was surprised when some of the tickets actually sold the night of the first show."

"No bet, Mallory. I'm sure you're right. Koozeman does have an interesting sense of humor. Let me see if I can guess where you're going with this. You think Koozeman was setting up Dean Starr to look like a fool in public, am I right?''

She nodded. He continued. ''When Starr was a critic, his writing showed a lack of native intelligence. Odds are the joke would have gone over his head. So the scheme would suggest some animosity, a—''

''A falling-out among killers?''

''That's reaching, Mallory.''

''Not really. Koozeman still owns the old gallery in the East Village. He rents it out through a real estate agent. According to the agent, he put both of the galleries on the market this morning. He's planning to liquidate and run.''

''That theory won't hold up,'' said Charles. ''He'd be running very slow, given the current real estate market.''

''He's greedy. He wants to leave, but he can't let go of the money on the hoof. The tickets are worth money, but only if he sells them fast. It all hangs on money, the old murders and the new one.''

She seemed so comfortable inside of Koozeman's skin, it seemed a shame to point out the obvious flaw in her logic, which was also the flaw in Mallory. ''You always force everything to a money motive. And I blame this on your father. That was his all-time favorite, wasn't it? But twelve years ago, most people just looked at the evidence of butchery and said, 'Psycho.' ''

''Charles, twelve years ago, *Quinn* didn't buy the psycho theory. Makes you wonder, doesn't it?''

As J. L. Quinn approached them, Mallory turned and glided away. The critic stopped and watched her back for a moment. Then he smiled at Charles. ''She asked you about the scar?''

''Yes, but I put her off.''

''You must tell me how you did that. I've never met anyone more tenacious than Mallory.''

''It's an old magic trick.'' Charles pulled a coin from his pocket, displayed it in his spread hand, and then made a fist. "You do it with distraction, replacing one thing with another." When he opened his fist again, the coin had become a twenty-dollar bill.

"I'm in your debt, Charles."

"Good. Perhaps you could explain something to me. I understand you think the tickets were Koozeman's idea. I like that theory. It suits Koozeman. But it doesn't explain why people are actually *buying* the tickets. They're all grown-ups. Not a four-year-old in the pack."

While they discussed the big production of the little tickets, Charles took slower, more careful measurements of the man who might be stalking Mallory. Jamie Quinn was a cool one, and always had been. Charming manners and eyes that chilled. As Quinn had once instructed him in the art of fencing as a child, he now guided Charles Butler through the unfathomable.

"So, it's just business? If you don't have the talent of an artist, you can make do with the talent of a businessman. Close?"

"Yes, Charles, it's very close." Quinn pulled a pack of cigarettes from his pocket. "But why not carry it just a bit further?"

"Somebody makes it, somebody else sells it, and some other somebody buys it."

"Yes, go on." Quinn lit his cigarette, disregarding the laws against smoking in public buildings.

"So the sellers and the buyers are cutting out the middleman. They're cutting out the artists."

"And so a new order replaces the old, entrepreneurial talent supersedes artistic talent. Superb reasoning, Charles, as always. My compliments."

The hidden door in the wall opened a crack, and a hand deposited a standing ashtray on the floor next to Quinn. The door had closed again before Quinn looked down at the ashtray. He seemed to take its presence for granted as he deposited an ash. So Quinn knew about the door and never thought it worth mentioning to Mallory.

"If this movement ever caught on, what would happen to the real artists?"

"You mean," Quinn corrected, "the artists of the old order."

Charles sensed that roads of deep feeling and roads of conversation were merging here. Perhaps in Quinn's mind the farce was already a sad *fait accompli.*

"Some will drown and some will be absorbed," said Quinn. "Others will become accountants, perceiving accountancy as a related field. And it is."

"Is that woman sucking on a rat?"

"Yes."

The performance artist nibbled on the rat's ear, basking for three seconds in J. L. Quinn's glance as he turned around to confirm that she was indeed sucking vermin. Then the performance artist jammed the rat back into her sleeve and hoped it would suffocate. Nasty creature. It gave her the creeps.

She turned her attention back to the blind portrait artist. He had misplaced his white-tipped cane and was currently at her mercy in his quest for directions to a drink. He was a sour man, not at all the cheerful cliché she had anticipated.

"I think it's so brave of you to go into portraiture without being able to see the model." She stretched out one foot to nudge his fallen cane against the wall. "It's a new frontier, isn't it? I mean, working with color you can't even—"

"Could you point me toward the bar?" His voice was plaintive, whining.

"I give you so much credit for being blind."

"Being blind is a pain in the ass. Could you—"

"And all that corporate grant money. I was wondering how you pulled that off. I had a double mastectomy. Do you think I could use that as a—"

"Point me toward the bar, you moron."

She obligingly turned him around and gave him a push in the direction of a blank wall, and the blind portrait artist promptly smashed into it.

Koozeman leaned against the back wall, eyes trance-gazing on the line of Mallory's cheek. His mind was completing a pratfall that had begun twelve years ago. If she turned now, if she saw what she had done to him.

He took his seat on the platform. A woman was standing before his chair, inquiring about a ticket.

"What? Number fourteen? Just a moment." Koozeman squinted at the sheet of paper in his hand and simultaneously appraised the value of the diamond bracelet on the woman's arm. "Oh, yes, fourteen. Mr. Starr's idea for that one is a big red wheel a quarter mile across. It's being airlifted by a blimp, you see? And it's absolutely useless because it has no reason to be there, but there it is."

Off to one side, Mallory suddenly appeared. She was watching him sweat. Now she came closer, walking slow. What beautiful green eyes, eyes of an assassin. A muscle in his chest constricted. Her voice was soft in the mode of casual conversation.

"I understand you still write art reviews. Charles gives you a lot of credit for never reviewing your own stable of artists."

"I try not to be obvious."

"Now that artist who died with Aubry Gilette—Peter Ariel? Before Ariel was one of your artists, you trashed his work in a review. I read it. Pretty brutal stuff."

"Peter's work improved considerably over the next season."

"Then it's lucky you didn't kill him earlier."

"What?"

"Quinn tells me your reviews were better at killing emerging talent than nurturing it. I suppose it's wise to stick with what you know best—the butchery."

And now she looked down at her empty hand. She turned around, head bowed, searching the ground for something lost. She slowly walked away from him, her eyes scanning the floorboards.

Sweating profusely, Koozeman rose from his chair and walked around to the back of the platform. He pressed his hand to a place on the wall, and the hidden door swung open.

A minute after he had closed the door behind him, two muffled, angry voices were bleeding through the wall.

Mallory kept her eyes to the floor, looking everywhere for the lost red ticket, her gift from Charles. He would be hurt if he thought it meant so little to her that she could lose it so easily. Though this was true.

She drifted near a small cluster of people and glanced up to see a blind man delivering a lecture to a stone pillar, as the surrounding people, including Charles, politely watched on.

"You're showing your ignorance, Mr. Butler," said the blind man to the pillar. "Sabra was overrated. Women will always hold an auxiliary place in the art world. They haven't sufficient power of personality to create meaningful work."

Mallory backed up a few steps to the spot where she had seen a dead fly. She scooped it up and pitched it into the blind man's wineglass and continued scanning the floor for her lost ticket.

The small group surrounding the blind man wondered, each one, if it might be rude or, worse, politically incorrect to mention the dead bug in his glass. Wouldn't that call attention to his blindness?

Ah, too late.

A small group of prospective ticket buyers had collected around the chair on the platform. Koozeman was unresponsive to any of their questions. He had a red ticket in

his teeth, and the number was just visible. When the matron from Ridgewood, New Jersey, consulted the sheets
in Koozeman's lap, she found the line giving the artist's
idea for that number. The original description had been
a reconstruction of elephant jokes, using dead elephants.
How amusing. All but the heavily underscored word
"dead" had been crossed out with the line of a pen.

Dead?

She stared into Avril Koozeman's unblinking eyes for
a full minute more. Then her own eyes drifted down to
the small spot of blood on his chest, and she began to
shriek. Four gallery boys converged upon her with the
mistaken idea that she had run out of wine.

Her hands fluttered, and she nearly dropped her glass.
She turned in time to see a young blond girl disappear
into a solid white wall. The matron put her glass on the
floor, and then she put herself down beside it.

Behind the wall, Mallory ran down a narrow corridor and
collided with a gallery boy, knocking him to the floor.
"Did anyone come this way?"

"No, ma'am." On hands and knees he scrambled after
a rolling wine bottle. "I didn't see anybody."

"Could anyone have gotten past you?"

"I don't know, ma'am." He got to his feet and slapped
at the dust on his black pants. "I just came back from
the main room." He was staring at the wine bottle in his
hand. "Damn, the label is torn."

Mallory turned back the way she had come. With the
brightness of the gallery behind the seamless door, one
shining point of light stood out from the rough boards.
She put her eye to the pinhole. It gave her a view of
gallery patrons gathered near the wall.

"This hole?" she prompted the boy, who had come to
stand beside her.

"The peephole. Yes, ma'am, that's so we don't open

the door and jostle a wineglass in someone's hand. You could get fired for that."

She reentered the main gallery and grabbed a cellular phone from the hand of a collector, disconnecting his call and giving curt instructions to the operator. As she came closer to Koozeman's body, she noticed the ticket number was forty-four. Her lost ticket.

Koozeman left the gallery in a zippered body bag. Heller and his forensic team stood with Jack Coffey and Mallory at the far end of the room.

"Well," said Heller, "the wound is from the front. That usually means it's someone the victim knew, but under these circumstances, anyone could have gotten close enough to kill him."

Charles Butler joined them. "Actually it could—"

Mallory took his arm and walked him away. "Charles is a little drunk," she said over one shoulder. "I'll be right back."

"I'm not drunk, and you know it. I was just going—"

"You were going to tell them about the door in the wall. I don't want you to do that."

"But you know it could have been Oren Watt."

"No, Charles. It couldn't. Don't muddy up the water, okay? I want you to go home now. It's going to take a few hours to clean up loose ends and do paperwork."

"But you must—"

"Good night, Charles."

This time Riker heard her coming up behind him with the tap of high heels. He turned around to the rare sight of his partner stalking across the roof in the soft rustle of black silk. An ancient schoolboy's drill of lines crowded his mind with images of the tiger "burning bright in the forests of the night."

He smiled. "Mallory, I wish I'd memorized more poetry when I was in school. 'Dynamite' just doesn't do you justice.''

She ignored him, letting his words go by with no nod or thank-you. He knew she distrusted every compliment on her beauty. If only Markowitz had found Kathy the child before the damage was done. What twisted thing did Mallory see when she looked into the mirror every morning?

She glanced over the edge of the roof, and quickly ducked her head back. Andrew Bliss was looking skyward in all directions.

She turned to Riker. "Quiet night?"

"A lot quieter than yours, kid. Did Coffey ream you out?"

"No, he was even sympathetic when I told him Koozeman was murdered right under my nose." She seemed almost disappointed in Coffey.

"Wait till the press gets onto this." Riker made a mental note to caution Coffey never to go easy on her again; it was costing him respect. "Too bad you're so damn photogenic. You know the newspapers are gonna run a picture."

"Maybe after Coffey sees the morning paper he'll decide to pull me off the case."

"No, I don't think so. When they turn on the heat downtown, Coffey will tell them you had a good instinct in going to the gallery. He'll hint around that you were following a lead. He knows how to work the brass and the press." But that didn't seem to cheer her up at all. "Mallory, don't worry about it. Go get some sleep."

"No, I'll take the late shift," she said. "I'm just going home to change clothes, okay?"

"Take your time, kid. Andrew's not going anywhere. Oh, he's run out of candles again. And I was right about him developing a new religion." Riker pointed down to the late edition of the newspaper lying over the rifle at his feet. "The press is off the fashion terrorist angle. Now they're calling him the messiah of Bloomingdale's. Fits nicely with the altar, doesn't it? That mannequin is really weirding me out.''

"Yeah, but think of what it's doing to Andrew."

He didn't really want to think about that. He worried about the little man on the roof below, and the slow disintegration of Andrew's body and his mind.

And what was this case doing to Mallory? "You know the FBI is gonna love the Koozeman murder. It's a bona fide serial killing, and that's where they shine—if you believe their own quotes to the press. We have to come up with our own profile to keep that idiot Cartland locked out of the case. You got any ideas?''

"Well, this killing was different," she said. "I don't think it was planned. This time it *was* the bartender's pick. We found blood traces, but the pick was too short to reach the heart. Slope thinks the assault brought on a massive coronary. When he cracked Koozeman's chest he found evidence of heart disease and a valve—''

"Hold it, Mallory. Slope did the autopsy *tonight*? How'd you get him to do that?''

"He owes me a favor."

"Slope might owe Markowitz, but he doesn't owe you anything. You're not shaking him down, are you, kid?''

Now why had he said that? Slope was the last honest man in New York City. What could she have on him? Well, maybe the scenario just fit so well with Mallory's own character.

She turned away from him. "Something happened in that gallery tonight, and it set the perp off. I told Slope I didn't have time to sit around waiting on him—I might lose another taxpayer. There was a lot of thought behind the first kill, if this one was done in anger—''

"A copycat killing?''

"No, it's the same perp.''

He bit back the impulse to argue the difference between what she knew and what she wanted to believe. It was all the same to her. She was leaving now, crossing the roof, when she turned around with one last detail. ''Oh, and now I've got Quinn on the site of three murders.''

Mallory locked her apartment door and headed for the bedroom, unzipping as she walked. After stepping out of the black sheath and stripping off the nylons, she opened a dresser drawer to stacks of expensive, but identical blue jeans. In the next drawer, her T-shirts only varied in the selection of color, and the materials of cotton and silk. Her everyday wardrobe had been designed for efficiency—no time lost in deciding what to wear. White running shoes were for daytime, black for formal wear. It had never taken her more than three minutes to dress—until tonight.

She pulled on the blue jeans, but left them unzipped. Her reason to hurry was forgotten as she stared at the candle on her bedside table.

When she was only ten, she had asked Helen Markowitz for candles, and Helen had bought her a night-light, believing the child must be afraid of the dark. Young Kathy had insisted on candles, and then Helen bought them in every color of the spectrum, and candle holders for every surface of the bedroom. When the child lay in her bed, between waking and sleeping, Helen would steal into the room and blow the flames out. And so her foster mother had become intertwined with this nightly ritual.

Now Mallory could not light one candle without thinking of her. But this candle habit had begun years before life with the Markowitzes. She had lost the origin of the ritual somewhere on the road. Why had she ever lit the candles? It had all slipped away from her.

Early on, Helen had tried to uncover her past. Forays into this area had been gentle, never pressing, but the child had only folded into herself. *Don't touch me there,* said her posture and her eyes. *It hurts*. Every memory had hurt her.

Mallory sat down on the bed and lit the candle now, as she did each night without fail. She stared into the flame, searching for a memory, yet fearing if she concentrated, it would come and catch her in the dark.

Confront your demons, the priest had counseled her when she was fourteen years old. And she had done just that. She had hunted through the halls of the private school for girls, stalking the nun. And when she had found her, she made the woman scream. The priest was startled when she told him she had only followed his advice.

She never saw Father Brenner again.

The candle had burned down some before she found Helen's old address book in the wooden box at the back of her closet. Mallory had never completed the task of clearing precious things from the old house in Brooklyn. And why should she? It was home, and it would always be there waiting for her. Home was where memories of Helen and Louis Markowitz were piled from the basement record collection to the store of school uniforms in the attic.

But in this wooden box, she had the personal things, papers which had belonged to Markowitz and might be dangerous, and small pieces of Helen—a thimble, her reading glasses. And now she held Helen's address book, a connection to all people and things past. She flipped through the pages of the *B* section, and dialed the number. She finished dressing before the third ring was answered.

"Hello," said the old priest, roused from sleep. "Hello, is anyone there?"

"It's Kathy," she said, in the presumption that he might recognize her name and voice out of all the students who had passed through the private school.

After a moment of silence, Father Brenner said, "Sister Ursula misses you. She tells me her shin still smarts on rainy days, and this reminds her to light a candle for you.''

''Why does she light the candle?''

''I believe the thrust of her prayers is that you'll be better-behaved in the future. . . . Kathy? Are you still there?''

But what do I light the candle for?

''Yes, I'm here.''

And who was Andrew praying for? The dead Aubry? There was no one in life he cared for. No parents. He'd been raised by a trust fund since birth. Who was he praying for? Or what?

''Kathy, may I tell Sister Ursula that her candles have had some good effect?''

''Tell me all the reasons for lighting the candles. What about guilt? Forgiveness for your sins?''

''No, that's the province of the confessional. What sort of sin?''

''Suppose you're a witness to murder and you never tell. Is that a mortal sin or a venial sin?''

''I'm so pleased that you remember all the buzzwords. Now, what murder did you witness, Kathy?''

''A woman. Let's say it was my mother.''

''Oh, no, let's not say it was Helen.''

''My mother before Helen. So what's the payoff if I tell, and what's the penalty if I don't?''

''That neatly sums up your childhood philosophy of 'What's in it for me?' Oh, and there was the companion tenet, 'What'll you do to me if I don't?' I believe those were your two guiding principles while you were with us.''

''So?''

''Well, the ultimate payoff is forgiveness—you won't die with a stain on your soul. But before you can be forgiven, you must confess your sin, and there must be an Act of Contrition and a devout intention never to repeat your sin, a sincere desire to change your ways.''

"Did you ever light candles when you were a kid?"

"What? Well, yes. For my father. He died many years ago when I was a boy. But I still light the candles.''

"So he won't get lost?"

"Yes, something like that. People do get lost in time, don't they? Images and memories fade. But when I was very young, I think I lit the candles so *I* would not be lost. . . . Kathy? . . . Kathy?''

She stared at the candle, transfixed by a memory of hell. And the old priest continued to call out to her across the wires of the worldly telephone company.

Andrew's eyes scanned the clouds for the hide-and-seek stars which winked on and off, appearing within holes in the overcast sky and then gone again. The night was chilly and he gathered his blankets about him, but never took his eyes from the heavens.

It was like waiting up for Santa Claus, who never showed until all the children of the house were fast asleep in their beds. He feigned sleep, lying back and closing his eyes to slits.

He had no sooner done this than he heard the sharp thwack on the roof. When he opened his eyes, three votive candles rolled out of a brown paper bag which also contained another small loaf of bread. He turned his face in time to catch the fleeting glimpse of his savior's head, a cap of moon-gold curls in flight just beyond the edge of the roof. Slowly, he crept to the retaining wall and looked over the side, afraid of what he might see.

No one there.

He knelt down to light his candles, and an hour later, he was still on his knees.

CHAPTER
6

"BUT THE HOMICIDE RATE HAS GONE DOWN."

"Well, it's an election year. The mayor won't let us drag the East River," said Riker, over the rim of his coffee cup. "Don't worry about it, Charles. We'll snag all the bodies next year and bring the stats back up."

Riker was reading Charles's magazine, which detailed the new and improved New York. "Hey, Mallory, listen to this. 'Fashionable New Yorkers *adore* the subways.' "

"They didn't print that," said Mallory.

"The hell they didn't." Riker slapped the magazine down on the kitchen table beside her plate.

Mallory set down her coffee cup and picked up the magazine. She leafed through the pages, frowning. "Why do you read this stuff, Charles?" Her tone implied that she had caught him with a porno rag and not an upscale magazine for well-to-do New Yorkers.

"I rode the subway once," said Charles, as though this were an accomplishment. "But now that I think about it, it was an abysmal experience. The train was supposed to be a local, and then it turned into an express and dropped me a mile out of my way."

Mallory leaned toward Riker. "Did Markowitz really

buy that fairy tale about Quinn showing up at the gallery late because he took the subway?''

"Not at first," said Riker. "But Quinn's private car was parked in his garage all night. The garage attendant verified that, while Markowitz kept Quinn busy. It's not like he had time to bribe the kid. And the only taxi log was for the dancer. Now if Quinn was running late, he might have taken the subway. Maybe he'd worry about a cab getting bogged down in traffic. He wouldn't want his niece to spend any time in that neighborhood alone. The subway would've been the fastest way to get there."

"Yeah, right."

"That's why *I* took the subway," said Charles. "It was urgent that I—"

"And Charles screwed up too," said Riker.

Mallory scanned the article titled "Gilette's Last Building." The unveiling of the plaza was slated for the day after tomorrow according to an interview with Emma Sue Hollaran. She closed the magazine. "Riker, what do we know about Emma Sue Hollaran?"

"I never heard of her."

"She's the chairwoman of the Public Works Committee," said Charles. "That's the group that made Andrew Bliss a respectable shoplifter."

"And she was an enemy of Gilette's," said Mallory. "I got that from Quinn."

"Waste of time," said Riker. "The old homicide wasn't a woman's crime."

"I'm a woman."

"Okay, we'll put her on the list." Riker pulled out his notebook and made a scribble of Hollaran's initials to pacify Mallory.

"Actually, I was thinking Hollaran might make a good victim. I've got two dead critics now. Maybe it's worth a stakeout." She turned the magazine facedown and smiled at Riker. "Speaking of critics, you know that scar on Quinn's face, just above the moustache? He told me Charles did that."

Now Charles had Riker's complete attention as a coffee cup hovered in midair.

"It was a fencing accident," said Charles.

Riker's cup settled to the saucer with a small crash, and Mallory's eyes were bright as she leaned forward. "You scarred him with a sword?"

"Well, it's a long story."

The detectives looked at their watches. "Give us the short version," said Mallory.

"It started with my acceptance to Harvard. I didn't want to go." No need to explain to them that he was only ten years old on the eve of his freshman year at college. "My mother asked Jamie Quinn to talk to me because he had just finished his junior year, and she thought he might be able to convince me that I would like Harvard."

Young Jamie Quinn had immediately understood the problem of a child leaving the shelter of a school for the unreasonably gifted to matriculate among tall people of normal intelligence.

"He gave me a fencing lesson. He thought it might be a good sport for me. He said it would give me confidence." And it might prepare him for the more subtle combat of navigating among the older students as a child with freakish intelligence which exceeded all known scores.

"So we went out on the terrace of his parents' apartment. He gave me the sword he had used as a child. But he had noticed the rust on the old mask and insisted that I wear his new one."

Mallory had done some fencing in college, but Charles was certain that Riker had not, and so he described the mask as a protruding steel mesh that allowed for peripheral vision. "It fits on the head like a protective cage. It

has a padding around the face, and there's a biblike padding at the throat to—"

"Could we cut to the good part, Charles?" Riker
poured another cup of coffee, and looked at his watch
again. "I'm gettin' old here."

"Yes, of course, sorry. It was a freak accident—in
fact, a combination of accidents. My saber was at least
ten years old and it had—"

"Sabers? Like the cavalry?" Riker cut a Z in the air.

"Yes. Well, no. I do have an antique set of cavalry
sabers, but the saber you fence with is more of a vestigial
cavalry sword. There's no cutting point, no cutting edge.
It's a tapered rod of steel with a blunted metal bulb at
the point. Unless you're using a sword that's electrified
for competition, and then, of course, the tip is quite—"
He noticed Riker's eyes glazing over.

"Sorry. It doesn't look much like the old cavalry saber, but the motions are the same. You make the slice
and the stab, just as you would if you had a cutting edge
and point. So I was using Quinn's old saber. The sword
seemed to be in good condition, but you can't detect
metal fatigue with the naked eye. He was going to give
it to me as a gift, so I could—"

Riker made a rolling motion with his hand in an attempt to speed up the story.

"The tip of my sword broke off while we were fencing, and it made a jagged point of the blade. It was my
first time with a saber in my hand. I was rather clumsy.
I didn't realize the blunt bulb was gone. I made a wild
swing, and my sword went through the mask where the
metal had rusted, and Quinn was cut."

"I'll bet he was pissed off," said Riker.

"Actually, no. After the doctor patched him up, I tried
to apologize. He just waved me off. Said he was honored
and rather liked the scar. Then he thanked me for it. He
really is the quintessential gentleman."

"But you were just a kid," said Mallory. "He must not be a very good swordsman."

"He was superb, an Olympian. He was only nineteen years old when he won his first gold medal."

"But if a little kid can beat him," said Mallory, "he must have a weakness, an opening."

"None that I'm aware of. And I didn't beat him. I made a wild swing." He turned to Riker. "You see, after a point is scored, you break apart. But I didn't realize that, and I made the swing when he wasn't expecting it."

"So he was unprepared for the unexpected, and he's well mannered to a fault." Mallory turned to Riker. "I've got fifty dollars says I can beat him."

"With a saber?" Charles stared at her as though she had proposed a flight to the moon. "You can't be serious. A few fencing lessons at college do not prepare you to beat an Olympic champion. You can't possibly win against him."

"If you want to bet against her, I'll take a piece of it," said Riker. "Is a marker okay, Charles? I'm short this week."

"Riker, I won't take your money. She can't possibly win."

"Then why not bet with him, Charles? You don't do well at poker. I'd think you'd want to win at something."

"This is ludicrous. Quinn's been a swordsman all his life. You fenced for one semester at school."

"She's half his age," said Riker, "and she fights dirty. I think she can do him."

Riker's cellular phone beeped. He extended the antenna, and as he listened attentively, he made a fist. When he ended the conversation and folded his phone away, he turned to Mallory. "That was an old friend of mine in Blakely's office. I hope you got what you wanted off Koozeman's computer last night. Blakely's boys impounded it, and they got all of Koozeman's books."

"How's the chief going to justify that?"

"He won't have to. We're officially off the case. Blakely's turning it over to a third-rate dick, and the FBI offered to assist. They're giving a joint press interview right now. Special Agent Cartland is playing it as a stranger kill."

"A what?"

Riker drained his cup. "A random murder, Charles. The perp doesn't know the victim. It's the crime where the FBI really shines. Cartland's a local PR jerk, but their team at Quantico is first-rate."

"But it's clearly not a stranger kill," said Charles. "How could Coffey go along with that?"

"He didn't, and that's the worst of it," said Riker. "Coffey wouldn't play along with Blakely, and now he's going down. The paperwork is in the machine for a demotion on grounds of insubordination and disobeying a direct order. There's another list of bogus charges that might force him out of the department."

"Blakely will never make the charges stick," said Mallory. "Coffey goes by the book." And by her tone, Charles knew she considered that one of Jack Coffey's flaws.

"Blakely can do whatever he wants with Coffey." Riker's voice was all resignation. "Internal Affairs hasn't gotten any smarter since the Dowd fiasco. Coffey's going down, kid. Count on it."

"No. I can fix this. A lot of the people on Koozeman's A list were in city government, the mayor, the ex-commissioner, the lieutenant governor—"

"No you don't, kid. You don't go near any of those people. You think you've got more power than you have. You can't blackmail the politicos to keep them in line, not even to save Coffey's tail. The job is to keep the law, not to break it."

"The ends don't justify the means? You're beginning to sound like Charles."

Charles sat between them, sincerely not knowing whether or not to take offense.

"I was hoping one day *you* would sound more like Charles. I don't expect that anymore." Riker's mood was darkening. "Don't go near Blakely. He'll get you. Don't think of him as just one old bastard, think of the whole machine. It's an ancient thing. You've got the talent, but you're just not old enough to be that mean and dirty. Markowitz would tell you the same. You can't save Coffey. He's dead meat. Don't go down with him."

"Riker, I thought you liked Coffey in your own twisted way."

"I got a lot of respect for the guy. But you're the one who needs looking after. You think you're such a hotshot. You don't ever go after a cop—you got that?—and never a top cop. You think you've got your own power base, but you—"

"I do—in spades. Between the data off Koozeman's computer and Markowitz's old case notes, I can hurt Blakely."

"Don't ever tip your hand, Mallory. Don't ever let on you've got those notes. What the old man put down in writing is court evidence. Don't make Blakely feel threatened."

"Markowitz would have covered Coffey's tail."

"Yeah, he would've. But you're no Markowitz, kid. He used finesse you use a hammer."

Mallory did not stand at attention before the chief's desk. Nor did she wait for an invitation to be seated, a courtesy Blakely rarely granted to those with the rank of sergeant. Uninvited, she settled deep in the chair opposite his desk and crossed her legs. He did not look up. The only clue that she had annoyed him was in the crumple of the paper in his hands.

"I want you to reconsider taking us off the Dean Starr case." Her tone of voice did not frame this as a request.

The sheet of paper he had been reading was now a crushed ball flying into the wastebasket. "No deal. Now get out of here, or I might forget how much I liked your old man."

She sat well back in the chair and gave no signs of going anywhere.

"Move your ass, Detective, or you'll be going down with your boss."

She was smiling when she said, "I don't think so, Blakely."

"You know the drill, Mallory. You will address me as *sir* or *Chief*, and those are all the choices you get."

"Makes you wonder what I've got on you, doesn't it? But I'm not here to talk about how you got your job."

"Careful, Mallory."

"I bet you're wishing the old police commissioner had been more careful about the way he spent his payoff money—he's a senator now, isn't he? That must put a lot of pressure on you."

"Mallory, don't push your luck with me."

"Milking the payoff from a mob bodega was really ballsy, Blakely. I liked that a lot. It made me wonder how much hard evidence you had on that operation to make them come across with the money."

He was rising from his chair.

"I did a little digging in Markowitz's personal notes," she said. "I came across an interview with a dealer who did business out of that same bodega."

He sat down again, slowly. She continued. "Quite a busy place, between the drug deals and the racketeering. Their delivery boys covered three states, didn't they?"

His chair squeaked as he swiveled around to face the window. "So what're you planning to do with all this crap, Mallory?" His fingers drummed softly on the red upholstery.

"Nothing. I'm sure the feds would like to know you shielded an interstate operation—but I don't owe the FBI any favors, do I?'' She looked down at her red fingernails. ''So that's old business. Right now, I'd rather discuss Lieutenant Coffey. You see, when you climb up his back, he climbs up mine. And I really hate that. So you will back off, won't you? *Sir?* I think you can trust Coffey to assign his own detectives.''

''Anything else?''

She knew his voice was too calm. But he was not fighting back, so it was all going well, wasn't it? ''You attached a lot of charges and a bad review to Coffey's record—you might want to rethink that. Markowitz always said, 'What goes around comes around.' ''

She could hear the old man saying that now, but Markowitz was saying it to *her*—a prickling warning from the back of her mind.

Blakely was silent. She wished she could see his face. He continued to stare out the window, and the only sound in the room was the soft drumming of his fat fingertips on the red leather arm of his chair.

Well, what had she expected, a signed contract? Their deal was concluded. There was nothing left to say. But she stood up with the uneasy feeling of unfinished business.

Mallory was across the room and through the door before she heard the squeak of Blakely's chair swiveling around again.

Riker sat at the desk in Mallory's private office, holding a telephone to his ear, and making an occasional scribble with his pen.

Charles sat down in the metal chair opposite the desk. He hated the decor of this room and wished Mallory would let him furnish her office with a few Oriental rugs and perhaps a desk from the last century. But he knew she was more comfortable in this atmosphere of stark simplicity.

Riker was speaking into the telephone. ''What's Blakely doing with the inventory sheet on Markowitz's house?'' And now he listened and his face was clouding over with anger. "Robin Duffy was the family lawyer. He got a ruling on the old man's personal papers. All the personal papers belong to the estate and the estate belongs to Mallory. There's no way he's gonna get any of it.'' Now he covered the mouthpiece with one hand and spoke to Charles. "You got a number for Duffy?''

"He's on a fishing trip in Canada. He's due back in a few days, but I suppose I could track him down if it's important.''

Riker shook his head and spoke into the mouthpiece again. "Duffy's out of town. I'll have him call Blakely's office when he gets back. . . . Right.''

Riker put the receiver back on the cradle of Mallory's state-of-the-art phone center, which spread tentacles to a fax machine, a recording device, and other equipment Charles could not readily identify.

Riker was not a happy man. "That was Coffey. He says Blakely wants all of Markowitz's personal notes, and he's doing paperwork with the DA's office right this minute. Claims they relate to an ongoing case. Now I've got a charge on my record because my name is on the inventory for the old house in Brooklyn. Blakely claims I improperly handled department property.''

"This sounds serious. Let me track down Robin. He can probably fix this with a phone call.''

"A phone call from God wouldn't fix this—not unless He's got some good dirt on Blakely.''

The old Koozeman Gallery in the East Village was on a narrow street in Alphabet City, and just off a lettered avenue which had boasted ten predators to every taxpayer in the days when Koozeman ran this gallery. On foot, artists and hookers had passed through this neighborhood they called home. Yuppies had only come by cab and limo, reveling in dangerous chic. That trend had passed, and the galleries abandoned this section of town, moving to the safer chic of SoHo and its better class of criminals.

The storefronts had For Rent signs on the doors. Mallory stared at the dark windows, up and down the street. This was a good place to do murder with no witnesses. But even twelve years ago, the artist and the dancer could have screamed all through the night and no one would have come to their aid. Such sounds were common then—like crickets to country people.

She never turned to look directly at him, but she was aware of the thin man walking toward her at a cautious pace. As he slowed his steps, she realized she was his mark. The body movement she detected in peripheral was twitched and jazzed. A crackhead. Closer now. He must be thinking this was his lucky day—a woman alone on the street, and the nearest branch of authority was the Hell's Angels clubhouse on the next block. Lucky day for the junkie—no waiting in line to pick off the suckers at the cash machines. Would he rush her? No. He would wait for the fear response, and then use it to his advantage. Closer now, all excited, he could probably taste her money, feel it gliding into his veins or up his nose in a cloud of white dust.

Mallory continued to stare at the building across the street, never even turning to look at him, and that made him a little crazy. He had to know she was aware of him. He circled around in front of her, and now she saw the perp in all his sick glory, eyes runny with infection, sores on his face. He smelled rank from soiling his clothes with his vomit and his bowels.

Did she want to touch that?

No way.

Hands behind her back, she worked on a pair of kidskin gloves.

He was grinning at her, hovering. One hand was in the pocket of his jacket, and that would be where he kept the razor or the knife. There was not enough bulk for a gun.

The hand was pulling slowly from the jacket pocket. But now the junkie was all surprise as Mallory's arm flashed out, and his straight razor went flying into the gutter. He was even more surprised to find himself kneeling on the sidewalk, feeling the pain in his testicles and staring at the hard steel of a large gun forced into his mouth. The gun barrel was set between an old man's rotting rows of teeth, but he was just twenty-one, if that.

A car with NYPD markings was gliding silently to the curb alongside her. She never took her eyes off the terrified thin man, not even when she heard Heller's deep voice.

"Mallory, you know the rules. If you can't play nicely with the animals, you can't play with them at all."

After the backup unit arrived and the debris of the mugger was cleared off the street and shoved roughly into the back of the car, Mallory and Heller were alone again in front of the deserted gallery.

"Poor bastards," said Heller, staring after the departing vehicle. "Their car is gonna smell like a junkie for the rest of their shift."

He turned around now to see Mallory working a wire in the lock of the gallery door. It opened under her hand. Heller took her by one arm and pulled her away from the door. He reached around the wooden frame to depress the lock button in the knob, and then pulled the door shut. Mallory only stared at him as though he had lost his mind.

"Markowitz never taught you that," said Heller. "I gather you don't have a warrant."

"I'm not supposed to be working the old case. How am I going to get a warrant?"

Heller said nothing. He only looked at her the way Markowitz did when he was waiting on a better explanation for what she'd done wrong this time.

"I'm not violating anybody's civil rights. Before he died, Koozeman put the gallery up for sale. If you want,

I'll go find the real estate agent. But that will take time. This is—''

"Do that. I'll wait."

"Heller—''

"Get the key from the real estate agent. Do it right."

He was a solid man, a large bear of a man. Bears did not back down. Why should they?

She returned to the gallery twenty minutes later, her wallet lighter by one fifty-dollar deposit, and she was holding the legal key. Heller was waiting by the door, comfortable in his slouch and his cigar.

"It was a sad business," said Heller as they legally passed through the door and into the small reception area. He flicked on the wall switch. A panel of fluorescent bulbs made buzzing noises overhead as the lights flooded the main room of the deserted gallery.

"We found the artist and the dancer over there." He pointed toward the center of the back wall.

Mallory reached into her tote and pulled out a floor plan. According to the crime-scene diagram, this part of the gallery was sixty feet in length, and twenty-five feet wide. Beyond the side wall was another five feet of storage space running the length of the room.

"We were a long time recovering the body parts," said Heller. "The heads were spiked on the rods, and the bodies were wrapped with wire." Heller opened his briefcase and folded back papers until he found the plastic slide sheet. He pointed at the first slide pocket. "Now this is what Ariel's work looked like before he died and became part of it. That hunk of metal used to be a car."

She held the slide sheet up to the ceiling light and looked at the rusted metal sculpture with two iron rods shooting straight up from the center of the car, which had been crushed and compressed to the size and shape of a steamer trunk.

Now she walked the length of the side wall, until she found the gouge in the baseboard. She beckoned Heller to join her. "Wait here. I'll be right back." She walked to the rear storage area door, counting her paces, and passed into the narrow hallway which ran alongside the gallery space. Just as Charles had done, she entered the gallery through the hidden door in the wall behind Heller's back. She tapped him on the shoulder, and he whirled around to face her.

"Jesus! Don't you *ever*—" Suddenly dumbstruck, Heller stared at the open door. His eyes traveled over the interior side of wood slats. "I can't believe this. I checked out the storage area. I must have taken this for part of the wall."

"Not your fault. The door is a perfect job. No seams, no knobs." She closed it again, and pushed on the edge. It popped open. "Pressure lock. You'd have to know just where to press. See the nick in the baseboard? Koozeman has the same door in his new gallery in SoHo."

Heller bent down to see the small gouge in the board at the base of the wall. "So, the killer might have hidden back there—"

"And come out of the wall to join the crowd before the uniforms showed up to chase them out."

"Shit, it could've happened that way. Markowitz figured the perp cleaned himself up and left the gallery. We found blood in the bathroom-sink traps. But I guess he could have stayed."

Mallory pressed her floor plan to the wall and penciled in the site of the door. "That night, did Markowitz figure the girl for the primary target?"

"No, not at first," said Heller. "But we got the prelim from the ME before I finished reconstructing the scene. I fixed Aubry's blood type to the victim who took the most abuse."

"You did a reconstruction?" Damn Markowitz and his tabloid paranoia. How many pieces of this case was she going to find squirreled away in someone else's mind, someone else's notes? "I thought the reporters botched all the physical evidence."

"Oh, those bastards." Heller's words were hard, his head was shaking—unforgiving after all these years. "They tracked blood everywhere. The reconstruction took days, and days—and then the jerk confesses. All that work for nothing."

"Did you work up any of the hair and fiber evidence? I've got all these bags and no—"

"No. The money for the case dried up after Watt confessed. There was no budget to do any tests. It would have been a waste of time anyway. This was a public place—people coming and going. There's no way to tell when materials were left on the scene. So hair and fiber evidence wouldn't have held up in court, even if we could've sorted out what belonged to the reporters. Same problem with latent prints."

"But Markowitz the detail freak, he talked you into running tests off the books, right?"

"Sorry, Mallory, it didn't happen that way. I gave him what I could on a cursory examination of the bodies—colors of stray hairs and some speculation on the clothing fibers. That was it. It's no more good to you now than it was to the old man."

"Go back to the early part of the night." Mallory was looking at the entrance to the gallery. "Watt delivered the pizza and went back to the restaurant to collect his check. After he left the gallery, Peter Ariel would've locked up behind him. Didn't you figure the next one through that door had a key?"

"No. Dr. Slope said the Ariel kid was really flying on dope. I don't know that he would've bothered to lock the door."

Mallory pulled out a notebook and flipped through the pages of her father's scrawl. "Slope says the killer did the artist first, then spent some time torturing the girl." She found the page she was looking for. Markowitz had underscored the word "torture" and added three question marks. "Did Markowitz have a problem with that?"

"Well, yeah, he did. The blows were pretty vicious, like the perp really wanted to kill her with every stroke. It wasn't so much a drawn-out kill, not like torture. It was more like a botched kill. Aubry just wouldn't lie down and die for the bastard. She was fighting to stay alive. That was one thing that really got to Markowitz, that and her freckles—just a light sprinkle across her nose. I think the freckles destroyed him."

Mallory held out the notebook and pointed to the word "cavalry" followed by a question mark. "Any idea what that means?"

Heller smiled. "Markowitz thought the kid was probably raised on old cowboy movies. So Aubry was holding on, waiting for the bugle call and the cavalry charge to come over the hill and save her."

"This is what Koozeman said." She read from the notebook. " 'The gallery was full of reporters when I arrived.' You know, Koozeman could've come out from behind the wall when the room was packed with sightseers. The reporters would have been at the back of the room, looking at the bodies."

Heller shook his head. "That scenario works just as well for Oren Watt, and he was definitely on the scene that night. We took his footprints. He had blood on his shoes."

"Everybody had blood on their shoes. The pizza place was six blocks west of the gallery, and Watt's apartment was three blocks east. After he picked up his check, he probably killed an hour scoring some dope and then walked home this way. All that noise, all those people. Of course he was going to go inside." She pulled a diagram from her tote bag. "Markowitz always had a problem with the time frame. Can you remember how you reconstructed the scene?"

"Like I'm ever gonna forget. I still have dreams about

this one.'' Heller walked to the back of the room and hunkered down to inspect the floor. Mallory knelt beside him. He took out a penlight and aimed the beam low. ''Look close and you can still see the axe marks in the wood. This is where the artist's body was cut. The wounds were all postmortem. There was blood, but not the same kind of flow you'd get if the heart was still pumping. Splatter patterns and blood type show all the work on the artist was done here. The girl was killed at the front of the room, and her body was dragged back here and laid three feet away from the artist.''

Heller moved over to his right and swept the dusty floor with his hand. His penlight picked up the indentations in the wood. ''These are the marks for the dancer. Dismemberment was done after death. Small mercy, huh? There was blood trapped between the floorboards to separate her site from the artist's. I tracked blood from the artist's body to the site of the first strike on the dancer.''

Mallory marked the axe scars on her diagram. She pulled out the bundle of floor photographs and riffled through them. The boards were awash in blood pools, drops, smears and tracks. ''And you found tracks? How?''

''Not tracks—drops of blood from the weapon and the first splatter pattern. I followed a line of drops from the artist's body to the first attack on the girl. The reporter's tracks passed through it and smeared it here and there, but it was still a definite line. It was Peter Ariel's blood. That's how I figured the perp was working on the artist's body when the dancer came into the room. Then he went for her and the blood dripped from the axe as he was crossing the floor.''

Heller stood up and moved to the center of the long room, with Mallory following. ''The drops were elongated, so the perp was moving fast. I figured the first blow was struck here. It was a hard blow to the neck to bring her down. She began to crawl.'' He walked closer to the front of the gallery. "Bloody handprints toward the door. Then she was herded back." He walked toward the center of the long room. "Here's the spot where she made it to her feet, God knows how, but there were two partial prints matching her shoes. And then she was brought down again."

Mallory was marking the strikes, when Heller took the floor plan and the pencil from her hand. "I'm gonna teach you a trade secret, kid." He made lines on her diagram. "This is how I knew how many times he cut her before she died. I never even had to look at the bodies. Slope agreed with my figures."

Now her diagram showed a march of lines moving across the floor and then changing direction and moving back. He handed it back to her. "Every time the attacker pulled the weapon back for another strike, he sent out a flying line of blood from the axe to the floor and part of the wall. That's how you can tell where he was, what direction he was walking in. So here, you can see him walking along beside her, making the blows while she crawled." He pointed to a change of line angles. This is where Aubry turned and made one last try for the door."

He walked back to the front of the room. "She's crawling toward the door, and this is where the killer made the fatal strike. This is where I found skull fragments in between the floorboards. And then the body was dragged to the back of the room."

Mallory walked back to the site of the first blow. "It doesn't work. She didn't have to come this far into the room to see what was happening to Peter Ariel's body. She would have turned to run long before she got this far."

"She could have fainted or frozen with the—"

"Aubry was no helpless bimbo. She was a dancer with good reflexes. She was young with good eyes. She wanted to live just like the rest of us. Maybe there were two killers."

"Markowitz didn't figure it that way." Heller's tone was skeptical.

"How do you know he didn't? The old man was always holding out. He held out on everybody else—why not you? But this time, he played it too cagey. Everybody got information on a need-to-know basis. If he'd laid open all the problems with the case, Quinn might have told him about the ritual of whitewashing the gallery walls and waxing the floor the day before every opening. Peter Ariel's show was scheduled for the next day."

"Oh, Christ, all the—"

"Yeah, if you'd only known, you might've gotten latent prints and worked up the hair and fiber evidence. But I'm sure Koozeman never volunteered that information. And he never mentioned the door in the wall either. Not your fault, Heller."

But Heller didn't agree. He stared up at the ceiling, shaking his head, his expression wafting between anger and frustration. "So, what now, Mallory?"

"Well, Starr and Koozeman would make a neat party of two."

"So you're trying their murders together with a revenge motive?"

"Maybe. When Dean Starr was a critic, he gave Peter Ariel two rave reviews. Suppose Koozeman wasn't the only one who owned a piece of the artist?"

"I can still run the old physical evidence. Would that help you any?"

"I can't have any paperwork on a case I'm not supposed to be working."

"I'll do it off the books. I can bury the cost in other investigations if I spread it around."

"You won't let me break into an empty gallery, but you'll risk your job to work evidence off the books?"

"If I break the rules, I've got a good reason. You break rules because you can get away with it. It's a game to you. Time to grow up, kid."

"Heller, I don't want any—"

"Grow up or fake it. At least try to make it look like Markowitz raised you right."

Blakely parked his car on Mott Street and fumbled with the childproof cap on a small medicine bottle. He dry-swallowed a pill as he looked down the street to the line of three limos along the curb. Young men, wearing dark suits and dark glasses, walked between the cars, carrying coffee containers and slips of paper. Blakely walked up to the second limousine in the parked parade. A conversation passed between a man wearing driver's gloves and his passenger beyond the crack of the tinted-glass window. The car's rear door opened and Blakely bent down to shift his bulk into the spacious compartment. He sat down beside an old man with yellow teeth and listless black eyes. The air smelled like a sickroom.

After a few minutes of Blakely sweating through his story, the old man laughed.

"She made you shit in your pants, Blakely." And now the laughing man began to cough into a handkerchief, and small spots of red bled through the white linen. The handkerchief disappeared into a massive hand with bulging blue arteries, crepe flesh and a vestige of power in the clenched fist. "Markowitz did a good job raising his kid. You know, I always liked that old bastard. I even turned out for his damn funeral."

"She knows all about the bodega," said Blakely, listening to the desperate notes in his own voice. "She could cause us both a lot of trouble."

"But she won't. Sounds like she has Markowitz's style. You know, if her old man had been for sale, he would have been chief of detectives, not you."

"But you did a deal with him on the—"

"Not what you're thinking, Blakely. It wasn't a pay-off. And why doesn't it surprise me that you don't know the details? What *do* you know about what's going on with your own department?''

''I know he backed off the—''

''Markowitz didn't care how you bought your job. He didn't have any hard evidence, but I didn't know that then. He ran a bluff on me, and it worked. But it was never about money. He only wanted that freak who was killing all the winos, and you wouldn't give him the manpower to do the job. So he and I, we did a trade. I put a small army on the street for three days and three nights. One of my boys delivered the freak to Special Crimes, and without a scratch on him. A nice clean job, and the deal was done.''

''He might not have had any evidence then, but the kid has something now.''

''So? She won't use it. Her old man made a deal, and his kid will honor it.''

''Mallory doesn't have a sense of honor. She's a loose cannon. I know her.''

''*She's* a loose cannon? I think you're confused, Blakely. Look at you. You're sweating like a pig. You're a man on the edge of a heart attack. You come to me to put out your fires? You have no control over your own people, and you know why? They don't fear you.''

''It's more than the bodega connection. She's going back into the Oren Watt case.''

''What's that to me?''

''Senator Berman collected the ghoul art. He's one of the—''

''The senator? That clown is going down in the next election. *You* might owe him something, I don't. I'm cutting my losses on him.'' He began to cough again. ''I'm thinking of getting out of politics. It's not like the old days. If you want to buy a politician, you have to outbid all those special interest groups. There's so many of them. They grow like cancer. This town is going downhill, you know that? It's one big flea market of souls for sale.''

The old Mafia don turned his head sharply, to stare out the window, and what he saw made him angry. Then the anger resolved itself into a sigh of resignation. ''Blakely, do you ever think about retirement? No? Perhaps you should. You see that?'' He pointed one palsied finger at the window.

Across the street a young Hispanic, walking at a leisurely pace, led an entourage of men all decked out in fur coats, though the day was mild. The sun glinted off the gold jewelry at the young men's throats and the diamonds at their ears.

''Crazy bastards,'' said the old man in disgust. ''They shouldn't be here, not today. But they've got no sense of fear, you know? That's what makes them dangerous. Now watch our people, see what they do.''

Two well-dressed young men in dark suits stood at attention, faces swiveling slowly, tracking the walking men. Now they were in motion, moving in concert toward the troop of furs and jewels. The furs smiled at the suits, flashing every tooth of white mixed with crowns of gold.

The old man turned back to Blakely. ''If I don't call the boys off, the razors and the guns come out. I don't like a bloodbath in my neighborhood. The one up front, the Dominican punk, knows that. He's counting on it. He's just playin' with us, you see? But he doesn't know I'm dying. So—not today—but one day soon, I won't call my boys back.''

Rolling down the window, he barked a short burst of commands to the men in suits and gave the fur men the finger as he closed the window again. The men in suits retreated to stand at attention beside their respective limousines. The smiling parade of fur coats and insulting hand gestures passed by, unmolested.

''The Dominican is your future, Blakely. He's dangerous because he's crazy and stupid and hot. If he thinks you're crossing him, the razor comes out and your nose is gone. Or maybe he'll take an ear, and then he'll make you kiss his shoe. And you will do that. After I'm dead, you will sleep in a bath of sweat every night that's left to you. If you can't handle a little girl, what chance do you have against the Dominican?''

''I can get a handle on this case.''

''No, you can't. Let Senator Berman go down. It's going to happen anyway, and I want him to go down for something that isn't tied to me. In fact, I like this a lot. He'll be turned out of the Senate, but he won't do jail time, so he won't be looking to make any deals with the feds. And don't interfere with Jack Coffey. You're too clumsy, too obvious. It'll come back on me, so I'm telling you to let him alone. Mallory did a deal with you, and it's in my best interests that you honor it.''

''Coffey disobeyed a direct order. The son of a bitch gave me attitude, and then he worked around me.''

''So? Markowitz's kid did a lot worse. She made you eat shit. But maybe she'll save you from the punk in the fur coat. Maybe you'll become her dog instead. Damn Markowitz had all the luck. Mallory should have been *my* kid.''

''I can't let her get away with this.''

''Well, you're right about that. Never let your people muscle you. But you've got enough dirty cops to do any job you want. You only ask me to handle it so it won't come back on you. Well, if you wanted to go behind my back, I suppose you could get one of these Young Turks to do it.'' He gestured to the man who stood outside the car. ''These boys have no respect for the old ways. They're punks, no style, no honor, not one good brain in the pack. Yeah, one of them might do the job for you, maybe figuring I'd never find out. They'd be wrong about that. I don't miss much. If one of them tried to touch

Markowitz's kid, it'd blow up in your face and mine. I'd have to get you for that."

"I need your—"

"If you can't control Mallory, then maybe I bought the wrong man for the job. I'll give you my advice, and then you and I will have no more conversation on this business. We will never speak of it again. Is that understood?"

Blakely nodded and the old man continued. "Fear works. Remember, you can't touch her. All you can do now is teach her to fear you. But to pull that off, you'll have to become a better man than she is."

Long after Heller had gone, she sat in the center of the floor with crime-scene photographs and diagrams spread on the dust. Now she cleansed the room in her mind's eye. She painted the walls white and waxed the floors to a high shine. After looking around at her imaginary handiwork, she began the slow work of willing the room into a bloodbath, just as it was on the killing night.

She looked down at the diagram of the crime scene, which exactly placed the spot where axe slices had been found in the floor. This is where the artist had been cut to pieces half an hour after he was dead.

She took out a gold pocket watch and opened it. She depressed the stem to check the stopwatch function. In the facing circle of gold was the inscription of her own name, just Mallory, which followed the generations of names back to Markowitz's grandfather.

She imagined Peter Ariel lying on the floor and set the watch to Slope's estimate for his time of death. Another half hour must pass before the first postmortem cut.

What was going on? What was the killer doing, saying?—conversation? Was there more than one person in the room?

Mallory stood up and began to pace back and forth between her mental re-creations of the artist's body and the sculpture of iron rods and a rusted, crushed car. She went to the back room where the hanging wire was kept and brought the imaginary spools back to the gallery.

She looked down at the watch and allowed a few minutes more for the time the killer might have taken to remove his clothes and pile them away from the mess of the makeshift abattoir. Only minutes had passed. What was the killer doing with the time?

She moved the watch ahead, and knelt down beside the body that was not there. She began to cut away at Peter Ariel with the imaginary axe, a few sure blows for each of the hands and feet, a bit more work for the head. The axe blade was dulling with every cut. The meat was splaying out instead of the clean sever. It was harder work to sever the torso into two parts, to hack through the spinal column and the meat. She would need to rest periodically.

The minute hand of the watch swept several times around the dial, allowing for the rest period. Before the mutilation was half done, her watch said it was time to bring on the dancer.

Mallory looked toward the main entrance and created a vision of Aubry Gilette. She brought the dancer through the door with slow grace.

"Hold it, kid."

She stopped the action in her mind and listened to another voice.

"Naw, that's all wrong, Kathy," said Markowitz. Though he was dead and in the ground, he sat beside her in the dust on the floor. *"This is a critical moment. What's Aubry thinking and feeling as she comes through that door?"*

"I don't know," Mallory whispered to the dead Markowitz. "I can't go where the ballerina goes."

"You can do this, baby. Hell, a bright chimp could work it out. Now think. Aubry's a young kid in a strange neighborhood after dark. She doesn't carry a gun like

you—she's got no defenses at all. So you bring her in cautious, all tense, all eyes. She thinks something's wrong. The message said it was an emergency, right? So she's moving faster. Her face is all worried—she's looking for bad news."

Mallory turned her watch back for the next try. Now the twenty-year-old dancer came through the door with more tension and energy. If Madame Burnstien told the truth, this would be a strange place to her—she would be wary. Mallory brought young Aubry across the small reception area and into the main room. Mallory rose and moved toward her, holding the axe high. The phantom Aubry turned and ran.

"Stop!" Markowitz called time out. And Mallory stopped the watch.

"She's looking at a body hacked up in pieces and someone standing over it still hacking. Give her time to take it in, to be sure it's not her uncle. Then give her credit for world-class reflexes and adrenaline, pure fear feeding her veins, giving her speed."

Mallory set the watch back thirty seconds. She made another whack in Ariel's torso and looked up to Aubry, allowing time for the shock to set in, then the fear. Mallory had already taken up the chase as the dancer was turning. Mallory ran fast, but not fast enough to overtake a dancer at physical peak and with a head start of at least twenty feet. No, Aubry would be out the door and into the street by now.

Mallory turned back her watch. This time, when she ran at Aubry, she created a companion phantom with no face. She placed this figure near the door. As Aubry recovered her wits and turned to run, the shadowy phantom reached for her and dragged her farther into the room. The body of Peter Ariel was thirty feet from the first spill of Aubry's blood. Mallory was halfway across the room now, swinging the axe high over her head and bringing it down on the dancer's neck.

Aubry would be screaming, so Mallory aimed the next blow at the front of the neck. This would have been the blow that flooded Aubry's throat with blood, making breath near impossible. The dancer was down, rising on one arm to lock eyes with Mallory. Aubry's young face was gone to shock and wild panic, not believing that this could be happening to her. Her hands flew up to ward off the next blow to create the defensive wounds found on her corpse.

Mallory swung again, and again. Aubry was crawling now, clawing her way back toward the door, as the axe came down again, and again. Mallory followed her victim the length of the floor, bringing the axe down with a rhythm as she walked.

How had Aubry managed that? She was choking on her own blood, every wound was a mortal wound.

"Why don't you die?" Mallory said, as she raised the axe again.

"*She thinks help is on the way,*" said Markowitz, standing off to the side of her mind, watching his own child hacking up the dancer as though he were supervising Mallory's school homework assignment.

Mallory brought down the axe to strike the blow to Aubry's head. Bits of the dancer's brains leaked to the floor, near the door where the skull fragments were found.

At last, Aubry stopped her struggles and lay dead. Mallory reached down and picked up the phantom dancer under the arms and dragged her body along the floor as though the imaginary Aubry had real weight. When she reached the body parts of Peter Ariel, she set down Aubry's body a few feet away, where the second set of slices still marred the floor.

Here she inflicted one last stroke to the dead body of Aubry, the only assault wound made after death. It was a listless stroke, only a drag of the axe across the body as a final token wound. And this might be more evidence of a conspirator in the room, a more withdrawn, not at all enraged conspirator.

Then she began the work of cutting up the dancer's body in a more businesslike fashion, the same sure strokes, the same rest periods. She pulled off the ripped clothing. The shreds came away easily, so she allotted only a small amount of time to this task.

Now she was ready to create the sculpture of body parts. She skewered the severed head of Peter Ariel on one of the rusted upright rods. The crushed car was the level of a bench. She seated the lower male torso on the metal and bound it to the long spike with the wire which had been taken from the gallery's storeroom. She completed this torso with the upper half of Aubry's body, carefully binding it in place to create one body of the male's head spiked above female breasts, and a penis below. It was close to the old Egyptian model of a god.

She moved on to the work of the second mismatched torso, skewering Aubry's head to the second rod. The male chest was set above the female nether regions. She mismatched the legs which required no wire, but only needed to be settled in place on the bench and then intertwined. The feet of Peter were set below the bloody stumps of Aubry's well-muscled legs. Her dancer's feet now supported the hairy legs of the artist. The arms were more difficult, placing them into bloody proximity of open wound sockets and forcing them to intertwine, then reinforcing positions with wire, which cut into the bloody skin. At last, she bound the woman's hands to the man's arms, and his to hers. Their heads faced forward, eyes open, staring at the artist turned spectator, Mallory.

She stepped back in her mind to admire her artwork, the ghastly embrace of two crimes against nature. It was a hundredfold more intimate than sexual intercourse. Blood was everywhere, and she layered the stench of mingling body fluids and feces over this.

It was sensational, the crime of crimes, the mother of

all horrors. And yes, there was dark genius here. Kooze-man might as well have signed it.

Her next thought was that this was the kind of thing guaranteed to sell a million newspapers. Publicity savvy was Koozeman's other signature.

She looked down at her watch. Quinn would have shown up at the gallery to discover the murder an hour ago. So the time frame didn't work, unless two people were working on the bodies. One person working alone could not have done it all in time. She turned around to look at the shadowy faceless one who had dragged Aubry back into the gallery. Now this one took the form and face of Dean Starr.

She allowed time for another pair of helping hands, and turned back her watch, leaving time to clean up and get behind the door in the wall. The time was still tight. Could there have been more than two of them? She looked back to the door. Time for Quinn to show up.

In a grisly stage direction, she brought her last known player onto the scene. She had Quinn enter slowly.

"*Kathy,*" said Markowitz, in a cautioning reminder.

"Right." Quinn was running late. He would be anxious to see that his niece was all right.

She backed up the watch and made her phantom art critic enter the gallery, not running, but moving quickly. She had him freeze as he took in the horror of the back wall.

She watched him for a moment more.

"Quinn, do you know what you're looking at?" she whispered.

There was so much blood, he would not immediately recognize his niece from this distance. Mallory let him come closer, stepping slowly, disbelieving, and finally recognizing the head on the right-hand post as his niece. And now there is blood on his shoes.

She stood up and walked over to him. "What are you thinking?" She stood beside him, watching the sudden lift of his chin, the awful realization that he was late, that if he had only come in time—

He couldn't know that his niece had come early to the gallery. The medical examiner would have to tell him that later.

Mallory came back to the most nagging puzzle. It had taken a long time to kill the dancer. What had kept Aubry alive so long after the first stroke of the axe?

"She was waiting for the cavalry," said Markowitz.

Mallory nodded. There might be something to that. Aubry had been a protected child. She must have been thinking that rescue would come, it would surely come. Quinn would be there any minute. A child raised on the street would have given up her life much sooner, knowing that the cavalry never came.

Minutes ticked by on her pocket watch as Quinn took in the total horror. Finally his eyes bludgeoned his brain to accept it. Now what? Would he fall to his knees? No. According to the old reports, there had only been blood on his shoes. He remained standing. Though he had been mortally wounded in his mind, he could not fall down and die. There was no escape from this.

"So much pain." She bowed her head.

Markowitz, standing in the blood and the stench of murder, was smiling. For this had been Mallory's longest lesson, and she had finally made the breakthrough to empathy.

The room was so quiet, she could hear the tick of Markowitz's pocket watch, steady as a heartbeat. Five minutes had gone by since Quinn's arrival. In another twenty-five minutes, Quinn would call the police. What did he do with the time?

She moved in front of him and looked deep into his eyes. "Did you cry?" she whispered.

Hard to imagine those eyes with any emotion in them. She let him stand there, knowing that this was wrong. What did he do with the time? It might have been different if there was someone else in the gallery. Then there would be conversation, planning, questions asked, plans laid.

But he had told Markowitz that he came alone.

"Well, that wouldn't be your only lie, would it, Quinn?"

And now she created a shadowy figure to stand beside him. But who could it have been, and why would Quinn shield this player who had accompanied him to the gallery? She stared at this second dark form, the one made wholly of shadow. Who was it?

And then she knew.

She stood before the shadow figure. "I've seen your face before, haven't I?"

Now the shadow wore Sabra's face as Mallory had constructed it on her computer.

Suppose the brother and sister had both visited their mother that night, and both had come to the gallery. So this was what sent Sabra over the top of her mind—not just the news that her only child had died horribly, but the sight of Aubry in this horrific work of art. Perhaps it had been Sabra's fault that they were late getting to the gallery. That would have bent her mind even more. If they had come in Sabra's car, and if she had left by herself, then Quinn's story about the subway would have a reason.

Mallory closed her eyes and ended the gory art show.

At last she understood the crime. The artist and the dancer were very different kills, for different reasons, only coming together when the body parts were assembled into a single piece of bloody sculpture.

There was no one at home in the old house in Brooklyn, no one to hear the footsteps on the cellar stairs, squeaking under the old wood, nor the softer steps across the linoleum of the kitchen and the slam of the back door.

It began in the basement. Louis Markowitz's collection

of rock'n'roll records melted in the heat, the album covers turning brown and bursting into flames. His old recordings of the Shadow and other superheroes of radio days were consumed by fire.

Smoke wound up the stairs, invading the kitchen, where Helen Markowitz had made meals for the small family. The flames captured Helen's sewing basket, then raced up the stairs to the room which had been Kathy's, a room Markowitz had preserved until the day he died, a constant reminder to him of his only child. The flames licked down the hall to Markowitz's den and ate his letters and his books, and at the bottom of his desk drawers it ravaged the pictures of Kathy Mallory's growing up, beauty flowering into a woman who amazed him.

When Mallory entered the Gulag, Sandy the waitress was leaning on the counter watching the clock, probably counting off the last minutes of her shift. Sandy looked at Mallory with annoyance, her eyes saying, *Go away*.

Quinn stood up and waved to Mallory from the far table. Suddenly the waitress's attitude changed. With a tired but pleasant smile, Sandy plucked a menu from the rack on the counter and handed it to Mallory.

Quinn was delighted to see Mallory, but even his own mother would not have noted the difference between this display of emotion and his facial arrangement for stepping on a dog turd. He was well aware of his own uncommunicative shortcomings, his limited repertoire of expressions.

Mallory ordered the cheeseburger on his recommendation, but when it arrived, she ignored it. She was gazing at him steadily, and he was quietly coming unhinged, but he was also assured that this would never show.

"Will you explain to me how a little weasel wakes up one morning, decides he's going to be an art star and lands a one-man show in an important gallery?"

"Dean Starr wasn't really an overnight success," said

Quinn. "He used a lifetime of public relations and marketing skills to pull it off. And his timing was good. His targeted market was a generation with conversational points of reference taken from the constant repetition of fifteen-second television commercials. This was the perfect age for it."

"I like to keep things simple. I think he had something on Koozeman, something big—say the murders of Peter Ariel and your niece. I think he was there that night. Starr made a lot of money after those murders, but then most of it went into his arm with a heroin habit. So he was looking for another hype. So he went to Koozeman, the genius of hype. Wasn't that what you called him?"

"Well, I suppose that would fit rather nicely, but it's a moot point now that they're both dead. If you're quite sure that Koozeman was the murderer, then you've finished your father's case, haven't you?"

"I still have the small detail of who's killing the killers. You didn't think I was just going to leave that hanging, did you? Quinn, if I can prove you're mixed up in that, I'm going to get you for it."

"And how can I help you toward that end?"

"I need some background on Emma Sue Hollaran. What kind of critic was she?"

"Are you figuring her for the next victim? I did notice a plethora of critics in this case. But I think you're wasting your time there."

"Maybe the old case isn't wrapped yet."

"Seriously, you're still looking for another killer?"

Mallory looked up as a new waitress, just starting her shift, refilled their coffee cups and then left them alone again. "She has the same name tag as the other one. Why are all the waitresses named Sandy? And why does a dive like this have real gold name tags?"

"The owner bought the name tags from a liquidator, who bought them from a bankrupt jeweler. And you're right, they are real gold. But since they were already engraved, he got a good price.''

He went on to explain that the name tags had been the deluxe business cards of a prostitute named Sandy. The cards were all paid for, cash in advance, but never picked up because Sandy had died of a severe asthma attack. Her nine-year-old daughter waited an hour for the ambulance to come, not believing it would never come. Next, she called the fire department. The firemen were there in three minutes, but Sandy had stopped breathing five minutes before that. ''And so, the phone number of Sandy's answering service was covered with a pin glued to the back of the cards, and all the waitresses are called Sandy.''

''You went to a lot of trouble to find that out.''

''Yes I did.''

''You remind me of Charles. He's a puzzle freak. He can't let go of a problem until he's worked it out. Hard to believe you ever stopped looking for Sabra—or the man who killed your niece. You had to wonder what had happened to your sister. You would have kept at it until you found her.''

''I never said—''

''A morgue attendant tells me you were first in line to view the body of a homeless woman, a jumper from Times Square. Did you think it was Sabra?''

He looked down at the table. Given his limited range of expression, he knew this simple aversion of the eyes must be tantamount to a confession.

''One more thing.'' Her voice had a cold edge to it. ''The night Aubry died—Sabra was in the gallery with you, wasn't she?''

He lifted his face, and discovered that his expressions were not so limited after all. Mallory was nodding in agreement, as if he had answered her question aloud. Apparently, pain was something she could read in his face, for her voice was softer when she said good night.

• • •

On the bedroom bureau sat a wedding photo in a silver frame. Youthful and smiling, Louis and Helen Markowitz stared out of the frame. Two pairs of young, laughing eyes watched the flames racing toward them, consuming everything in sight, every memory of home and family until, mercifully, the glass of the picture frame was coated with soot and ash, blinding their eyes to the end of memories stored away in precious, irreplaceable things.

Mallory stood by the open door of her apartment, taking in the damage of pulled-out drawers, overturned tables and broken glass from the bulbs of fallen lamps. The doorman followed her into the front room.

"I swear I don't know how he could've got past me, miss."

"He probably walked in behind a tenant. If they want to get in, they will. There aren't any safe places in this town."

She walked into the kitchen to stand amid shards of crockery. The burglar had wiped the shelves clean of dishes and cups. Canned goods lay on the floor alongside the contents of her refrigerator. A canister of sugar was spilled over the contents of the flour canister.

Thorough little bastard.

Her den was less damaged. Since she had moved all her computer equipment to Charles's building, Mallory had not thought to put this room to any better use than storage. Clothes were spilled out of trunks and onto the carpet, and the few remaining computer manuals had been ripped.

Not just a robbery.

She picked up a winter dress of good wool and found it slashed with a razor cut. In the bedroom the carpet was littered with silk blouses slit the same way. More drawers had been pulled out, and a wide selection of running shoes were strewn all over a jumble of blue jeans and blazers, linen and nylons. The mattress had been gutted and its stuffing coated the room. The feathers from her pillows lay on every surface.

The doorman was fidgeting beside her.

"It's okay, Frank. I'm fully insured. Now tell me everything that happened. Who told you about the break-in?"

"A tenant. Mrs. Simpson. She comes down and says a cop told her to get me up here. He was waiting for me at the front door."

"Are you sure he was a cop?"

"Yes, miss. He showed me a badge and his identification. And he gave me this." The doorman put a white business card in her hand. "He said he'd get back to you for a list of what was missing, and I should tell you that you don't have to file the report. He said he'd take care of it."

Now she read the card and recognized the name of Blakely's gofer. A push for a shove? She went to the bedroom closet and pulled out the side wall. Nothing had been touched, he had missed this cache where her valuables were stored.

"Thanks, Frank. You can go now."

"I'm sorry, miss."

She looked at his face grim with worry over his job. Well, she wasn't about to break in an entirely new doorman. "I don't think I'll be mentioning this to the management company, Frank. And I'll talk to Mrs. Simpson, all right?"

"Thank you, miss."

It took twenty minutes to determine that nothing had been taken. Simple harassment? No, Blakely had probably sent his gofer out to find something. Did Blakely know about the office in Charles's building?

● ● ●

The sirens were screaming down the road as the flames shot up to the rafters of the attic, where Helen Markowitz had stored Kathy's baseball glove and her school uniforms. The family albums of five generations were all burning. The book of photos on the top of the pile was stubborn, only smoldering, then finally catching fire, burning all the pictures of a child's growing years from ten to seventeen, when she had her full height. Before the siren screamed up to the front door, every trace of young Kathy Mallory had vanished in the smoke.

She unlocked the front door of Charles's building. He would be asleep now. She took the stairs slowly, gun in hand, listening for sounds that did not belong in this quiet building of sleeping tenants, but she heard nothing out of the ordinary. On the second floor, she walked the hall silently, approaching the office of Mallory and Butler, Ltd. She fit her key in the lock and worked the tumblers quietly, entering with no noise at all.

Nothing in the reception area had been disturbed. She opened the door to Charles's private office. Nothing was out of place. She found her own office in the same perfect order. She settled down in the chair behind her desk and waited in the dark. If Blakely knew about this place, his gofer would come here next. She might have some time to kill.

She reached out to the desk phone and dialed the priest's number. And she knew from the weary "hello" that she had awakened him.

Well, tough.

"Father Brenner, what's the religious penalty for defiling a corpse?"

"You woke me for *that*?"

"It was my mother's corpse. This is under the seal of the confessional, right? You can't tell?"

"Oh, God. Yes, if you wish. Kathy, is this real?"

"Oh, Father, it's as real as it ever gets. Let's say I lost

my mind. Maybe it was all that blood, and the *way* she died. I had to leave her, but I couldn't leave. But it was too dangerous to stay. I had to go, to run and right now. So I took a little bit of my mother with me—her brain.''

And now she looked down at her fingernails, examining the polish for chips. ''So, Father, what's the penalty for that?''

''How old were you, Kathy?''

''I was almost seven.''

''The church doesn't expect a small child to reason out morality when the child is half crazed and in fear of its life. You must have—''

''Let's say I wasn't a child. Suppose I was a normal, moral person.''

''All right, let's use our imaginations.''

She could hardly miss the sarcasm in his voice, and the creep of skepticism. ''Rabbi Kaplan won't like it when he finds out you're doing his act.''

''He steals my jokes. Well, I suppose we share them. We shared you once. We talked about you behind your back, and we worried over you. We split up the prayers. Less work. I liked that.''

Time for a little side trip to hell, Father.

''The killer used an axe on my mother. He hit her over and over again. There was blood everywhere. It was like a slaughterhouse. I can still smell the blood, Father. She was crawling toward me, holding out her hand. She thought I was going to save her. But I didn't. I ran away.''

''You were only a child.''

His voice was strained, he was buying it—all of it.

''What's the penalty, Father?''

The beep came from the cellular phone in her pocket. She hung up on the priest with no goodbye, and pulled out the cellular phone, lifting it to her ear. ''Mallory here,'' she said, and listened to the stone silence on the other end.

"Mallory," a voice whispered at last. "Your house is on fire."

It was only a whisper—familiar though.

Blakely's voice.

She stood in the front yard of the old house and watched the firemen wetting down the rafters of the attic, black charred ribs smoking and steaming under the arching waterfall from the hose.

"It was arson," the fire chief was saying, though she barely heard him. "The guy didn't even try to cover his tracks. We found the gas cans in the yard. Any idea who'd want to do this to you?"

"No," she lied.

"Don't bullshit me, Mallory. It's like somebody went out of his way to leave you a message. Now is this connected to an ongoing case or not?"

She didn't answer him, seemed not to see him anymore. Her eyes were fixed on the husk of the old house, her home. All gone now.

The fire chief leaned into her face and moved his hands across her eyes. She made no response. He drew away from her and turned to the man next to him. "There's a doctor's house three doors down the street. Go get him."

She stood alone on the lawn, as firemen, going to and fro, made a wide circle around her. She stared at the ruins and rocked back and forth in a cage of solid hatred for a thing she could not put a name to. It was such a large beast, it threatened to become the whole earth.

Somewhere behind her, another siren was screaming up to the house. Now a car door was slamming, footsteps running.

The house was gone, that solid anchor to the world, all gone. She was airy and light, and in danger of being drawn up with the smoke. It was the sudden tight wrap of Riker's arms about her that kept her bound to the earth. She was engulfed in rough tweed and the familiar scents of cigarettes, cheap spot remover and beer.

"So you went after Blakely," said Riker, holding her close and watching the smoke twisting up to the sky. "Now how did I know that?"

Charles opened the door to Riker and Mallory. She walked past him, through the foyer to the couch in the front room. Charles turned to Riker. "Is she all right? Does she need a doctor? Henrietta's just up the stairs."

"No, she's okay. I just didn't feel right letting the kid go back to her condo. Some bastard trashed it. So put her up for the night, and don't ask her any questions. If she cries in front of you, she'll never forgive you for it." Riker handed Charles her duffel bag. "I gotta go, Charles. Somebody has to look after Andrew Bliss."

"There must be something else I can do."

"If you really want to do something for the kid, send Mrs. Ortega over to clean up the place before Mallory goes home again."

"You know the old house in Brooklyn was her real home."

"Yeah, well, the condo's all she's got left now. Good night, Charles."

Mallory was sitting on the couch when he returned to his front room to lay the duffel bag at her feet. "I've made up the bed in the spare room."

Seconds crawled by before she seemed aware that he had spoken to her. She looked down at the duffel bag by her feet as though it had appeared there by magic.

"Are you all right?"

She nodded.

Clearly, she was not all right. He detected the signs of shock in her eyes, which had gone to soft focus, staring inward and not liking what she saw there. He hunkered down before her and gently turned her face to his.

"Would you like me to call Henrietta Ramsharan?"

"I don't need a shrink." Her words were slow to come out.

"But Henrietta is also an M.D., you know. She could give you something to help you sleep."

"I don't need her."

She turned away from him to say that she didn't need him, either. But when he took hold of her arm and guided her body up to a standing position, she allowed it. He carried her duffel to the back room and opened the door for her. Every stick of cherrywood and oaken furniture and even the patchwork quilt and the heavy velvet drapes could be dated to the early 1800s. The bedding of the antique four-poster was turned down, awaiting this child of the late twentieth century.

She looked so tired and worn. Without her energy and easy confidence, she seemed to have lost some of her size, and he worried over this.

Well, perhaps with rest, she would grow.

On the Upper East Side, a priest was turning in his bed, periodically rising to lean on one elbow and stare at the phone by his bed, wondering where she was and how she was. Finally, he tired of willing the telephone to ring, and Father Brenner burrowed deep into his blankets. Then came the misstep at the border of sleep, the foot kicking out into air, prelude to the long dark free fall into dreams.

In the first gray light of an indecent hour, the telephone did ring, awakening him. He knew it was her. It had to be. No one else would do this to an elderly priest. His first feeling was relief, and then he prepared himself to be disgruntled and short with her. Eyes stuck fast with sleep glue, he reached out one blind hand to grasp the receiver and hold it to his pillowed head.

"All right, what is it now?"

The only response was a stutter of breath brushing up against his ear, soft as moth wings. In the strange twilight state between waking and sleeping, only half shaken from dreams, he truly believed he detected the sound of rolling tears.

Now a small voice whispered that ancient complaint of the lost child, "I want to go home."

CHAPTER
7

IT WAS HENRIETTA RAMSHARAN'S DAY OFF FROM THE psychiatric clinic. Today the doctor wore a pink sweat-shirt, faded jeans and bare feet. Waves of dark hair, salted with white strands, hung down her back as she sat across the kitchen table from her landlord and friend. Charles Butler was not wearing a tie with his suit this morning, and she recognized this as his idea of casual dress.

Henrietta poured herself another cup of coffee and wondered why she had ever bothered to decorate her living room. All the important conversations of life took place in kitchens. "You should have called me right away."

"Mallory told me she didn't want a doctor—she didn't want anybody. And it was very late." Charles had the sad, distracted look of loss, as though his own house had burned and not Mallory's.

"Charles, we're friends, aren't we? The next time you have a problem, call me. And I don't care how late it is. Where is Mallory now?"

"I made her coffee this morning. She's gone now," he said, as though Mallory had been vaporized. "She acted as if nothing out of the ordinary had happened. But I know how important that house was to her, especially after her father died. How much can she internalize before she breaks apart? She's taken entirely too many blows to the heart.''

Henrietta wondered if it might not be Charles who had been taking all the blows lately. Mallory would probably be just fine. Charles sometimes forgot that Mallory didn't have a heart, and perhaps it was that which made her more resilient than the rest of them.

"Henrietta, do you think she might become more reckless now, take more chances? She really should be relieved of duty for a while.''

"Charles, I wouldn't even suggest it to her. She'd only take it as a criticism, and you know she never takes that well.''

Henrietta leaned back in her chair and regarded his gentle face. He stared down at his plate of untouched scrambled eggs while his coffee cooled in the cup. Charles was a classic study in misery, a man in love. She had seen his counterpart in her own reflection.

"More coffee, Charles? No?'' *Oh, and did I ever mention that I love you?*

Because he had been so straightforward, so forthcoming, she had learned a great deal about this man in the first moments of meeting him a little more than a year ago. He had left the safe, elegant aerie of an uptown highrise to live among buildings more to human scale in SoHo. He was a warm man who genuinely liked people.

"Here,'' she said, pulling a slice of bread from the toaster on the table between them. "You have to eat something.'' *And I'll love you till I die.*

When she had met Mallory for the first time, Henrietta understood him better. Charles loved Mallory, and Mallory loved no one. Henrietta held out no hope for any of them.

Oh, Christ! It's in bed with me!

Andrew Bliss sat bolt upright, eyes wide and frightened. As he fought with his quilts, his panicked heart pounded on the inside wall of his chest. The brown rat slithered out from under the bedding and scurried across the roof.

Andrew fell back on his pillow, exhausted and sweating, until his breathing was normal again. His hand fluttered over his head to chase the bugs out of his hair.

Perhaps the rat had taken him for dead, and thus, fair leavings. Well, was he not? He hadn't bathed or brushed his teeth in nearly a week. Would road kill smell as sweet?

Oh, sweeter, surely.

And while he was in the revulsion mode, he had one particularly vile act to perform, and he might as well get it over with. He walked to the most distant corner of the roof, squatted down and dumped his bowels with the shame of a fanatically housebroken dog, unable to hold back anymore. This shame was the cost of the loaves of bread which dropped from the sky.

And *now*, of all the hours of the day, *now* the damn traffic-watch helicopter flew overhead. As it hovered above the roof, the wind of the whirling blades sent every loose thing flying, and stirred up funnel clouds of dust. The distressed canopy of Armani raincoats swung back and forth on its armature of ropes and wildly waved its sleeves.

Andrew pulled his robe closed and stood up as the woman in the helicopter addressed him from a bullhorn.

"How are you this morning, Mr. Bliss?"

Andrew was moving slowly as he crossed the roof against the stiff wind of the helicopter blades. He picked up his own bullhorn and turned it skyward. The woman had put away her loudspeaker to shoot him with a video camera, to take his portrait with matted hair and a scraggle of beard. He made the appropriate obscene hand gesture, and then released a golden arch of piss.

She lowered the camera.

"That blue jumpsuit is more pathetic than the last one, my love!" yelled Andrew, sinking down to a tired cross-legged sit. "Were you raised in a discount store? Do you want God to strike your helicopter down? Get a long-line girdle from Intimate Apparel on the fourth floor! And now, would you like to discuss that brassy, bimbo-blond hair while there's still time to repent?"

Apparently not, for the helicopter was veering off. The bullhorn fell from his hand and rolled off to one side as his head sank to his chest. His chin lifted slightly as he tracked a quirky movement across the roof out of the corner of one eye.

The rat was back.

The animal was getting bolder, coming out in the broad daylight. It trotted up to his splayed hand and sniffed it, checking the fingertips for signs of life. Andrew snatched his hand back to his chest, but the rat didn't run away. It only sat there, watching him. The creature seemed to grow in size as it walked around his knees and stood in front of him, slowly lowering itself on its haunches.

Perhaps this was the devil come to sit with him awhile. If the being who left his bread and flew from the roof was his Sunday school angel, replete with moon-gold hair, then there must be a devil, too. And didn't the devil also have a long switching tail?

Oh, where was his guardian angel now? He looked up to the heavens, and the sun seared his eyes, but he felt no pain anymore.

Where was the angel?

Mallory stood just outside the ring of television cameras, boom mikes and round, bright lights on stalks of steel. A technician was attached to each piece of equipment. Other workers milled around inside this loop of machinery, while the pedestrian watchers stood behind the ropes which cordoned off the East Village gallery. Oren Watt's head made furtive, jerky turns as he looked Mallory's way from time to time, perhaps not believing she was still there, still doing this to him.

The man acting the role of Oren Watt wore clothes soaked in Technicolor blood. On cue from the director, the actor burst out the door of the old East Village gallery and ran down the street.

"You're a lousy technical advisor, Oren." Her voice was just behind him. Only a second ago, she had been at the edge of the crowd. "Everybody knows a junkie can't run that fast. And you only had blood on your shoes when you left the gallery—that's another mistake. How did you get rid of the rest of the blood, Oren?"

Watt was rigid now, never acknowledging her, but reflecting every verbal blow in some stiff movement of the head or shoulder. She looked down to his hands in spasms of clenching and unclenching.

She turned away from him to scan the crowd of pedestrians behind the ropes, wondering who else might have been attracted to the reenactment of New York's most famous crime. Her eyes fixed on an old woman in layers of shabby clothes. The woman cradled a tea tin in her arms, rocking it like a baby. Now the gray head bowed down to speak to the tin as she tied it to the top of her wire cart with a bungee cord.

Very crazy, very old.

Or maybe this woman was not so ancient as she seemed. Life on the streets of New York was a rapid aging process. The average homeless person could expect to die in twelve years.

Mallory stripped the woman with her eyes, taking years off the bent body, looking beyond the matted strands of gray hair to see what lay beneath the deep-etched lines of the face. The gray head turned toward her, and Mallory was staring into familiar eyes, large and expressive.

Sabra?

The woman dragged her cart backward into the crowd. A path was made for her by those who dreaded head lice and the stench of the homeless. Mallory moved forward, crossing the space between the television crew and their audience. Her long legs easily swung over the restraining rope, and she was pushing her way through the crush of people.

A man grabbed her by the arm. "Who do you think you're shoving, sister?"

She stopped to open her blazer and retrieve her shield and ID. The man let go of her arm. It was the exposed gun that spoke to him, not the badge. It was a very large gun.

Mallory pressed on and broke through to the other side of the crowd. Sabra was turning a corner at the end of the block and disappearing down a side street. Mallory followed from a distance as they moved south across Houston.

On Essex Street, Sabra settled her cart by the wall of a boarded-up building. Mallory watched as the woman pulled wood slats from a basement-level window. With no hesitation, Sabra lowered her cart through an exposed black hole and followed after it with the ease and confidence of long practice.

So this was home. Well, good.

It was best to meet on Sabra's own turf. From what she'd been told of this woman, intimidation would not work. They had to talk on Sabra's terms, or she would get nothing.

Sabra's hands reappeared at the hole between the boards. She reached out to retrieve the slats she had removed, and now she was pulling them into place, fitting them back into the nail holes.

Mallory gave her a four-minute lead. Then she knelt on the ground and gently, soundlessly pried one board away from the basement window. She looked in on a shallow, dark space, accented by one blurred rectangle of bad light streaming in from the street. She pulled away the rest of the boards and eased herself through the opening.

Her running shoes touched down on a surface too high to be the basement floor. Her eye adapted, but there was little to see. She was standing on a large wooden shipping crate. Directly before her was a plywood wall. On her right was a crude staircase made of smaller crates in staggered sizes. It led down to the basement level and turned a corner into perfect blackness.

Mallory reached outside the window and pulled the boards back in place, fitting the wood to the window frame in the manner of politely closing a door behind her. When the last pinhole of light was gone, the space had become so dark, her eyes had lost their purpose—she was blind.

Welcome home, said the darkness as it closed in all around her in the suffocating embrace of old acquaintance, *and where have you been all these years, Kathy Mallory?*

One hand drifted to the gun in her holster, to the touch of something real and solid. As her hand dropped away, her mind was in free fall again, no up nor down, no compass point. She made her way down the short flight of crates which passed for stairs. Her fingers grazed the wall and trailed along its rough surface. When the wall ended, the floor became even and cement solid. She entered a space which might have been a closet or a football stadium. Picking her steps with great care, she walked forward with the sense of something looming in front of her. Her hand reached out and connected with a solid wall. Her fingertips walked along the wall, guiding her until she touched on a cluster of living, squirming things, and now one of them was crawling up her hand. She flicked her wrist and shook it off.

The nest of roaches was not the worst thing she had ever touched in the dark. Once, on a moonless night by the river, under the piers, a ten-year-old Kathy Mallory had encountered a soft obstacle in her path. Night blind and curious, she had made out the shape of the thing on the ground by running her hands over the long hair and the cold dead face of another child. Stunned by this discovery, she had sat down beside the girl's body and not moved for hours. But before the dawn could shape the corpse and prove its reality to the child's eyes, young Kathy had crept away in the dark to tell herself lies: that it had not happened; it was in the dark, and so it did not count, this evidence of a child's mortality; that it could never be herself laid out like that, killed and thrown away.

She would survive. She *would*.

And then Markowitz had found her, and she had gone to live with him and Helen in the old house in Brooklyn. From then on, it had been a life lived largely in the light.

Stone blind now, guided only by the flat wall under her fingertips, she crept forward into black space, along a floor which might, at any footstep, turn into a great yawning hole. Her other senses were adapting to the loss of her eyes. The smell of roaches and dust mingled with urine and rotted food. She knew the crumbling sounds inside the walls were made by tiny feet, and something rat-size was slithering across the floor. Now there were high-pitched sounds, whistles and squeals—the conversations of vermin.

And what of Sabra?

Mallory could not put one sound to a human being. Had the woman found her way out of the cellar? Mallory stood dead still in the pure blackness until she lost the sense of her own body. She reached out with her hands and encountered another wall. On again, moving slowly, listening to the rats' feet and the sound of water dripping from a leaking pipe. Her fingers found a wet stream with the rank smell of rusted plumbing.

The wall turned a corner, and the next panel was made

of something less substantial, she guessed plywood. Reaching out with the other hand, she discovered another partition of the same flimsy material. She was in a narrow passage. Exploring hands found the seam of a door, and farther down, the knob. She pressed her ear to the wood and knew there was nothing living on the other side of it, nothing larger than the cockroaches. The musty odor of their pollution was everywhere. She found another door on the other side of the small passage. No one home there, either.

She stopped to listen for the larger creature, as if believing she could detect the heartbeat of a human apart from the collective life signs of rats and insects.

But the woman *was* here. Mallory could feel the presence, the tension of one who waited and listened. It was guarded intuition, the awareness of a nearby animal set to spring. Mallory wandered farther down the passage, passing other doors. She guessed this basement had once been rented out for storage rooms. A good guess. She turned another corner and found herself in an identical row of facing doors.

"Tell me what you want with me," commanded a woman's voice, floating free in the black space.

There was no way to orient the sound except by the distance, which was neither near nor far. Mallory revolved slowly in the dark.

"Tell me what you want," said the voice.

This time, the voice came from behind her. She turned around. "My name is Mallory."

"I know who you are, Detective. I asked you what you wanted."

The position had changed.

"I only want to talk to you," said Mallory. *And I wonder, do you read the papers, Sabra? Or did someone tell you my name and rank?*

She had a vague direction now, and she moved toward

it. A rat ran over her foot and squealed in terror as she kicked it.

"Stay where you are, Mallory. Don't come any closer. I wouldn't like that. You may be younger, but I know the terrain and you don't."

"All right, Sabra, we'll do it your way," she called into the void, moving forward with softer footfalls than any of the other creatures in the basement.

"You have no children, do you, Detective Mallory?"

"No, Sabra. No children, no family."

"You can't know what it's like to have your child slaughtered."

"I've seen the crime-scene photographs." And what had Sabra seen? The real thing?

"Photographs won't show you the half of it, not the pain she was in, not any of the terror. Is there anything in your experience that can tell you what that was like?"

You and the priest and the rabbi. You all want a piece of me. All right, I'll play.

"I saw my mother slaughtered before I was seven years old. I know exactly what it's like."

She stopped moving in the silence and waited for the voice to begin again, to give her bearings and direction.

"I'm sorry. So sorry." The voice softened now, a mother's voice. "It's incomprehensible, isn't it? You can't quite believe that you'll never see the one you love again. How could it be possible that this person could just cease to be? Detective Mallory, how did you feel when you finally understood that you would never kiss your mother again?"

Was the voice farther away now? Mallory moved forward in the dark, making no sound. "That was the thing I missed the most—the kiss. For a long time, I couldn't go to sleep without it. The dark was always difficult for me. The dark of night and no mother. I'm afraid of the dark, Sabra. Can we go somewhere in the light and talk? Can we, please?" Wheedle of a child to a mother.

"Perhaps." Sabra's voice was edging away.

Mallory stepped forward again.

"Tell me about your mother," said Sabra.

You and the priest and the rabbi.

"I think I look like my mother," said Mallory. "For years it drove me crazy because her face was slipping away from me. And then one day, there she was in the mirror. But by then I had another mother—Helen Markowitz. Helen was wonderful. I loved her, too. And then Helen died a few years ago. I was very angry with her. Does it sound strange to be angry with someone for dying?"

She waited for Sabra's answer. And waited.

And now Mallory knew she had been abandoned. She had been talking to no one.

She moved forward with speed, too reckless, and her blind feet stumbled over a crate. Her shin hit the wood, but she did not cry out. Mallory felt her way along the corridor of doors to empty rooms. She stopped and listened to the sound of the boards being pushed out to the pavement beyond the window. Moving forward again, she hit a wall in a blind corridor, a dead end. She turned back, moving faster now in her familiarity with space already covered, rounding a wall of lockers, and then another. But she realized too late that she had lost her orientation. She was heading deeper into the room, and away from the window.

Sabra was gone by now, slipped away down some street in the invisible cloak of poverty. No one on the sidewalk would be able to point the way she'd gone, for who ever looked at the face of a bag lady?

When Mallory rounded the storage cabinets into the next row, she saw a flickering light leaking out from the crack beneath one of the doors, and she hurried toward it, flying through the suffocating darkness.

She pushed open the door, knowing that no one would be there. The tiny room was lit with candles. Newspapers lined one side of the room with black-and-white pictures of Oren Watt. Color photographs of a child were pinned to the opposite wall. Cracked dishes were neatly stacked in a corner. It was too familiar.

The storage room was small and close. The photographs of the child gave Mallory glimpses into a background of more open spaces and graceful living, a happier time in Sabra's life. All around this cramped space were the signs of obsession. The woman must have collected every newspaper article ever printed about the murders. Mallory understood obsession. It was a basic thing. It was important to find a place to put your hate. She understood, but it would make no difference.

I have to get the press off my back and the feds out of NYPD or I lose my case.

The bedding on the floor was a rotting blanket pulled over a makeshift mattress of old clothes and newspapers. One photograph lay on a tattered pillow. It was Aubry dancing. How beautiful she was. Mallory looked closely at the photograph, then turned it over facedown.

Sabra, it's a big mistake to get between me and a case.

She turned to see another photograph pinned to the wall, and this one was startling. Sabra smiled for the camera as she was holding Aubry on her lap. The resemblance between mother and child was a strong one. This might be the only likeness of Sabra in existence, the single breach of her fanatic rejection of portraits. It must have meant a great deal to her. It must have been hard to leave it behind. Sabra's eyes stared into Mallory's.

You lose, Sabra!

In the shimmer of candlelight, the walls seemed to move. The candles were everywhere. Mallory walked around the tiny room, blowing them out in the familiar manner of an old ritual, until there was only one candle left to illuminate the photograph of mother and child. Aubry was perhaps four years old. Sabra was planting a kiss on her cheek, as Aubry was squirming free to mug for the camera, eyes crossing, laughter spilling out of the photograph.

The kiss.

Sabra would never kiss her child again.

Mallory did understand. *I was there before you, I know what you think, what you feel, I remember the kiss.*

She sank down on the floor, pulled up her knees, and bowed her head. In memory, she was a child again, sitting in the discarded refrigerator carton that had once been her home for a few days in winter. She remembered lighting a candle and casting her child-size shadow on a plywood wall. She had stolen all her candles from the churches, and she lit one each night without fail, only dimly remembering the candle had some purpose beyond the light.

She remembered pulling the two dishes from her small store of belongings, which might be discarded the next time she had to run. Young Kathy had carefully emptied the food from her pockets onto the plate and poured the contents of a soda can into the cup. The dishes were somehow important, and whenever she lost a set on the run, she would steal another as the first order of business.

After the meal she would wipe her face with a dry square of cloth, in vague semblance of a forgotten bedtime ritual. As a child she had pulled together these simple conventions of home, the makings of sanity. And last, it had been her habit to blow out the candle and pull a blanket of newspapers round her, tucking herself in.

One thing that was lost to her was the kiss before sleep. But so much had been lost. The child had become resigned to this and ceased to cry over it anymore. Over time, the baby hard case had come to take some pride in the dearth of tears, and hard anger had displaced each soft and childlike thing about her.

On the night Helen Markowitz took possession of her, that good woman had gone through all the rituals of the meal, the bath, and then the forgotten customs of the nightclothes, brushing teeth and braiding hair. Last in the order of familiar and forgotten things, Helen had turned out the light and bowed down to kiss the small child in her protection.

After this gentle woman had left the room, the little hard case turned her face to the wall and cried in eerie silence, tears only, but so many—so important was this small act which was committed all over the world between mother and child.

Brilliant sunlight illuminated the stained-glass windows of the cathedral. Arches curved heaven high. The priest and his altar boys were steeped in the ritual of communion, the eating of the flesh of Christ and the drinking of His blood in the form of bread and wine. One young woman listened carefully as the priest spoke to the parishioners kneeling at the railing before the altar. He offered them the flesh and then the blood wine. This woman was at attention in every part of her being, as though committing the service to memory.

The elderly priest faltered in the words when he saw Kathy Mallory standing at the back of the church. Then the words began again, his mouth apparently not requiring his full attention, so accustomed was he to the ritual. Not one parishioner noticed his absence in spirit.

Father Brenner watched her as she walked to an altar where a score of candles were lit beneath the statue of Saint Jude. Ten years had passed since he had seen her, but he knew her at once—that face, that incredible face. God's grace was writ into the very shape of it. Kathy Mallory even walked in grace—while Sister Ursula still limped when it rained.

So Kathy had come to God's house. This was a miracle, or at the very least, he could tell an elderly nun her prayers for the born-to-stray lamb had been answered.

He watched the prodigal child steal a handful of candles from the altar of Saint Jude. Then she slipped out the door.

Well, some things never changed.

Charles was bewildered. Mallory only slathered mustard on her sandwich and behaved as though she had just told him that the mayonnaise had gone bad. He sat down at the table, still wondering if he had heard her right.

"Sabra is living on the street?"

"That's right," she said. "Pass the cheese plate, will you?"

Sabra is homeless and pass the cheese plate. He remembered a time when there had been a predictable and tranquil sameness to his days. Then along came Mallory, and soon the world was a jarring, unnerving place where logic ruled if she could twist it her way—otherwise not. And humanity was a weakness she tolerated in fools like himself.

And now Sabra was homeless, and Mallory was building a triple-decker sandwich.

"You have to find her and right now. Can't you put out an all-points bulletin or something?"

She reached over to grab the cheese plate herself. "No. Sabra hasn't broken any laws."

"Couldn't you make up some plausible reason for it?"

"That would be against the rules, Charles." She selected the Swiss cheese.

"But under the circumstances . . ."

"The end never justifies the means," she said, throwing his own words back at him, shutting him down with his own rules. "And suppose one of Blakely's boys turns her up before I do?" She cut her sandwich on the diagonal and paused to admire it. "I'll never be allowed to talk to her. They'll lock her up someplace. Is that what you want? You think Sabra wants that?"

"Mallory, she's obviously not in her right mind."

"You don't know that."

Perhaps he had erred here. It was never a good idea to suggest she had missed the obvious, but he was about to do it again. "She's living in filth on the street, and her family is worth millions. That's your idea of sane?"

"Well, she never cared about their money, did she? That's what you told me. Her kid is dead, and she's living with obsession and hate. Trust me, she could care less about the surroundings."

"It's madness."

"Maybe it is, but I *understand* it."

There was a warning edge in her voice. He chose to ignore it. "You have to find her and get her to a hospital."

"I'll find her eventually. It's going to take some time."

Her responses were crisp and growing cooler.

"Mallory, you *must* find her right now. It's your duty to find her. This poor woman—"

"That's *enough*."

Something in her tone of voice made him lose the place-marker in his mind. Now his face was one naked question mark, and she rose from the table to come closer to him, the better to explain all the errors of his ways.

"I live in the real world," she began, as though instructing an idiot child from some fraudulent planet. "All I care about is the murder of Dean Starr. It's going to lead me to the evidence for the murders of the artist and the dancer. You must realize that nobody actually wants me to work that one out—not the commissioner, or the mayor, not the city attorney or the chief of detectives. It's dirty laundry, big-time embarrassment and potential lawsuits."

"But Sabra hasn't harmed anyone. Justice dictates that—"

"There is no justice." She left him to fill in her pause with the implied, but unspoken, *You imbecile*. "New York cops are paid to keep the city from sliding into a cesspool—that's it! There is nothing in the job description about justice. Sabra didn't get justice for Aubry.''

"But you could help this woman if you—''

"No, Charles, I can't. I can't fix the world for her and put everything back the way it was. Her kid will never come home again. But Sabra can help *me*. They all want the case buried, Charles. Do you like the idea of people getting away with a thing like that?''

"It's your job to—''

"Back off!''

He did back off, and back up, and he would have backed out of the room, but she was standing in the doorway.

"I'm doing my job,'' she said—spat. "So Sabra goes on, and I go on.''

She stalked down the hallway, crossed the front room and slammed the door behind her to say she had not appreciated his criticism very much, not much at all.

Charles pulled a blanket around his shoulders and surveyed the roof which overlooked Bloomingdale's. This was penance for crossing Mallory. This was what it had taken to pacify her. His mistake was asking what he could do to help. The next thing he knew, she was handing him a blanket, a building key, binoculars and a cellular telephone. And now he was doing time on a roof, baby-sitting the lunatic Andrew Bliss.

He turned to Henrietta Ramsharan, a good friend and a good sport, who probably had other things to do this evening. But she had come when he called. "So what do you think?''

"Long-distance psychoanalysis isn't in my bag of tricks, Charles.'' Henrietta lowered the binoculars. "But I think you may have underestimated the case. He's not unraveling, he's unraveled.''

"Perhaps I should try to convince Mallory to bring him down from the roof.''

"Have you considered the possibility that Andrew's state of mind is Mallory's work?"

"No, I just assumed it was. How badly damaged is he?" And how badly damaged was Mallory? That was the question he really wanted to ask, but he didn't really want the answer.

"Well, Charles, talking to the mannequin is not a good sign." She raised the binoculars again. "I'm looking at wine bottles all over the roof and no sign of food. So, the aberrant behavior might be a temporary delusion brought on by fasting and alcohol abuse. If I'm right, it's not irreversible damage. But he's hardly moving now. Physically, he's in very bad shape."

He thanked her for coming, and walked her across the roof to the door. She was reluctant to leave him alone here, but he was even more reluctant to impose on her anymore. His good-mannered insistence won out, and she left him. It was his only clear win of the day.

He returned to his lonely outpost at the ledge and focussed his field glasses on the hapless Andrew, who at least had the mannequin to talk to. Henrietta had been gone for an hour when he turned to the sound of footsteps.

"Hey, Charles." Riker leaned a rifle against the retaining wall and glanced over the side to the roof below. "So Mallory talked you into roof duty, huh?" He set a paper sack on the ledge. "You can go home now. I'll take it from here."

"No, I'll stay. Mallory's coming to relieve me. She wanted me to tell you to go home and get some rest."

"Thanks, I could use a decent night's sleep." He handed the sack to Charles. "Here, you can have my sandwiches and beer. Anything else I can do for you?"

"Look out for Mallory?"

Riker smiled. "Mallory will be all right. She knows the rules. She pushed Blakely too far. She saved Coffey's ass, and she paid the bill with her house."

"The house? You think Blakely did that?"

"I don't think it, I know it. Heller jumped into the arson investigation and pulled a print from the gasoline can and another print from inside the house. We bagged the perp who set the fire. He's one of Blakely's men. Now we get to hold the guy for seventy-two hours without charging him. That's gonna make Blakely real nervous, maybe nervous enough to cut a deal with Robin Duffy."

"Robin? He's involved—"

"He's known Mallory since she was a puppy. We couldn't keep him out of it. There was no arson coverage on the house. Duffy was pressuring the department for an investigation so he could sue somebody to cover the damage. We had to cut him in, or he would've blown the scam."

"The scam?"

"Yeah, it's a thing of beauty, Charles." Riker hunkered down beside Charles and took back the paper sack. He pulled out two sandwiches and a six-pack of beer. "Blakely keeps his payoff money in a nice fat offshore account—more than enough money to pay for the kid's house and—"

"Just a minute. A lawyer is conspiring with police officers to blackmail the chief of detectives into paying for the arson with his bribery money. Am I following this?"

Riker nodded, popped the tab on a beer can and handed it to him. Charles thought, yes, he would very much like a drink just now.

"It gets better." Riker slugged back his beer and grinned. "If everything goes well, Blakely is going down, resigning without a pension. That's part of the deal. He's going to walk away with no jail time, but he'll be dead broke. Mallory only has to stay out of Blakely's way for a few more days—just long enough for him to realize that he can't dig his way out of this."

Charles took a healthy swig of beer. "You think he might go after her again?"

"Well, she's got him cornered, and he's making a fight of it."

"So Mallory's involved in this?"

"Charles, do you know anyone else who could've put this scheme together?"

No, of course not. What had he been thinking of? "I don't suppose this could've been managed in a clean, law-abiding fashion?"

"Naw, that almost never works." Riker settled himself on the ground beside Charles and grabbed up a blanket from Mallory's duffel bag. They sat together on the floor of the roof, cross-legged in the storytelling fashion of nearly forgotten summer camps.

Riker pulled a fresh pack of cigarettes from his paper sack and began the evening's entertainment with a metaphor which was far from a child's campfire. "Just think of corruption as cancer in an animal. So maybe forty years ago, the cancer overtook the animal that was New York City, and then the cancer *became* the animal."

Riker lit a cigarette, and the ember glowed in the dark.

"Ah, Charles, the city even steals from the kids. You know, by the time the money travels through the bureaucrats, the kids get damn little. Stealing from babies is pretty low." He took a long drag on his cigarette, and they watched the smoke curl up to the moon.

"Don't I just love this town?" Riker said this as much to himself as to Charles. "But now I'll tell you what really scares me. Mallory fits into this system so beautifully. She plays corruption like a piano. She did make Blakely back off of Coffey. Not only that, but the paperwork for his promotion is in the hopper. He'll make captain before the month is out. You gotta wonder what she had on Blakely to pull that off."

"You don't know? But the payoff money in the—"

"Oh, it's an open secret that Blakely is a dirty cop.

Naw, she made her deal with him and she stuck by it. She won't share the details. Coffey thinks it's a mob connection, but only Mallory knows for sure. I'd bet even money she could get the dirt on any poor bastard that gets in her way. I feel sorry for Quinn if he's holding out on her."

"She won't get any dirt on Quinn."

"She can get anybody, Charles."

"Quinn is an honorable man. His wealth comes from inheritance and a clever way with stock manipulation. He doesn't steal, cheat or lie. I know this man."

"Look, if you won't bet that Mallory can stick him with a sword, I'll bet you that Quinn is more like Mallory than you know."

"No bet. I believe there is a sense of honor in Mallory. It's a bit twisted but—"

"Charles, that's not exactly what I meant, but never mind."

"No, please go on."

"Twelve years ago, Quinn pulled political strings to keep the police away from the family during the murder investigation."

"But those people were falling apart, they couldn't take any more."

"Everybody gets ripped up in a murder investigation. There's a lot of breakage, but it's necessary. We couldn't do the job with Quinn's interference. People in high places owed him favors and he called them in. He obstructed a homicide investigation—that's a major crime, and you've gotta have a lot of dirt on the right people to pull it off. That's why Markowitz brought Quinn into the case and made him part of it. You see how it works?"

Charles shook his head. "The correct—"

"The correct procedure would have been for Markowitz to lose his job slapping Quinn with a charge of obstruction—Quinn and every politician he knew. So instead, the old man made use of Quinn and his connections. Clever? Well, Mallory learned a lot from her old man. The kid turned out to be a natural. You know, she works the weasels better than Markowitz ever did. It cost her one house to learn how far she could go, but she's the new master.''

Riker said his good night as he stood up. He ambled off toward the roof door. Then he stopped and turned to face Charles. ''The kid's all grown up now. I feel like I'm out of a job.''

Charles smiled. Riker did not.

For another hour, Charles continued to sit on the roof with a blanket around his shoulders, staring at the lunatic on the roof of Bloomingdale's. He looked at his watch. The minute hand was coming up on the hour when Mallory would relieve him, and she was never late.

''Hello, Mallory.'' He said this to the night air, for he had not heard her open the door, nor any footsteps. He had absolutely no sense of her presence.

''So, how's it going, Charles?'' She settled a grocery bag on the ground beside him.

Did she seem disappointed that he hadn't given her a chance to sneak up and frighten him? Yes, she did, and he was delighted. Mallory had a strange and unsettling sense of gamesmanship, but he was definitely getting the hang of it.

He lowered his binoculars. ''I think Andrew might be dying.''

She took the binoculars from his hand and stared at the thin figure of Andrew Bliss lying on the down quilts, barely moving anymore. ''No, he's okay. I just saw him twitch. Good night, Charles. Thanks for the help.''

And now he pressed his luck. ''You know this man is obviously not in his right mind.''

''He's hiding out from a killer. That sounds like a pretty sane game plan to me.''

''Hiding out on the roof of Bloomingdale's with full

media coverage from dawn to dusk? This is hiding? This is sane?''

Oh, right.

It was, now that he thought about it, and smart too. And after dark, Andrew could be assured of a hundred voyeurs among the thousand windows that looked down on the roof. If they could count on a sane killer, and Mallory certainly did, then who would be fool enough to harm the man without cover? Yet Charles could not shake the idea that this poor lunatic was Mallory's idea of a good piece of lean meat, a bit of bait for a serial killer.

It was with some reservation that he made his way across the roof and left a helpless fellow human in the hands of Mallory. And now another thought occurred to him as he descended the stairs: She would always view civilians as a class of defenseless, witless sheep, and she would lay down her own life for any one of them, without hesitation. She was a cop.

If God was not listening to Andrew's prayers, Mallory was, and she had grown tired of the slow drone of intonations. She lowered her directional microphone, picked up her cellular phone and dialed the number of the priest. Before she could speak, she heard the old man's voice saying, ''Yes, Kathy?''

''I want to make confession, but I don't remember the words.''

''There's a good reason for that, Kathy. You never made a confession in your entire life, not in or out of the church.''

''Tell me what to say.''

''Do you remember the last time we discussed confession in my office? I remember your very words. 'That's not the way it works,' you said. 'If you can't catch me doing it, then I didn't do it. I've got rights, and you can

call Markowitz, he'll tell you. I don't ever have to confess to anything.' "

"And did you call Markowitz?"

"Yes, Kathy, I did."

"And?"

"He said, 'The kid is absolutely right.' Then he hung
up on me."

"So tell me the words. I want to take communion. I
can't do that until I confess my sins, and I need the damn
words."

"Actually, the church has loosened up a bit since you
were with us. You can take communion if you—"

"No, I want to do this right."

"Why don't we just talk about it first?"

"Is this under the seal of the confessional? You can't
tell anyone, right?"

"That's right. You were so young when your mother
died. There is no fault attached to your actions. You were
frightened, you ran away. That's what children do. I only
wish you had told me about this when you were still a
child. You shouldn't have had to carry that—"

"You would have told the others."

"Still the same trusting little soul you always were."

"Sarcasm is unbecoming in a priest. I think you spend
too much time hanging out with Rabbi Kaplan."

"An occasional poker game."

"I knew it. If you'd known, you would've talked. You
would have told them all."

"No, that would never have happened. But what if
they had known? Helen wanted to adopt you. If your
mother was dead, that would've been possible. Was your
father still living?"

"This is not about my father."

"You witnessed your mother's murder?"

"I saw her after the bastard left her for dead. She was
crawling toward me, covered with blood. Any one of
those wounds should have killed her. You know what

kept her going? She had to crawl a long ways with mortal wounds. But she thought I would get to her in time to save her. That's why she was holding on.''

''No, Kathy. She wanted to touch you before she died, to say goodbye. That's what kept her going. It was for you that she kept going. She must have loved you more than her own life.''

''No. She believed I was going to save her. But I ran away.''

''And you survived. So she did not go through that ghastly ordeal for nothing. Do you know who killed her?''

''No. I never saw him.''

''You never spoke of this to anyone?''

''No.''

''That would explain a lot.''

''The bruises on Sister Ursula's shins? She had that coming.''

''I won't argue that. But you know, there's a kind of innocence in insanity. Ursula still wonders what you're up to. If she knew this about your birth mother, she would send up the flames of a thousand candles each night for the rest of her life. You tend to linger in her memory. You have that effect on people.''

''You can't tell her or anyone.''

''Of course not. Why are you telling me now?''

''I'm confessing. Now what do I do with the guilt? I've confessed. What now?''

''You were a blameless child.''

''I don't want to hear that crap, Father. So let's say I'm guilty, and I've confessed. What now?''

''God forgives you.''

''That's it?''

''That's it.''

''Yeah, right.'' She hung up on him.

•   •   •

He walked around the roof, occasionally pausing to anchor himself by touching the corner of the table or some
object, fearing he might float away if he did not hold on
to something solid, something real. He picked up an
empty wine bottle and set it down again. At each turn of
the roof, he kept his eyes to the design of the plush rugs
which carpeted the tarpaper. He avoided looking at the
decorative mirror in a small art deco frame, skirting it
with a tremor of terror. The last time he had looked at
his reflection, it had been like viewing the remains of a
familiar corpse.

His eyes, oh his eyes.

There were two dead flies lying on the table, sun-dried
and so light, they were carried off on the next breeze. He
turned away. His hand worked over his eyes and left
them closed, the way that service was done for the deceased.

He sat down on the tarmac and addressed the upholstery of the chair. "I couldn't stop what happened."

There was no response from the upholstery.

"There was nothing I could have done."

He took the chair's quiet repose for agreement. He
opened his eyes and leaned over to touch the brocade
arm, as though to gain the chair's confidence, and then
he went on in a louder monotone. "What good would it
have done to tell?"

He stood up and walked twice around the chair in the
way of a child who believes that the circle has a magical
and protective charm. He came to rest beside the chair
and put one arm around the back of it. "Oh, what would
have been the good of it?" His voice was rising more.
Hysteria came stealing up his throat, surprising him and
scaring him with a shrillness in his voice. "Well, it's
crazy, that's all—just crazy!"

One hand clawed through his matted hair. "Am I
screaming?" he screamed. "Do I sound a little frantic?"

The chair withdrew into prolonged silence. He turned away, tears running freely.

When he turned around again, a beautiful woman was sitting in the chair. He recognized the moon-gold hair, though in the better light of the standing lamp, it was closer to burnished copper, and her eyes were long slants of green. The tailoring of her blazer was superb. This was definitely his angel.

"Good evening, Andrew," said the angel, in a soft, silken voice. It was nearly music.

"Good evening." And now he wished he had paid more attention to the nuns' instructions on the order of cherubim, seraphim, and assorted supernatural messengers.

"I understand you've been praying for a sign." She perused the labels of a small store of wine on the side table and found a bottle of red that she approved of. "Andrew, I really worry about you, up here all by yourself." One long red fingernail split the skin of the seal around the cork. "Anyone can get at you. . . . Anyone."

She held a small silver device, which she now opened to expose a cruel screw of metal. She smiled. Andrew tucked in a breath and held it. She drove the point of the screw into the heart of the bottle cork and began to work it deeper and deeper.

Her blazer opened as she leaned forward to pour the wine into a silver goblet which had suddenly appeared on the low table. He saw the gun in her shoulder holster. Well, that was intriguing.

Now he was afraid.

So this was not his guardian angel at all. She was an avenging angel. He supposed that was only fair. So be it. "I see you carry a gun."

A vertical line appeared between her eyebrows, only a faint line to show her annoyance. Andrew lowered his foolish eyes to look down at her feet, which were inexplicably encased in rather expensive running shoes. "It's just surprising to see a gun. I suppose I expected a sword, a great shining sword.''

"Well, the world changed, Andrew." She replaced the bottle's cork. "We use revolvers now."

"I suppose vengeance is vengeance, sword or gun."

"You got *that* right." She brought a handful of communion wafers from her pocket.

"How shall I address you?"

"Mallory—just Mallory is fine." She set the wafers on the low table near the wine goblet and her cellular telephone.

"Mallory? Is that from the order of Malakim, the Virtues?"

If so, that would be good news. The Virtues liked everybody, and never slew anyone as far as he knew.

"Just Mallory."

"I don't know that one. No disrespect intended, but what rank is that?"

"Don't piss me off, Andrew."

"Oh no, I wouldn't dream of it. I'm sure it's a very high rank. I'll just assume it's right up there with the archangels."

"Right. I'm a damn angel." She picked up one of the wafers and held it out to him. As he took it from her hand, she said, "This is the body. Take this body and eat." And then she picked up the wine goblet and offered it to him, saying, "This is the blood. Take it and drink."

He looked down at the wafer and the wine goblet and then looked up at her with a mixture of fear and sadness. "But I can't take communion. You see, I haven't made confession for my sins. I can't even remember the last time I made confession."

"Yeah, right. That *is* a problem."

"Will you hear my confession, Mallory?"

"Oh, sure."

His speech was slow and slurred as he began to describe his sins. Far into his confession, which she could make nothing of, he fell asleep, and the only sound on the roof was the steady rhythm of his snoring.

The angel brought her fist down on the arm of the chair with enough force to make a loud crack in the wooden frame.

The penitent slept on.

CHAPTER
8

HE AWOKE TO A PAIR OF STARING EYES, TINY AND RED. The angel was gone, the rat was not. The beast was only a foot away from his face. He waved his hand lethargically, but the rat did not move. Andrew felt weaker today than yesterday. Would he be able to fend off the rat when it came for him in earnest?

A loaf of bread lay a few inches from his hand. The angel must have left it for him. He was reaching out for it when he heard a beeping noise. He looked up to see the cellular phone on the table by the chair. She must have left that for him, too. But why?

He picked up the phone and extended the antenna. "Hello?"

"Is Mallory there?" asked the brisk voice of a man in a hurry.

"The Archangel Mallory?"

"The what?"

Now the man recited a telephone number, and Andrew confirmed that this was the same number printed on the phone. "But she's not here now. Can I take a message?"

"Yeah, my name is Coffey. Tell the little angel to get lost for a few days. Tell her our negotiations have hit a snag. The chief is sending uniforms to pick her up. He wants her now.''

Father Brenner was not wearing his priest's collar. He had spent the morning working in his garden, and he was still dressed for a day in the soil and the sunlight, wearing a flannel work shirt and a pair of old trousers. He passed through the cordon guard of nurses and receptionists without the protection of a priest's vestments to elicit their best behavior. Today, he felt very much a man like any other, and perversely, he believed that he was getting away with something. For one guilty moment, he wondered if he hadn't left his proper dress at home for the sheer pleasure of getting a rise out of Sister Ursula.

The old woman was one of perhaps forty people seated in the lounge area, yet he picked her out of the crowd immediately. He fixed on her dark, angry eyes before there was time to register the white wimple which hid all but her face from the eyes of fellow earth people, most of whom she doomed to the low-rent echelons of hell. She was dressed all in white, as she was on the day she had been wedded in the church. She looked very much the elderly bride of Christ in her flowing robe and slippers.

Robe and slippers?

Perhaps he had gotten his days mixed up. He was getting to that age. But he could have sworn that today was the day they had agreed upon to pick her up at the hospital and drive her back to the rectory in Manhattan for a proper dinner and a long visit with her only tie to the world, himself.

''You're not dressed,'' said the priest as he sat down beside her.

''And neither are you.'' Her appraising gaze wandered over his person and found him wanting. In most respects she was solidly entrenched in the old ways, but she had never kept to the custody of the eyes. She looked at him squarely, all disapproval.

"You came early this time," she said. "You've never done that before." And there was an implication that he should not do that again. Ursula was death on punctuality. "We have to wait until the proper time before some young puppy will give me my clothes."

Only a few minutes into a polite conversation about weather, flower gardens and hell, said young puppy in nurse's garb arrived by Ursula's chair and led the old woman off to change her clothes. He supposed this was a reasonable precaution in such an institution. It wouldn't do to have the inmates wandering out the door, unescorted and dressed for the unsuspecting world.

A few minutes later, Ursula was back, striding down the hall, moving very fast for a nun in full regalia. She was no modern woman of the church, no short skirt and lipstick fashion sister, but a dress-code nun, a great black warship at full sail. Her heavy crucifix swayed from side to side as she closed in on him.

Father Brenner tried to see her from the point of view of a small child. He closed his eyes against that vision.

When they were in the car and heading toward the city skyline, Ursula broke her stoic silence. "Tell me more about Kathy's extraordinary new habit of stealing candles from the church. What do you suppose she's up to this time?"

Father Brenner winced. He should have known better than to tell her, but under the circumstances, the theft of candles was the only cheerful note he had to offer the elderly nun, all that he was not prevented from repeating. And surely Kathy was safe from Ursula now. All the children were safe.

Though he had never liked this woman, she was continuity to him, a last tie to the old days. He suspected she would live to speculate on whether or not his immortal soul had been admitted above or below.

"I'm glad to see you looking so well," he told her in all sincerity.

"Thank you, Father. Now, about Kathy."

"I was rather pleased that she remembered where the candles were kept. Sorry I can't enlighten you further, Sister Ursula, but she didn't stop to chat."

"How many times do you think she's done this?"

Perhaps Sister Ursula's true vocation was police work. Interrogation had always been her forte.

"She's only stolen candles once that I'm aware of, but the candles have gone missing several days in a row. So it would seem she *is* coming to church on a regular basis. I thought that might make you happy."

"She can buy votive candles in any supermarket or bodega for a few dollars. Doesn't it make you wonder why she steals them from the church? Don't you wonder what dark things she might be doing with them?"

This had been a grave mistake, he could see that now. Ursula had something new to fixate on, to draw out into long strings of conspiracy. Why had it taken him so many years to rechristen her eccentricity as madness?

"Well, I'm pretty confident that she's not selling the candles on the black market."

The nun glared at him, to let him know his levity was not appreciated. "I know she's doing something we would not approve of. She's certainly not burning those candles to the glory of God."

The priest sighed. Ursula was a compulsive soul who would harbor dark suspicions of any parishioner who had not died the minute after baptism. She had been this way even in her young days.

No, now that he thought of it, she had never been young. Even when her face was fresh and unlined, she had been dry as a stick, humorless and without mercy, condemning children to hell in her mind for the sins of youth and beauty, knowing to what use they would put those attributes in adult life.

Kathy Mallory had been the supreme target, wild of spirit, possessing grace in the body and uncommon intelligence. But the little girl's worst crime had been her lovely face. In Ursula's mind, such a child should have been hidden from the world, so as not to create temptation in every man who encountered her.

This beautiful child had brought home the truth that Ursula was quite insane. Among all the generations of children passing through the school, only Kathy Mallory had struck back.

"Stealing candles from a church. Well, I'm not surprised. Once a thief, always a thief," said Ursula. "I always wanted to catch her red-handed."

"Well, you broke up the floating poker game. That was something."

"But even under the threat of everlasting damnation, the other children wouldn't give her up. It was never a clean win. She was only a child, yet she was the most worthy adversary I ever had."

Sister Ursula's devotion to God was beyond the pale, and she could not have told a lie under torture. Young Kathy had been a gifted liar, an amoral character, a thief, a sinner only Nietzsche could love. Her simple creed in those days had been the child's code of honor: Thou shalt not rat on anybody.

And yet, on the last day of the world, when the earth gave up all its mysteries and all questions were answered, it would probably not surprise him to learn that God loved Kathy Mallory best—because she had not ratted on the nun.

The child had taken her revenge, cradling a broken wrist in her good hand as she kicked the nun's leg out from under her and brought the screaming Ursula to ground. Then Kathy had stalked off, never to break her silence, never to give in to the Markowitzes' questioning or his own. She had been utterly satisfied with her revenge, and in the child's mind, the affair was settled.

Kathy's old enemy now sat beside him, an aged monster at the end of her ruthless quest to suck the spirit from generations of children, an overzealous vampire in the service of God.

"Thank you, Father, for bringing me this new information about Kathy."

"What are friends for?"

This was not friendship, of course, for he suspected Ursula did not like him, and proximity to madness had always made him nervous. Whatever their relationship was, it would continue until one of them gave up the ghost.

It is penance.

He nodded at this new insight.

When Mallory was certain there were no stakeout vehicles near her condominium, she stepped into the street, heading for the front door. A long black limousine stopped in front of her, a window rolled down and a familiar face nodded her back to the curb. She waited on the sidewalk as the car pulled up. A door opened and she slid into the rear seat beside the aged Mafia don.

He smiled at her, displaying red, receding gums and broken, crooked teeth with wide gaps between them. She knew his type. He would take great pride in having all his own teeth, however rotted they might be. He was probably unaware that it gave him the look of an old dog who could no longer chew.

He turned to face her. His breath reeked. "I hope those offshore account numbers were of some use to you."

She nodded.

He leaned over to speak more intimately. "Mallory, have you ever thought of getting into another line of work?"

"No. I like being a cop. I'm good at it."

"You take after Markowitz." He reached out one gnarly hand to touch hers. She balled her hand into a fist to warn him off. He did pull back, but he also smiled, as if he found her gesture of violence exquisitely charming.

"I suppose you learned a lot from your father."

She nodded again. "So the sooner you retire, old man, the better."

His cracked lips spread wide over the yellow teeth, and his frail body shook when he laughed. The laughter turned into a barking cough. He reached out to the bar recessed into the back seat of the limo. Where the booze should be, there was a water pitcher and a portable pharmacy of medication. He fiddled with a plastic mask attached to a small bottle of oxygen. He clasped it over his face and inhaled deeply.

Enjoying the good life, old man?

Mallory glanced at her watch while she waited out the dregs of the coughing spasm. "I haven't got all day," she said. "What do you want?"

He removed the mask. "I came to warn you." His every breath was a ragged piece of work. He held up one hand to call for a time-out. In another minute, he was himself again. "Blakely tried to hire one of my boys to whack you. I put a stop on that."

"How comforting." She touched the glass partition that separated the driver from his employer. "Bulletproof glass?"

"Yes, and soundproof—very private. I conduct all my business in this car, so my driver checks it for bugging devices every morning."

She could only see the dark hair of the man behind the wheel. He stared straight ahead. "And who checks the driver?"

"He's family—my nephew's youngest boy. Satisfied? Now listen to me, Mallory. Don't underestimate Blakely. He's scared now—not thinking straight. Next, he'll lean on one of his own people to do the job. He's gone underground. It may take me awhile to find him. But I can give you a good bodyguard—"

"I don't want your bodyguard. And you don't touch Blakely—you got that? You can't kill all your mistakes, old man. Blakely is being threatened with tax evasion, not mob connections. There won't be any investigation. I keep my bargains—you better keep yours."

The driver's head turned slightly to find her reflection in his rearview mirror. He looked away quickly, as though she had caught him at something.

Now what was that about?

"I want you to take the bodyguard." The old don's voice was insistent, but not so confident anymore. "I'm going to give you a man I would trust with my own life."

"So you're still worried that it's all going to come back on you." And if she didn't live through the night, it would. Buying Blakely had been a bad mistake, and the payoff trail to a senator had left the old Mafia don vulnerable. It was only a matter of time before his own people realized what a liability he was.

She caught the eyes of the young driver in the rearview mirror. Was this man suddenly worried too?

"Cops don't need bodyguards." Her eyes traveled over the car's lush appointments, looking for the thing that didn't belong here.

"Cops don't usually have gunmen after them," said the don, as though explaining elementary facts of life to a small child.

"Yeah, they do—every time they hit the street." Her eyes were fixed on an irregular upholstery stud near the glass partition. She leaned closer. The black stud was not leather but plastic, and it had three machine-made holes. She pulled it from the plush leather. It came out easily, only anchored by a pin. She blew a shrill whistle into the small plastic transmitter.

On the other side of the glass wall, the driver put one hand to the ear where the receiver must be hidden. There was real pain in the mirror reflection of his eyes.

The old man looked from the driver to the eavesdropping device in Mallory's hand. Eyes rounded with shock, he knew he had been betrayed, yet he tried to deny it with the slow shake of his head.

Mallory knew everything in the don's mind: This could not be happening, not to him, not at the hands of his own family.

"Soundproof? Bugproof? Don't you wonder who your driver reports to?" Mallory touched the button to lower the glass partition. "Let's ask him."

The man at the wheel was turning around, one hand fumbling in his coat where the holster would be. She was already pointing her revolver at the driver's face—and the bulletproof glass was sliding down.

The driver left the car at a dead run. Across the street, Frank the doorman was averting his eyes from the running man with the gun in his hand. Frank was a good New Yorker. What he did not see, he could not witness to in court at the cost of a day's pay.

When the running gunman was out of sight, Mallory holstered her revolver and turned back to the old don. "Was that one of your hotshot bodyguards?"

Angry now, the don reached for the car phone. "That punk is a dead man."

Mallory grabbed his wrist. It took very little effort to restrain him. "Who are you going to call? Another bodyguard? One of your nephew's kids?" She sat quietly for all the time it took him to grasp this simple thing—*he* was the dead man.

She opened the door and stepped out of the car. "Might be smarter to call a cab and head for the airport." She closed the door slowly, saying, "Don't light in any one place for too long. You know the drill, old man."

Mallory crossed the street to the condominium. Frank the doorman was smiling as he held the door open. "Two cops came by, miss." He followed her into the lobby. "They showed me their badges and told me to let them into your apartment." He pushed the button to fetch her an elevator. "But they didn't have a warrant, so I told them to go screw themselves into the ground. I hope I did the right thing."

She put two twenty-dollar bills into his coat pocket to tell him he had done exactly the right thing.

The elevator doors opened, and she looked up to the mirror mounted high on the back wall. It gave her a compressed view of an empty interior. When she stepped off the elevator at her floor, she had her revolver out of the holster. The gun preceded her into the apartment. After checking all the rooms and closets, she sat down on the couch and rifled her tote bag for the cellular phone.

It was gone. *But where*—

She checked her watch again. Now she reached over to the standard telephone on the end table and dialed Father Brenner's number.

Where is the damn cellular?

While she talked to the priest, she searched the drawer of the table—a futile activity. Mrs. Ortega, world's foremost cleaning woman, had put the apartment back in order after the robbery. So what were the odds that a single item would be out of place? Where had she lost the damn cellular phone?

She finished her instructions to Father Brenner. "I want you to say a mass for her."

"Consider it done, Kathy. What was your mother's name?"

"You don't need her name. When you talk about her, just say she was a woman who was brutally murdered. And leave me out of it."

She glanced at the messages accumulated on her answering machine.

"Kathy?"

"That's all you get. It's enough, isn't it?"

"Yes. I'll say the mass tomorrow."

"No, do it tonight, I need it tonight."

"All right, tonight it is. So you're not looking for spiritual comfort for yourself?"

"No. You can save that routine for the believers, the suckers."

"Are you still lighting the candles, Kathy?"

Mallory hung up the phone.

She emptied the tote bag on the coffee table, and spread the files and notebooks—not here. The last time she had seen the cellular phone it was in this bag, wasn't it? No, wait. She remembered sliding it into the pocket of her blazer last night. She reached out for the desk phone, ignored the pulsing light of the messages waiting, and pushed the buttons for the number of her cellular phone.

"Hello?"

The voice was Andrew's. So she had left it behind on the roof. "Hello, Andrew. How are you?"

"Oh, Mallory. I was hoping you might call. Shall I give you your messages?"

"Sure."

"You have one from Jack Coffey. He says the chief's boys are after you with orders to bring you in. Oh, and J. L. Quinn called and asked for you. But he didn't leave a message."

"Did Quinn say anything?"

"Well, we did have a lovely chat. But there's no message. He said he'd probably catch up with you later in the day."

"Thank you, Andrew."

Picking up a spare phone from her office was next on her list of things to do. It was shaping up to be a busy day. She pulled out her notebook and ticked off what she would need from her apartment.

The doorman called on the house phone to announce J. L. Quinn. She should tell Frank to turn the man away. Time was precious, and she had already stayed here too long. What could Quinn want now? Perhaps his long chat with Andrew had raised a few questions.

"Send him up, Frank."

When she admitted Quinn to her apartment, he was wearing his courtesy smile. She was learning to categorize his facial expressions, discovering small variations in the mask. He casually examined the surroundings, as if he were looking for something.

She remained standing and folded her arms to let him know he would not be staying long. When he turned to face her, his smile was unaltered, but his eyebrows were raised, and she knew he was going to apologize.

"Sorry to drop by without calling first, but if you recall, the only number you gave me was for the cellular phone, and it seems that Andrew Bliss has that."

He glanced at the long leather couch, probably waiting for an invitation to sit down. She ignored the subtlety.

"So, Quinn, I understand you had a long talk with Andrew."

"Yes, he told me he made a confession to a green-eyed angel. I was surprised you hadn't arrested him."

"Andrew's idea of confession is my idea of a rambling drunk. I think we got as far as the sins of puberty. What do you want, Quinn?"

He was staring at the walls, bare but for the single clock, a piece of minimal design with dots in place of numerals. The furnishings of her apartment were expensive, and stark. There should be nothing here to give away any shading of her personality. But by the faint nod of his head, she knew these environs were what he had expected to find; that much was in his face when he turned back to her.

"Mallory, I wonder if you'd have dinner with me tomorrow night. And perhaps the theater."

She turned away from him and covertly scanned her front room as though for the first time. What did Quinn see in this place? Perhaps it was what he did not see: no personal items to connect her to another human being, no dust, nothing out of place, and no wall hanging to indicate an interest in anything but time. The large clock dominated the space. The furniture was arranged in precision symmetry.

And now she understood.

This extreme order had not created the intended false front of a guarded personality—the real effect was all too personal, next to naked exposure. It was an effort to shake off the feeling of violation.

"I'm free tomorrow," she said. "Would you like to do something a little more exciting than dinner and the theater?"

"Name it and it's yours." One splayed hand indicated that his offer included the whole earth. "Anything."

"A fencing match."

His smile was back, but only for a moment. "So Charles told you about the scar." He walked over to the couch and ran his hand over the back of it, approving the quality of the leather, and perhaps wondering how she had managed it on a cop's salary. "A fencing match. Well, that does sound more diverting."

She sat down in a chair and gestured to the couch. "Do you still keep your hand in? You have a membership at a fencing club?"

"Yes, on both counts." He settled into the plush leather cushions and crossed his legs. "What's your background, Mallory?"

"One semester of fencing classes at school, but I think I can take you."

It was predictable that he would not smile at this. He would never be rude enough to suggest that she was blowing smoke.

"The agility of youth goes a long way, but it won't take you all the way. Don't count on an easy win."

"I can beat you. I'm willing to place a bet on it."

He shook his head. "I won't do money with you."

"Not money. I was thinking along the lines of anything I want, against anything you want."

"Those are outrageously high stakes, Mallory. I won't take advantage of you. No bet."

How predictable.

"You shouldn't be afraid to bet—unless you're afraid to lose." She looked at the clock. She must leave soon.

"You can't possibly win, not with your limited experience. It's not a fair wager."

"I'm not worried. If you do win, I know you'll pick a forfeit I can easily make." She had to do this quickly.

"You know that for a fact?"

I know you.

"It's your character, Quinn. Charles tells me you're the quintessential gentleman—I know the breed."

"You're right. I would never ask a forfeit you couldn't afford. So I'll concede that you know me very well." He stood up and turned to face the clock. "But no one knows very much about you, Mallory—not even the people who knew you best."

He moved to the window and spoke to the glass. "Your origins are a complete mystery. You wouldn't give the necessary information to the Markowitzes so they could formalize your adoption. Child Welfare made an exhaustive search, but they could never trace your family. Juvenile Hall records show two brief incarcerations at ages eight and nine, but no success in learning your right name. And they were never able to hold on to you for more than a few days each time. There's a note in a folder with your photograph. It says, 'Brilliant child.' "

He turned around to see what effect his words had on her. He seemed pleased with the result. "My own investigators are very thorough. They're the best in the world, and they have no idea where you came from. Suppose your forfeit was to tell me everything I wanted to know about you, your history, everything. Could you afford that?''

She had underestimated him.

''I keep them in here.'' Charles stood aside to let her pass through the door. Mallory had never been in his bedroom before. She did not seem overly excited by the seventeenth-century dower chest at the end of his hand-carved bedstead. She probably thought if she had seen one precious antique, she had seen them all. What captured her attention was the glass case mounted on the wall over the chest. It contained a pair of crossed swords.

''Charles, they're wonderful. These are nothing like the sabers we used at school.''

''You trained with a blunt saber, right?'' He opened the closet and took out a long brown leather bag and unzipped it. He carefully lifted out a pair of swords. Holding one in his right hand, he sliced the air with its tapered rod. ''Now this is what you'll be using with Quinn. It's a competition saber. It's wired so you can be scored on a machine that—''

She wasn't listening. She put one knee on the carved chest and reached up to the case, looking to him for permission. He nodded. She opened the case and removed one saber from the rack. She eased off the chest and stood at the center of the large room, hefting the sword in her right hand. Now, with utter disregard for the weight of the steel and its sharp edge, she easily slung the handle through the air from one hand to the other. She held the edge up to examine it. She smiled to say, *Now this is a weapon.*

''This has a really wicked point.'' She touched the sharp edge of the blade. ''It could use some sharpening, but not bad.''

''Well, it's the real thing. It's much heavier than what you're accustomed to.''

''No, it's about the same.''

What? Oh, of course. She was comparing the weight of the sword to the weight of her gun.

"The pair was an heirloom of the Quinn family. Jamie made me a present of them after I'd scarred him. It was an outrageous gesture. They're very old and quite valuable. I think he gave them to me because he was afraid that the accident might put me off the idea of fencing."

"He *is* a gentleman, isn't he?"

"To the nth degree. He's also the finest swordsman I've ever met."

"But you scarred him."

"That was an embarrassment, not a victory." Oh, wait. That wasn't properly translated into Malloryspeak. "It was a pure accident, a fluke." He held up the competition saber. "This is a very good blade. You'll need a mask—I've got that. Now the fencing jacket. I have an old one that might fit you. And the vest, the body wire—the club will have those items, no need to buy them."

She kept her eyes to the sword in her hand. "I wish we could fence with these."

"Not a chance. He'd never agree to that. These are not sporting weapons. He wouldn't risk hurting you. You know, you can't beat him, Mallory."

"I have to beat him. The stakes are very high."

"I know this man. He won't hold you to the bet. I'm sure he didn't want to make it in the first place."

"I have to win."

"I don't think you understand what it means to be an Olympic champion. You don't respect your opponents, and that will cost you."

He took the cavalry sword from her hand and replaced it with the competition saber. Next, he handed her a white fencing jacket he had worn as a child, albeit a rather large child. "See if this fits."

When she had zipped up the jacket and fastened the high collar, only the wide shoulders were outsized.

He reached up to the top shelf of the closet and pulled

out two white helmets with dark steel mesh. "Put this on." He threw her one mask. She caught it easily and put it on, slipping the strap over the back of her head, and settling her chin into the screen cage. He didn't like the sight of her in the mask. It made her face a near-black oval, and gave her the appearance of an unfinished machine, an imitation of a human without a face.

He pushed the few pieces of obstructing furniture to the wall and moved to the center of the wide room. She gracefully followed him into the *en garde* position, feet placed at right angles with space between them, her body straight and evenly balanced between her heels.

She did not wait for the courtesy of the saluting swords. With no warning, she lunged, arm and sword extended for the thrust to his midsection. Her speed was astonishing, but he easily parried the thrust and sent her blade away from his body.

"If you're counting on the element of surprise to beat him, you will lose in that first move, and you'll have nothing left. Strategy is everything, and it's intricate."

He lunged and feinted the sword to her left, then quickly described a half circle in the air to make a strike to her right side. She parried, but badly and too late. One hour later, he could not fool her with that maneuver, but she had made very few strikes and lost every bout.

He ended the last round by removing his mask and saluting her. She followed his every move, bringing the hilt of her sword to her lips, blade pointing straight up, and then down.

He settled into a chair by the wall. She sat on his bed.

"You need a strategy to win, Mallory. But you haven't the experience to formulate one. Every move you can make will be predictable to him. Experience and skill are everything. Your reaction time will be twenty-five years younger, but that won't save you. You're very fast, but he'll destroy that edge by always being moves ahead of you."

She seemed skeptical of this.

He sighed. "It's rather like a chess match. Now aren't you sorry you wouldn't let me teach you that game?" Apparently she was not. She only stared at the tip of the sword.

He stood up and crossed the room. Gently, he lowered the point of her blade to get her attention away from it. "Every time you angle your saber, you telegraph the move you'll make, and he's there before you. You see?" No, she didn't. She saw nothing but the sword in her hand.

"Mallory, you can't beat me, and I can't beat him. You are nothing if not logical. So, you can see that this is a lost cause."

Riker looked up as she walked into her office with a leather bag slung over one shoulder. It was shaped like a basketball with a rifle barrel.

"What's in the bag, Mallory?"

"A sword and a mask."

"You're joining the opposition? A thief with a sword? I like it."

"It's for the fencing match with Quinn. But, yeah, I might be crossing sides for a while. Coffey says Blakely's after me. It looks like he's going to put up a fight."

"It figures. That stupid bastard doesn't know how to lie down and die right."

"I need a place where Blakely wouldn't think of looking for me. A hotel is a bad idea, and I can't stay with Charles again. I don't want him involved if this all goes bad on me."

"Well, I'm taking the graveyard shift with Andrew tonight. You can use my place. No one would ever suspect you of hiding out in a smelly ashtray. But the decor might put you off."

"Decor? You mean the spiderwebs in every corner,

the garbage piling up in the kitchen, and the forty-two mostly empty pizza cartons? That decor?''

''Yeah.''

''As I recall, it was only the plastic Jesus night-light I really hated. Very tacky. You can kiss that thing good-bye. Thanks, Riker.''

''You'll need a way in.''

''You mean a key?''

''Sorry. Sometimes I forget who I'm talking to.'' And now he grabbed her hand and pressed the key into her palm. ''Use it. And where are you going now?''

''You know where I'm going.''

The main room of the East Village gallery was a blaze of television lights. The script girl was making him wild. She questioned every little thing. She found fault with every item in his story as she was working out the motions of a murder. ''Mr. Watt,'' she said, ''I just have one more question. How could it have happened that way if you—''

''I don't know!'' yelled Oren Watt.

The script girl backed away, eyes a little more open now, perhaps suddenly remembering that this was the Monster of Manhattan who was screaming at her.

''Get out of my face! I don't know!'' He pushed the girl out of his way, and she left the lobby at a run. The director called for a break, and the crew members withdrew to the far side of the long room to light up cigarettes and squat in conversational groups. Only the cop remained with Oren.

He blamed his loss of temper on Detective Mallory. She had a gift for getting on his nerves.

''That's the trouble with lies, Oren. They only look good on paper. They never work out in real time and space. Now would you like to tell me how Senator Berman fits into this murder?''

''I don't know.''

Mallory stood beside him, edging closer, saying, "My father used to say we all know more than we know we know."

What was good enough for the script girl might be good enough for the cop. He grabbed her shoulder and shoved her back to the wall. She gave him no resistance, but she showed no fear either. And now she was even smiling at him. He had always been comfortable in the sure knowledge of his own sanity. It crossed his mind that she might be the crazy one.

"Oren, aren't you going to tell them about the Outsider Artist scam? Big names, big scandal for the evening news. It might boost the ratings if you nail Senator Berman."

Enough! Bitch!

He put one flat palm against the wall close to her head. "Now listen, honey—"

He heard the click of metal before he saw the handcuff dangle from his wrist. In the next moment, he was being spun round and knocked off balance. His cheek was pressed to the hardwood floor when he heard another click of the cuffs, and his left hand was prisoner to the right.

All the following moments were barely comprehensible to him. He was on his feet, being hustled toward the square of daylight in the distance. As he rushed his body forward, she kept him off balance. He was staring at the floor now and fearing that he would fall on his face. Then he was out on the sidewalk, and she was pushing down on the top of his head, forcibly seating him in the rear of a small tan car. In another minute, they were rolling, speeding through the streets, ignoring stop signs and lights, barely avoiding a collision with a bus.

He was sweating profusely when the car pulled to a curb in SoHo. She pulled him out of the car and escorted him in a quick shuffle through a door and into an elevator, then down a hallway and into a room luxuriously decorated for another century. They passed down a short hallway and into another room of computers, modern furniture and a familiar face he had not seen in years. What was this cop's name?

"Hi, Riker," she said, answering his question.

Riker seemed stunned.

"I want my lawyer," said Oren Watt.

"Up to you, Oren," said Mallory, pushing him roughly into a chair. "But if we call your lawyer, then we have to go down to the precinct and go through all the damn paperwork, pressing charges for an assault on a police officer."

"I did *not* assault you!"

"You've been away a long time, haven't you, Oren? Eleven years? It's a new world. There's a huge political base out there that says I get to lock you up just for calling me *honey*. Yeah, the assault charge will stick. Four people saw me identify myself as a police officer while the cameras were still rolling. And there are a few old charges I could make stick."

"The statute of limitations was over—"

"Is that what you were counting on, you idiot?" She brought her face close to his. "Murder never goes away. You didn't do it, but you're tied to it. You might need police protection, so play nice."

"Protection?"

"The whole scam is coming apart now, Oren. Koozeman and Starr are both dead, and I think you'll be the next man down. Want to come in out of the cold?" She leaned down to forage in a cardboard carton. When she stood up again, she had an axe in her hand. "Last chance, Oren."

"This is insane!"

"Isn't it? A bit like a bad acid trip through Wonderland." She slammed the axe down on the table with great force. Oren Watt stiffened. "Well, come on, little Alice, it's time for the unconfession. No? I wonder if the killer will use an axe again? The last murder had a little more creativity. Koozeman died eating the artwork. He was a greedy bastard, wasn't he? Everything he saw was food, animate, inanimate. Now you sell drawings of body parts. Yeah, I think the killer will use the axe for you. It's so fitting, isn't it?''

"I'd go to jail if I told you anything. You said obstruction of—''

"Ease up, Mallory." Now Riker spoke to him in a rational voice, almost kind. "This is the way it works, sir. The last one to cooperate loses immunity and takes the fall.''

"Seven years in a cell, Oren," said Mallory. "Or maybe I could arrange to have you shipped back to the funny farm for three more months of unrestricted television privileges if you cooperate. But that shrink of yours is definitely doing time for this. If you don't recant that confession, I'm going after him. Then you know what happens? He throws you to the district attorney as a bribe. If he rolls over on you, he gets immunity from prosecution. He walks, and you do the hard time by yourself.''

"That's enough, Mallory. Stop badgering him,'' said Riker. "You really want to think it over, sir. But don't talk to your doctor. She's right about him, you know. He will give you up in a heartbeat. He couldn't care less what happens to you. He's a profiteer first. I'm not sure he ever was a doctor. I don't trust any of those bastards.''

"You're both nuts.''

She leaned down, her eyes level with his. "High praise from you, Oren, considering your mental history. Markowitz asked you if you had any trophies from the kill, maybe a body part. What did you tell him?''

"I don't remember. I was high, I was jazzed. I swear I don't remember what we talked about.''

"I'll give you one more chance. You tell me what

piece of the body was missing. If you guess right this time, I'll leave you alone.''

''Her heart.''

''Too poetic. You lose.''

Now she left her seat to walk around the table and stand behind his chair. ''Let's try an experiment, shall we?'' She pulled the chair out from under him, tumbling him to the floor.

''Mallory!'' The other cop was leaving his chair, moving toward her.

She gave Riker a look to say, *Back off or you're next.*

Oren watched her walk around the side of the desk, and now she was advancing on him, hands clenched into fists. He managed to right his body to a sitting position. Working legs and rear end like an inchworm, he scooted back to the far corner of the room, tucking in his head to protect it from the rain of blows that was surely coming. She pursued him on cat's feet, slow and quiet. One hand came from behind her back, the hand that held the axe. That hand was rising now, and he was crying.

The other cop came up behind her and took the axe away. Riker pinned one of her arms behind her back and dragged her from the room and into the outer office. The door was slightly ajar. Oren watched the other cop slam Mallory's body up against the wall as he yelled at her.

''I can't trust you anymore, Mallory!'' Riker reached inside her blazer and took the gun. ''You know, you were right. Watt didn't do it.'' He slapped her face. ''But you've snapped, kid. You're a loose cannon now.''

Suddenly, it was Riker's turn to be surprised. He was being lifted bodily off the ground, and then he was flying toward the couch, landing there in a tangle of arms and legs. He looked up to see Charles advancing on him in slow deliberate steps, as Mallory moved quickly in the other direction to shut the door to her office.

Charles's mouth was set in a grim tight line of anger,

an expression Riker had never seen on the gentle giant's face before. He knew that at any moment, this large man he dearly loved could take his head off with one blow, and by his face, Charles meant to do just that. Riker still held Mallory's revolver in his hand, and Charles didn't like the gun at all, not in this proximity to Mallory, and he showed no fear of it.

"Stay back, Charles." But Charles was still coming. Now Mallory had moved between them.

"Charles," she hissed, "stay out of it! Back off."

He did stop, but his face showed no signs of abating anger, and he was not backing off. So Mallory only held the giant on a string for the moment.

Riker untangled his legs and placed them squarely on the floor. "The game is called good cop, bad cop, Charles."

He could almost see the mechanics of Charles's beautiful brain rapidly processing this information, realizing what he had done, and changing his mood from rage to unbearable sadness. Charles turned and slowly walked back to his own office, pulling the door closed behind him.

"It's time," said Mallory, motioning Riker toward the door.

He entered Mallory's office alone. Oren Watt was still shivering on the floor. Riker crossed the room to kneel down beside the man, and this made Watt drive his body deeper into the corner.

"Oren, I'm sorry about this. Look here," said Riker in his normal, amiable tone of voice. "Whatever happens, I want you to know that I really did try to get the gun away from her. She kicked me in the balls."

"She's coming back? And that big guy? Him too?"

"Yeah, 'fraid so. You know, she never levels with me. I really got no idea what she wants from you."

"She wants to know who killed the artist and the dancer. And she wants to know why, but I don't know, I swear I don't know.''

"So you never killed anyone.''

"No, I never did. She already knows that. Ask her. But I don't know who *did* kill them. And I don't know anything about Dean Starr's murder or Koozeman's. It's the truth, I swear it.''

"I'll tell you what, Oren. If you help me, I'll help you. And when she comes back, I promise I won't let her hurt you. Deal?''

"What do you want?''

"You met a woman at the mental institution. She was very attractive, fortyish, short black hair and large blue eyes, very white skin.'' He held up the photo Mallory had manipulated on her computer.

"Yeah, I remember her. She was my friend.''

"Suppose I told you she was a famous artist under an assumed name. Who would she remind you of?''

"Oh, shit, there are thousands of people in the famous-artist category. Who can keep track?''

"You remember when she left the hospital?''

"Yeah. It was the day they took her last dollar. She was worse off when she left, and I don't mean the money. When she first came, she was very strong. I wondered what she was doing there. She never said. So she came in larger than life, and left when she was small. It was sad.''

"She was your friend.''

"My only friend.''

"You were close.''

"I miss her. I think about her all the time.''

"Do you know where she might have gone?''

"No. I wish I did.''

"Okay, you were very close to her. You confided everything to her. You told her something about the murders. What was it?''

"I told her the truth. All I did that night was deliver the pizza and the drugs."

"You never heard from her again?"

"Oh, she keeps in touch. Sometimes she calls me, but she never leaves a number. I don't know where she is, and that's the truth."

"Did you give her the connection between Koozeman and the murders?"

"What? You're not gonna hang anything on me. I didn't—" And now Watt's eyes were showing entirely too much white.

Mallory was standing in the doorway. Riker got to his feet, dusted his pants and walked toward the door.

"Hey, Riker," said Watt, voice straining, breaking. "We had a deal."

"I lied," said Riker, closing the door behind him and leaving Oren Watt to Mallory.

He walked to the door of Charles's office and knocked.

"Come in." Charles was slumped behind his desk, staring down at the blotter. "You'll never forgive me, will you?"

"There's nothing to forgive, Charles. I'm really glad you tossed me around. Ah, you think I'm kidding?" He sat on a corner of the desk. His smile was wasted. Charles would not meet his eyes. "I used to worry about the kid. I mean, suppose something happened to me?" Something like his rainy day bullet, which would not wait forever. "Now I don't have to worry anymore. I know you'll always be there for her."

Riker put out his hand, but Charles only stared at it.

"You're just gonna leave it hanging out there in the air that way?"

Charles grasped Riker's hand, but his face was a long way from coming to terms with what he had done, and what he had planned to do.

"Snap out of it, Charles. You're breaking my heart

here. I don't need that kind of crap from you. I got Mallory for that.''

''Oren, I already know how scum like you happen to be on such friendly terms with a senator. He buys your work. That bastard is one of the ghouls, the crime scavengers.''

Oren Watt had recovered a bit of his emotional stability now. Mallory had trained him like a rat. As long as he answered the questions, she kept her distance.

''No, that's not exactly right. He's not a collector, he's only in it for the money, the turnover profit. He's part of the start-up market. He makes the initial investment.''

''Then he makes his profits in the secondary market after he and his friends drive the price up.''

''Right.''

''So it's a cartel?''

''Nothing that sophisticated. He's just an individual buyer. He bought Peter Ariel's work, too. And then he made big bucks after the murder.''

''Could Berman have had anything to do with the murders?''

''That ass? Oh, give me a break. No. Let's just say the money he made on Peter Ariel whetted his appetite for crime art. He also bought John Wayne Gacy's work. He held it until after the execution, and then he made a bundle. And there are eight or ten minor mass murderers who paint. Berman buys ghoul art by the carload and makes a huge profit on volume. He gets it from prisons and mental institutions. It's just business. He unloads it as fast as he can.''

''He used Koozeman to broker all the deals quietly, right?''

''Lots of people went through Koozeman.''

''I found your shrink's name in Koozeman's computer,'' she lied. ''It looks like they started doing business about twelve years ago.''

Oren Watt was nodding his head. All she'd been able to turn up were code names and dates. Blakely probably had the Rosetta stone to break that code. If so, it was burned by now.

"So Koozeman had a lock on the sickness market? He was the one who did the deal with the shrink for your confession, right?"

"Yeah, he snagged me outside the gallery the night of the murder—right after the cops let me go. He told me to go to his apartment building, and he put me into a cab. That night, we all met at Koozeman's place. I signed an agent contract with the shrink, and the shrink did a contract with Koozeman. Koozeman had the lists of people who would pay the moon for art connected to high-profile crimes. No one seemed to care that I couldn't draw."

"Koozeman and the shrink I can almost understand. But it's a funny business for a senator, making profits on murdered taxpayers. So Senator Berman must have gone nuts when there was another murder in one of Koozeman's galleries."

"He went through the roof. He thought it would all come out if Koozeman was investigated. Lucky the senator has powerful friends in the same funny business."

"You mean the lieutenant governor?" The ex-mayor of New York.

"Sure. Why do you think that little bastard's so in love with the damn death penalty? Every time one of those murderers dies, the price of their work goes up."

Father Brenner would give Kathy Mallory a worthy performance. He was still doing penance for the sins which could not be put to Ursula, for she was truly insane, and therefore blameless. The sins of blindness were his own.

What he had prepared was a small miracle, given the time he'd been allotted to pull it off. And throughout the day, Ursula had been invaluable in putting the fear of

God into lapsed Catholics, none of whom wished to be on the bad side of a mad nun on a mission.

This was to be his finest mass. The music would be Mozart's *Requiem*, for this was the piece which the precocious young student orchestra had been rehearsing when the priest made his begging call to the music school. A former student, a somewhat lax and guilty parishioner, was now the director of that school. Father Brenner had been refused with a hail of excuses from scheduling problems to personal problems. He had been told it was quite impossible on such short notice. Sister Ursula had then taken the phone, and the school's director learned, once again, that it was a dreadful mistake to get between Ursula and God's work.

And so, the holy stage was now set with the well-scrubbed faces of music students. And he had packed many pews with their proud parents. It was a good turnout for the death of a woman whose name would mean nothing to any of them.

The young musicians' feet shuffled and tapped with stage fright as they held fast to their bassoons and bass horns, strings and trumpets, trombones and timpani. Father Brenner had pulled out all the stops for this most special occasion. The chorus would be sung by every gifted voice of choirs past and present whom the beleaguered choirmaster had been able to corral into service.

Both choirmaster and conductor had told him it was insane to attempt the chorus without a proper rehearsal with the orchestra. The priest had counseled faith, and counted on good memory, for the *Requiem Mass* was not new to any of them.

A parishioner who owned a mortuary had been leaned on to provide the flowers which graced the altar, a profusion of lilies and orchids borrowed for a few hours from the viewing room of the uptown funeral parlor. Actually, since some bereaved family had paid for those flowers, this might be considered a theft of sorts. But that was almost fitting, considering who he had in his front pew, the thief of candles.

He was touched that Kathy had brought a recording device, which sat on the space beside her. So she wanted to preserve her mother's mass. He was confident that both Helen and the birth mother would have been proud to see how far their child had come in her spiritual growth.

He remembered the day twelve-year-old Kathy had stolen the communion wine from the school chapel and made herself sick on it. That day she had sat in his office, drinking strong tea and memorizing lines of scripture, preferring that to the alternative of his calling Markowitz at work to tell him his child could not hold her liquor.

That was the day he had noticed the fresh bruise on the side of her face, and not asked where she had gotten it. There had been other days and other bruises—more blindness. Helen Markowitz had asked her about the bruises, and then written a note asking that Kathy be more closely supervised during rough sports. He had found the note curious at the time, for there were no rough sports at the academy. More blindness.

Now the electric lights of the cathedral were switched off, and a score of candles flared up in the hands of the altar boys. The white flowers took on an eerie glow as the priest announced that this was a mass for a woman who had been brutally murdered—the very words Kathy had requested. He never mentioned that this woman had a beautiful child—as he had been requested to leave her out of it. But because he had known this woman's child, he was able to summon up a passion he thought was lost to him.

He looked back at Kathy. How young she seemed, how little changed. The last time he saw her as a student, she had been carried into his office in the arms of the janitor who had found her at the bottom of the cellar stairs. She was unconscious as the janitor gently laid her slight body down on the couch. But she had rallied long enough to do some damage before the ambulance came for her. And the last time Sister Ursula ever saw Kathy Mallory's face, the old woman was lying on the floor holding on to a freshly fractured leg and screaming in pain. That had also been the last time the priest ever saw Kathy smile. At the time, he had been startled, for the girl's smile had a touch of evil to it. And in that same moment, he realized that it was Ursula's own smile thrown back at her. And then the blindness was ended.

Ah, but hadn't he always suspected?

The young music students took up their instruments, and the music blended with the voices of the chorus, building from the delicate sweet notes of a soloist, and swelling to the full accompaniment, rising, surging with beauty and power. Above the altar, a statue of Christ hung on a cross of gold and gazed down on the bouquets at His feet. In the flickering play of candlelight, lilies and orchids seemed to move to the genius music of Mozart, an illusory resurrection of cut flowers. A spate of "Ah"'s came from the pews as the music rolled through the church to its conclusion.

Applause broke out like sudden gunfire. This was wholly inappropriate behavior for the mass, but Father Brenner never noticed, never saw the rows of clapping hands and the rapturous faces. He looked only to Kathy as the sound of applause thundered all around them.

She nodded to him, and in that simple gesture, she managed to convey that a debt had been paid.

He hoped she would stay to talk with him awhile, but instead she unplugged the microphone from her recording device and left the pew. Apparently, she had more pressing business elsewhere. She moved quickly toward the door, and he wondered if he would ever see her again. Would there be no more calls in the dead of night?

She slowed her steps at the altar of Saint Jude and pocketed a few candles in passing.

• • •

Mallory opened the door to Riker's apartment, and flicked on the wall switch. An overhead light illuminated the whole ungodly mess. It was much worse than she had remembered. Cockroaches fled to the dark cover of the take-out cartons and into the mouths of discarded beer bottles. The crumbs embedded in the rug under her feet gave new meaning to the cliché of a floor you could eat off of. Some of the grazing roaches seemed too bloated to run very fast. There was no single uncontaminated place to set down her duffel bag.

With the risk of a hotel room in mind, she walked to the telephone on the far wall. Her hand hovered over it for a moment, hesitating to touch the receiver, which bore every fingerprint from the day it had been installed.

A half hour later, she was back from the corner bodega with a bag of supplies—cleaning solvents for window glass and mirrors, for porcelain fixtures and metal fixtures, linoleum and wood. She set the bag on the kitchen countertop and pulled out a roll of paper towels, a new sponge for the mop, a pair of plastic gloves, and an aerosol can with a label that promised to kill even saddleworthy mutations of roaches.

Her face was grim as she gathered up her arsenal. Cleaning house was not something she usually objected to. Her own condominium was spotless, dustless, without blemish of any kind, and she was near fanatical in keeping it that way. On the Saturday mornings of her childhood, she had helped Helen in the ritual of cleaning. But Helen, the world's champion homemaker, had always begun with a perfectly clean house.

It was late when Mallory returned from the laundromat. She put down the bag of clean towels and sheets, what must be several months' worth of them. Leaning back against the door, she brushed a damp tendril of curls from her face. She was tired, but if she sat down, she would lose momentum.

She dragged her bucket and mop to the bathroom, the last room to clean. And there she was confronted by the plastic Jesus glowing in the dark. She pulled the night-light out of its electrical socket and tossed it into the hamper, where she would not have to look at it.

A white-haired man stood alone in the plaza. Behind him, the door of the wooden fencing lay in splintered pieces. He made one slow circuit of the plaza, beholding the ghostly white tarpaulins covering every bench, blanketing the fountain, and extending in a pale virus up the walls of the building facade.

This was Gregor Gilette, whose work one critic had described as almost like a song. Critics had always floundered for the adjectives. They wanted very much to call him classical, and every instinct sought this word. It was the classic lines of nature which made the inhabitants of Gilette's buildings feel so perfectly in accord with their environs, in the same way that classical music kept to the rhythm of the human heart. His work never recalled the classic forms of European architecture, but the motion of the river, majestic heights that eagles might inhabit, and the feminine elements of a graceful nude. This was Gilette.

He had been elated when he finally received the portfolio of photographs. The plaza was about life, and it was good that there had been people to fill all the spaces he had lovingly created for them, as though they had not been strangers to him, but invited guests. Such was his feeling for all his creations. But this building was most special. He would end his career at the height of his powers with this, his greatest piece of art.

He also approved of Jamie Quinn, who had visited his house tonight. Had he been planning ever to create another work, he might have stolen a line of elegance from Jamie's face and another from the body and then incorporated the man into something of marble. Only marble would suit the critic's cool, smooth, graceful exterior. There were no cracks or seams through which the uninvited might intrude on him.

An hour ago, Gilette had listened as his brother-in-law explained the purpose for his visit, as he described the Public Works Committee's choice of art for the plaza. Gilette had listened, but he had not believed. What kind of an animal would do such a thing?

Emma Sue Hollaran. A dumb, slow-witted animal, Jamie Quinn had gently explained. The artist was Gillian, the vandal.

Gilette had come to the plaza to see for himself. Heavily veined hands reached out for the first tarpaulin and ripped it from the mooring pins with ferocity, and then the next and the next, until the floor of the plaza was covered with the white canvas. He stood by the fountain at the center of the plaza, taking it all in. And now he believed.

A fifteen-year-old boy, with the aimless walk of a vagrant, was making his way down the sidewalk, past the wooden fencing, adjusting the straps of his knapsack as he walked. The sack was heavy with the weight of his best pair of jeans and all the rest of his possessions.

When he came to the small pile of boards on the sidewalk, he turned to see the splintered opening in the fence. He stepped lightly over the remnants of the wooden door and slipped quietly through the hole, wondering if this might be a good place to spend the night, perhaps to sleep through until morning without the rude awakening of a cop kicking him in the side to move him along. He was sick, flesh hanging on his bones, and he could not afford another injury. It took so long to heal now.

Once he was through the fence, his eyes became accustomed to the poor light leaking through the hole, and the pale light of the moon overhead. He moved cautiously under the high marble arch and into the plaza.

Someone else was there ahead of him. It was an old man with a bowed back. The boy held his breath as the old man settled wearily to a bench that had been cracked and smeared with paint.

Now the boy's gaze traveled up the length of the walls to see the crude paintings of muggers and subway trains, and the big red blob in the center of it. Painted across the stone face of the building were the words "Welcome to the Big Apple."

The fountain was also smeared with paint and gouged with something that had left tracks of rust in the wounds. The vandal had gone too far. A delicate arm of the fountain had been broken off and lay in the water like a severed limb.

Again, the boy read the writing on the wall. "The Big Apple." That was what his mother called New York City, the Big Apple. And what he saw in this wreckage was so New York. It was his mother's building one block from a soup kitchen. It was the dark man on the corner who sang, "Come kiddy come. I got crack and I got smoke, and come kiddy come kiddy come." It was the flowers that his mother could never put in the first-floor window box without seeing them broken-stalked and stolen by the day's end.

He could not get out of this town fast enough.

The old man was rising unsteadily to his feet. The boy, sensing some remainder of authority here, melted back into the dark of the broken ash trees as the old man quit the plaza.

The boy walked over to the pile of rubble and old paint cans at the base of the wall. He knelt down and selected a can of red. He made a tentative squirt in the air, and then he froze.

A shadow loomed on the wall alongside his own, and it was growing larger.

He looked up to see the face of an old woman. She never spoke to him, but only extended her hand to the paint can. She wanted it and there was a look in her eyes that said, *Don't fool with me, boy, just give it to me.*

He had seen that look so many times. Now it was a reflex action to surrender whatever he had in his hands. He gave her the can of spray paint and stepped back.

She turned away from him and pressed the nozzle close to the ruined wall. She walked along the stone facade, writing in a giant scrawl of red paint, "Apple, Apple, in the river, all you do is make me shiver."

The boy read the line and said, "Amen."

Gregor Gilette left the after-hours bar with a weaving walk and wandered down the street, hearing nothing, seeing only the pavement before his shoes, until he passed by another man who was walking in the opposite direction. The other man had ragged clothes draped on a stick-figure body. His arms made wide circular motions in the air, arm over arm, swimming to Fifty-seventh Street.

This was madness Gregor felt more comfortable with. His mind did not stray back to the wreckage of the plaza, for that was dangerous ground tonight.

Now he thought to look for a cab, but the street was deserted and it had begun to rain. He stared at the open mouth of the subway. He and Sabra had come a long way since the days when they rode the underground, unable to afford a taxi during the young years of the struggle to make it here.

He descended into the darkness beyond the shattered bulb intended to light his way. He bought a subway token from the man behind the glass of the booth and barely registered the fact that the cost of his token had gone up 500 percent. He passed through the turnstile to stand on the platform and wait through the dregs of night ending, a drunk slowly sobering, waiting for the train which takes its own time.

An announcement was being made on the public address system.

Even a native New Yorker could not actually understand the individual words that came out of the subway speakers, but he knew the words would only be a variation on the same theme: Your train will never come, so go away now.

Two stragglers on Gregor's side of the tracks took this message to heart and exited through the turnstiles. The platform on the other side of the tracks had also emptied. One overhead bulb spread a pool of light on the far platform, creating the illusion of an abandoned stage.

Gregor was stubborn. He would stay. He would wait to see if the announcer lied. In the old days, half the time they lied.

He shrugged against the post and sluggishly meditated on the upside-downness of drinking through the nights and sleeping through the days, eking light and warmth from electric bulbs. He pushed cigarette stubs and wrappers with the toe of his shoe, looking for friendly omens in the dirt tracks and the trash.

He stared over the side of the platform at the tracks below. A small brown shape scurried between the rails. Gregor remembered Sabra's old game of making a wish on the first rat of the evening. His footing was a bit unsure; tipsy still, he moved back to sag against the tiled wall.

He was not alone anymore. Someone spoke to him. Sabra's voice? A hoarse, hollered whisper, calling his name. From where?

There—across the tracks, waiting for the train that goes the other way. She was peeking at him from behind a post, coming out now, walking into the pool of light. Her wide eyes were smiling and not. Then, a grotesque, clown-face smile split her face.

But it was not Sabra—only an old hag, almost spectral in her long rags. One hand clutched a tin and the other held on to the handle of a wire cart.

A train passed between them on the middle rails. He

stared through the lighted square windows of the cars. There were no passengers. It was a ghost train, traveling empty to some maintenance depot. It passed on, and he could see the woman once more. Poor, pathetic, broken thing. How could he have taken her for Sabra?

His northbound train was approaching. He could hear it in the tunnel. He could see the light growing larger. There was a little moment of terror before the train pulled in and blocked her from sight. The woman's mouth opened wide and round. The brakes of the approaching train screamed. Her arm shot up like a referee of the game. And then she was lost from sight again, the entire platform blotted out by the tons of screaming, steaming metal.

He boarded his train, tired and shaken sober. He never looked back through the windows of the car, but as the train picked up speed, he wondered if she looked for him in these quick squares of light.

The cellular telephone rang. Andrew opened his eyes to the dark canopy of raincoats. When at last he had the phone in his hand, he said, "Hello?"

"This mass is for a woman who was brutally murdered," said a man's voice. In the litany that followed, Andrew realized it was a priest saying mass for the dead dancer.

Mozart and a ghost choir spilled out of the magical telephone and filled his senses. Moving along on his knees, he crawled out from the cover of his canopy and looked up to the ceiling of the sky with its faint sprinkling of stars. Mozart's *Requiem* filled a cathedral of his mind's making. Hooded monks paraded past his eyes, candles became torches, and there was blood on the altar and blood on the floor, a river of it winding and washing through the belly of the church, churning beneath his feet.

Aubry crawled down the aisle under the falling axe. Her heart still beating with seconds of life. Everything was pulsating red. The exposed organs beat out their independent lives and deaths as they failed her, each one in turn.

He reached out his hand to her too late. Her face was gone to dark sockets and a death's-head grin. He knelt on broken glass in shock beyond pain. And there was a new fear in his eyes, which were blurring with tears, as he stared up at the final horror of the night—the stars. In a suicide of heaven, the stars were going out.

And now, all the brighter lights of New York City also failed him as he pitched forward in a faint.

CHAPTER
9

IT WAS PAST TWO IN THE AFTERNOON WHEN RIKER walked in the door, his eyes closing to narrow slits. He set his small bag of belongings on the coffee table, and sank down on the couch in the front room. He laid the assault rifle on the floor and slid it underneath the skirt of the slipcover and away from his host's sight.

"Thanks, Charles. I really appreciate this."

"My pleasure." Charles was standing at the hall closet, pulling blankets and sheets from the top shelf. He was also making rapid calculations on the toll of sleep deprivation upon a man of Riker's age, who drank too much and smoked too much. There were slowed reflexes to consider, and then—

"Mallory's holed up at my place," said Riker. "I'm looking at maybe six hours of sleep before I take the night shift with Andrew."

"Couldn't someone else do it?"

"It's not a problem."

Charles wondered if he had offended Riker, for it suddenly occurred to him—he would never have made that suggestion to Mallory. Oh, and there was one more thing to worry about. He tucked the bedding under one arm and searched the mantelpiece until he found the detective's card. He handed it to Riker. "About an hour ago, this man came by with two officers in uniform. They were looking for Mallory."

Riker held the card out at arm's length. "Kinkaid? You didn't tell this cop anything useful, did you?"

"Certainly not," said Charles, as though cooperating with the authorities were something a gentleman would never consider. "But why does she have to hide? You don't think Blakely would really harm her, do you?"

"No, not now he wouldn't. He might want to kill her, but when he resigned this afternoon, they made him turn in his gun. And Robin Duffy didn't leave him with enough money to hire a shooter."

"So it's over?"

"The business with Blakely? Yeah. Now she's only in trouble with the commissioner." Riker held up the business card. "This cop, Kinkaid? He's attached to the commissioner's office. Beale wants to have a little chat with her about the proper form for arresting suspects while cameras are rolling. She made the evening news last night."

"But the worst is over, and Mallory is all right?"

"She's fine. She called Coffey this morning. He got on her case right away. Told her it was her lucky day that Oren Watt wasn't pressing charges for abuse of power, and if she ever pulled a stunt like that again, he'd suspend her in a heartbeat."

"But under the circumstances—"

"He had to rag her. If he didn't, she'd walk all over him. I taught him that." Riker obviously took some pride in this. "Coffey still has a lot to learn, but he does learn fast. So then Coffey tells her, real sarcastic, it might be nice if she showed up for a meeting once in a while. And the kid says, 'Why should I? All the important meetings are in the men's room.' Coffey told me that in the men's room of Peggy's Bar."

Charles carried his bundle of sheets and blankets to the

spare bedroom. When he returned to the front room, his houseguest was sitting up straight enough, but the man was fast asleep.

Charles gently lowered Riker's body down, and then lifted his feet to the cushion and began to untie the shoelaces. When he was done with the pillows and quilts, one would have to admit that Riker's own mother could not have done a better job of tucking him in.

Quinn stood by the large window in the dining room, watching the river rolling by, no longer aware of the Chopin étude in the background. In a polite ripple of baroque chimes, an antique mantel clock consulted with him about the passing time. His first appointment of the evening was with Gregor Gilette.

There was nothing he could do to ease the pain which Emma Sue Hollaran had caused, but he could do something to Emma Sue. He had tried to stop her, even threatened her, and the woman's own stupidity had foiled him. She truly did believe she was invincible, and she would continue to believe that until she lay crushed beneath the wheels of the machinery he had put into motion. Too late for Gregor, however. The damage could not be undone. Revenge was only the next best thing, but he found it a necessary thing.

Quinn packed his sword and his mask in preparation to meet with Mallory later in the evening. As he packed the formal white fencer's uniform, he planned out Mallory's future as he would a military campaign. It was a strange warfare, this, for all his strategy was toward embracing the enemy, and preventing her from ever leaving him.

He avoided his reflection in the mirror above the mantelpiece as he zipped up his fencing bag.

Other women had come to him, not believing that he could care for them. Nothing in his eyes ever led them on, ever promised them anything. They had come to him without expectations; they left him without rancor. And it was always they who left him. For even when he did care for a woman, even when she moved him, his eyes were disbelieved. The woman would put all her faith in the unintended counterfeit contempt of his expression, and having a better opinion of herself, she would leave him.

It would be different with Mallory. She would never look outside herself for affirmation of her worth. She was made for the battle between man and woman. She promised an exciting tension that would last, always challenging, never abating, for she was young and had little need for rest. Tonight, he would beat her in the fencing match, and she would make him pay for that.

He smiled, or thought he did. The expression never made the translation to his eyes, and so it was unrealistic, unbelievable.

He wanted Mallory more than he had ever wanted anyone. He wondered if she knew that. No, of course she didn't. He could depend on his cold eyes to never give away an honest emotion. But if he *told* her what she was to him, would he be believed? No. His eyes would always foil him. Perhaps one day he would tell her in the dark.

Charles watched over Riker as the man turned in his sleep. The room had grown dark. He pulled on a delicate chain, and a glass lampshade of colored panels cast a small pool of warm light. Now he could read the dial on the alarm clock he had placed by the couch. It was set to go off at eight-thirty, when Riker would rise to take his tour of duty on the roof. It was nearly time. But surely Riker needed more rest. Tonight the man looked ten years older than he should.

Charles leaned down and gently switched off the alarm. He pulled an old knapsack from the hall closet and began to pack Riker's binoculars, a blanket against the chill night—what else? Riker would probably need his cellular phone, so he should leave that behind.

Riker rolled over in his sleep and never heard Charles stealing out the door to do his time on the roof.

Central Park was the only place where a New Yorker could be alone after dark. The average New Yorker seldom took advantage of this well-known fact. The rare tourist was sometimes found there, having parks that one can freely roam in his own part of the world. Such people's bodies were usually recovered from the bushes in the early daylight hours by the sanitation crews, whose job it was to clean up the litter of tourists and muggers alike.

Even the muggers entered the park with some trepidation. They had been known to become confused and attack one another, anger escalated by the mutual insult of having been taken for an ignorant tourist. Though a police station was nestled in the heart of the place, the police never went walking in the park after dark.

Sabra did.

She came walking across the wide-open expanse of the great lawn, showing some strain, as though the cart she pulled behind her on the grass might be a solid block of lead.

She was headed toward the dark cover of trees. Coming finally to the footpath at the edge of the lawn, she dropped to a bench. The thousands of city lights, bright eyes above the tree line, had been following her, tracking her across the grass. They vanished now, blotted out by leaves and branches. She sat in near blackness, owing to a string of broken path lights.

Her body had become too heavy to drag around anymore. Would that she could leave the weight of it sitting on the bench, just abandon this body, this sack of ailments and sores, and go on her way. In a second more, she realized that this was possible, that the method was in her reach, resting on the top of her cart in the form of a discarded butcher knife. The handle was old and cracked, but there was nothing wrong with the blade. Why not? She hadn't the energy to fight the city anymore.

Portrait of a falling woman, deadfall, making no shrieks, no useless flailing motions of the arms and legs. Ah, but the night was not over yet. There were places to go and things to do. Yet she found it near impossible to rise from the bench.

The near-dead always weighed more.

The high ceiling of the gymnasium was aglow with bright panels concealing long fluorescent tubes. Yet the flood of light was so diffused, it seemed to come from nowhere and everywhere, refracting off the cream-colored walls and illuminating every part of the room. And so, the lone swordsman dressed in white had no shadow.

He fastened the collar of his fencing jacket as he walked to the center of the hardwood floor. He stepped over the painted blue line which defined the narrow rectangle of the fencing strip—the field of combat. All the important lessons of Quinn's life had taken place within this six-by-eighteen-foot boundary. Here, he had been taught philosophy and human nature, honor and deception. Despite his gold medal, he had also learned humility, for he well understood there was always something more to be learned on this strip.

His mask lay on the floor near his feet as he swung the sword and parried with an invisible partner. This would be an easy win, for he already understood Mallory's style. In every conversation, she created a false opening, an invitation, and then she stabbed him in the heart. What was a fencing bout but a conversation of swords?

And now he realized he was no longer alone.

Mallory was standing just behind him. When he turned to face her, she was looking up at him. In the next moment, he had the disorienting impression that their eyes met on a level plane.

"How long have you been there?"

"Awhile." Her body was a lean dark silhouette against the light walls, attired in blue jeans and a long-sleeved black jersey of silk.

"May I?" She held out her hand to take his sword, and he gave it to her. Her black running shoes made no sound as she moved across the room to the long brown leather bag by the door.

The door—how disconcerting. It was closed, and a chair was wedged under the knob. He gathered she didn't want the match to be disturbed. Or perhaps she didn't want any witnesses. If she had only done that to unnerve him, he would have approved.

She knelt down to unzip her fencing bag and free a pair of sabers. Now she slid his own sword into the bag and zipped it up. She came back to him again, carrying one cavalry saber and swinging the other, slicing the air in front of her as though she were cutting a path to get at him. She handed one sword to him, and he recognized the family heirloom.

"Charles loaned you these sabers?"

"No, I stole them."

He touched the cutting edge of the blade and then the point. "You've been busy with a whetstone, haven't you?"

"Yes. Razor edges and needle-sharp points."

"It's an interesting choice of weapons, Mallory, but too dangerous for sport. We'll use my fencing sabers. My pair is rigged to score electronically." Now he noted the round bulge in her fencing bag. So she had at least brought a mask and perhaps a glove, but apparently no jacket. "I have a body wire, all the electronic gear. You'll find a spare jacket and everything else you need in the locker room.'' He pointed to a door at the back of the gymnasium. ''You can change clothes—''

''Thanks,'' she said, hefting the antique saber, testing the weight of it. ''But I'm already dressed.''

''Mallory, that silk jersey is too flimsy. Even with the blunted swords, you need the proper costume for protection. I won't fence with you until you're suited up.''

''I won't need any protection. And we *will* use the cavalry sabers.'' She pointed her sword to the mask on the floor. ''Pick that up and put it on. I want to get this over with.''

He shook his head, incredulous. What was she playing at?

She dipped her sword into the helmet that lay by his feet, and raised it up to the level of his hand. He took it off her sword, but only cradled it in his free arm. ''I won't fight you with these sabers. It's too dangerous.''

''Yes you will.'' She backed up two paces and assumed the *en garde* position.

He smiled. This promised to be a marvelous evening. ''No, Mallory. Even with the cutting edge and the point, you're still at a great disadvantage.''

''You also have a cutting edge and a point. I wouldn't like anyone to say I didn't give you a sporting chance. Put on the mask, Quinn. You'll need it.''

''You can't be serious. I don't think you really understand the damage—''

''Oh, I know all about damage.'' She jabbed the sword close to his face and pulled back.

He never flinched, and he wondered if that didn't disappoint her. ''I won't fight you while you're defenseless.''

''I may be the least defenseless person you ever met.''

''You don't understand.''

''*I* don't?'' She slashed the air in front of his face. ''This is a free kill for me, if that's the way I want to play it. You're the one with protective gear—not me. The

bet is well known. I can get away with this. Put on the
damn mask and put up your sword, or I'll do you right
now.''

''I won't cut you.''

''Oh, I know that—I'm counting on it.'' She lashed
out with her sword, this time with the unmistakable intention of cutting him.

He quickly stepped back out of the reach of her blade.
He put on the mask and raised his sword to *en garde*
position. She followed him with a burst of short, unnerving jumps and lunges, her sword arm extended and the
point within an inch of his chest, driving him back, slicing the air with her blade. He retreated with long steps
to keep the distance between them. Where the line of the
strip was marked on the floor, he held his ground and
met her sword with parries, neatly killing the action of
her swings in a long phrase of sharp reports, steel clashing on steel.

''You're very selective about sportsmanship, Quinn.''
She lowered her sword and stepped back to the line at
the edge of the narrow playing field. ''Koozeman didn't
have a sporting chance, did he?''

''Neither did Aubry.''

It was eerie to meet an opponent who lacked the cover
of a mask. Within the cage of steel mesh, his own mask
of a face was an accident of birth, an illusion, a counterfeit. Her naked automaton face was the genuine article.

She advanced on him in long steps. ''And what about
Sabra?'' Her sword was aiming a slice to his head. ''Now
that's what I call real damage.''

He parried, raising his sword to block the swing of
hers. *Oh, bloody hell.* Without the offensive strike he was
only treading water. She had all the reckless energy of
youth, not even heeding his own sharp point.

''I've seen your sister, Quinn. I've talked to her.
You're a real piece of work, you bastard.''

Anywhere he touched her with the sword, he would

draw blood. He could not come to grips with the idea of maiming her. It was ludicrous. This could not be happening. It was a fight to restrain the reflex instinct of the strike. "I tried to help my sister."

"Yeah, right." She made a thrust to his mask, and she did it with enough power to foil his parry, and to spread the metal mesh and send the point an inch inside the mask.

Her blade pulled free of the mesh and left him stunned. By this time, he should have been long accustomed to attack and well beyond shock. It was late to be learning the difference between games and life.

She walked away from him. His old lessons of humility deepened. She thought nothing of turning her back on him.

She spun around to face him, hovering on the strip, and hovering in time—waiting.

"I put Sabra in the best hospitals money could buy. She kept running away from them."

Mallory rushed him, and he warded off her blade with a defensive fly of steel. She came at him again, and he parried this attack too, metal crashing again and again. "You put your sister in the same asylum with Oren Watt." She was backing him to the wall. "You think that was a good idea?"

"No, Orwelhouse was her own idea." He glided to the right.

She followed, advancing on him, relentless, thrusting toward his center. "So the institutional route didn't work." She made a slice to his head, and he blocked her swing. "And then you decided to help your sister in another way."

He stepped back to parry another slice to his head.

She followed him with her eyes, her body and her sword, all parts of the same relentless machine. "You've been feeding Sabra information you got from me." Her sword rose to the level of her hips. It hung in the air. He froze, waiting to see which way the blade would fall.

"You used me to feed her obsession." Mallory's sword angled in a half circle to strike his side. He met her blade with his, and parried ten times before one of her strikes broke through his guard. She cut the thick material at the throat of his mask. The padding spilled out in clumps. He warded off her next attack with a beat of his blade, and she stepped back.

"Poor crazy Sabra. Revenge is all she's living for, isn't it?"

"You don't know what it was like, Mallory. You had to be there, to see what I saw."

"I've been there." She lunged and cut to his head, bringing her steel down on his blade again and again, as he held his sword high to fend off the rain of blows.

"Oh, God, the places I've been." Her next slice was lower, and he parried to the right. She lowered her own saber and threw it from one hand to the other. It was an unnerving play he'd never seen before. And now the sword flew back to her right hand to cut his undefended side. He heard the material rip along the midsection of his jacket.

Sweat ran into his eyes, but she was dry, cool, so single-minded in her cutting and stabbing. Her reaction time was twenty-five years younger, and her speed was astonishing. She was a slicing machine—she never tired. He listened to his own ragged breath inside the mask.

She left the marked outline of the strip, going outside the parameters of the combat field. That fit so well, he should have seen it coming. Of course she wouldn't recognize boundaries. Now all the wheels and works of his brain were stripping gears in their speed to devise a strategy to match hers.

Too late. She rushed him from the side, slashing at the padded bib beneath his mask. This time he felt the point close to flesh. Only the jacket's high collar, one thin layer of material, protected his throat.

"How many times do you suppose I have to do that before I get down to the real thing?" Her sword was lowered to her side. It rose swiftly, faster than his eye could follow. She stabbed his mask at the level of his eyes, and he jumped back, hitting the wall, the last possible step of retreat.

"Can't you guess?" She turned her back on him and walked to the far end of the strip. He moved away from the wall and resumed his own place within the marked outlines of the field. They stared at one another across this space.

"You watched me work over Koozeman at the gallery. Then you passed your guesswork along to your sister."

There was no warning before the rush. Long-stepping, she came after him, jabbing holes in the air, coming closer, now lunging to thrust, recovering her move and lunging again. "You damn amateur!" Every attack maneuver was hers, leaving him only the defensive moves and the escaping backward steps.

"You've made so many stupid mistakes, Quinn. Aubry wasn't the primary target. You were wrong about that." Steel clanged with rapid strikes and counterstrikes, and in her swings he discerned the rhythm of a hammer on a nail.

"How can you possibly know—"

She broke off the attack and stepped back. "It was always a money motive." She lowered her sword. "The killer stood to make money on the death of the artist, Peter Ariel. Aubry came in while they were cutting up his body."

"No, it didn't happen that way. I was called there to discover the bodies because Aubry was one of the victims. The setup was planned before she even died!"

"No, Quinn. The killers needed a critic to kick off the hype. Koozeman probably figured the police were too stupid to recognize a dead body as a work of art. So he used Aubry's name as bait for you. But she was never meant to show up at the gallery. That was an accident. Something went wrong.''

She was dangling the sword carelessly in her hand. Now it rose suddenly to attack position. Forgetting forty years of training which told him to wait on her advance, he stepped back too soon, his sword rising to parry. But she never left her place on the strip. Now she let her saber dangle again. And his own sword came down. She smiled, and in that smile, she told him that she owned him now.

''Let's go over the lies you told to Markowitz. You were late getting to the gallery that night.''

''Yes, but I explained that.''

''You lied to Markowitz. You'll have to do better with me.''

''As I *explained* to your father, the cab was caught in a traffic jam on a street where a film was being made. So I had to get out and take a subway. I'm no good at navigating subways. I'd never used—''

''Markowitz knew you lied to him. I found his copy of the shooting schedule for that old movie and all the city location permits. It took me a while to work it out. The film location wasn't between your apartment and the gallery. And that's all the old man knew—that you lied. He never got to interview the family. He didn't know Sabra was meeting your mother that night. But I did— after I talked to Aubry's father. Then I noticed the shooting location was midway between your house and your mother's. So you and your sister saw the movie crew on the way to your mother's house. I even know you drove there in her car.''

''Sabra was never—''

She rushed him with long steps, a swing and a cut to the arm. His parry was too late. He looked down to the blood drops staining his sleeve. She had bloodied him, and yet he remained true to the brotherhood which refused to believe that the female could be the deadlier sex.

The wound was hard evidence against her gender, and still he would only defend and retreat. His mind was coming apart; his code remained intact. He could finish her with one thrust, and yet he would not.

And she knew it.

"What's the point of lying anymore?" She lowered her sword and stalked off to the far end of the strip. "You got the message at your mother's house—you called the paper or they tracked you down. Then you and Sabra drove her car to the gallery. You were late, but not late enough to account for the delay in calling the police."

"You couldn't possibly know that."

"Oh, no? Tell me what doesn't fit. Sabra saw what they'd done to Aubry, and she went right over the screaming edge. You needed time to calm her down and get her safely away—time to plan. You had to keep the police and the media away from Sabra. You decided she couldn't stand up to an interrogation—what a gentleman. You made up the subway story to explain why you were late calling the police, why there would be no record of a cab log. So they couldn't follow the trail back to your mother's house and Sabra. That was the first lie."

She left the strip to walk around him, making side circles, slow and quiet. This was no maneuver learned at school—she was playing with him. His life had been lived within parameters of form, where all the moves were familiar, almost a ballet. Nothing in his experience had prepared him for what lay beyond the boundary lines. The sight of Aubry had ruptured his mind and not taught him a thing.

He turned to watch Mallory, moving as she moved, revolving to keep pace with her circles. All the aggression was hers, she picked the shots, began the dance and stopped it when she wished. She controlled the court, the game, himself.

She was so sure she was going to beat him—that much, but no more, was in her face. And worse, it was in his own mind as Mallory danced up to the mark to play, ignoring his blade, she thought so little of his chances.

His concentration was broken. He missed the parry and let her through to bloody his side. She backed away again to the center of the court. And now she broke with any pretense of form, running across the floor, her saber describing circles in the air. When she had closed the distance, she dropped to one knee and sliced low toward his unprotected thigh, a forbidden zone which no opponent ever aimed for.

He cursed himself for not anticipating her. He had heard the rip of material, but he would not look down. If she had cut him again, it would do him no good to see the blood. He parried the next rush, doing twice the brainwork to cover his body and his legs.

She broke off, stepping back, light as a cat, to the end of the strip. When she moved forward again, it was still on cat's feet, an unhurried, stalking advance.

She began this bout in slow-action time, the cadence of casual conversation, as her blade met his in easy strikes and counters. The swordplay accelerated with more rapid strikes, but still no force, light touches only— *You kiss my sword, and I kiss yours.* Faster now, and faster—quick reports of steel sounded on steel. The tempo was more the breathless pace of something carnal, heart pounding—

Suddenly, Mallory broke with him and retreated to the edge of the strip.

Sweat blurred his eyes as she came dancing back to him with short steps and a rather ordinary gambit. He parried easily, and this should have made him suspicious. Instead of answering his parry with a riposte, she let her steel slide down his sword until she closed with him, hilt to hilt, swords pointing up, only a few inches between their bodies. She pressed closer until they stood *corps-à-corps*, in the forbidden contact of opponents.

Softly, she said, "I'm going to take you now."

And he believed her. He was staring into the long slants of her green eyes. Her sword was disengaging, lowering. And this was the moment where he lost the match, even before he felt her metal slipping into the handle of his saber. With one elegant move, she backed away and ripped the steel from his hand with the pry bar of her own sword and sent his saber flying across the court, clanging to the floor.

He glimpsed the bright triumph of a child in her stance and in her eyes—and then the child was gone. Deadly serious now. "I won."

Stone silence. She stepped forward, sword rising.

"Oh, I'm sorry," he said. "It was my job to keep score, wasn't it? Well, would you like me to tally up the bloodings?" He looked down at the cuts, thin lines of blood on his side, his arms and one leg. "There are a few tears in the material that didn't get through to the skin, but of course they count too."

"I want to collect my bet now."

"Suppose I sign a confession to the murders of Dean Starr and Avril Koozeman. Would that be satisfactory payment?"

"No. You're not the type. You won't even make a strike to save yourself. And leaving your sister out in the rain—well, that doesn't count as violence."

"What was I supposed to do? Lock her up in a maximum-security ward for the rest of her life? She'd rather be dead."

She moved in close to him. "I think you meant to say that she'd be better off dead." Too late, he felt her leg hook around his own, unbalancing him as she pushed him to the floor. She stood over him with the sword to his throat. "Pay up! I want Sabra."

"I don't know where she is."

"Liar!" She pulled the sword back only a little, slowly angling the point to his face. She thrust it into his mask again and again. "How many drives before I get your eyes? I won! Deliver what you promised."

"Wait!" He raised one hand, and she stopped. He removed the mask and held it out to her. "This should make it easier for you."

Her blade came closer. He no longer believed he understood her well enough to anticipate her. But he had well understood Louis Markowitz, and now he was betting his eyes on the man who had raised her.

She put up the sword. "You know, there's stabbing, and then there's stabbing."

She backed away from him. "Aubry was never meant to die that night. I figured it out with the messages. You didn't know about the message left at the ballet school, did you?"

He shook his head, and she continued. "I got that from my interview with Gregor Gilette. You figured they already had her when that message was left at your paper, right?"

He nodded and closed his eyes. Her next words came from behind him.

"According to her father, Aubry's message was a long one. That's what made me think she was being sent somewhere else—so you wouldn't be able to reach her by phone when you got your own message. Aubry's was garbled by the clerk, too many instructions to write down in a hurry. So she killed a lot of time trying to decipher the message, and then more time trying to locate you. Finally, she called your newspaper. By then, a message had been left for you. A receptionist probably checked your message box and confirmed the meeting at the gallery. It's the only scenario that fits the two messages. Too bad you wouldn't let Markowitz near the family. He could've worked it out twelve years ago. It only took me five minutes with Gregor Gilette."

"Oh, God."

"Markowitz usually went for the money motive. My

father was a smart cop, but with Aubry as the primary target, he had nowhere to go with this case.''

She was very close to his side, speaking into his ear. ''If he'd only known that Aubry was there by accident, he would've gone after the man with the profit motive to kill Peter Ariel, someone who knew your family connections.''

He opened his eyes. She was in front of him now, leaning down, her face close to his.

''Everything pointed to Koozeman,'' she said. ''The killers would have been jailed—if you'd only stepped out of my father's way. And Sabra? She's been strung out on the street all these years for nothing.''

His head lolled back, eyes rolled up to the ceiling. He felt as though he had been mortally wounded. As she had said, there was stabbing, and then there was stabbing.

''So, Quinn, would you call this a clear win?''

He nodded.

She sat on the floor beside him and laid down her sword. ''You knew the link between the old murders and Dean Starr. How did you know he was one of the killers? Did Sabra tell you, or did you tell her?''

''I didn't send that letter to Riker.''

''I never said you did, Quinn. I know who sent that letter. I figured that one out a long time ago. How did Sabra know about Dean Starr's connection?''

''Sabra surfaces now and then. When she turns up, I give her walking-around money and a place to stay. I keep an apartment for her—she keeps losing the key. But there are times when she seems fairly rational. She visits old haunts, old friends. For a while, she's almost herself, almost sane. But then in a few days, she's back wandering the streets again, looking for—''

''Answer the question! How did she know about Dean Starr?''

''I'm trying to tell you she doesn't exist in a vacuum. She has sources in the art community. Koozeman has no idea how much the gallery boys hate him—they talk about him incessantly. So she was in Godd's Bar one night and heard something strange, just snatches of conversations among the gallery staff. Sabra thought Starr might be blackmailing Koozeman. She asked me to find out more about it.''

"And did you?''

"Yes. It only cost me a few hundred per gallery boy to get all of it. It didn't really sound like blackmail. Starr was only pressuring Koozeman to make him into a hot artist. Starr said he wanted to use the same scheme he used for Peter Ariel. I never heard Koozeman's end of that conversation.''

"Is that all you told her?''

"That's all there was to it.''

"She was crazy, you knew that. You just let her draw her own conclusions?''

"Well, they were the right conclusions, weren't they? I gave her whatever she asked of me.''

"And then you went down to the morgue to view the remains of the jumper, the homeless woman who died in Times Square. You thought Sabra had killed Starr and then killed herself, right?''

He nodded.

"But now you believe your sister killed them both, don't you? Starr and Koozeman?''

"We never discussed the murders.''

"How convenient. Was that on your attorney's advice? Were you worried about conspiracy charges?''

"Mallory, I have an idea you know that feeling of nothing left to lose. So does Sabra. She can't depend on the police to finish it for her, can she? Look at the way they—''

"Are you telling me she's not done? There's another one on her list? You son of a bitch! Who is it? Andrew Bliss? Did you give her Andrew as a murder suspect? I told you his pathetic little confession was nothing—''

"What does it matter? Andrew is well away from harm on the roof of Bloomingdale's."

"Your own mother could make it up to that roof. Anyone who wants him can get at him."

"But you have people watching him, right?"

"Yes, from the distance of the next roof and a street. If she goes near him with a weapon, she'll be shot down. I selected that assault rifle to make a big hole. She won't survive."

The rain shower had ended. Charles wiped the lenses of the binoculars and looked again. He believed he was watching a religious ceremony—a baptism or purification rite. Andrew had been on his knees in fervent prayer for a long time. Then he had removed all his clothes.

Now he was standing in a circle of candles and pouring champagne over his head, letting the liquid run over his naked body. Andrew looked up at the mangled staircase twisting away from the roof door. He turned and stared at the storm cellar door of the second exit. The ground door was more than half covered by steel beams and large wooden crates. Andrew put his shoulder to a crate and tried to move it. No luck. He slid to the ground and banged his fist on the door handle like a tired child begging to be let back into the house. The door fell away under his hand, opening downward to expose a square of dull light.

Charles focussed on the opening in the roof. So the heavy material blocking half the door had never been an impediment. Mallory had been right. All this time, anyone who wanted Andrew could have gotten at him by simply opening the door inward.

Andrew was climbing down the rungs of an interior ladder, disappearing through the square of light and below the level of the roof, wearing nothing, only carrying a cellular phone.

Charles was thinking of the cellular phone he had left

behind on the coffee table by the sleeping Riker. How foolish. That was the one thing he should have brought with him. Well, at least Andrew was moving slowly. Charles's own roof had more floors. He would have to hurry.

When Charles emerged on the ground floor, he ran across the street to the fire exit Mallory had diagrammed on her bulletin board. He looked around in all directions. Andrew had not yet emerged.

He began to turn around at the sound of a squeaking wheel, but he was not fast enough. He felt the blow to the back of his head, and he was falling to the sidewalk as Andrew exited by the fire door, setting off the alarm.

Riker awakened under the cover of a toasty quilt. He looked to the clock on the end table by the couch. He was slow to register the fact that he had overslept—and there was no one watching over Andrew Bliss. He sat bolt upright.

"Charles?"

He knew there wouldn't be a response. The apartment had an empty feel to it. He was alone.

Now he saw the sheet of paper on the coffee table. It was Charles's note to say he had taken the tour of duty on the roof. But the rifle was still under the couch, and the cellular phone was lying on the table.

Charles would never make it as a cop.

Riker threw off the quilt, smashed the phone into his pocket and looked for his shoes. When his laces were tied, he put on some speed, gathering up his gun and the rifle and heading out the door.

The alarm for the department store continued to scream and wail. Cars drove by, drivers hazarding a quick look at the trio on the sidewalk and then driving on.

"Is he all right?" Quinn raised his voice to be heard above the alarm.

He knelt down beside Mallory as she ran her fingers over the back of Charles's skull. Next she rolled the large man's unconscious body onto his back and gently pulled back one eyelid. She moved her hand to create extremes of shadows and light. Satisfied with the reaction time of his pupils, she nodded. "He'll be okay. It's just a scalp wound. I'm guessing she came up behind him and hit him with a bottle."

"You don't know that Sabra did this."

"I know Andrew didn't do it. He couldn't beat up a bouquet of flowers—not in the shape he's in."

She pulled out the antenna of her new cellular phone and punched in the number for Riker's. "Riker? It's Mallory. . . . Yeah, I'm here now. . . . How far away are you? . . . Fine." Closing the antenna, she turned back to Quinn. "I want you to stay with Charles until Riker shows up."

"Where are you going?"

"I'm going hunting for Sabra. His wound is fresh, so she can't be far away."

"If you take her in, you know what will happen to her. She'll be a circus freak for the media. Just let her be. I promise you I'll find her again, and I'll find another hospital. She's weak and sick, she can't do any real damage."

"She did Charles in rather nicely, didn't she? I think you know exactly what she's capable of."

"You don't know what she's been through. You can't. Aubry's skull was split up the back. Her brains were falling out through the bone fragments. I watched Sabra trying to force the tissue back into Aubry's skull. And then the back of it fell off, and it was all in her hands, a piece of the skull, the blood and the brains. She was trying to fix the skull when I pulled her away. She was trying to fix her dead child."

"That's why it took you so long to call it in. You took her to a safe, quiet place and then you went back."

"Yes, you were right about everything."

"You believe she killed Starr and Koozeman. And you *gave* her Andrew. You told her about that pathetic little rooftop confession—all the sins he ever committed before the age of twelve. But all that Sabra knows is that he confessed. Am I right? For all I know, Andrew is already dead. Now I'm going to get Sabra, and you're not going to stop me."

He pushed her into the doorway and blocked her escape with outstretched arms, palms pressed to the stone wall on either side of her. He was surprised to see the gun in her hand. It just appeared. He never saw her pull it from the holster, and now it was leveled at his heart.

"Get out of my way, Quinn."

"No, you won't fire that. The game field is all different now. Different rules and weapons. I'm unarmed, and you're a police officer. I know you a little better now. You do have rules, Mallory, and I don't think you'll break them. You wouldn't maim me with a sword when I was helpless, and you won't shoot me now."

Mallory shot him.

He was so startled by the explosion of sound and the sight of the blood, he never felt the butt end of the gun as she pistol-whipped him and sent him to the ground.

A naked man can walk unmolested down any street in New York City. It is a place where people rely on peripheral vision for the imminent dangers of day-to-day living. If no figure rushes at them in peripheral, then no one else exists. There should be no eye contact with lunatics; they all agree on this. When the eye of the New Yorker does fall upon an unfortunate whose mind is absent without leave, said New Yorker's eye, in the interest of preserving the life of the body, will often fail to inform the brain so long as the lunatic remains on some outer periphery. Eye contact might draw the crazy closer. Eye contact, they tell their young, is to be avoided.

And so it was that Andrew crossed all the traffic lanes of wide streets without incident or interference. No homeward-bound commuter, no hack-bound cabdriver ever thought of pulling over to alert the authorities. So Andrew continued to walk north, wearing only a broken smile that tipped up on one side of his mouth and down on the other.

Two men, standing on a street corner, were speaking in heated, rapid Spanish. He passed by them without causing a lull in their conversation. Near Seventieth Street, he walked by a young woman who was debating the affordability of a cheeseburger. After he passed by, she decided, yeah, she might as well spend the money. An old woman carrying a bag of groceries came out of the deli on the corner of Lexington and had to make a detour around Andrew when he paused on the sidewalk. The woman's mind only registered the darkness. She wanted to be off the street while it was still only a semi-savage hour.

The naked man walked on, stopped by no one, safe in the constant that a cop was never where a cop was needed.

The cellular phone beeped. He raised the antenna. "Hello?"

"Hello, Andrew."

"Oh, Mallory." She asked where he was, and he told her.

"Look out for a bag lady, Andrew. I'm on my way."

Mallory was coming for him. He had not long to make his last act of atonement. He should hurry.

He crossed the street.

Charles heard the beeping noise and opened his eyes to focus on the burning ember of a cigarette dangling from the side of Riker's mouth. The spinning cherry light of a police car was illuminating his immediate surroundings in revolving bright red flashes. It was clear that he was not in his own bed, but spread out on the concrete. Riker's worried face was relaxing to a broad smile of relief.

"Riker, I think your phone is beeping." Charles put one hand to the back of his head where it ached with dull, throbbing pain. When he tried to sit up, it hurt more. He lay back again, staring at the sky.

Riker was speaking into the phone. "Yeah?" He listened a moment and said to Charles, "It's Mallory." Into the phone he said, "Naw, Charles is fine. The other one's still breathing too. . . . Sure. No problem."

Charles propped himself up on one elbow and looked down at Quinn's prone body. He reached over and placed one finger on Quinn's jugular. As he felt for the pulse, he was wondering if Riker might think it was rude of him to double-check on Quinn's continuation among the living. Above the bloody wound on the man's arm was the makeshift tourniquet, an Irish linen handkerchief with the initial *M*.

"Riker, did you call an ambulance?"

"What—for a little flesh wound like that? Naw, think of the paperwork. And Mallory would have to take another psych evaluation. It's standard after a shooting. How many of those tests do you think she can take before the department finds out what they've really got here?"

"He has a big hole in his arm, Riker, and he's losing blood."

"Oh, I've seen a lot worse wounds than that one. She put the shot where she wanted it. That's the least amount of damage it's possible to do with a cannon like Mallory's. And I've got twenty bucks says she didn't even fracture his skull with the gun butt. Look at that scalp wound," he said, turning Quinn's head to the side and pointing at the cut as though offering up something to be admired. "See how low it is? She laid him out right. Her old man would've approved."

"He's not conscious, Riker. He needs medical attention, and right now."

"When he gets to the hospital, they'll file the mandatory report for a gunshot wound. No way you can pass that off as an accident with a knitting needle. If he mentions that a cop shot him, we'll be going round and round with the paperwork and the newspapers for weeks. Quinn's not gonna like that any better than we will. We'd have to nail him with obstruction charges to cover for Mallory, and her career would still go down the tubes. It's just not a real good idea, Charles."

"He's right," said Quinn. His eyes were not yet open as one hand was going to the base of his skull where Mallory had kissed him with the butt of her gun. "I'm sure we can manage without the ambulance."

"You need a doctor."

"But I don't need the media circus. And then there's Mallory to consider."

Riker gave him the thumbs-up sign. "You're a good sport, Quinn."

Now Charles realized that he and Jamie Quinn had a great deal more in common than fencing. First she shot him, and now Quinn would rather bleed to death than damage her in any way. And Riker was right. She would not go on with her career after shooting a prominent art critic. It would not play well in the newspapers or the commissioner's office.

"Jamie, you still need medical attention. There's a doctor in my building who could patch that up in a hurry." He watched Quinn's face go slack again, fading out of consciousness.

Riker stood up and signaled to a uniformed officer leaning against a police car. "Charles. That kid'll take you wherever you like. So I can tell Mallory we're bypassing channels on the shoot, right?"

"Right."

Riker held up his phone. "You need this?"

"Yes. Thanks." Charles took the phone, and Riker stood up and walked to the car to speak to the young uniformed officer.

Quinn was back among them again, his eyes opening as he struggled to raise himself on one arm. "Charles, we'll have to come up with a plausible story for your doctor friend."

"Oh, I don't think it will be much of a problem. Henrietta will understand."

"According to Riker, she's bound by law to report the bullet wound. It's highly unlikely she'd risk her license for neglecting that bit of paperwork."

"We'll see." Charles picked up Riker's cellular phone and punched in a number. "Henrietta? It's Charles. . . . Fine, thank you. I've got a slight problem, an emergency really, with a bit of blood. Do you have your medical bag handy? . . . Good. Could I drop by in a few minutes?"

The doorman recognized Andrew Bliss immediately. He also recognized that Mr. Bliss was stark naked but for the telephone clutched in one hand. He wondered if he was expected to do something about that. He only had fifteen minutes to go before his shift was over, and so he elected to assume that Mr. Bliss was a mugging victim on his way to visit the friend who lived nearest to the scene of the crime, possibly seeking comfort and clothing.

Yes, that was a reasonable assumption.

And since Mr. Bliss had brought his own telephone, the doorman felt relieved of any necessity of making a police report. Now Mr. Bliss was entering the elevator, the doors sliding shut behind him. The doorman's problem was out of sight, and therefore it did not exist.

However, when his gaze fell on the bag lady, that was another story. He knew his duty now, and he quickly shot out one arm, palm to her face, to block her way without the necessity of actually touching her and possibly contracting the dreaded head lice which New Yorkers feared more than AIDS. He was quite sure the old hag would get the message via his angry scowl and the flat of his palm. These people were only lazy, not stupid.

The motion was so quick. He saw the flash of light on metal, and then his white-gloved hand was a bloody rag of ripped cloth and flesh. The woman passed by him, entering the stairwell, as he sank to the floor with the shock of seeing the white bones of his hand exposed to the light.

"Andrew, you smell." This was Emma Sue Hollaran's first observation when she opened the door to him. He walked past her and entered the apartment in the manner of a sleepwalker. She waved the air between them to chase the odor away. Then she walked over to the French windows. "Andrew, let's go out on the terrace, all right?"

He nodded, following docilely behind her as she opened the doors and preceded him into the night air. The deep cover of potted trees gave them privacy from the windows of the building across the way, but a scattering of small, bright eyes looked down on them from the sky.

"There has to be a confession," he said, "and an Act of Contrition."

"So you knew."

His head tilted to one side, and his face gave the impression that some part of his mind might have tumbled out of his head. "Of course I knew. How could I not—"

"Have you discussed this with anyone?"

"No. Emma Sue, you must listen. I don't know how much time we have. The confession is very important. I don't want you to die with a stain on your soul." His face turned up to the sky, and he was suddenly preoccupied with the stars. The clouds were parting to clear a wider space in the heavens so more of them could watch.

"Now don't excite yourself, Andrew. If it will make you happy, I'll confess, all right? But you know, I wouldn't have killed Dean if he hadn't been so greedy."

Andrew was moving his head from side to side, as though that would help. What was she saying? How could—

"Dean was starting the old scam all over again with Koozeman." She walked to the French windows and turned back to face him. "You know those tickets were Koozeman's concept, not Dean's. I think it was his idea of a joke. He couldn't believe that people would buy them. Could you move back just a little, dear?"

She pressed on his chest to gently push him farther into the cover of the trees. "I didn't want any part of it. Too risky."

Emma Sue bent down to a large ceramic planter and began to root around in the dirt. "That little bastard Dean threatened me. He was still a junkie, you know. All junkies are dangerous. You can't trust them. Then Koozeman figured it out. He read the article about the long pick."

She pulled an ice pick from the pot and shook the dirt off its gold handle. "It is unusually long, isn't it? Do you remember this, dear?" She held it up to Andrew's passive face. "No? Well, Koozeman did. He asked me if I was still chipping ice with the murder weapon."

Wiping the rest of the dirt off the pick with the hem of her dress, she polished the gold handle till it shone. "Then that pig Koozeman said I'd have to go along with the scam for a second showing of the tickets. He needed to make his profit fast."

She held the pick up to the light of the door, and nodded in satisfaction with her cleaning job. "I think he was planning on leaving the country. He was going to have problems unloading those stupid tickets, and he needed me to prime the pump with publicity and a list of new

suckers. I told him he couldn't blackmail me. He was
part of the original crime, wasn't he? He laughed at me.
Said that line hadn't worked when he tried it on Dean.
But Dean was only threatening to expose Koozeman's
list of clients in the ghoul market. Koozeman said, in my
case, he could supply the police with physical evidence.
Then, at the gallery, he pointed out a cop, a blond cop
in a black silk dress.''

Emma Sue held the long ice pick out to Andrew. He
only stared at it. She picked up one of his limp hands
and closed his fingers over its handle. "Just hold on to
that for a minute, Andrew. I'll be right back."

She disappeared from the terrace and reappeared a moment later. He looked at the gun in her hand, and then
dropped the ice pick to the stone tiles of the terrace. It
rolled to a rest at Emma Sue's feet.

"Pick it up, dear." She kicked it back to him. "Oh,
do pick it up, Andrew. I really want to give you a sporting chance. Think you can beat a bullet? Want to give it
a try?"

"You killed Starr and Koozeman?" He said this
slowly, as though trying to make sense of a foreign
tongue.

"Yes, dear. And it was just a matter of time before I
got around to you. Ah, but now you've come to me."

"Why did you have to—? No, wait. Perhaps it
wouldn't be proper for me to hear any more of your
confession. We'll wait till she comes."

Emma Sue put up the barrel of the gun for a moment.
"Who's coming, Andrew?"

"An angel. She'll hear your confession. But while
we're waiting for her, we could pray together and ask for
forgiveness." He sank down to his knees.

"No, Andrew. It's really better if you stand. The police can be such sticklers for details. I don't want to have
to think up a scenario for shooting a man on his knees.
Now take the ice pick and stand up."

Andrew only bowed his head and clasped his hands together in prayer.

"Oh, well, a little improvisation." She knelt down in front of him and leveled the gun at his chest. "The reporters have gotten bored with you, haven't they? But you had enough time to make your voice heard. It was very considerate of you to demonstrate your insanity to the whole world. When they find your prints on the pick, I think I'll have a credible case for self-defense."

"How can you do this?" There was no panic in his voice. He felt very calm. He was trusting in a higher power—Mallory.

"You were always the weak sister, Andrew. Koozeman even mentioned that. And now you're just not dependable anymore. You're the last witness."

Mallory found the doorman slumped to the floor just inside the glass door and cradling his bloodied hand. A woman with a grocery bag was kneeling beside him, only staring at the wound, making no move to actually help the man.

Mallory bent over the doorman. "Who did this to you?"

There was no response. He seemed utterly fascinated by his own blood. She looked closely at the hand.

A knife wound. Not a pick.

She hovered over the woman, who only now noticed the large gun in Mallory's hand. "Did you call for an ambulance?"

"No, I didn't." The woman's eyes were panic-round and full of the gun. "I'm not good at emergencies."

"Call nine-one-one and tell them an officer needs backup and an ambulance. Do you understand?"

The woman nodded, and Mallory tossed her the cellular phone. "Plan on being here awhile. The response time for the ambulance is the pits, even in this neighborhood." Mallory stopped to consult the mailboxes, then passed up the elevator and took the stairs at a dead run.

Andrew lifted his head to the sky. The field of stars was fading. He watched the slow creep of cloud cover blotting them out one by one. The gun barrel was rising. He stretched out his arms in the posture of supplication, and his head lolled back as he waited for death.

He heard the first shot, his eyes closed tightly, but he never felt the bullet. Then a second shot. And still he remained alive. When he opened his eyes, Emma Sue Hollaran was lying at his feet, hands stretching up to ward off the dark creature. The knife point was glinting in the light, the handle clutched tight in the fist of a woman in rags.

There were two bloody holes in this strange woman, this apparition from hell, and small rivers of blood pouring out of her. So she had taken Emma Sue's bullets and Emma Sue had received this woman's knife into her own body. Now the blood of the old hag merged into the blood of Emma Sue Hollaran, as the woman brought the blade down again and again. And all the while, someone was pounding on the door.

Behind him he heard the explosion of another gunshot. He turned to see the splintered wood of the door just before it flew open. The Angel Mallory with her avenging revolver was coming toward him with long strides.

His knees and his feet were wet with blood from the body of Emma Sue. He looked down at the eyes of a stunned animal, throat slashed. Her screams were gurgles as she strangled in her own blood. Just like Aubry.

The angel called out, "Sabra, stop!"

Sabra?

Was it possible? Yes, it was she, a dark animalistic form, rags flapping like bloody wings, bending over the body, cutting up the meat. Emma Sue's hair had blended from brassy blond waves to bloody ropes that curled like

snakes with each thrust of the knife, until the eyes of the
Medusa head rolled up to expose solid whites.

Sabra bent low to look into Andrew's eyes with all the
hate in the world. Her knife raised up again. And the
Angel Mallory raised her gun and yelled, ''No!''

The two women stared at one another above his kneeling body.

''You don't understand,'' said Sabra, as she retreated
a few steps.

''Everyone tells me that, and I'm getting damned sick
of it,'' said Mallory. ''I understand revenge—I understand obsession. I've understood these things for a long,
long time.''

Sabra looked down at Andrew's sorry face, raising her
knife, not heeding the gun Mallory leveled at her head,
but only advancing on her next target—himself. He
bowed his head. He was ready.

Mallory lowered the gun barrel and moved her own
body between Sabra and Andrew. One hand flashed out,
and she was holding Sabra's knife hand by the wrist.
Something close to perfect understanding passed between
them. Mallory released her grip on Sabra's bloody wrist,
and the woman backed away from her, nodding. Mallory
inclined her head in homage to the pain and rage in the
older woman's eyes. She stared into Sabra's face as
though it were a looking glass, a view into the madness
of long-unfinished business, obsession without end.

''Andrew's not a killer. Trust me to know my killers,
Sabra. It's my gift. Your brother told you about the letter
that came to us with Andrew's review?''

She nodded, and Mallory went on. ''Andrew wanted
the truth to come out. That's why he wrote that letter.
He wanted everyone to know. And now you have to let
him live so he can tell the story. The story is important.
It's the end of unfinished business. It's what you've
wanted all these years. Let Andrew tell it. How could
you live without hearing it? I couldn't.''

Sabra sat down on the terrace flagstones.

Mallory looked at the blood on her hands. It was Sabra's blood, streaming from the holes in her body. The gun in Emma Sue's frozen grip was a .22. Still, the shots were well placed. What kept this woman going she did not know, unless it was this, the end of the story.

"I believe you, all right? I'm sure Dr. Ramsharan is a very decent person."

Quinn had always genuinely liked Charles Butler. But early on, he had realized that this charming man didn't live on the same planet with the rest of them. On Charles's homeworld, people were all good neighbors and exceedingly kind to strangers. The lions all lay down with the lambs, and discord was restricted to the screams of fresh-cut flowers. He wondered how Charles's ideal world fared in tandem with this stroll down the hall in the company of a man who was dripping blood on the carpet.

As they waited for the elevator, Quinn was saying, "We should agree on a story for the doctor. We'll tell her I had an accident while I was showing you my gun collection."

"Do you have a gun collection?"

"No, but it doesn't— Oh, I see your point. Best not to clutter it up with unnecessary lies. We'll say I slipped on a scatter rug while holding a gun. Now that's reasonable. Most New Yorkers have at least one gun."

"Do you have one?"

"Yes, everybody has one."

"I don't. And you were showing it to me? Henrietta knows I don't care for the sight of guns. So it's hardly likely that—"

"All right. I was removing the gun from my desk drawer to get at something *beneath* the gun."

They stepped into the elevator, and Quinn slumped against the back wall, leaving a bloodstain there. As

Charles pushed the button for the third floor, the large man's face gave away his deep concern.

Quinn closed his eyes. So tired. His left hand was slick with the blood which leaked from the hole in his arm. His eyes opened again at the prompt of a gentle tug on the sleeve of his good arm.

"Now about the scatter rug behind the desk," said Charles. "Odd place for a rug, isn't it? And wouldn't the desk chair tend to keep the rug from slipping around?"

"All right. I was removing the gun from the drawer of a *table*—which has a scatter rug in front of it."

"Bit clumsy slipping on the rug that way. And do you usually keep loaded guns about?"

"So I'll admit to being slightly drunk and inexperienced with firearms." So tired. Not thinking straight, not straight at all. "Now you'll swear you were there and witnessed the whole thing. That might persuade her not to file a report. But if she still insists on it, I can always buy her off. You can buy anyone in New York City. Remember, Mallory's name shouldn't enter the conversation."

He had the idea that Charles was not listening to his instructions. The soft-spoken giant seemed somewhat distracted as they emerged from the elevator and walked toward the door of apartment 3A.

"Charles, perhaps you'd better let me handle it from here on. Somehow, I don't think guile is your forte."

Charles smiled gently as he nodded and pressed the doorbell. When the door was opened by a dark-haired woman in a long white robe, he pointed to Quinn's bloody arm, saying, "Mallory shot him, and we want to hush it up, all right?"

"Yes, of course," said the woman. "Come in."

Quinn lurched forward. His last thought before he fainted was that this woman must hail from Charles Butler's planet, for she opened her arms wide to receive his falling body and to stain her robe with the blood of a stranger.

"No one murdered Peter Ariel," said Andrew, as he began his story in a monotone. "He was stoned on drugs and very clumsy. I was there when the artwork fell on top of him. He was killed instantly. Koozeman was furious. All that planning and promotion for nothing. He'd done such a brilliant job launching this career, despite the lack of talent. He had Emma Sue and myself as the critics to promote Peter in newspapers. Dean Starr doubled as a critic and a publicist. That's all his art magazine ever was, you know, a public relations plug for artists who were willing to pay for their reviews. But then it was all for nothing. The artist was killed by his own work, a potential joke of the art world.

"By the time Emma Sue arrived, Dean had come up with the idea to make it look like murder, to sensationalize the death and try to salvage something from sales of the artwork. Well, what was the harm in that? Peter Ariel was already dead. We'd pooled a lot of money to grease a lot of hands—editors of art magazines, and a promised slot in a museum group show. It was a major investment for all of us."

He fell silent for a moment, losing the threads to this ramble. Mallory touched his shoulder and asked, "Was it Koozeman's idea to butcher the body and work it into the sculpture?"

"Yes, Koozeman's idea. . . . Starr loved the concept and so did Emma Sue. All they had to work with was the fire axe from the box with the extinguisher. They underestimated the time it would take to cut up the body parts. All three of them took off their clothes and went to work. I stood by the door to keep watch. It was hard work, cutting up a body with that small axe, but once they got into the rhythm of it, it went much faster. My job was to call out if anything untoward happened—say if Quinn showed early. Had we left him a message then? I can't remember. If anything happened, if anyone came, I was to call out and give them time to get through the door in the wall. I had no blood on me. I would say I'd just discovered the body. We'd thought of everything, almost everything.

"I could hear what they were doing in the room behind me. There was no door I could close. The noise was as sickening as the stench. Once, I turned around. It was an incredible sight, the three of them, naked and bloody, working over the body.

"It was then, while my back was turned, that Aubry came in. I swear I believed I had locked that door. But I was drunk that night—I've been drunk every night since. Aubry shouldn't have been there. We'd left a message to send her to New Jersey. It was so incredible that she should show up at the gallery. It was the last thing we expected. We'd only meant to use her name to bait Quinn into coming. We needed him, his name linked to Peter Ariel in the press. Koozeman said Quinn would not be able to resist a comment on the artwork of the butchered body. You see, Koozeman had been a promising sculptor once, and now he was determined that this was to be the best piece of work he'd ever done. But now here was Aubry, and the whole thing was coming undone.

"I tried to stop her—to turn her around before she could see. 'Don't go in there,' I said. She misunderstood. We'd left a message to say it was an emergency. She thought something had happened to her uncle. I couldn't stop her. She ran into the room. And then she stopped, frozen. Koozeman was just turning around, naked and holding the head of Peter Ariel in his hands. Aubry turned to run. Emma Sue screamed, 'Stop her!' I did stop her, I was even trying to explain when Dean Starr dragged her back into the room. Emma Sue was already running across the floor. She brought the axe down on Aubry.

"No one had expected that to happen. Emma Sue did it again, and again. The others stood back, and I turned away. Aubry was screaming to me to help her. I'd known her since she was a little girl. We were friends, you see. And now she was bleeding, dying, and she was asking me for help. I turned my back. Then, all I could hear was the gurgling. I closed my eyes. It went on for a long time."

And now he put his hands over his eyes as if it were all happening again. "She would not die. I listened to the sounds of the axe, the scrabbling on the floor. She was crawling back toward the door. Her hand was within an inch of me when I turned to see Emma Sue strike the final blow to the back of her skull." His hands fell away from his eyes. "That ended it."

He turned to Sabra. "Then the others made the pact. They were all involved now and there was no way out. They each took the axe and made a cut in her body. And then they came for me. They forced me to take the axe. Starr pressed my hands around it and dragged it across her throat.

"They sent me back to the window. Quinn was due, but Koozeman, that crazy man, he was intent on his work of art. Starr and Emma Sue left the gallery. I stayed by the window, crying, waiting for it to be over. When Koozeman was done with them, he forced me to look at what he had done with the bodies."

Andrew looked at Sabra. "Well, you saw what he did. You were there. When Koozeman had cleaned himself up and put on his clothes, he dragged me through the door in the wall. You and your brother were just coming in as we were leaving."

He bowed his head. "I remember you wore that fabulous multicolored coat. I saw you as the door was closing. You looked so much like Aubry. Koozeman watched you and your brother through the pinhole. He couldn't resist. He wanted to see how his work would be received. You were to be his first critics. I left by the back door. I ran all the way home.''

When the story was done, Sabra rose and walked to the back of the terrace where the fire escape ladder cropped up from the low wall. She reached out to the curled rail of the ladder.

Mallory lifted her gun. ''I can't let you go.''

''I don't think I'll get far, but I don't want to end here.'' Sabra lifted her head. ''You understand?''

Mallory nodded. ''But I can't—''

Sabra walked back to her. She brought her face close to Mallory's and kissed her cheek. ''Yes, yes you can.'' Then Sabra returned to the low wall at the edge of the terrace and lowered herself over the side and down the rungs of the fire escape.

Mallory walked to the ladder and watched the descent. Sabra climbed down slowly; blood smeared the handholds and dripped to the rungs below her feet. She slipped and lost one foothold and then the other. She hung there for a moment, and then she was falling, screaming out as she fell past all the dark windows. She landed on a large metal trash bin parked below. She lay spread-eagled among the garbage, her head twisted at an unnatural angle.

An ambulance was parked outside the apartment building. The screaming sirens of two police units pulled up alongside of Riker's car, all their spinning cherry lights flashing codes of fear and urgency to all the civilians hanging from open windows and clustering on the sidewalk. The young uniformed officers moved quickly out of their cars and into the building, guns drawn. As Riker left his own car, he heard the scream. It came from the alley to one side of the building.

He ran into the narrow breach between the brick walls.

An old woman was spread out on the trash, which was piled high and overflowing the large metal bin. He didn't need to reach out and touch her to know that she was dead. He stepped back and looked up to see Mallory leaning far out over the ledge of a terrace.

"No!" she yelled, as though ordering him to undo this death.

He held his breath as she swung her long legs over the side of the building and hung for a moment in the air, trying to gain a foothold on the slippery ladder, descending now to the fire escape. She skimmed the stairs with her running shoes, moving with fluid speed down the zigzag of the ironwork. When she was level with the trash bin she jumped from the fire escape and landed on her feet beside the body of the old woman.

"She's gone, kid," said Riker, as she knelt down beside the corpse. "I'll put in a call for the meatwagon."

Mallory eased herself off the trash bin, her running shoes slapping hard against the cement. She reached over the rim of the bin and tugged at the body.

"Hold it, Mallory. The meatwagon will take her."

"No! Not like this." She pulled Sabra's body into a slide, passing it down the rubble of ripped plastic bags, eggshells and coffee grounds. She received the dead woman into her arms, and stood there for a moment, holding this ragged burden as though it weighed nothing. Then, slowly, so gently, Mallory laid the body down, taking great care in settling the corpse to the ground, as though afraid of causing the dead woman any more pain.

The alley was protected from the flashing lights, the noise and energy of the street. No wind blew here, no dust stirred as Mallory arranged the body in the pose of sleep.

"I'm sorry," she said to the dead woman, as her hand moved across the face to close Sabra's eyes. She folded the rag doll arms across the breast. "I'm sorry."

Riker watched Mallory at her ministrations, gentle as

a mother with a child. Deep inside of him, permanent
damage was being done as the roles reversed again, and
he watched the child bending down to the mother to kiss
her brow and say good night.

When Mallory stood up and moved toward him, there
was no emotion in her face, and that frightened him. He
reached out to catch her arm as she stalked past him. She
shook him off and continued down the alley toward the
street. He watched her retreat for a moment, then looked
back to the corpse on the ground. Caught in that sad
middleground between the living and the dead, he didn't
know his own place in the world anymore, but thought
he might have overstayed his life.

The first thing Riker noticed about his apartment was the
smell of fresh air which had displaced the stale odors of
garbage and ashtrays filled to overflowing.

He turned on the light and blinked twice. He had forgotten the color of the braided area rug in the living
room. Gone was the litter of pizza boxes and old newspapers which had once protected it from dust. And he
could see city lights beyond the window glass for the
first time in the ten years he had lived in this apartment.
The two-years-dead houseplant had been replaced with a
live one.

He moved on to the bathroom. Everything was in order, every fixture sparkled and the porcelain gleamed. He
pulled back the shower curtain. The garden of fungus no
longer grew on the tiles of the stall.

Oddly enough, she had not made good on her threat
to toss out the plastic Jesus night-light. She had only
cleaned it, and now it glowed even brighter. Perhaps she
thought he might need guidance in the dark hours when
his drunk's bladder awakened him.

It was predictable that the kitchen would be spotless,
but inside the refrigerator all his beer bottles were upright
glass soldiers, standing in formation. He pulled out one

cold bottle and wandered into the bedroom.

He opened the drawer by his bed to see each thing perfectly aligned and all debris cleared away. In the back of the drawer was the small yellowed envelope with his wedding ring and the rainy day bullet with his name on it. He picked up the envelope, hefted it in one hand and found it was light by a few ounces. He crushed the paper in a tight fist and felt only the hard substance of the ring.

Mallory. She had stolen the bullet.

He sat down on the bed, popped the cap off his beer bottle, lit a cigarette and decided to live.

"When will you people ever learn to lock your doors? This is New York City."

Charles looked up as Mallory cleared the foyer of Henrietta's apartment and entered the front room.

Oh, God, no.

There was blood on her face and the front of her T-shirt, and smears on the arms of her blazer. He was rising from his chair when she raised one hand to stay him. "Charles, it's not my blood. Sit down." He did as he was told.

Mallory in bloodstains and blue jeans was so at odds with delicate flowers in crystal vases, small pieces of sculpture and rose-colored afghans—all the ultrafeminine trappings of Henrietta's front room. Mallory slung the fencing bag on the floor and knelt beside it to remove the antique sabers. He had not missed them all day.

"Thanks for the loan, Charles."

The loan? You stole them.

"Mallory!" Henrietta was standing in the hallway, her face in shock.

"It's not my blood," said Mallory, weary of having to explain this simple fact to everyone.

Henrietta came into the room as the swords were pulled from the long leather bag. "Well, that explains a lot.'' She walked over to the couch where Quinn lay in his bandages, a blanket and a deep sleep.

"Quinn didn't tell you about the fencing match?"

"No. I did ask him about the cuts while I was stitching him up, but he wouldn't talk. I told him he was going to have some scars, and he didn't seem to mind that at all. I think he was almost pleased with them. *Men*," said Henrietta, as though that word encompassed the explanation for every flaw of his gender.

Charles wondered what word she might choose to explain Mallory. No doubt it would be a long word with a psychiatric subtext.

Henrietta was holding Quinn's wrist and looking at her watch, timing the pulse.

"Will he be all right?" Mallory might have been asking if Henrietta thought it would rain.

"He's lost a lot of blood," said Henrietta, "but he'll be fine in the morning. I pumped him up with antibiotics and gave him a strong sedative. He'll sleep for at least another six hours. I'll take good care of him." Henrietta handed Mallory a wet cloth which had been intended for Quinn's brow.

"Thanks." Mallory rose to her feet, and now Charles could see the day had taken a toll on her. She was tired, and moving sluggishly as she wiped the blood from her face.

"I have to change clothes, and then I've still got lots to do before the night is over. When Quinn comes to, tell him I was there when Sabra died. Tell him she finally got what she wanted. That'll be important to him."

"Oh, no," said Henrietta, sinking down to the armchair beside the couch. Charles covered his eyes with one hand.

"Don't worry," said Mallory. "Quinn will take it very well. He's been expecting it." She walked over to Charles's chair and lightly touched his hand to bring it down so she could see his face. "I know how much you cared about Sabra. But the only thing that was keeping her alive was unfinished business—she saw it through, and then she died. It wasn't the worst death.''

"Why don't you rest awhile? I'll get us some coffee.'' Henrietta took the bloody cloth from Mallory's hand and turned toward the kitchen.

"Nothing for me, thanks,'' Mallory called after her. "I have to go.''

No, don't leave.

Mallory was moving into the foyer, and then she stopped, seeming to hover there with an afterthought. She turned to catch Charles staring at her.

Stay. Please stay.

She walked slowly back to him and stood before his chair, and closer now to stand between his parted legs. She leaned down, placing one white hand on each arm of the chair. Closer. He could feel her breath on his skin, and the delicate feathering touch of her hair, which smelled of some exotic flower that never grew in New York City. Closer now, her eyes growing larger, flooding his field of vision and coloring it green. She pressed her mouth to his, gently, softly, her lips opening to him as she fed him a paralyzing current of electricity and flooded his body with heat and butterflies. And now, pressing into him, she was waking the last of his senses—he could taste her.

She pulled back, startled..In the flicker and widening of her eyes—a flash of discovery—Mallory had finally been taken by surprise.

And then she was going away from him again, moving swiftly to the door, saying, "Goodbye, Charles.''

He sat very still, listening to the sound of the door closing behind her.

Goodbye? Not good night?

She was precise with her words, not liking to waste them.

Goodbye?

He left his chair and walked to the window. He parted the curtains and watched the dark street below until she appeared there, crossing the paving stones, making a long shadow by lamplight. He leaned his forehead against the cool glass as he watched her enter the small tan car and drive off down the street. Behind his back, he heard slippered footsteps and the sound of a cup settling to the coffee table. Without turning, he said to Henrietta, "She won't be back. It's over."

"What's over, Charles? You never told her what was going on."

"Well, how could I? She thinks of me as an old friend of the family. It would put her in an awkward situation. Don't you see? It would be an *imposition*."

"That's not a word in Mallory's vocabulary. I wouldn't worry about good manners, Charles."

"I can't. I'm afraid she'd—"

"Now there's the key word. That young woman walks around in bloodstains, and look at you—you're *afraid* of an imposition. I think civilized behavior is overrated."

The only one to see her enter the church was a cat which had crept in with another parishioner and hidden itself away in the alcove, resting on the vaulted relic of a saint. Now the cat, in haste to hide itself a little better, knocked over a candlestick and startled a man in the pews.

His lined, pale face, roused from prayers, turned round. The old priest rose from the pew and stood in silence by a column, covertly watching a young woman with lustrous golden hair and a dark stain on her hand. She lit a candle to the patron saint of lost causes.

The lamb had come back.

With a shuffle of slippers on stone, he walked around the column and into the light. "Kathy?"

"Father, you're up late." She never turned away from the candles, lighting one after another.

"There's something I have to know. About your mother—"

"I made it up." She raised her eyes to the statue above the flames.

"I don't believe you." He reached out and touched her shoulder.

Now she did turn to face him, to shake off his hand. "It was another woman who was murdered. So what? It was a beautiful mass. My compliments, Father."

"You lied?" He shook his head in disbelief. "You could lie about a thing like that? So your own mother—"

"Who knows? I don't remember her."

She averted her eyes and moved away from him. He walked toward her, and quickly, to close the space between them. "Are you lying to me now?"

Mallory turned her cold eyes on the priest, and then turned her back. As she was walking toward the great doors and the night, the old man called after her, "Where are you going?"

"I'm going home."

"Did you pay for those candles?" One white, gnarled hand emerged from the folds of his black woolen shawl and pointed at Mallory's retreating back. "You haven't forgotten the poor box, have you, Kathy?"

"That's *Mallory* to you." She kept walking, saying, "And no, I didn't forget to pay the poor box. Now I suppose you'll want to check the serial numbers on my bills." With that, she was gone through the studded oak doors, her form fading into shadow, all but the gleam of bright hair, and then that gleam winked out in the dark.

Father Brenner's hand hung in the air for a moment, and then quickly delved back into the folds of his shawl as though he were pocketing a soul.

Charles cased Mallory's apartment house with the eye of a burglar-in-training. He approached the doorman with a twenty-dollar bill and a story about leaving an envelope under her door. He rode the elevator to the roof and exited by the fire door, coming out onto a clear night of shimmering city lights and the moon-bright slick of the Hudson River. He could smell the salt air, and he felt exhilarated.

The wind was on his face as he crossed over to the roof of the adjacent building and climbed down a fire escape ladder, a remnant from the old days before Mallory's building had been joined with this wall to create a common air shaft.

Now he was level with a window on the opposite wall and looking into Mallory's front room. Her apartment was a fortress. Only this window was not barred, the only portal inaccessible from the outside of the building by fire escape or terrace. It was a great expanse of glass from ceiling to floor.

He pulled a chunk of concrete from the depths of his coat pocket and hurled it at the window with all his strength. The plate glass broke into a million tiny pieces. When the violence of shattering glass had dissipated into a tinkling rain, he was staring at an enormous, jagged hole—and he was quite proud of it. His eyes adjusted to the dark beyond the window frame. He could see his missile lying amid the wreckage of a glass coffee table.

Better and better.

The alarm went off in a shriek of outrage.

Better still.

And it shrieked after him as he ascended the ladder to the roof door and made his escape.

She would find his message among the shards of glass when she returned home. The rock had a bit of paper wrapped round it and tied securely with a shoelace. His note bore that simple timeworn thing which he had found no way to improve upon: *I love you.*

And then the gentle man, unaccustomed to violence, unlawful trespass and destruction of private property, was exhausted from having done all of this. He walked homeward, slowly, hands in his pockets. She had broken his heart; he had broken her window. It was a break-even day.

EPILOGUE

MALLORY WOULD NEVER READ CHARLES'S NOTE. SHE was already miles gone.

The window of her compartment was one of a hundred points of light which trumped the stars in their brilliance and speed. She was running along the iron rails, propelled by a powerful engine with no mercy for anything in its path, cutting a swath through the dark with the blinding brightness of the train's electric eye.

Staring into the window glass, she recognized another woman's face in her own reflection, a gentle presence floating beside her. Two suitcases sat by Mallory's feet, but she carried no stitch of formal identification that would tie her to a name or a place. This was the way she had come to New York as a child, with only her wits and a bit of a mother's blood on her hands. And this was the way she voyaged out again, out of New York City and into the great sprawling landscape of America, which was another country.

Turn the page for a special excerpt from
Carol O'Connell's novel

SHELL GAME

Available in paperback from
Berkley Books

PROLOGUE

THE OLD MAN KEPT PACE WITH HIM, THEN RAN AHEAD in a sudden burst of energy and fear—as if he loved Louisa more. Man and boy raced toward the scream, a long high note, a shriek without pause for breath, inhuman in its constancy.

Malakhai's entire body awoke in violent spasms of flailing arms and churning legs, running naked into the real and solid world of his bed and its tangle of damp sheets. Rising quickly in the dark, he knocked over a small table, sending a clock to the floor, shattering its glass face and killing the alarm.

Cold air rushed across his bare feet to push open the door. By the light of a wall sconce in the outer hallway, he cast a shadow on the bedroom floor and revolved in a slow turn, not recognizing any of the furnishings. A long black robe lay across the arms of a chair. Shivering, he picked up the unfamiliar garment and pulled it across his shoulders like a cape.

A window sash had been raised a crack. White curtains ghosted inward, and drops from a rain gutter made small wet explosions on the sill. His head jerked up. A black fly was screaming in circles around a chandelier of dark electric candles.

Malakhai bolted through the doorway and down a corridor of closed rooms, the long robe flying out behind him. This narrow passage opened onto a parlor of gracious proportions and bright light. There were too many textures and colors. He could only absorb them as bits of a mosaic: the pattern of the tin ceiling, forest-green walls, book spines, veins of marble, carved scrolls of mahogany and swatches of brocade.

He caught the slight movement of a head turning in the mirror over the mantelpiece. His right arm was slowly rising to shield his eyes from the impossible. And now he was staring at the wrinkled flesh across the back of his raised hand, the enlarged veins and brown liver spots.

He drew the robe close about him as a thin silk protection against more confusion. Awakenings were always cruel.

How much of his life had been stripped away, killed in the tissues of his brain? And how much disorientation was only the temporary companion of a recent stroke? Malakhai pulled aside a velvet drape to look through the window. He had not yet fixed the day or even the year, but only gleaned that it was night and very late in life.

The alarm clock by his bed had been set for some event. Without assistance from anyone, he must recall what it was. Asking for help was akin to soiling himself in public.

Working his way from nineteen years old toward a place well beyond middle age, he moved closer to the mirror, the better to assess the damage. His thick mane of hair had grown white. The flesh was firm, but marked with lines of an interesting life and a long one. Only his eyes were curiously unchanged, still dark gunmetal blue.

The plush material of the rug was soft beneath his bare feet. Its woven colors were vivid, though the fringes showed extreme age. He recalled purchasing this carpet from a dealer in antiquities. The rosewood butler's table had come from the same shop. It was laid with a silver tray and an array of leaded crystal. More at home now in this aged incarnation, Malakhai lifted the decanter and poured out a glass of Spanish sherry.

Two armchairs faced the television set. Of course— one for the living and one for the dead. Well, that was normal enough, for he was well past the year when his wife had died.

The enormous size of the television screen was the best clue to the current decade. By tricks of illness and memory, he had begun his flight through this suite of rooms in the 1940s, and now he settled down in a well-padded chair near the end of the twentieth century, a time traveler catching his breath and seeking compass points. He was not in France anymore. This was the west wing of a private hospital in the northern corner of New York State, and soon he would remember why the clock had sounded an alarm.

A remote control device lay on the arm of his chair, and a red light glowed below the dark glass screen. He depressed the play button, and the television set came to life in a sudden brightness of moving pictures and a loud barking voice. Malakhai cut off the volume.

Something important was about to happen, but what? His hand clenched in frustration, and drops of sherry spilled from his glass.

She was beside him now, reaching into his mind and flooding it with warmth, touching his thoughts with perfect understanding. A second glass sat on a small cocktail table before her own chair, a taste of sherry for Louisa— still thirsty after all those years in the cold ground.

On the large screen, a troupe of old men in tuxedos were doffing top hats for the camera. Looming behind them was the old band shell in Central Park. Its high stone arch was flanked by elegant cornices and columns of the early 1900s. Hexagonal patterns on the concave wall echoed the shape of the plaza's paving stones, where a standing audience was herded behind velvet ropes.

Above the heads of the old magicians, a rippling banner spanned the upper portion of the shell, bright red letters declaring the upcoming Holidays of Magic in Manhattan.

The preview—of course.

So this was the month of November, and in another week, Thanksgiving Day would be followed by a festival of magicians, retired performers of the past alongside the present flash-and-dazzle generation. Beneath the image of a reporter with a microphone, a moving band of type traveled across the width of the screen to tell him that this was a live performance with no trick photography. The cameras would not cut away.

Malakhai smiled. The television was promising not to deceive the viewers, though misdirection was the heart of magic.

The plaza must be well lit, for the scene was bright as day. The raised stone floor of the band shell was dominated by a large box of dark wood, nine feet square. Malakhai knew the precise dimensions; many years ago, he had lent a hand to build the original apparatus, and this was a close replica. Thirteen shallow stairs led to the top of the platform. At the sides of the broad base step, two pairs of pedestals were bolted into the wood and topped with crossbows angling upward toward a target of black and white concentric ovals. The camera did not see the pins that suspended the target between the tall posts, and so it seemed to float above the small wooden stage.

Memory had nearly achieved parity with the moment. Oliver Tree was about to make a comeback for a career that never was. Malakhai leaned toward Louisa's empty chair. "Can you find our Oliver in that lineup of old men?" He pointed to the smallest figure in the group, an old man with the bright look of a boy allowed to stay up late in the company of grown-ups. The scalp and beard were clipped so short, Oliver appeared to be coated with white fur like an aged teddy bear.

"Where has he been all this time?" Even as Malakhai spoke these words, he recalled that Oliver had spent his retirement years working out a solution to the Lost Illusion.

The crossbow pedestals were made of giant clockwork gears, three intermeshing toothy circles of brass. Soon their weapons would release arrows in mechanized sequence, four time bombs set to go off with the tick of clocks and the twang of bowstrings. All the sights were trained on the oval target. The television camera narrowed its field for a close look at the magazine on one crossbow. This long narrow box of wood was designed to carry a load of three arrows.

The camera pulled back for a wide shot of two uniformed policemen on top of the platform. One of them held a burlap dummy upright while the other officer manacled its cloth hands to the iron post rings. Then they both knelt on the floorboards to attach leg irons to the widespread feet. And now the mannikin was splayed out across the face of the target. Standing below on the floor of the band shell, the newsman was speaking into his microphone, probably giving the history of the Lost Illusion and its long-deceased creator, the great Max Candle.

Malakhai inclined his head toward Louisa's chair. "I never thought Oliver would be the one to work it out."

Indeed. The retired carpenter in magician's silks had once been the most ordinary member of the troupe, a boy from the American heartland, stranded in the middle of a world war and without a clue to get himself home. So Oliver had only made it as far as New York City. Perhaps Paris had spoiled him for the midwestern prairies that spawned him.

And now Malakhai remembered one more thing. He touched the arm of the dead woman's chair, saying, "Oliver made me promise you'd watch this. He wanted you to see him in his finest hour."

The camera was panning the plaza. "There might be a thousand people in that park. Millions more are watching this on television. No one in our crowd ever had an audience that size."

Oliver Tree had surpassed them all.

More lost time was restored to Malakhai as he reached down to the cocktail table and picked up the formal invitation to a magic show in Central Park. He read the words in elegant script, then turned to the woman who wasn't there. "He's dedicating this performance to you, Louisa."

The rest of the text was a bit cryptic for Oliver. A hint of things to come?

Malakhai faced the screen as the two policemen finished cocking the crossbow pistols. The gears of the pedestals were all set in motion, toothy brass wheels slowly turning. A clockwork peg rose to the top of its orbit and touched the trigger of a crossbow. The first arrow was launched and flying too fast for the eye to track it. In the next instant, the burlap dummy was losing stuffing where the metal shaft had torn its throat. The next bow fired, and the next. When every missile had flown, the cloth effigy was pinned to the target by shafts through its neck, both legs and that place where the human heart would be.

The uniformed officers climbed to the top of the platform, unlocked the irons, and the demonstration dummy fell to the floorboards. They picked it up and carried it between them. The sawdust bled down the stairs in their descent. They made one last tour of the pedestals, cocking the weapons, allowing more arrows to drop from the crossbow magazines.

Oliver Tree stood at the base of the stairs and handed his top hat to another magician. Then he donned a scarlet cape and pulled the monk's hood over his white hair. As he slowly climbed toward the target, the long train of material flowed over the stairs behind him.

When the old man reached the top of the staircase, he stood with his back to the crowd and raised his arms. The cape concealed all but the top of the oval target. The scarlet silk sparkled and gleamed with reflections of camera lights. Then the cape collapsed and fell empty to the wooden floor. In that same instant, as if he had materialized in position, Oliver was revealed facing the crowd, spread-eagle across the target, bound in chains by hand and foot, himself the target of four armed crossbows. The gears of every pedestal were in motion. Soon the arrows would fly.

Malakhai clapped his hands. So far, the timing had been flawless. If the volume had been turned up, he might have heard the first round of applause from the audience in the plaza. Oliver Tree had grown old awaiting this moment.

The magician jerked his head to one side—the wrong side—as the gears on the first pedestal stopped and the bow released its arrow. Oliver's face contorted in a scream. There was blood on his white tie and collar. His mouth was working frantically, no doubt begging his captors to stop the rest of the crossbows from firing their arrows and killing him. Oliver's cries for help went ignored by the policemen and the reporter. They had apparently been informed that the great Max Candle had used these same words in the original act—just before dying in every single performance.

Another arrow flew, and another. While Oliver cried out in pain, the young reporter was smiling broadly for the camera, perhaps not understanding that the old man high above him on the platform was mortally wounded. Possibly this grinning child of the television era did not realize that all blood was not fake blood, that the arrows pinning the old man's legs were quite real.

The crowd was staring agape. Though uninitiated in the art of magic, they knew death when they saw it, when it came with the final arrow swiftly ripping a hole through Oliver's heart. The old man's screaming stopped. He dangled from his chains, not struggling anymore. His eyes were wide, unblinking—fixed in fear.

Malakhai had much experience with death. He knew that it never came in an instant. Perhaps, just for one moment, Oliver was aware of a few people in the crowd moving toward the platform, coming to help him—as if they could.

The newsman was laughing and waving these rescuers off, yelling and gesturing, no doubt assuring them that death was part of the show, a special effect for their viewing enjoyment. Then the reporter looked up at the chained corpse, and he lost his professional smile, perhaps realizing that trick photography was not an option here.

This was what death looked like.

The police officers, better acquainted with mortality, had already reached the top of the stairs. They unlocked Oliver's manacles and gently lowered the body to the wooden floor. Women covered the eyes of their children. The cameraman was ignoring the wild, waving hands of the reporter, who was mouthing the words to make him stop the pictures. But the lens was so in love with its subject, narrowing the focus, closing in on the fear-struck face of the dead magician and his true-to-life blood.

Louisa's sherry glass fell to the floor, and the dark red liquid spread across the pattern of the carpet.

Malakhai's hands were rising of their own accord. It was an act of will to keep one from touching the other, so as not to harm Louisa with a sound that aped applause. His lips spread wide with a silent scream, a parody of Oliver, whose volume had been turned off even before his life was ended. Then Malakhai's hands crashed together, slapping loudly, again and again, madly clapping as tears rolled down his face and ran between his parted lips in warm salty streams.

What a worthy performance—murdering a man while a million pairs of eyes were watching.

·

Also from *New York Times* Bestselling Author

Carol O'Connell

WINTER HOUSE

Never has Mallory faced as many surprises as in this case. It seems cut-and-dried at first: A burglar has been caught in the act and killed by a scissors-wielding homeowner. Except that the homeowner turns out to be the most famous lost child in NYPD history, missing for almost sixty years, thought to have been kidnapped following the massacre of her family: five siblings, father, stepmother, nanny, and housekeeper—nearly the entire household wiped out…with an ice pick.

AVAILABLE IN PAPERBACK

penguin.com

More from *New York Times* Bestselling Author

Carol O'Connell

DEAD FAMOUS

Jurors on a controversial trial are being killed off one by one, and only Detective Kathleen Mallory can figure out why. But the FBI has told her to lay off and leave it to the Feds. That's never stopped Mallory before.

AVAILABLE IN PAPERBACK

M145T0310

- fruits + veg.
- limit sweets
- $\frac{40-50\%}{Carb.}$ $\frac{30}{F}$ $\frac{30}{Prot.}$

- $\frac{200}{C}$

- reduce flour + sugar
  - breads
  - snacks
  - pretzels

- Br. rice
- beans, s.pot.
  w. squash
- X ↑F corn syrup
- 600 F cal.
- less but less fatty M
- use EVOO
- No hydrogenated oil
- avacado + nuts